The Path of the Four Lions

AJ Treloar is an Australian author of intelligent, atmospheric thrillers that weave history, theology, and conspiracy into gripping narratives. His stories invite readers to question the comfortable narratives of history — and to imagine what else might have been. A lifelong reader, Andrew grew up in a household where books were a birthright, passed down from his father alongside a love of dusty archives, improbable adventure, and unanswerable questions. That spark has never left him — and his novels aim to share it, offering readers not just entertainment, but a reason to think and feel differently about the past.

Before turning to writing, Andrew served as an engineer in the Australian Army, worked as a contract electrician, and built a career in project and construction management — experiences that left him equally at home building something with his hands or deconstructing an official narrative on the page.

His debut novel, *Textus Haereticorum*, has been praised by readers for its confident prose, deliberate pacing, and willingness to challenge established truths without veering into mere cynicism.

The Path of the Four Lions is the second novel in the Alex Carey series

When he's not writing, Andrew can usually be found in the quiet sanctuary of his rural Queensland home or astride his Triumph Tiger, chasing silence and stories down forgotten dirt tracks.

This novel is dedicated to my loving family – my wife Andrea, my son Mitchell and my daughter Kyniska and daughter-in-law Michaela, without whose support and encouragement this book could not have been written!

The Path of the Four Lions

BOOK ONE – TO SAVE A KING

Act I (March 641 CE) - The Desert and the Dead

Chapter 1

Abu Nas'r ibn Talib moved with brisk purpose through the crowded streets of Alexandria, his sandaled feet whispering against the worn limestone slabs. The city hummed around him—a discordant symphony of merchants bartering in multiple tongues, oxen groaning under the weight of goods, and criers announcing news from Constantinople. Despite the familiar bustle, an air of unease threaded the morning air like incense before a storm. Alexandria, jewel of the Mediterranean, was not what it once had been—but it remained a city of consequence. Under centuries of Roman, then Byzantine rule, it had grown beyond its origins as a mere Egyptian port into a metropolis of commerce, culture, and learning. It had long eclipsed Memphis in size and stature, becoming the second largest city in Egypt and a proud cornerstone of the Eastern Roman Empire. Greek philosophers, Persian astrologers, Coptic monks, and Jewish scribes still debated in its courtyards and scribbled in its scroll-rooms, though the golden age of such discourse now showed signs of fading.
And now, a new force was gathering beyond the desert's edge.

The Rashidun army, under the command of the Arab general Amr ibn al-ʿĀs, had crossed into the Sinai. Word from the eastern provinces was grim. Byzantine forces had been scattered near

Pelusium, and the invaders advanced westward with alarming speed and divine conviction—much like the Romans themselves had done six centuries earlier. If their march remained unchecked, Alexandria would fall within months.

Abu Nas'r's jaw tightened beneath his neatly cropped beard. The city's famed garrison, long the deterrent to southern incursions, had begun mobilising eastward in haste—too little, too late, he feared. As newly appointed Custodian of the Great Library, Abu Nas'r bore a heavier burden than most. He touched the bronze medallion that hung against his chest, etched with the mark of the Curatorship—a symbol of scholarship and stewardship, now as much a target as a title.

He turned onto the grand avenue leading toward the Royal Quarter, the hem of his robe flaring slightly with each stride. Around him, Alexandrians prepared for what many feared would be the end—scribes bundling scrolls into trunks, Greek merchants shouting over berths in the harbor, and Roman matriarchs ushering their households toward safety. The scent of saltwater mixed with sweat and anxiety. The port, Portus Magnus, would soon be overflowing with ships bound for Crete, Antioch, or any haven beyond the tightening grasp of war.

The Great Library, formally part of the Mouseion, still stood—stately, if scarred by time and the shifting priorities of distant emperors. Under the Roman Empire, it had languished for decades in disrepair, but under recent Byzantine governance, a modest revival had taken place. Now it thrived again as a beacon of scholarship, containing not just papyri and codices, but minds capable of interpreting them. Abu Nas'r had dedicated his life to those minds—and to the belief that knowledge must outlast empires.

As the sun climbed above the harbor's edge, casting long gold lines across the marble facades, he caught sight of the library's

portico. He paused for a breath. Inside waited his fellow scholars—
and the Ahl al-Khidr.

Today, they would make a choice—not just for the city, but for
history.

Abu Nas'r ibn Talib was born in Qift—Coptos to the Greeks—a
sun-scorched city cradled in the bend of the Upper Nile. Once a
proud node of priestly power and intellectual trade, Qift had long
since faded into the bureaucratic hinterlands of empire, but its
memory lingered in stone and ink. Nas'r's family, Muslim in creed
but shaped by centuries of syncretic tradition, had served for
generations as scribes and translators. Their ancestors once
inscribed prayers to Thoth on temple walls before turning their
pens to Greek scrolls, Roman ledgers, and finally Byzantine
decrees. By Nas'r's time, they could write in Demotic, Greek,
Coptic—and, crucially, Arabic.

His father, Talib ibn Omar, had been a legal translator under the
Byzantine provincial court, a quiet man with precise fingers and a
reverence for the written word. He taught Nas'r to wield both
qalam and kitab, pen and book, with discipline. The family lived
modestly, but in a house where words carried weight and the
margins of old papyrus scraps were more precious than coin.

Even as a boy, Nas'r unnerved his elders. He asked questions that
unpeeled the skin of tradition. At eleven, he began studying under
a reclusive Persian exile in nearby Qena—an aging scholar who
had once taught at Gundeshapur. It was under him that Nas'r
encountered the forbidden fire of Zoroastrian cosmology, Greek
mathematics, and Indian star-charts scratched into clay. He read
obsessively, memorized easily, and believed nothing without
dissection.

By twenty, Alexandria called to him—a decaying metropolis of
fractured glory, where imperial decrees echoed off broken
colonnades and Christian bells rang beside crumbling statues of
forgotten gods. He arrived with no patron, no protection, and only
a satchel of copied texts to his name. He found work in the

shadows of the Cæsareum, transcribing imperial edicts, translating
between Greek and Coptic, and eventually into Arabic—a talent
rare enough to draw cautious interest from a few progressive minds
in the city's fading academies.

He published his first treatise at thirty-one, a slender argument on
the reconciliation of Aristotelian logic with Qur'anic metaphysics.
It made him enemies. Coptic clerics called it heretical. Byzantine
scholars called it subversive. But others—quieter, older, more
secretive—took note. Among them were members of the Ahl al-
Khidr, the invisible society of guardians, watchers of time and ink.
They saw not only brilliance in him but alignment. Patience.
Purpose.

Then came the appointment.

The city bristled with unease in the early months of 641. Rumours
flew like ash on the desert wind—Arab armies were crossing into
Egypt, Byzantium was retreating, the end of the old world was
near. In the midst of this uncertainty, Cyrus of Alexandria, the
city's pragmatic governor and Melkite patriarch, did the
unthinkable. He named Abu Nas'r ibn Talib the new Custodian of
the Great Library, recently revived and reconstituted within the
Royal Quarter.

The reaction was instant and furious. The Coptic Church, already
suspicious of Cyrus, accused him of handing the intellectual keys
of Christendom to a Muslim. The Greek intelligentsia balked—too
Arab, they whispered, too modern. Yet Cyrus stood by his
decision.

"The library holds the wisdom of many gods," he was heard to say.
"Let it be watched over by one who worships knowledge above
them all."

Nas'r accepted the post without ceremony. He did not wear jewels
or robes of silk. His garb was simple: undyed linen, a leather sash
for his inks and tools, and a single scroll—Aristotle's Ethics—
tucked into the folds of his belt. Around his neck hung the bronze

seal of the Curatorship, an old medallion depicting Athena and a falcon in flight—symbols of wisdom and watchfulness, forged when Egyptian and Hellenic worlds had still coexisted.

He lived alone in Rhakotis, the city's oldest quarter, near the harbor where Alexander had once stepped onto Egyptian soil. His home was modest, airy, lined with scrolls that rotated weekly depending on his studies. From the rooftop, on clear nights, he could see the flicker of the Pharos Lighthouse, still standing though less visited now. Scholars came to him quietly—from Antioch, Harran, even distant Gundeshapur. Some came to argue. Others to listen. All left changed.

Nas'r believed three things with equal intensity.

That knowledge was divine, eternal, and borderless.

That empires would fall, but ideas must endure.

And that the written word—be it scratched into palm fronds or inked onto calfskin—was the soul of civilization, entrusted to the few, judged by the many, and forgotten only at humanity's peril.

He did not guard the Great Library for glory or vanity. He guarded it because it was the last breath of memory before the tide came in.

And now, as war crept westward and fires burned in the Sinai, Abu Nas'r stood in the shadow of marble colonnades and papyrus shelves, listening to the wind as if it, too, could read.

He knew what was coming.

He only prayed the words would survive it.

The Library came into view just as the sea breeze shifted, laced with salt, kelp, and the sharp tang of fish unloaded at the eastern docks.

It stood on a rise of carved limestone, just beyond the Royal Quarter, where the older colonnades gave way to newer vaults and mosaic courtyards. The building itself was a composite of ages—Ptolemaic foundations, Roman archways, and Byzantine renovations fused by time and ambition. Pale sandstone walls caught the sunlight in shimmering tones of gold and chalk-white.

Marble steps, broad and slightly worn, led up from the mosaic plaza in front, where traders and scholars alike gathered in shaded cloisters, murmuring beneath palm fronds and arched porticoes. Above the grand doors, framed in bronze and cedarwood, the ancient inscription remained:

ΜΟΥΣΕΙΟΝ – ΤΗΣ ΣΟΦΙΑΣ ΚΑΙ ΤΗΣ ΑΛΗΘΕΙΑΣ
Mouseion – Temple of Wisdom and Truth.

It was not a temple in the religious sense, but it had always been sacred.

The dome that crowned its central rotunda—rebuilt after the Aurelianic destruction—gleamed with new tiles inlaid with Coptic crosses and ancient Greek patterns: a quiet marriage of creeds. From the steps, one could look past the grain warehouses and fishing piers, out across the eastern harbour to where the great Pharos Lighthouse still pierced the sky. The wind carried with it the sound of gulls and dockworkers, and the ever-present scent of brine and scale. Alexandria was a city of sea and stone—and here, at its intellectual heart, one felt both eternally present.

Nas'r paused as he reached the final steps, his hand brushing the smooth banister. He always did. It was not superstition, but recognition—a silent moment of respect before entering what he considered the last sanctuary of truth in a crumbling world.

Once, it had been unmatched.

At its zenith under the Ptolemies, the Library of Alexandria had been the soul of human memory. No port in the known world equalled its collection. Merchant ships arriving in Alexandria were required—by royal decree—to surrender any books or scrolls on board. These were copied by trained scribes, and the originals were added to the library's holdings. Works from India, Babylonia, Carthage, Athens, Judea, Persia, and even the far west of Hispania lined its shelves. No scholar was turned away on account of race, color, tongue, or creed. Greek philosophers debated Indian mystics. Jewish scribes compared their scripture to Egyptian hymns. The only rule was this: seek knowledge, and share it. This—this openness—had made it unique.

But greatness is never without enemies.

In 30 BCE, after the chaos of the Battle of Actium, everything changed. Octavian—soon to be Augustus—defeated the combined forces of Mark Antony and Cleopatra, the last queen of the Ptolemaic line. The Roman fleet swept down the Nile like an iron scythe, and Alexandria fell. Cleopatra died, and with her, Egypt's last sovereign dynasty.

But the Library was spared.

Legend held that Julius Caesar himself—in life an ally of Cleopatra, and in death a name revered by Octavian—had once ordered it preserved. Nas'r had read the scrolls: poetic fragments claiming that Caesar, during his own campaign years earlier, had urged Octavian to protect the Library *'for it holds more empire than Rome itself.'* Whether this was true or merely a later embellishment, Nas'r had always believed it. The fire that consumed the docks during Caesar's siege spared the main repository—a miracle attributed to either divine mercy or the clever misdirection of local scribes.

Still, Rome brought with it a slow corrosion.

Under Roman rule, the Library suffered from neglect. Politicians, not philosophers, now held sway. Funding waned. Curators were replaced by bureaucrats. Scrolls were pilfered, sold, or shipped to Rome. Over time, the Library became more a symbol than a sanctuary.

Then came war.

In 272 CE, the Emperor Aurelian marched on Alexandria, bent on reclaiming it from the forces of Zenobia, queen of Palmyra. The fighting was brutal—street to street, wall to wall. Parts of the city burned. Much of the Bruchion district, where the Library's sister

archives had stood, was reduced to rubble. Entire wings of papyrus were lost, their ashes carried on desert winds.
What remained fell silent for nearly a century.

It was only under the Byzantine revival that the Library—damaged, scattered, but not destroyed—began to breathe again. Coptic monks, imperial archivists, and surviving Ptolemaic blueprints helped to reassemble its core. A new wing was built beside the old rotunda. What could not be replaced was rewritten, translated, or sought in far-flung monasteries. It became a hybrid sanctuary, half museum, half monastery. Still, it retained its original mission: to be a house of memory.

And now, in 641, as war crept again toward Alexandria's gates, the Library stood renewed yet imperiled once more—a fragile flame in the gathering dark.
To Abu Nas'r, it was not merely a building.
It was a threshold.
The last breath of wisdom before the silence of swords.
He entered it as a man enters prayer.

Chapter 2

Abu Nas'r pushed open the great cedar doors, their bronze hinges groaning with age and authority. The familiar scent of parchment, beeswax, and ink enveloped him immediately—a fragrance more sacred to him than frankincense. The interior rotunda was awash with movement and murmur. Scholars in loose linen robes bent over desks beneath high windows, their quills scratching methodically. A Persian mystic and a Jewish rabbi debated quietly beneath a dome of painted stars. Two Coptic scribes whispered verses of Aristotle back and forth in translation drills, while a Nubian monk traced fine calligraphy onto fresh papyrus with a steady hand.

There were no guards, no priests of the sword—only priests of the word.

Here, the disciplines blurred: astronomy and theology, medicine and metaphysics, logic and law. Shelves reached upward like palm trunks, heavy with scrolls and bound folios. Dust motes danced in slants of sun, and low voices echoed off the stone walls in Arabic, Greek, Syriac, and Latin. Nas'r passed them all with gentle nods, unnoticed save by a few young acolytes who briefly paused in deference.

He made his way through the east colonnade, past the restored Mosaic of Hermes Trismegistus—a relic from the old Museion—and into a quieter annex where the air grew cooler and the light thinner. At the far end stood a door of dark acacia wood, its iron handle warm from years of use but untouched by any hand but his. He opened it and descended.

The steps were narrow, worn in the middle from centuries of passage, and led downward in a gentle spiral. A faint lamplight flickered at the bottom. This chamber, originally part of the Hypostyle Vault—the Library's oldest surviving section—had once been used for restoration and conservation. The humidity was controlled here, stone walls lined with cedar and bitumen to keep rot and mildew at bay. The very foundations of the Ptolemaic library lay buried in this space, hidden from the world but pulsing with its echoes.

Here, he had called the meeting.

At the center of the chamber sat seven figures, arrayed in a semi-circle around a low marble table etched with ancient Greek and Aramaic script. No banners marked them. No titles were spoken aloud. But these were the Ahl al-Khidr—the People of the Verdant One.

Not a formal order, but a society of guardians.

Keepers of continuity.

The unbroken thread.

They hailed from different lands—Egypt, Persia, the Levant, even farther south. Scholars, mystics, healers, and scribes. Some wore the robes of monks, others the simple dress of travellers. One bore the marks of Zoroastrian initiation; another wore a talisman shaped like a lotus blossom. They were not of one religion or culture, but of one purpose: to safeguard true knowledge—the kind that outlives kings and outlasts empires.

No official leader presided over them. But they deferred to Nas'r. Not by vote, not by oath.

By recognition.

He carried no staff of office. No ring or crest. What he had was memory—deep, exacting, endless memory—and the burden of choosing what must be preserved when the flames came again. He entered the circle and sat opposite the official scribe, a quiet Ethiopian man named Malik, who inked the minutes of each meeting in a bound codex, carefully coded in script that could not be deciphered by the casual reader.

They waited for Nas'r to speak.

The only sound was the whisper of Malik's pen and the distant drip of condensation along the stones. Above them, the Great Library hummed with the traffic of living minds. But here, in this quiet crucible of preservation, the future of that knowledge would be decided.

Nas'r called the meeting to order. There was no hymn, no chant, no prayer—only the low rustle of robes and the soft scratch of Malik's pen poised to begin.

He glanced toward Malik, seated with a reed pen poised over parchment.

"For the record, mark today: the fourth day of the month of Baramhat, in the year 641 of our Lord."

Malik nodded and inked the line without a word.

"I have called this meeting of the Ahl al-Khidr with great urgency. As all of you know, my brothers—" he looked at each of them in turn, eyes shining beneath heavy lids—"a storm is on the horizon. The forces under Amr ibn al-'Ās have crossed the Sinai and are now pressing toward Pelusium."

A murmur swept through the chamber. Pelusium—the easternmost gate of Egypt. The very place where Persian kings and Roman legions had once stepped into the Nile Delta. If it fell, Alexandria would not be far behind.

"The garrison has been recalled," Nas'r continued, "and is being deployed to meet the Rashidun army near Balbeis, along the route from Sinai to the Delta. But I fear, as I am sure you all do, that it will not halt the tide."

A low voice answered from the semicircle, its owner cloaked in deep red linen and marked with the tattoos of the Kushite priesthood.

He looked around the semi-circle of faces before him—Copts, Jews, Persians, Nubians—each marked by age, wisdom, and fatigue.

"I have called this meeting of the Ahl al-Khidr with great urgency," he began. "As you all know, brothers, a storm is upon us. The forces under Amr ibn al-ʿĀs have crossed the Sinai and are now encamped near Pelusium. They will be at Alexandria's gates within weeks."

A low murmur rippled through the chamber. All of them had heard the rumors: the Rashidun armies sweeping across the Levant, the fall of Jerusalem, the burning of imperial outposts.

"The Alexandria garrison has been deployed east of the Delta," Nas'r continued, "attempting to stall Amr's advance along the coastal road. But it will not hold. Not for long."

One of the elders—a thin, sharp-eyed Jew named Baruch of Antioch—leaned forward. "Who commands now in Constantinople? Heraclius is dead, is he not?"

"Yes," said Nas'r. "He died in February. His son, Heraclius Constantine, has taken the throne—young, sick, and caught between the factions of the court. Byzantium is fractured. No aid is coming."

Another voice, deep and weary, came from the Nubian scholar Amon-Sa. "What are we to do, Nas'r? We cannot take everything. The books alone would fill ten caravans."

"And where would we go?" asked Stephanos, the last of the Greek mystics still loyal to the old Platonic schools. "We are men of ink and scrolls, not swords."

"Cyrus of Alexandria has written to Constantinople for reinforcements," Nas'r said. "But even if Heraclius Constantine responds, it will be too late. This meeting is not to wait on emperors. It is to decide what must be done, now."

Then another, the youngest among them—a Copt with fire in his eyes—interjected, "Should it not be Pope Benjamin who appeals to the emperor? This is a matter of the faith."

That stirred a round of muttering, heads shaking. Nas'r raised a hand and quiet fell like dust from the vaults above.

"Benjamin is in hiding," he said. "The Chalcedonians still seek his exile. Cyrus may be imperialist and hated by our own, but he alone has the reach to Constantinople. This debate is meaningless. Irrespective of who writes, aid will not arrive in time."

The scribe's pen paused. Nas'r looked to them all, his voice hardening.

"This meeting is not to bemoan what cannot be undone. It is to decide what must be done. If we are to preserve the heart of this library—its soul, not its stones—then we act. Not later. Now."

"What do you propose, Nas'r?" asked the Kushite. "We have no soldiers. No ships. All we have are scrolls—wisdom written on leaves that would burn on a whim."

Another chimed in: "It is obvious we cannot go east. Damascus is lost. Jerusalem, taken. There is only west."

"Or by sea," said Nas'r quietly.

Murmurs rose again. One of the older members shook his head gravely.

"The Rashidun navy already marauds the coast. Their fleet patrols from Al-Arish to Damietta. Even reaching Crete would be suicide. To flee to Greece now is to sail into death."

Nas'r lowered his eyes. A long silence passed as he unrolled a large vellum map across the marble table. Egypt, the Sinai, the Red Sea. His fingers traced the old trade routes—the desert roads, the Coptic monasteries, the hidden wells.

In his mind, he saw another man, hunched over another map. Theodore, commander of the Byzantine defense, doubtless weighing the same grim variables from a tent in the Delta marshes. He pitied him.

Then Nas'r looked up.

"We sail," he said. "But not north. South."

They stared at him. It was the Copt who broke the silence, incredulous.

"South? Toward Yemen? Toward the Caliph's territory? There are Rashidun ports all along the Arabian coast. The Bab al-Mandab is likely blockaded. Even if we reached it, we'd never pass into the Gulf of Aden."

"We aren't going through the strait," Nas'r said. He tapped a remote point on the map. "Our destination is here."

They leaned closer.

A shaded crescent nestled in the highlands west of the Red Sea. Inland, beyond the reach of the sea, yet connected by old trade roads still guarded by desert tribes and Christian allies.

Meroë.

The ancient Nubian stronghold.

Once the capital of the Kushite kingdom, its pyramids older than Rome, its priests once protectors of Egyptian secrets. Its royal libraries, long forgotten by the world, still existed—hidden in sandstone catacombs and guarded by bloodlines that traced back to Amun.

"It is remote," Nas'r continued, "but reachable. The Blemmyes still roam the Red Sea hills. They are no friend to the Caliphate. And the Christian kings of Nubia remain autonomous—if not allied, at least not hostile."

"You would have us bury Alexandria's knowledge in Kushite soil?" the Cyrenian asked softly.

"No," Nas'r said, with conviction. "I would have us plant it. So it may grow again, when the world is ready."

No one spoke for a long time.

Then Malik, the quiet scribe, looked up from his inkstone and asked the only question that mattered.

"How many ships do we need?"

Nas'r considered this.

They would need more than a scroll or two carried under the arm. They would need dozens of carts, a fleet of ships, and the cooperation of men with more power than conviction.

He leaned over the map, his fingers pressing lightly along the route that curved across the desert from the Nile to the coast.

"We will take the overland route through Misr—the old city south of Babylon Fortress," he said, referring to the ancient settlement now sitting atop what would one day become Cairo. "From there, we will push east toward the port of Berenice Troglodytica."

Baruch frowned. "Berenice is deserted."

"All the better," Nas'r said. "It is far enough south to remain free of Rashidun control—for now. They concentrate their presence near Qulzum and Ayla. Berenice is forgotten—and that makes it perfect."

He looked at them sharply now.

"We will commandeer every cart, every ox, every camel in Misr. I will ask Cyrus to write the order. Baruch—" he turned, voice commanding—"I entrust to you the assembling of the fleet. I know it is a mighty task, but you have dealt with merchants before. Once you have Cyrus's seal, travel south and begin preparations at Berenice. Hire crews quietly. Buy what ships you can. Patch together what you must. But no word of this is to escape the coast. Not a single whisper."

Baruch inclined his head. "I will see it done."

Nas'r turned next to Stephanos.

"You will oversee the gathering of carts and animals. Horses, oxen, donkeys—whatever can bear the load. Buy them if you must. Use the library treasury; it is what it was saved for. Many will flee the city in the coming weeks—use that to our advantage. Seize every idle cart. Have them covered and ready by the next full moon."

He paused, eyes narrowing as his thoughts turned south.

"Amon-Sa," he said at last, "you must send word to King Pachomius in Nobatia." He looked directly at the tall Nubian. "I will draft the letter on behalf of the governor, as the Curate of the Library, and beg him for divine intervention. He may yet remember the vows made between our forebears. Tell him our mission is not of war, but of salvation—for all peoples."

Amon-Sa bowed slightly. "He will listen, if the gods still bless my tongue."

Nas'r's eyes drifted back to the map. He traced a line down the Red Sea to an ancient name: Adulis.

"We shall come to Adulis by the closing days of the flood season, when the Nile's waters crest high and the winds still favour southern sail. Expect us no later than the new moon of Misra, and if God wills it, even sooner. The coastal winds will shift by then—from north to south—and with them, so must we."

There was silence. The weight of the moment settled like dust across old vellum.

Nas'r straightened. "This is our charge. If we fail, it will not only be Alexandria that burns. It will be the memory of the world."

He looked around the room, into each face.

Chapter 3

Malik interrupted them as he set his quill aside, voice low and urgent.

"Nas'r," he said, "this is a fine plan—and if any plan is to bear fruit, it is this." He gestured toward the map spread across the table, its worn parchment soft under his ink-stained fingers. "But before we adjourn, I must remind the Ahl al-Khidr that Alexandria is more than scrolls and books and codices. It is more than the Great Library. It is more than the wisdom it guards or the scholars it shelters."

He paused, looking slowly around the chamber, the torchlight casting his face in flickering gold and shadow. "We possess, by default, something greater than all of it."

"Greater than six centuries of collective wisdom?" scoffed Father Athanasius, the aging Copt. His voice carried that unmistakable rasp of disdain only a lifetime in monastic silence could sharpen. "What, Malik, could possibly be greater than that?"

Malik met his gaze without flinching.

"Dhu al-Qarnayn himself."

The words struck the room still. Even the distant shuffle of guards outside seemed to halt.

The other men exchanged glances.

"You cannot mean—" began Baruch.

"I do," said Malik. "I mean exactly that. Alexander. The Macedonian. The world-shaper. The city's founder. His body still rests here, entombed in the heart of this city. Hidden, yes. Forgotten by many. But not by us."

There was a long silence. The name alone—Dhu al-Qarnayn—
carried a power few dared speak aloud.

"Why?" whispered Stephanos. "Why does this matter now?"

Malik turned, his voice taut with controlled force. "Because the
Muslims—those marching beneath the green banner of the
Caliphate—do not know where he is buried. But they believe in
him more than the Greeks ever did. To them, he is not simply
Alexander. He is Dhu al-Qarnayn—'The Two-Horned One'—a
righteous king spoken of in the Qur'an itself. Not a myth, not a
fable. A divine agent. A warrior guided by God, who travelled to
the ends of the earth, who built walls to keep out the cursed tribes
of Gog and Magog."

"They revere him?" asked Athanasius, the bitterness draining from
his voice.

"With holy fear," Malik replied. "In their eyes, he is a prophet.
Perhaps even a man blessed with knowledge from the heavens.
Some call him half-divine. He is a symbol of just kingship. Of
sacred order."

"Then surely they would not desecrate the tomb," said Baruch
cautiously. "Surely they would protect it, if they knew—"

"And that is the danger," Malik interrupted. "They do not know.
And should they find it accidentally, they may treat it as loot, as a
relic of blasphemous empire. There is no guarantee Amr ibn al-'Ās
will restrain his men. No guarantee he himself will even recognize
the tomb for what it is. What the Qur'an calls sacred, the sword
may still destroy."

Nas'r's jaw tightened.

"So you believe the city may fall," said Stephanos, "and the
tomb—"

"Could be lost. Defiled. Burned. Forgotten." Malik's voice
dropped lower. "Can you imagine what would be lost, brothers?
The body of Alexander the Great—Dhu al-Qarnayn—cast into the
street, stripped of its sanctity, reduced to ash. What would that do
to the very idea of Alexandria? To history itself?"

Baruch slowly crossed himself again.

"We must take it with us," said Nas'r. The words came with the weight of an oath. "No matter how impossible it seems."

"It will be difficult," said Malik. "It will require the utmost secrecy. Perhaps a false trail to deceive the Rashidun army."

"Then so be it," said Nas'r. He looked to each of them in turn. "We save the scrolls. We save the codices. But this—this we must preserve with our lives. For if Alexandria is destroyed, and the library lost, it may rise again in time. But if the body of the Two-Horned King is desecrated, something sacred dies forever."

The torchlight flickered across the chamber's domed stone ceiling, shadows dancing behind each man as if listening too. The air smelled of myrrh, ink, and old limestone—of history itself. Malik finished recording Nas'r's final instructions and set the quill down with care.

Nas'r leaned forward, his eyes sharp beneath the cowl. "Malik, before we adjourn—there is one more task. Perhaps the most difficult."

The scribe raised a brow. "Name it."

Nas'r gestured to the library above him.

"Somewhere, in this great library, is hidden the Khitābāt al-Maqbarah—the Grave Scrolls. They were entrusted to us a century ago, hidden within the Great Library under codex names. Translated fragments from Ptolemaic priests. They claim to hold the clues to Alexander's resting place."

A sharp breath escaped one of the elders.

"You believe they're still within these walls?" Malik asked, voice hushed.

"I believe," said Nas'r, "that they are our only chance. We do not know where the Soma lies—only that it still exists, somewhere beneath this city or perhaps within its ruins. Your task is to find and study these scrolls, cross-reference the old temple registries, city maps, anything you can. If the sarcophagus is still here, you must find it." He stepped closer to Malik, lowering his voice.

"You are the only one who has read the old registry in full. You know the scribe marks, the Ptolemaic numerals, the misfiled scrolls. You must find them."

Malik nodded once, the weight of the charge evident.

Then it was Baruch, the older Copt, who spoke first. "And when we do find it, what then? Do we carry the tomb with us like priests of Osiris across the desert?"

The room tensed. Baruch's tone was not mocking, but heavy with uncertainty.

Stephanos folded his arms. "He cannot go to Meroe. It's too far. Too exposed. If we are found, everything—everything—is lost."

"But we cannot leave him here!" Amon-Sa barked. "If the Rashidun find his tomb, they may desecrate it, plunder it, or worse—convert it to their own ends. Alexandria is no longer sacred to them. Dhu al-Qarnayn may mean nothing to Amr ibn al-ʿĀṣ."

"Or everything," Malik muttered, almost to himself.

The men looked to him.

"Alexander was more than king to the early Muslims. The Dhu al-Qarnayn of the Qur'an was righteous, favoured by God, a bringer of justice, builder of the wall against Gog and Magog. Some even say he was a prophet. But that reverence may not stay the sword of conquest. This army," he pointed towards the east, "seeks dominion, not relics."

Nas'r stood again. "Which is why we will divide our burden. The scrolls and the contents of the Library—every codex, every piece of knowledge—will go south, to Meroe, hidden along the Nubian trade route. But the sarcophagus..."

He pointed to the western edge of the map.

"...will go west. To Siwa."

The chamber fell still.

"To Siwa?" Baruch repeated.

"A desert temple," Stephanos murmured. "A ruin."

"A sanctuary," Nas'r corrected. "Siwa was the oracle of Ammon. It is where Alexander journeyed alone to learn the truth of his lineage. It is where he wished to be buried, not here. Ptolemy took that from him. We will restore it."

"But it is deep in the sand. No roads, no fresh water," said Amon-Sa.

"Which is why they will not look for him there," Nas'r replied.

The men exchanged glances. No one objected.

Malik exhaled slowly. "Then we sever the soul of Alexandria—wisdom to the south, the king to the west."

Nas'r nodded, solemn. "Not sever, my friend. Scatter. We scatter the soul, like seeds before the flame. We divide our labour, divide our burden, and divide our inheritance—so that something, at least, may endure the fire."

There was silence. Then Malik, the elder scribe, picked up his quill again.

"Let it be written."

The next morning the sun cast a pale fire through the clerestory windows of the library, filtering dust motes like motes of gold through the cavernous, vaulted chambers. The Ahl al-Khidr were gathered once more beneath the dome of the central rotunda, a hush of solemnity resting over them.

Nas'r stood with a scroll in hand, its ribbon sealed in red wax and pressed with the Great Seal of the Library—the owl flanked by papyrus reeds, beneath the inscription: Σοφία διατηρεί την ελευθερίαν — Wisdom Preserves Freedom.

"This," he said, holding the scroll reverently, "is addressed to King Pachomius of Nobatia. A plea for alliance. For sanctuary. For preservation."

He turned to Amon-Sa. The Egyptian bowed slightly as Nas'r handed him the sealed letter and a leather pouch.

"Two gold solidi," Nas'r said, "and five dirhams in silver. For bribes, tolls, silence. Spend it as you must."

Amon-Sa nodded, accepting the weight with practiced discretion. "You know the path," Nas'r continued. "Follow the Nile south. Pass through Babylon Fortress under pretence—perhaps as a grain merchant. From there, cross east to Berenice Troglodytica. Once you reach the coast, find passage aboard a felucca. Hug the coast down to Adulis and assess the port."

"I will scout ahead, Baruch," Amon-Sa said, turning to his friend with a firm clasp of the shoulder. "If anything is untoward, I'll leave word beneath the old lintel at the well in Berenice."

"May the waters of the Nile carry you safely," Baruch said quietly. With no further ceremony, Amon-Sa gathered his satchel and disappeared into the rising morning.

Nas'r then addressed Stephanos. From beneath his robe he drew another pouch, heavier than the last.

"Ten gold solidi from the treasury," he said. "Start today. Focus first on wagons—many will be abandoned in panic. Seek the cartwrights, the mulemen, the bathhouse porters. Offer coin, or prayers. It does not matter. We look at the animals last—less cost to feed, less risk until we move."

Stephanos bowed, eyes already scanning the possibilities. He took the pouch with care and departed in the wake of Amon-Sa.

Only five remained.

Nas'r turned to Baruch and Malik. "Baruch, until we have the letter commandeering the fleet from The Governor, you will assist Malik. Both of you - have the hardest road. The Khitābāt al-Maqbarah must be found. Without them, we are blind."

The two men exchanged a look—quiet understanding, tempered by gravity. Without a word, they gathered their tablets and lamps, and disappeared into the labyrinth of staircases leading to the library's deepest vaults.

Now, only the scribes remained.

Nas'r turned to the final trio.

"Father Athanasius," he said, addressing the elder Coptic priest, draped in black wool and white beard. "Brother Yohanon," he added, gesturing to the young Copt, no older than twenty, still pink of cheek and fire-eyed. "And Theonides the Cyrenian," he said, naming the final, pale Greek who had long kept to the corners of the library.

"We hope carry it all. But that may not be possible. So you will prioritize. Begin cataloguing the corpus. Start in this order—burn it into your minds. One mistake could cost us a civilization."

He unfurled a scrap of papyrus:

> *The Corpus of Euclid*
> *The Commentary on Galen*
> *The Coptic Gospels*
> *The Babylonian Star Charts*
> *The Sanskrit Sutras of Patanjali*
> *The Complete Works of Ptolemaeus*
> *The Map of Eratosthenes*
> *The Oldest Torah Scroll*
> *The Book of the Hidden Names*

"Everything else follows. Sort by uniqueness, age, and irreplaceability. Work in shifts. Do not tire. You will assemble the volumes in the Great Vesica."

The Vesica was the massive, ellipsoid chamber beneath the central dome—a scriptorium turned staging hall. Its stone floor could hold twenty wagons, and its alcoves had once held statues of Athena and Isis. Now it would cradle what remained of six centuries of knowledge.

The three scribes bowed, almost as one. They turned wordlessly and disappeared into the adjoining galleries.

Nas'r stood alone beneath the rising columns of the rotunda.

The soul of Alexandria had begun to divide.

And finally, Abu Nas'r ibn Talib gathered his outer cloak, his ledger of seals, and the stamped scroll bearing the crest of the High Curators. He tucked them carefully into the folds of his satchel.

The time for quiet planning had ended. Now came the time for bold requests—and dangerous negotiations.

It would take no small amount of persuasion to convince Cyrus, the Imperial Prefect of Egypt and Patriarch of Alexandria, to issue a formal decree authorizing the commandeering of ships. The man was a devout Miaphysite, a cautious statesman, and surrounded by his own political enemies. In these anxious times, with the Rashidun army closing in, every ship was a precious asset.

But Nas'r had to try.

He descended the marble stairs of the library's western portico, the great cedar and bronze doors groaning closed behind him. The morning sun had climbed above the rooftops now, burning away the mist that clung to the alleyways.

Turning west, he set his course toward the Cæsareum, the former Roman temple now repurposed as the Patriarch's residence and seat of government. There, under its weathered columns, Cyrus held court with bishops and imperial secretaries alike.

Nas'r quickened his pace. His sandals struck stone with silent urgency.

The soul of Alexandria might be preserved in scroll and bone—but only if those still living dared to carry it.

Chapter 4

Two days had passed since Nas'r had first ascended the long
marble steps of the Governor's Palace. He returned now to the
library hall with a heavy scroll tucked under his arm—the fruit of
two full days of negotiation, rebuttal, and political pressure.
Cyrus had resisted at first, his treasury officials citing the urgent
need to preserve all remaining vessels for transporting soldiers
north, to bolster the defences around the Delta. Nas'r countered
with calm conviction: "Any troops not already on the move will be
stranded by the tide of war. By the time our ships launch, the
Rashidun will have taken what they will. This is not a matter of
arms. It is a matter of legacy."
And so, begrudgingly, Cyrus had relented. The decree bore the
Governor's seal and signature, and with it came sweeping authority
to commandeer, purchase, or otherwise acquire any vessel deemed
necessary for scholarly or ecclesiastical purpose, regardless of
ownership or destination.
That morning, the sun fell across the upper rotunda of the library,
casting long gold slants onto the great marble floor where the Ahl
al-Khidr gathered. The scroll of authority lay unfurled on a lectern
of Libyan cedar.
Stephanos arrived first, dusty and sun-touched. He reported
progress with the wagons—forty-seven already secured, with deals
in motion for twice as many more. "There are whole teams of
merchants who've fled their caravans and left wagons in the
southern quarter," he said. "They can be bought for silver weight,
or less."

Nas'r nodded. "We'll need one hundred. No fewer. The scrolls must be packed in hay, cloth, and order."

Malik arrived next, bearing with him an armful of texts—Greek, Latin, and early Arabic translations of Roman-era journals. He had begun comparing accounts of Julius Caesar's visit to Alexander's tomb, particularly the route Caesar's entourage had taken through the city. "There are fragments," Malik said, "descriptions of certain pillars, a reflecting pool, a temple with painted lions. I think I can map it. Slowly."

Father Athanasius, Theonidus the Cyrenian, and the young Copt, Brother Yohanon, stood before an ever-growing mound of scrolls, codices, tablets and parchment rolls. They had filled two corners of the Great Vesica. They had named it, unofficially, Hekatē Hall—after the goddess of liminality and preservation.

"We have begun with the Euclids and the Galens," said Theonidus. "The Coptic gospels are whole and many. The Book of Hidden Names we will move last, when the guards are changed."

Nas'r nodded. "You are the memory of Alexandria. Guard it well."

Now they turned to Baruch.

He had donned his travel cloak and carried a folded list of coastal holdings drawn by Malik, a gift of geography and hunches. Nas'r handed him the scroll bearing Cyrus's seal and a velvet pouch that clinked with weight.

"Thirty solidi and six dinars," Nas'r said. "Not nearly enough, but it will get you started. The rest will come from the Bishop's treasury in Qift, Cyrus has requested twenty solidi from the Bishop."

Baruch nodded gravely.

"Purchase, beg, or steal every dow, felucca, or barge that floats and holds sail. We will need every ship the Red Sea has to offer."

Baruch embraced Malik, nodded to the scribes, and pressed his hand to his heart. "I will meet you in Meroë," he said. "Or in the next world."

And then he was gone, slipping through the colonnades of the library and into the western quarter, where merchants still traded rumours for coin and old sailors waited for wind.

Nas'r turned back to the others.

"Five weeks," he said, looking at each face in turn. "Five weeks, and then we move. Let the world burn if it must—but we shall not let it forget."

And the work resumed, beneath the cracked dome of the last living library.

The Ahl al-Kidr met again one week later in formal council. Morning light pierced the high clerestory windows of the Great Vesica, casting long golden shafts across the floor. The once-solemn chamber—once used for public readings and royal decrees—was now transformed into a warehouse of civilization. Scrolls bound in linen, crates marked in Greek, Coptic, and Demotic, amphorae sealed with wax—knowledge packed and sorted by trembling hands.

It was a progress meeting.

Malik had spent every waking hour scouring the archives for accounts of Caesar's visit to Alexander's tomb in 48 BCE. From the fragments he uncovered, he gleaned identifiable geographic details—landmarks that no longer stood, but when cross-referenced with ancient city maps, they narrowed the possible burial site to within a few city blocks.

He had also searched for any mention of the visitations by Mark Antony and Cleopatra, but following the fall of the Ptolemaic dynasty, such references had been systematically erased—purged at the decree of Octavian himself. What remained, however, were scattered records of Septimius Severus, the Roman emperor who had famously visited Alexander's tomb and ordered its restoration. Malik was now chasing these elusive threads, hoping they had survived imperial censorship.

"We've found four distinct references to Caesar's visit," Malik said, holding up a thin papyrus annotated with careful markings. "All of them point to a subterranean chamber beneath the Soma. I believe we're close." He glanced at Nas'r, eyes sharpened with urgency. "I'll return again tonight. With luck, we'll have confirmation before week's end."

Nas'r stood at the head of the room, flanked by Malik and Stephanos.

"Sixty-nine wagons confirmed," Stephanos reported crisply. "Another twenty are under repair. We've scoured every stable and alley from Rhacotis to Canopus. Animals will come last, as agreed—oxen if possible, donkeys or horses if not. Camels for the long-haul travelers."

Malik nodded silently, the strain of sleepless nights etched into his face.

"And the manuscripts?" Nas'r asked.

Across the hall, Father Athanasius, Brother Yohanon, and Theonidus continued their monumental task. The Corpus of Euclid was already catalogued and crated. Galen's commentaries were halfway complete. The Babylonian star charts had been meticulously traced. Theonidus, ever meticulous, was fashioning lead-lined scroll cases for the Map of Eratosthenes. The pile of salvaged knowledge grew taller each day, and even Nas'r doubted whether one hundred wagons would be enough.

They had made staggering progress.

But so had the armies of the Rashidun Caliphate. Under General Amr ibn al-As, the invaders advanced with terrifying speed. News had reached them that the Caliph's banners now flew over Clysma - modern-day Suez - and the road to Alexandria lay open. The city had weeks—no more.

Nas'r didn't need to remind them. But he did, quietly:

"The fire draws near. We must outrun the flame."

It was the end of the third week, and as agreed, the Ahl al-Kidr gathered once more beneath the high vaults of the Great Vesica. The meeting took place at the same hour as before, the sun casting golden bars of light across the marble floor. Progress had been made—but so had the Rashidun.

Stephanos was the first to speak.

"We now have seventy-five wagons secured, including those salvaged from damaged stock. Most of the broken ones were beyond repair, but we're using them for parts to reinforce the others. We'll need to venture farther afield—beyond Eleusis district and into the outer villages. Many are fleeing west with their carts and beasts, and the supply is thinning. By the end of next week, we'll be finished with the wagons and begin securing animals. I'm praying we have enough. May God help us in this endeavour."

Nas'r gave a tight nod, then turned to the scribes.

"And the library?"

"As you can see," said Father Athanasius, gesturing to the increasingly crowded chamber, "the Great Vesica fills by the day. We've worked without pause, and by week's end, the first list will be complete." His voice swelled with pride. "But with your blessing, we ask for a second. We've barely scratched the surface, and without direction our work may waste precious time. You, Nas'r—you know this library better than any living soul. Help guide the hands that preserve its wisdom."

Nas'r paused, considering. The weight of it was immense. He looked around the hall, at the crates and scrolls, the tired but determined faces.

"Very well," he said at last. "You shall have your second list before the week is out. Your diligence honors the legacy we fight to protect."

Then he turned to Malik. "And what of the Two-Horned One? Has any light been shed?"

Malik's eyes gleamed with a spark of excitement.

"Yes. With Severus's account, we've confirmed the final resting place of Dhu al-Qarnayn. He lies beneath the ancient Soma, in a crypt deep below the old Macedonian necropolis—what once stood at the heart of the Serapeum complex. His tomb was restored during Severus's reign, likely sealed again and forgotten." Malik hesitated. "What we haven't found is the entrance. But Nas'r, we're close. We've narrowed the Khitābāt al-Maqbarah scrolls to one of three sealed alcoves in the east wing of the library. If Allah wills, we will have them by week's end. And if the scrolls are correct, they will lead us to the entrance."

Nas'r's shoulders eased slightly. They were doing all they could. Pushing harder would yield no more.

He offered quiet thanks to each man, then spoke again, his voice more somber.

"The Rashidun have now taken Clysma—the gateway to the Red Sea. Our final defenses there have crumbled. Pope Benjamin has come out of hiding and now seeks terms with Amr ibn al-As, but I fear it is too late. The general smells victory." He paused. "The last reserves have been called up. General Theodore hopes to intercept them near Pelusium, but the odds are long."

The chamber fell silent.

"We may have only a few weeks left," Nas'r continued. "Let us pray the Rashidun continue to march north—while we head south."

Another week had passed in the blink of an eye. Word had reached them from Baruch—he had made it to Fortress Babylon and was en route to Berenice. Reports spoke of marauding bandits along the southern roads, harassing villages and caravan routes. Local militias had begun fortifying the towns, bracing against both the Rashidun and lawlessness. Food was growing scarce. In some regions, villages were abandoned entirely—crops left to wither and livestock wandering untended through the fields.

Miraculously, Baruch had not yet needed to bribe anyone, and the sum entrusted to him remained untouched. It was a blessing, however fleeting.

As was his custom, Nas'r allowed the others to speak first.
Stephanos began.

"We have one hundred and five wagons," he said. "Some may not
survive the journey if fully loaded, I fear. Repairs are ongoing, but
the wheelwrights and cartwrights"—he paused—"what few
remained, have now fled the city."

He took a breath.

"Tomorrow, we begin collecting the oxen and other beasts. We'll
house them in the old stables of the Alexandrian Guard. They've
been abandoned but still hold hay and provisions. We will meet
our quota, Nas'r—but even so, it may not be enough."

He gestured to the growing rows of bundled scrolls, crates,
amphorae, and sealed tomes. The Great Vesica now overflowed
with the cargo of civilization. Shelves stood bare, alcoves empty,
thanks to the tireless work of the scribes.

"We've begun work on the new list," added Brother Yohanon from
behind a stack of scrolls. "The Mechanica of Hero of Alexandria,
more of Galen's treatises, fragments of the Aetia by Callimachus.
Even parts of the lost histories of Berossus and the sacred
geometries of Archimedes."

He sighed.

"We've enlisted every scribe and scholar we could find, but many
are deserting us now. Fear and inevitability weigh heavy. Perhaps,
Nas'r, a word to Governor Cyrus? We need more hands."

"I will speak to him," Nas'r replied solemnly. He too had noticed
the library's familiar rhythm fading—the hush of study replaced
with silence. The Rashidun were not famed for preserving the
written word. The Library of Ctesiphon and the ashes of
Gundeshapur were grim omens.

"And Malik?"

"We found the scrolls," Malik said, stepping forward, his face
drawn. "They were indeed in the alcoves we discussed. The text is
old—written in a mixture of late Demotic and early Coptic, with
occasional Greek notations for place names. It is not encoded, but

the script is faded and fragmented in places. Still, we are confident they will reveal the entrance to the tomb in due course."

Nas'r nodded in thanks to them all.

Then he spoke again, more grimly.

"I bring word from Cyrus. Palestine"—he glanced around—"or rather Palaestina Prima, as the Byzantines now call it—is lost. Caesarea fell after a brutal siege." He paused. "Patriarch Benjamin has fallen back to Nikiou. The horizon is black with smoke. War has come to our doorstep. We cannot delay. The enemy is near. News of our brother Baruch, he has held an audience with the Miaphysite Bishop of Qift and secured the twenty solidi promised by the Governor. This is a small mercy at least."

It was the eighth night Malik had gone without proper sleep. The narrow study chamber tucked behind the eastern colonnade of the Library was lit by flickering oil lamps, their smoke trailing like incense into the darkened vaults above. Around him, scrolls lay unfurled, annotated, and hastily stacked—an ocean of ink and linen washed over the low tables. Two scribes dozed in corners, exhausted. The room smelled of beeswax, parchment, and sweat. Malik hunched over the final scroll, its fibres brittle with age, the ink nearly vanished to the naked eye. He had enlisted a young apprentice—Aesclepius—to help trace the barely legible script with diluted charcoal. For two nights, they'd tried to make sense of the fragmented passages. And then, in the margins, buried beneath a redundant funerary blessing in late Demotic, it appeared.

A line, written in faint Greek.

ἐντός τοῦ νεκροταφείου Μακεδόνων, ὑπὸ τῷ πρώτῳ λίθῳ τῆς Σώματος

'Within the Macedonian Necropolis, beneath the first stone of the Soma.'

Malik froze.

He traced it again and again, calling to the others. Within minutes, the small chamber was alive with muttered translations and

overlapping voices. The full annotation, deciphered with careful cross-reference to similar passages in adjacent scrolls, read:
'The resting place of the King lies beneath the Soma. Seek the crypt in the earth below the first stone laid, in the shadow of the Heroon, where the gods of old once stood watch. The entrance is concealed, its seal made of Tyrian stone and lion-carved.'
Malik exhaled, a long breath that trembled on the way out.
"The tomb is beneath the Soma," he said aloud. "The original Macedonian necropolis… they buried Alexander beneath the sanctuary itself. The 'first stone'—the cornerstone of the structure—it marked the entrance to the crypt."
"But the Soma is long gone," said Theonidus, rising from his seat, bleary-eyed but lucid. "The necropolis was built over, layer upon layer. What stands there now?"
They unrolled the ancient topography maps of Alexandria, cross-referencing with Stephanos's recent urban surveys. Father Athanasius pulled down an updated layout compiled by local cartographers.
"There," said Malik, tapping a finger. "The ancient Soma would have stood here, near the intersection of the Canopic Way and the Street of the Sun."
"But that site is no longer open ground," said Stephanos. "The Roman basilica was built there in the third century. And more recently… yes, it became a public granary under the Exarchate. Now it's nothing more than a garrison depot. The guards quartered there call it the Domus Gravia—the heavy house."
Nas'r, summoned to the chamber by the urgency of the find, stood silent for a long moment.
"Then we must go. Tonight."
The others turned, surprised.
Nas'r's voice was low but resolute. "If the entrance still exists, it may be beneath the current structure—sealed, forgotten, built over. But if we wait, it could be lost forever. The Rashidun are weeks away, days perhaps. We will take the floor plans of the basilica and

the layout of the depot. We investigate in secret. If it is there, we find the crypt. If not... we move on with what we have."
Malik nodded, eyes heavy but shining. "I'll bring the original scrolls. And the lion. If the annotation is true, there should be a carving—Tyrian stone, and a lion."
"Then that is what we will seek," said Nas'r. "The lion that guards the king."

Chapter 5

The night air was thick with salt and smoke. Alexandria, once the brightest jewel of the Mediterranean, now whispered only in ash and fear. The stars above were veiled by low, drifting haze; somewhere to the east, a column of fire from a distant granary sent pulses of red into the sky.

Nas'r and the others moved in silence, cloaked in heavy wool, the hems of their robes soaked with dew and city grime. Over their tunics, they wore plain outer cloaks—hooded and dark—to avoid drawing attention. Each man carried a torch wrapped in cloth dipped in oil; they burned low, their flames flickering against shuttered windows and abandoned colonnades.

They moved in two files through the back alleys and covered arcades that branched off the Canopic Way, avoiding the central boulevards where soldiers or worse might still patrol. The journey from the eastern quarter of the Library to the old Roman depot—Domus Gravia—took just under an hour at this cautious pace. Longer than usual. They had to pause three times: once to evade a drunken gang of looters stripping bronze fittings from a disused bathhouse; once to help an emaciated boy huddled beside his dead mother beneath a portico; and once when a patrol of mounted militia clattered past the Serapeum, heading north with urgency.

"Even the shadows have grown teeth," muttered Stephanos.

They pressed on. By the time they reached the outskirts of the depot compound, the fires had dimmed behind them and the torches had been extinguished. Only Malik's smoldering wick remained.

The Domus Gravia was a squat, grim complex, set back from the main thoroughfare. Once a Roman basilica, its vaulted ceilings had long since collapsed; the remaining walls had been reinforced in the last century to serve as a granary, then barracks. Now, it stood deserted—the garrison having been summoned west to reinforce the final defensive line along the Nile. A crumpled standard hung limply from the upper parapet: the blue-and-gold banner of the Alexandrian cohort.

They entered through a side archway—once a servants' entrance—pried open earlier that day by looters perhaps. Inside, the building was deathly quiet. The air was cold and smelled of old wheat, sweat, and limestone dust.

Malik led them across the nave, consulting his sketches by the light of a small clay lamp.

"Look for the lions," he whispered.

They began their search—moving along the mosaic floors and ashlar walls. The iconography of the Macedonian era was largely lost beneath later Roman plasterwork, but here and there, faint outlines could be discerned.

"There," said Athanasius, brushing a palm across a flaking fresco. A lion—its eyes half-gone, its mane chiselled with care—was carved low into the base of a column. Across the room, another. Then a third, this time embedded in a corner slab, scarcely visible in the torchlight.

"A trail," breathed Nas'r.

Following the lion markers, they converged on a circular patch of stone in what had once been the central transept. The paving here was newer, but oddly set—tighter-fitting than the slabs around it. Malik knelt. He ran his fingers along the joint.

"This is it," he said. "The 'first stone'—or rather, the one that replaced it."

He took a rod from beneath his cloak—a tool for separating scrolls—and slid it into the hairline seam. With a slow, grinding creak, the slab shifted. It took three of them to shift it completely. Beneath it, darkness.

A shallow shaft revealed narrow steps cut directly into the bedrock, descending steeply into the bowels of the necropolis. The air that wafted up was damp and cold—heavy with the scent of old earth, myrrh, and stone long undisturbed.

Nas'r lit his torch again. The flame trembled but held.

And with that, one by one, they began to descend—leaving the ruined surface of the city behind.

The team of six descended slowly into the earth, their path lit only by the flickering glow of oil lamps. The narrow staircase spiraled downward in tight coils, carved directly into the stone, the walls close enough on either side to scrape their shoulders. The air grew cooler with each step, and the silence was broken only by the scrape of sandals and the soft hiss of breath. There were no railings, no handholds. One slip could send them tumbling— perhaps all of them—into the dark.

They had long since lost count of the steps when the sound reached them: water. Not a trickle, but the steady, rhythmic hush of flowing current. A subterranean stream. The temperature dropped sharply, the air moist and cool, carrying with it the scent of stone and deep earth.

At last, they reached the base of the stairs. It opened onto a narrow stone walkway, carved with precision and flanked on one side by a flowing canal. Malik held his lamp high. The tunnel they stood in stretched ahead and behind, twelve feet wide, vaulted and carefully laid with limestone blocks. The canal, about six feet across, ran down the middle, the water moving swiftly but without violence. The sound echoed in the vaulted chamber.

He crouched near the water's edge. "This was built," he said in quiet awe. "Not by chance. By design. The canal, the tunnel, the stairs—everything. This was engineered."

"Masterfully," agreed Threonidas, casting his light across the ceiling. "This work is far older than we imagined."

"What's striking," Father Athanasius said, his voice hushed, "is the absence of decay. No mold. No fungi. The air currents must keep the damp from settling."

Brother Yohanon peered across the canal. "But where does it come from? Where does it go? I've lived in Alexandria my whole life and never knew this waterway existed."

Nas'r stepped forward, eyes wide with reverence. "This was meant to be hidden. And yet here we stand, inside a structure that may be older than the city itself."

"I understand how the entrance remained hidden," Theonidas added, gesturing behind them. "For centuries, that granary floor was never disturbed. But this—this is magnificent."

Malik interrupted. "There are no markings. Which way? Upstream or downstream?"

They turned slowly, careful not to lose footing on the narrow ledge beside the canal.

"Upstream," said Nas'r at last. "We may not find the tomb, but we'll learn where the water begins. And if the builders meant to guard something, it would lie at the source."

One by one, they nodded. Single file, they followed Malik upstream, the current brushing against the edge of the stone ledge. Shadows danced madly on the tunnel walls as their oil lamps flickered, their light casting tall, warped silhouettes that seemed to move of their own accord.

After a hundred paces, the sound began to change.

The quiet hush of water gave way to a dull roar—like a hidden waterfall. Soon they entered a vaulted chamber, twenty feet across and just as high. It offered room at last to move freely, to stretch limbs aching from the narrow ledge.

In the far wall, four wide clay pipes jutted out high above the canal, disgorging streams of water that splashed into the trough below.

"It must come from Lake Maryout," Malik said, wiping moisture from his brow. "There is no other natural source for leagues."

"Surely not," Stephanos countered. "That's—what? Seven stadia? Ten? A massive distance underground."

"And not one mention of this in any map or archive," added Theonidas.

"But look around you," said Father Athanasius, sweeping his lamp across the chamber. "This is not for irrigation or utility. This—this was built for another purpose entirely."

"The tomb," Theonidas reminded them.

They turned slowly in place, the water behind them, the wall of pipes ahead. There was no exit. The vaulted ceiling offered no clues.

"Yohanon," said Nas'r. "Your lamp."

The monk handed it to him, and Nas'r edged cautiously toward the water. The ledge here was slick with spray. Malik steadied him with one hand on his belt as he leaned out over the canal.

Lifting the lamp high, Nas'r peered into the darkness across the water. "There's something there," he said. "Stone. Large. I can't make out the details."

"Allow me," said Malik.

He took the lamp and poured nearly all its oil into his own, creating a blaze twice as bright. Handing the half empty lamp back to Nas'r, he stepped forward, took aim, and swung his arm in a clean arc. The clay lamp soared across the canal and shattered on the far side.

Flames burst forth instantly, dancing across the oil-soaked stone. For the briefest moment, the chamber was lit like day—and what they saw stole the breath from their lungs.

A stone platform, worn smooth by time, supported a colossal sarcophagus—nearly twelve feet long, carved from dark basalt and gilded at the edges. Its sides were adorned with scenes: battle, triumph, a golden chariot pulled by lions, a young man crowned by Nike, the goddess of victory. Macedonian soldiers stood behind him, shields raised, spears held high. The lid was a single massive slab, fluted with ridges and carved with the likeness of a man—young, idealized, with the unmistakable features of Alexander the Great.

The flames flickered once more—then died into darkness.

No one spoke.

They had found it.

Not myth. Not legend.

The tomb of Alexander. Hidden for nearly a thousand years.

The six men moved like shadows through the sleeping city, retracing their steps with the same precision and care that had brought them there only hours earlier. Behind them, the stone slab had been returned to its resting place, sealing the ancient stairway and its secret once more beneath the ruined Domus Gravias. The alleyways of Alexandria lay deserted; only the cold sea wind whispered through the streets. Cloaks drawn tightly around them, the group arrived at the Library annex, now long repurposed as a safe haven for the Ahl al-Khidr.

Once inside, they lit a low flame in the hearth and shed their heavier garments. The room, sparse but fortified, buzzed with a subdued energy. It was here, in the flickering lamplight and under the silent gaze of old statues and scroll-lined shelves, that they began to speak—quietly at first, then with growing animation. Each man carried the weight of what they had seen, and though they viewed the discovery through different lenses—faith, duty, scholarship, awe—all were united in one belief: the tomb of Alexander the Great must be preserved at any cost.

Nasr stood at the centre, his robes still dusty from the descent, and raised a hand for silence. The room obeyed him.

"Brothers, time is as much an enemy as the Rashidun," he began,
his voice composed but heavy with tension. "We must act quickly,
but we must act wisely. Recklessness will doom us."
He turned to Malik, who was removing his sandals near the hearth.
"Malik, tomorrow night, you return. I can spare no men to
accompany you—all have their tasks. You will need poles—
hardwood if we can source them, from the old granaries or perhaps
loading beams from the disused warehouses at the waterfront.
Strong. Twelve cubits or more in length. And lashings—leather
cord if it survives, or hempen rope from the shipping stores. Build
yourself a temporary span. A bridge. Then take my qass al-
'imdad—the rod of measuring. You must assess the sarcophagus.
We need its length, width, height—and by that, we may estimate
its weight."
Malik nodded imperially. "I will make it so."
"You must work in the shadows Malik, none must know of our
discovery" Nasr continued. "But do not tarry. We must know what
we face."
Brother Yohanon raised his hand, his brow furrowed. "What is the
canal's significance? It is strange—out of place. Why divert a
stream so far below ground?"
Nasr gestured to the wall behind him, where an ancient map of
Alexandria was partially pinned.
"That is what we must determine next," he said. "There is only one
reason for a channel of that kind to pass through a tomb: access.
The sarcophagus—six, perhaps seven quintars in weight—cannot
be carried up those stairs, nor was it bought down from the top.
The passage is too narrow, and the weight would collapse the
structure. No, it was brought there early in the construction, before
the crypt was sealed. And so, it must leave by the same path: the
canal."
Father Athanasius stroked his beard. "You would divert the flow?
Or use it as a slipway?"

"I do not yet know," Nasr admitted. "But the way is there for a reason. We must learn where it leads. If the canal empties under Portus Magnus, we are doomed—too deep, and too exposed. But if it leads to a dry drain or empty cistern, then perhaps God has left us a way."

Stephanos stepped forward, crossing his arms. "What of transport? Even if we reach the surface, we must carry the coffin across a crumbling city without a whisper. We have no cart capable of bearing that weight."

Nasr looked to him intently. "Is there anything among the inventory? Something we've yet to inspect?"

Stephanos shook his head. "No wagon we've found can carry more than three quintars. Nothing close to what we need. Perhaps… perhaps in the barracks of the Augusta Legion—if the army under Benjamin haven't already seized it. The war-wagons, supply carts—they might still be there."

"Then search," Nasr commanded. "Make that your highest task. A useless tomb is no salvation."

He turned now to the scribes—Father Athanasius, Brother Yohanon, and Theonidas—who stood by the rear table, still clutching their ink-stained notes and dusty folios as if ready to get back to work despite the late hour.

"Enough for one night. All of you, return to your quarters. We reconvene at dawn. You have done well."

Each man nodded, fatigue beginning to show through the fire of discovery.

Nasr remained behind as they departed. Alone now, he took up a small oil lamp and carried it into the side chamber that had become his sleeping quarters. A woven reed mat—softened with wool and sheep hide—lay in the corner beside a scroll shelf. He unrolled it with care, laid down his cloak for warmth, and extinguished the lamp until only the distant crackle of the main hearth remained. He lay on his back, eyes open, the flicker of firelight playing against the ceiling.

It was not fear that kept him awake, but awe. Awe at the brilliance of the engineers who had constructed this tomb; awe at the staggering burden now laid at his feet; awe that the boy-king, Dhu al-Qarnayn himself, had rested there all these centuries, untouched. His thoughts turned, not to logistics, nor to secrecy, nor even to the dangers of the Rashidun—but to the shape of the canal, and the question that burned behind his eyes:
Where does it lead?

Chapter 6

Baruch's journey from Qift had been long and grueling, the desert stretches between the Nile and the Red Sea were unforgiving. After days of intense travel, he finally glimpsed the horizon where the jagged mountains met the coast. The ancient port city of Berenice Troglodytica lay before him like an aging relic of Rome's forgotten ambition, nestled against the desolate backdrop of the eastern desert.

Though it was mid-morning, the sun blazed overhead, casting harsh shadows along the narrow streets of the town. The air was thick with dust, the scent of saltwater, and the occasional whiff of dried fish—evidence of Berenice's once-thriving maritime industry. Though the city's walls still stood, their once proud stones now weathered and crumbling, it had fallen from its prime. He passed through the stone gate that once marked the grand entrance into Berenice, its watchtowers now abandoned. No guards stood sentinel. A single Arab merchant carrying spices on his back passed him, offering a quick nod of acknowledgment, before disappearing into a narrow alleyway.

Baruch moved through the town with purpose but careful consideration. Berenice had once been a jewel of the Roman empire, founded by Ptolemy II Philadelphus in the 3rd century BCE, and for centuries it had served as a vital trade post between Africa and the Arabian Peninsula. Its location along the Red Sea coast made it invaluable. But now, it seemed only a shadow of its former self, its vitality stolen away by the advancing tide of Arab control.

The eyes of the local population, still largely Coptic and Roman in
their heritage, were wary, though not hostile. The Arabs had yet to
fully integrate, and the city remained divided between those who
had accepted the new caliphate and those who resisted. Baruch
descended slowly, leading his exhausted mount down the narrow
path from the stone gate - once paved with Roman bricks, now
half-swallowed by the desert. At the outskirts, a weathered woman
with cataract-clouded eyes watched from beneath a threadbare
awning, her gaze passing over him as though seeing a ghost.
He found no soldiers. No patrols. Only the murmurs of sea wind
and the occasional bark of a mangy dog. A handful of sun-
darkened men mended fishing nets by the rocky shore. They
paused to watch him pass, then returned to their work. The harbor
was still functional, in its way—a few reed rafts lashed to rough
docks, and a solitary dhow bobbing in the shallows, its lateen sail
limp.
As Baruch made his way to the heart of the city, he couldn't shake
the sense that Berenice was now an occupied land, no longer a
place of commerce or power, but a broken crossroads of empires.
The once-strong Roman influence was being slowly replaced by
the Arabs' expanding dominion. He passed a small gathering of
local traders who whispered among themselves. They wore the
tunics of old, their robes still hinting at a time before the caliphate,
but their expressions betrayed suspicion. A few eyed Baruch as he
passed, no doubt wondering who he was and what business he
might have in this forgotten place.
Baruch made his way inland, past the ruined praesidium and
toward the high bluff where the Roman principia had once stood.
There, he found a Coptic chapel cut from stone and coral. He
paused at the chapel's threshold, the smell of incense and old stone
rising to meet him. If this place held answers—or allies—he would
soon find out.
Baruch stepped inside the small chapel carved from stone and
coral, its interior dimly lit by narrow shafts of sunlight filtering

through high, slitted windows. The scent of burning myrrh and beeswax clung to the cool air. Icons painted in the old Alexandrian style adorned the walls—faded gold leaf and ochre halos surrounding the saints who had once defended this very land.

A pair of monks in threadbare woollen robes knelt in silent prayer before the apse, their lips murmuring Coptic verses too low to understand. At the rear of the nave, a bearded man in a patched mantle stirred from his writing desk. He rose slowly—more from wariness than age—and met Baruch with a guarded expression.

Baruch bowed his head respectfully. "Peace upon you, Father."

The monk stepped closer. "And upon you, stranger. You are not of Berenice."

"I am Baruch, formerly of Alexandria, now in service to Governor Cyrus of Egypt. I bring orders—and coin—from Bishop Theophilus of Qift. I seek labor, aid, and shelter."

The mention of the Bishop seemed to soften the monk's shoulders. He introduced himself as Brother Stephanos, caretaker of the chapel and spiritual guide to the remnants of Berenice's Christian flock. Baruch explained the scale of the undertaking as simply as he could—he spoke not of names or relics, but of construction, secrecy, and the need for speed. The monk listened in silence, then called for the other brothers.

They gathered at a rough-hewn table in the chapel's side room, men of weathered faces and sand-chafed hands—no idle theologians, but fishermen-turned-monks who had chosen solitude over surrender. Baruch laid out the plan. A dock needed repair. A road down from the bluff must be cleared and reinforced. Timber would need to be found, rope fashioned, teams assembled. Ships— any vessels—must be gathered. And all of this in a town that barely held itself together.

"We cannot offer coin," Baruch finished, "but I offer something greater—purpose. You are not forgotten here. Your work will serve a cause sacred to all who follow the cross. And I can pay

laborers and traders, for I carry the Bishop's seal and twenty
solidi."
Brother Stephanos stood. "Then let this place once again serve the
Lord's work. You shall have our strength." He turned to the others.
"Go to the homes of our brethren. Tell them their hands are
needed. We build not for man or governor—but for legacy."
The monks dispersed at once, some with hoods raised, others
clutching shepherd's staves. A quiet energy filled the chapel.
Outside, Baruch moved next to the harbor. The sun was beginning
its descent, casting long shadows across the sand-packed streets.
He approached the fishermen by the rocky shore—rough men with
skin like leather and eyes narrowed from decades on the sea. Their
nets lay in coils beside them, their work nearly done for the day.
Baruch raised his voice. "Men of Berenice! I am Baruch of
Alexandria. I ask not for your fish, but for your sons."
This drew wary stares.
"I need messengers—fast boys, clever and sure-footed. One to sail
north along the coast. One to sail south. Every village, every inlet,
every fishing port—tell them ships are needed. Any vessel that can
bear cargo to sea. I do not ask for free service. For each ship,
payment will be given—by weight and by time."
One of the elder fishermen rose. "And what is this cargo that
cannot wait?"
Baruch met his gaze. "Something ancient. And something worth
protecting. That is all I can say."
There was a long silence, broken only by the call of a gull
overhead.
"I'll send my grandson," the old man said finally. "He knows every
rock from here to Myos Hormos."
Another nodded. "Mine too. The south route. He's restless
anyway."
Baruch thanked them and left behind one dirham to be split among
them.

As the sun began its slow descent behind the jagged peaks that loomed over Berenice, Baruch stood for a moment at the crest of the bluff above the chapel. The salt breeze tugged at his robes, carrying with it the scent of brine and dust. Below, the harbor shimmered faintly, a skeletal echo of Roman ambition. The day's efforts had exhausted him, but one last task pulled at his thoughts—the promise Amon-Sa had made before they parted in Alexandria.

'I'll leave word beneath the old lintel at the well.'

The well was easy to find. It sat on the southern edge of the forum ruins, a squat stone structure long choked with sand and time, but once central to life in Berenice. The surrounding buildings were little more than rubble now, their columns fractured, and cornices broken. But the lintel remained, a block of red granite balanced across two pillars, ancient and pitted, bearing a half-erased Latin inscription.

Baruch knelt before it, brushing sand from the base. His fingers found the edge of something tucked between stones—parchment, oiled to withstand the dry wind. He eased it free and unrolled it by the last rays of sunlight.

The handwriting was unmistakable: Amon-Sa's tight, angular script, hastily scrawled yet legible.

> *Baruch,*
>
> *I arrived the night before the full moon. The city is quiet. No signs of the Caliph's men. No bandits. I kept to the shadows, but the chapel stands, and the old harbor could yet be made to serve.*
>
> *I asked nothing of the locals. They watch, but they do not act.*
>
> *I have gone on to Adulis without delay. The gods willing, I shall return word before the new moon rises.*
>
> *— A.*

Baruch exhaled slowly, the tension in his shoulders softening just slightly. So, Amon-Sa had come and gone. No trouble. No delay. If the full moon had risen last night, then Amon-Sa was already two days ahead—perhaps more if he had secured fast passage south. He folded the message and tucked it deep into his robes, then looked east, where night crept steadily over the water. The message had arrived, as promised. Now, all that remained was to see if Adulis would answer.

Chapter 7

The last of the golden light filtered through the intricately patterned clerestory of the Great Vesica, casting long latticed shadows across the marble floor. Dust hung in the air like soft incense, drifting between shelves and scroll-racks that had once been full but were now being steadily emptied of knowledge. The hushed scrape of reed pens and the faint whisper of parchment filled the domed chamber. At the far end, beneath the great oculus, Nas'r stood hunched over a long cedar table, he rubbed his temple with ink-darkened fingers. Even here—surrounded by knowledge centuries old—the path forward felt uncertain, provisional. Their burden was not only to preserve, but to escape unnoticed and survive the road ahead.

Around him, scribes worked methodically—cataloguing, annotating, inventorying what they could of the stored relics – what to save and what to leave behind. Some were young, apprenticed in the monastery at Saint Catherine's; others were older men of the Church, lured from cloisters across the Delta to partake in what they understood was holy labour. Every page, every scrap of vellum, every reed-bound codex was treated with reverence. Every evening, Nas'r would consult the lists and decide what stayed and what was saved – a task he did not envy.

Nas'r dipped his pen into a jar of black gall ink, then paused. His other hand rested on a curled scroll of calculations—estimates for rations, water, and draft animals. The numbers were grim. "Ten weeks until we get to Berenice Troglodytica. Then another two weeks to Adulis. We cannot possibly carry all the provisions for man and beast to undertake such a journey. We will have to beg or buy. Or simply live off the land as we travel," he muttered to himself

He exhaled through his nose and turned back to the letter before him, addressed in large formal hand:

To His Excellency, Cyrus, Augustal Governor of Egypt, by Grace of the Emperor Heraclius.

The content, still in draft, was measured but pressing. He required Cyrus's explicit sanction for unimpeded passage south—not merely through the cities, but across all Roman roads. Without the decree, Byzantine patrols or rogue factions might challenge them—or worse.

Nas'r looked up as Malik entered silently, robes trailing faint dust from the colonnade.

"I have not heard from Stephanos. Has he sent word?" Nas'r asked without preamble.

Malik shook his head, brushing grit from his sleeves. "Not since morning. No word. No beast. No wagon."

"I would have expected him back by now," Nas'r muttered.

"Perhaps he ventured to Canopus today."

"He may be bartering still."

"Or worse," Nas'r said, voice low. "There are too many hands on every coin in this city. If he mentioned what the wagon was for…"

Malik didn't answer. The silence said enough.

Nas'r turned the parchment on his desk, placing the quill gently across its face. "Cyrus must sign this by week's end," he said. "I'd send it now, but without knowing his mood…" he trailed off, then added, "I almost think it would be better to ask Benjamin."

Malik arched an eyebrow. "The Pope?"

"He commands more loyalty than the Governor in much of the south. And his name carries weight among the desert Fathers. A decree from him would buy us obedience in the Coptic regions."

"But none from the garrisons," Malik replied. "Benjamin may hold the hearts of monks and farmers, but Cyrus holds the roads. And the blades."

Nas'r nodded reluctantly. "Which is why I need both. One for the men of God. One for the men of power."

Outside, a warm wind stirred the tapestries that lined the walls, fluttering them like sails. Darkness was settling over Alexandria, the purple hour painting the columns with shadow.

Malik glanced toward the stacks, then to the stout hempen rope tucked under his arm. "I will go to the Domus Gravias tonight," he said. "The timber for the span is already nearby, close enough to gather in the darkness but not too close to draw attention. By tonight, we will know what lies before us in moving Dhu al-Qarnayn."

"We need as much information as we can gather" Nas'r said, agreeing.

Malik offered a quiet nod, the mutual understanding between them unspoken but resolute.

"Be careful," Nas'r said.

"I always am."

Malik pulled up his hood and disappeared into the growing twilight, the echo of his sandals fading across the marble floor as the last of the sun bled out behind the Library's dome.

The night wrapped Alexandria in heavy velvet as Malik slipped from the alleyways into the shadowed forecourt of the Domus Gravias. The air smelled of salt and stone. His sandals made no sound over the worn flagstones. A thin crescent moon hung low behind a veil of cloud, offering no help. Perfect.

He moved quickly but with care, keeping to the shadows as he circled the abandoned barracks. No lamps lit the tall windows. No dogs barked. No voices murmured behind the columns. As before, the place lay dormant, hollowed out.

As before, Malik entered through the same side archway that had once been the servant's entrance. From beneath his robe, he produced a short iron crowbar, its edges honed earlier that day to his exact dimensions and profile. He set his oil lamp down on the mosaic tiles floor, with both hands he slipped the bar into the seam of the chosen flagstone, marked with a shallow gouge from his last visit.

He heaved.

The stone gave a groan, subtle but deep. He paused, listening, holding his breath. Nothing but wind whispering through the colonnade.

Another pry, another tilt—then with a damp scrape, the slab lifted. Malik eased it aside and propped it against the wall, revealing the black mouth of the stairwell below.

The air that rose up was cool, thick with the musk of long-sealed things. He closed the lamp's shutter to a pinprick and crept back into the shadows of the ruined portico, where he had hidden his cache. One by one, he hoisted the cut timber lengths—eight in total—balanced them over his shoulder and dragged them silently across the courtyard.

Each one dropped into the opening with a dull, echoing clunk, vanishing into darkness. The final beam gave a louder thud, like wood striking wood.

He froze. Waited.

Silence.

Then, satisfied no one had heard or stirred, he lowered himself into the stairwell.

The spiral steps were damp and uneven, worn down by centuries of use and neglect. His lamp flickered against the stone, casting long, jittering shadows down the coiling walls. The descent was slow, cautious—his hand brushing one side for balance, the other cradling the lamp.

At the bottom, the timber lay in a scattered heap, cast like bones across the narrow walkway that ran beside the subterranean canal. The black water glimmered dully, silent but powerful, flowing fast through the cut beneath the rock archway. The air was cool and moist, thick with limestone and silt.

Grunting with effort, Malik dragged each timber—one by one—along the narrow ledge, his sandals slipping now and then on the wet stone. Sweat slicked his face and soaked through his linen tunic. He paused only once to drink from a leather flask and wipe his brow.

The beams had now been assembled in the ante-chamber ready for the next phase.

Kneeling in the dust, Malik began to assemble the temporary bridge span. There were no nails. No bolts. But the cuts were clean. He laid five beams lengthwise across the channel on the stone coving blocks, then set shorter cross-braces perpendicular to these, three of them, lashing them tightly with hempen rope soaked in water for pliability. Every knot was doubled. Every joint pulled tight. He flipped it over with some effort.

By the end, his hands were blistered and his arms shook with fatigue—but the result was sound. A narrow walkway, little more than five planks wide, but strong enough to hold the weight of a man.

He tested it—first with a tentative foot, then both. It held.

Malik exhaled.

He turned to gather the rest of his equipment: his leather satchel, looped tightly shut; a bundle of spare oil flasks, wrapped in cloth; a bound sheaf of parchment pages tied in leather, what they called a mashaf in the scriptorium; his reed stylus, tucked into the binding; and finally the qass al-'imdad, the tool Nas'r had given him for measuring, weighted and elegant in its own wrapping of wool and oilskin.

Before he crossed the span to the tomb itself, Malik turned his attention to the canal.

He uncoiled a length of rope, tied a small oil flask to the end, and dipped it gently into the current. The flask jerked away in the flow, tugging constantly against his grip. He counted the time it took for

the flask to drag downstream before he retrieved it—roughly four
paces per heartbeat. A significant current.
Then, holding a weighted reed rod, he probed the canal's edge. The
water deepened quickly—the sides were vertical, and the bottom
slightly rounded, easily more than the height of a man – six cubits.
No way to wade this.
He made quick notations in his mashaf and stowed it all in his
satchel.
He turned to face the black mouth of the tomb across the water.
The oil lamp guttered as Malik crossed the temporary span he'd
lashed together. Each footfall creaked faintly on the damp wood,
but the bridge was sturdy. The canal gurgled beneath him—
sluggish, opaque, carrying centuries of detritus through forgotten
channels. He kept his hand near the dagger at his belt, eyes
sweeping the shadows along the chamber walls.
The sarcophagus waited as it had before, vast and unmoved, its
hulking mass of dark basalt rising like an altar from the stone floor.
The air here was still—oppressively so—pressing in like the
weight of time itself.
Malik approached slowly, the pool of light from his lamp casting
long shadows across the carvings. He paused before the massive
tomb, running his palm lightly along the cold stone. It was as tall
as his chest and nearly two men long, hewn from a single slab of
basalt, polished smooth on the faces but for the bands of carved
relief that wrapped around its sides.
The scenes struck him anew even in this second viewing—
Alexander at war, spear lifted in mid-thrust, a chariot drawn by
lions, the winged figure of Nike crowning him with a laurel
wreath. Macedonian soldiers stood behind their king, resolute, their
shields raised in salute or battle. It was less a memorial than a myth
in stone.
He moved to the front of the sarcophagus. The lid was a monolith
unto itself—a single, seamless slab, ridged at the flanks and carved
in high relief with the reclining figure of a youth. Alexander,

rendered in idealized repose, his head tilted slightly toward the viewer, hair curling like waves of bronze, a faint smile on his lips as though death had not been defeat, but apotheosis.

Malik knelt, setting down the lamp. He reached into his satchel and withdrew the iron bar he'd carried for this very purpose. Wedging the flat edge into a notch near one corner of the lid—likely once made for lifting pegs or ceremonial fasteners—he levered the weight with slow, quiet effort. The basalt groaned faintly in protest but shifted, just enough. He repositioned, braced his foot against the side, and pushed again.

The lid moved—half an inch, then another. He worked in silence, sweat dampening the back of his neck despite the chill of the air. A faint crack of old resin broke the stillness as a long-sealed seam gave way.

When at last the lid stood offset by nearly a hand's breadth, he fetched the lamp and raised it over the opening.

What lay within was unexpected—and extraordinary.

Set within the carved cradle of the sarcophagus was a second container, far smaller but no less remarkable: a coffin of bronze, dark with age but unmistakably intact. It lay nestled like a blade in its sheath, perfectly fitted, as though the outer tomb had been built around it.

The bronze had gone to a rich green-black with time, the surface mottled with oxidation. Along the upper band, just beneath the lip, ran a ring of Greek lettering—some words worn into obscurity, others still sharp enough to read:

ΑΛΕΞΑΝΔΡΟΥ ΦΙΛΙΠΠΟΥ ΜΑΚΕΔΩΝΟΣ
Alexander, son of Philip, of Macedon

Ornate bronze handles flanked either side, set in iron rings darkened with rust. Malik reached out and touched the surface—it was cool, not clammy, and rang faintly under his knuckles. A traveling coffin, not a fixed reliquary. This had been meant to move.

His breath caught.

The implications struck him in waves. The outer tomb—so immovable, so eternal—was symbolic, a temple to the myth. But this inner casket… this was the vessel of the man. Not just ceremonial. Practical. Portable. Secreted. If ever they needed to remove the body from this place like they had done at Memphis—whether to hide it, honour it elsewhere, or safeguard it from desecration—they could.

It also meant that the real question remained unanswered.

Was the bronze coffin occupied?

Malik hesitated. He would not open it tonight. Not alone, not in the dark.

Instead, he set the lamp down carefully and withdrew his mashaf and reed stylus. He took the qass al-'imdad, the inkwell-case Nas'r had gifted him, and began to sketch, taking down every dimension he could reach—length, breadth, the width of the ledge around the sarcophagus, the orientation of the figures in the reliefs, the width of the canal, and most crucially, the height clearance between the tunnel arch and the top of the bronze coffin. As he took this measurement, standing on the lid of the sarcophagus, he noticed heavy lifting rings of iron cast into the arched ceiling – the ancient engineers had left nothing to chance.

History had been laid bare here—but only just. The man who had wept because there were no more worlds to conquer had not vanished.

He had been hidden.

Malik turned down the wick on his lamp, pulled up his hood, gathered his belongings and disappeared once more into the shadows.

The stars were sharp and cold above Alexandria when Malik emerged from the Domus Gravias, the faint scent of wet stone clinging to his robes. His arms ached from hauling timbers and lashing the makeshift span into place, and his satchel—heavy with tools, empty oil flasks, and the damp qass al-'imdad—dragged at his shoulder. But his steps were careful as he crouched beside the open stairwell one final time.

With a low grunt, he reached for the broad flagstone he had pried up hours earlier. Its underside was smeared with damp earth and dust, and it scraped softly as he maneuvered it back into position. He pressed it down firmly, twisting it slightly until it sat flush once more with the surrounding floor. The grooves of the mosaic locked into place—nearly seamless in the moonlight.

Satisfied, he stood, brushed grit from his hands, and slipped silently back into the shadows of the alleyway.

The walk to the Library was quiet and untroubled. The streets had emptied, save for the occasional flicker of a distant oil lamp or the bark of a dog in the Greek quarter. Malik kept to the margins, ducking beneath colonnades and moving with the practiced silence of a man who had spent too many years avoiding attention.

When he reached the Great Vesica, the inner chamber of the Library was still aglow. From beneath the domed oculus, the warm amber light of a single lamp spilled across the marble floor in a flickering pool. Inside, Nas'r sat alone at his cedar desk, a sheaf of scrolls spread before him and a cup of honeyed wine cooling at his elbow.

He looked up as Malik entered, the lines of fatigue stark across his face, though his eyes remained sharp.

"The hour is late," Nas'r said mildly.

Malik lowered his hood and exhaled. "Yes. I built the bridge, inspected the tomb, and took measurements."

Nas'r sat back, setting his stylus down. "You have spent the time wisely. What more do we know?"

"The sarcophagus is enormous. A single piece. The stone alone would weigh more than three hundred talents. Ten oxen could not shift it—not without divine favour or some ancient cunning."
Nas'r nodded once. "I fear we are out of cunning." He stood and crossed to a nearby cabinet, pouring Malik a half-cup of wine.
Malik accepted the drink, his voice dropping. "But it is as we hoped. I believe there's a funerary casket of bronze inside. Smaller. Likely movable. I couldn't lift the sarcophagus lid alone."
"The inner coffin," Nas'r murmured. "A vessel within a vessel."
Malik nodded. "If it is what we think it is… we may not have long."
"And the weight?" Nas'r asked.
"Twelve talents. Maybe fourteen. No more."
"Could we float it out? Would it float?" Nas'r asked, now problem-solving aloud.
"We'd have to build a raft. Cedar, if we can find it. But that alone won't float the casket."
"Goatskin bladders?" Nas'r suggested.
"Possibly."
Nas'r drank quietly, then glanced toward the southern windows, where the wind stirred the long silk curtains. "Stephanos still hasn't returned."
Malik said nothing.
"I'll return tomorrow," he said at last. "We need to know the outflow of the canal."
Nas'r gave him a weary, grateful look. "Sleep first. You'll need your strength."
Malik nodded, drained the last of the wine, and turned toward the quiet dormitories in the east wing. Behind him, Nas'r remained at the cedar desk, staring down at his maps and calculations, the flicker of the lamp catching the faint ink stains on his fingers. Outside, Alexandria held its breath.

The next morning the Library was still cloaked in hush and lamplight when the heavy knock came at the northern portico. Malik looked up from the table where he was entering buoyancy calculations into a vellum folio. Nas'r, seated across from him, froze mid-sentence.

The knock came again—three hard raps, uneven, urgent.

Malik rose swiftly and crossed to the bronze-bound doors, easing one open just wide enough to see out into the fog of pre-dawn. Stephanos stood slouched in the archway, silhouetted by the dying stars, one arm pressed tightly against his ribs. His face was bloodied, his cloak torn, and the left side of his tunic soaked dark with something that had started as crimson and dried to rust. A swollen bruise covered one eye, and he limped as he stepped forward into the lamplight.

Nas'r was already on his feet, eyes widening. "By the saints—"

"They didn't kill me," Stephanos rasped, with a grimace that might have once been a smile. "But they damned well tried."

Malik caught him as he stumbled, helping him to the long bench beside the scroll cabinet. The stink of iron and sweat clung to him—old blood, fear, ash. Nas'r fetched a cloth and a basin of water, and Malik eased off Stephanos's cloak, revealing deep gashes along his forearm and a nasty welt on his temple.

"Tell us," Nas'r said, kneeling beside him.

Stephanos exhaled slowly, as if testing whether his ribs would allow speech.

"I found it," he said. "An ox-wagon. Heavy-bed, reinforced axle, iron bindings. It was in the yard behind old Kalbar's forge, near the Quarter of the Ironmongers."

"That's nearly to the water," Malik said, frowning. "Why so far?"

"I had to search far and wide. It's the only one that can take the weight," Stephanos replied. "I made inquiries. Quietly. A man at the docks pointed me there."

Nas'r handed him a cup of watered wine. "And then?"

"I had coin on me—to purchase it. But word's out. Gangs have taken parts of the quarter. Deserting soldiers, dock thieves, zealots. I was cornered near the old aqueduct. Four of them. Armed with blades and clubs. They took the purse, beat me half into the grave. Then I was arrested"

"Arrested, not taken to an infirmary?" Malik asked.

Stephanos nodded grimly. "A riot broke out just blocks from there. Fire. Looting. I must've looked like part of it. Patrol swept me up with the rest. They held us at the customs barracks near the eastern gate."

"You were gone all night," Nas'r said. "I feared the worst."

"I would've still been there," Stephanos muttered, "but the Captain of the Guard recognized my name. He knew I was yours. Said he owed a favour to Cyrus."

Nas'r's brow lifted at that, and he muttered a silent prayer under his breath. "Cyrus buys us more than time, it seems."

Stephanos sat upright, wincing. "There's more. At Kalbar's yard— beside the wagon—I saw them. A dozen oxen. Big ones, healthy. Still tethered in the rear stables. If we can get in... if we can get to the yard..."

"It's a miracle they haven't been taken already," Malik murmured.

"Or slaughtered," Nas'r added.

"They won't last," Stephanos said. "Once the gangs realize what's there..."

Malik looked to Nas'r. "We'll need men. Armed ones."

Nas'r nodded slowly, already moving toward the far cabinet, where his seals and official scrolls were kept. "I'll go to the Governor myself, at once. If Cyrus still holds sway, we may have a phalanx by midday."

Stephanos groaned and leaned back, closing his eyes. "Don't let this face greet them at the gate. I'll frighten the oxen."

"You'll frighten the Governor," Nas'r muttered with dry affection, placing a hand on his shoulder. "Rest. You've done more than enough." He quickly donned his cloak and headed for the heavy cedar and bronze doors.

Outside, the wind stirred through the cracked city, where statues toppled and fires smouldered in temple courtyards. Alexandria was breaking—but the tomb still waited, silent and undisturbed beneath its stone veil. And now, they had a way to carry its burden.

If the city didn't fall first.

Chapter 8

Evening blanketed Alexandria in sullen tones of ochre and smoke. Fires still smouldered in parts of the city; ash drifted like snow through alleyways once proud with merchant colour. Malik moved quickly but carefully through the streets, keeping close to walls and slipping into shadows at the first sign of danger.

The looters were more brazen now. Armed gangs roamed openly— some dressed in fragments of Byzantium armour, others in militia garb. The waterfront had become a gauntlet of lawless militia, temple loyalists, and deserters. Soldiers no longer obeyed orders; they obeyed hunger, fear, and whoever held the strongest fist. Malik avoided a group of men overturning carts near the old fish market and ducked through a passage beside the grain exchange. He moved east until the street narrowed and opened into the silent yard of the old Domus Gravias.

The old granary loomed like a forgotten tomb. He circled to the servants' door, pried it open, and stepped into still, musty darkness. No sound but the echo of his own footfall as he crossed the floor to the tile—the lion tile. He set down the satchel slung across his chest and pulled from it the short iron bar. It took several minutes of levering, but eventually the stone loosened, groaned, and lifted just enough for him to grip and slide it aside.

He lit a small oil lamp from his pouch and began the descent, step by careful step, into the dark beneath the city. The stone stairwell coiled downward like the gullet of some ancient beast.

At the base, the canal awaited. The water ran quietly, with the deep whisper of age. He knelt beside it and drew from the satchel a tightly wound goatskin. Shaking it out, he raised one leg of the skin to his lips and began to inflate it. It took effort; his lungs strained with each breath until finally the bladder was full. He tied it off with a piece of twine.

Then he stripped down to his loincloth, folded his clothes, and placed them carefully inside the satchel, tying it shut. He'd retrieve them if he survived the journey.

Sitting on the edge of the canal he lowered his legs into the flow, he flinched—the cold gripped him like a vice. He lowered himself in, clutching the float under one arm, the oil lamp in the other. Using his feet to press gently against the canal walls, he let the current take him.

It was slow at first. Silent. The only sounds were the soft lapping of water and the trembling hiss of his oil flame.

He flowed down the canal, without deviation for a long time. Then, something ahead—resistance.

He collided with iron. A rusted grate stretched across the canal mouth, half-submerged and eroded with age. The current pinned him to it like an insect on a screen. He reached up to wedge the lamp on the ledge beside the water, but his hand slipped. The lamp fell and shattered.

Darkness swallowed him.

Panicking, Malik gasped, then forced himself still. His heart thundered in his ears. He felt the grate—worn, ancient, pitted. He reached lower and found one bar eaten away with rust. He kicked it hard. Once. Twice. It cracked and gave.

Another bar next to it bent with a shriek under his sandal. He kicked again and it snapped. He had an opening.

He shoved the goatskin forward, but it snagged on a jagged edge. A loud hiss—then the bladder deflated.

Panic surged. The current pressed him hard into the iron. He couldn't breathe, couldn't move.

With a growl of effort, he ducked below the surface and pushed himself bodily through the gap. A tearing pain lanced across his side, but he was through.

The water surged stronger now, and the canal began to slope. Malik swam, kicking as best he could, but his strength was ebbing.

The roof above began to narrow, dropping closer to the surface.
Then, suddenly, it was just inches above his face.
There was no choice now.
He sucked in a deep breath and dove forward, letting the current
sweep him.
The roof was low. His head struck stone once, twice. He winced,
twisting sideways to stay beneath the ceiling. He was blind—no
light, no direction, only the feel of water pulling him forward.
His lungs ached. Limbs heavy.
Then—up ahead—something faint. A dull grey circle, far off, low
and small.
Light.
The end of the tunnel.
He flailed toward it. His body was screaming now, muscles
trembling. Just as his chest felt ready to tear open, he reached the
end. The tunnel spat him out in a rush.
He tumbled forward, the current hurling him into open water.
Cold silence. Stillness. Then moonlight.
He surfaced with a gasp, sucking in air like a drowning man
reborn.
All around him, the world shimmered in silver. The canal had
emptied into a quiet basin. Nearby, the rotted beams of a wooden
jetty stretched into the water.
Portus Magna.
Of course. The old port, disused for generations.
Around his legs he felt the colder stream of canal water mixing
with the saltwater port. He kicked slowly toward the jetty, found
the moss-covered ladder, and climbed up, hand over hand.
Soaked, half-naked, shivering. But alive.

He sat on the planks, breathing heavily. He was too cold, too tired
to feel triumphant. But still, as he stood and began the long walk
back toward the library, bare feet slapping on wet stone, a smile
crept across his face.

The exit was real.

The route could be done.

The tomb could be moved.

And now, the others would know.

The great doors of the Library creaked open, casting a flicker of torchlight across the stone floor. Malik staggered into the atrium, his skin pale and wet, his ribs heaving with each breath. His hair was still slick with canal water, and his feet left a glistening trail behind him as he made his way, half-naked, through the corridors of the grand old Domus. A servant, wide-eyed, rushed to fetch Nas'r.

Minutes later, Malik sat wrapped in a heavy wool cloak, the scent of cedar and old ink rising from its folds. A cup of warm, honeyed wine steamed gently between his hands as he huddled beside a brazier in the central chamber, letting the heat return life to his limbs. Across from him, Nas'r leaned forward at the long desk, inkpot and parchment ready, eyes locked on Malik.

Malik took a slow sip, swallowed, and began.

"I found the outlet," he said, voice rough. "The canal emerges beneath Portus Magna, just beside the old wooden jetty. It's well hidden, and difficult to reach—no wonder it was never found. I was lucky to survive the descent. But it can be done."

Nas'r's quill scratched to life.

"We'll need sturdy ropes," Malik continued, warming with the momentum of planning. "And pulleys—good ones. Assuming those iron rings in the ceiling of the tomb still hold weight. The lid of the casket—" he paused, brows drawn. "It will be the hardest part. It may weigh more than the casket itself. If we cannot lift it cleanly, we may need to tip it over the far side. Damage may be unavoidable."

Nas'r's eyes flicked up, but he said nothing.

"Once the lid is off, we insert stout cedar beams underneath the casket. Long enough to extend out over the edge of the canal. As we inch it forward, the beam will pivot and lower the casket like a ramp. Slower than building scaffolds or stairs, but steadier. The pulleys can be reused here—lashed around the sarcophagus, or if the lid remains intact, we can anchor to that."

Nas'r nodded, scribbling diagrams in the margins.

"The raft is our greatest risk," Malik went on. "We'll construct it down in the tomb, in pieces. Thick timber beams lashed together, with six inflated goatskin bladders—three on each side. Enough lift to keep the casket afloat. It must be tied tight, very tight, or one wrong tilt and it capsizes. We'll have two men in the water to centre it in the current, and two on the walls with rope to control its forward motion."

"And the grate?" Nas'r asked.

Malik nodded. "I reached it myself. It's old—cast with the canal, I'd wager. The underwater bars are severely corroded. A few iron rods and some leverage will break it open. Two men could do it quickly."

Nas'r raised his quill again. "Very well. But the incline after that—the canal slopes. You said the exit is submerged. How do you stop the casket from floating to the roof and jamming?"

"Neutral buoyancy," Malik said. "We bleed two of the central goatskins—just enough air to bring the casket down while keeping it afloat. The escaping air will give our swimmers air to breathe, too. It's risky—very. But I'm betting the casket is sealed, like the sarcophagus. If water gets in... then we've lost everything."

"And surfacing it at Portus Magna?"

Malik offered a faint smile. "We catch it like a fish. A net, stretched beneath the jetty, held by men on either end. Once it's secure, we drag it ashore, roll it up ramps, and place it on the ox-wagon."

Nas'r looked up from his notes, face lined with concern. "We assume a great deal with this plan, Malik."

"I know," Malik said quietly. "It will take strong men and many hours. And yes, it could fail at a dozen points. But I've been over it again and again. This is the only way that gives us a reasonable chance of success. And it will take time to prepare."

Nas'r exhaled through his nose. "Time is the one thing we lack. The Rashidun draw nearer by the day. The peace accord with Benjamin is not yet offered, and I fear it will do little to sate Amr's appetite for conquest."

He sat back, letting the full weight of their task settle over the room. Then, with a final stroke of his pen, he looked up.

"Very well. We attempt it the tomorrow night. You have one day to prepare your team. Stephanos and I will retrieve the oxen and the wagon. The rest will begin loading what we can."

Malik nodded slowly, turning the plan over in his head.

"And protection?" he asked.

"Cyrus has offered us a phalanx from the palace guard," Nas'r replied. "They'll defend the Library and accompany us on the first part of the journey. After that—" he spread his hands. "We are alone."

Malik looked into the fire. His skin still tingled from the cold. His muscles ached, and the smell of river sediment still clung to him beneath the cloak. But his eyes burned bright.

"Then we'd best not waste the day we have."

The morning haze lifted reluctantly over Alexandria, sea mist clinging to the lower streets as if unwilling to surrender the city to the sun. But there was no pause for the men of the Library. Time had become a currency too precious to squander.

Outside the fortified walls of the complex, Nas'r and Stephanos made their way along the eastern road, accompanied by six guards from the palace phalanx. Their scale armour shimmered dully beneath grey wool cloaks, helmets crested with horsehair. Each man bore a long spear and a curved kopis blade. Their presence drew wary eyes, but no interference. Word had already spread through the markets: the city was being emptied of anything valuable.

Stephanos moved stiffly, still in pain from the previous night's engagements.

The group approached the Quarter of the Ironmongers from the south. It was still alive with sound—the rhythmic clanging of hammer on anvil echoed through the streets. Kalbar's Forge stood near the centre of the district, not far from the wharfs and Portus Magnus. Kalbar himself, a squat man with forearms like tree trunks, was busy shaping horseshoes with precise, practiced blows. Nas'r asked the palace guard to remain at the front gate while he and Stephanos approached. They greeted the blacksmith with measured politeness before Nas'r turned to the matter at hand.

"Our apologies, master smith, but we're making enquiries about the stout ox-wagon and the dozen oxen in your yard."

"That would be mine," Kalbar said, not pausing in his work. "And who's asking?"

"I am the Curate of the Great Library. We require the wagon to move several large statues to the Grand Palace," Nas'r said, lying smoothly.

"They're not for sale," Kalbar replied flatly.

"For any price?" Stephanos asked, warming to the negotiation.

"You must be in desperate need, Curate, if you've come to bargain yourself."

"Perhaps. But I see they are not in use—perhaps surplus?"

"Nothing here is surplus," Kalbar said, spreading his arms wide. "Everything has its use, eventually."

Nas'r clenched his jaw. Time was bleeding away; he couldn't afford to haggle.

"Six solidi," he offered.

"Ten," Kalbar countered instantly, "and not a dinar less."

Before Nas'r could reply, Stephanos stepped in with a flourish.

"Eight solidi—or we take them by force." He gestured toward the phalanx waiting silently down the street, their attention fixed on the exchange.

Kalbar raised an eyebrow, then grinned.

"A very generous offer, to be sure." He waved toward the yard.
"Take them. They're yours."
With the help of the palace guards, Nas'r and Stephanos began
hitching several oxen to the wagon, leading the others by rope. As
they made their way back to the Library, Nas'r turned to his
companion.
"'We take them by force?'" he echoed, half in rebuke.
"They'll be ideal for moving the statues, Curate," Stephanos
replied, smiling as he walked.
While Nas'r and Stephanos negotiated the oxen and wagon beneath
the wary gaze of the palace phalanx, Malik remained within the
Library grounds—his thoughts entirely consumed by the physics of
impossibility.
He had eaten little since morning, a crust of bread forgotten on a
stone ledge as he paced and planned in the dusty side court of the
eastern cloister. The courtyard had become his improvised
workshop. Around him lay piles of thick cedar planks, coils of
rope, scraps of goatskin, and the heavy scent of pitch. The noise of
the city and the rising tension of Alexandria's streets were distant
echoes here. All Malik could hear was the imagined creak of ropes
under tension, the groan of bronze being shifted, the slap of water
against a narrow canal wall.
He knelt beside a long cedar beam and tapped it methodically with
a mallet, listening to the tone. Sound wood. Strong. He needed at
least four to serve as the base for the raft, another two for the
beam-pivoting mechanism that would lower the casket into the
canal. He marked them with a dab of charcoal, then moved to the
goatskins drying nearby—six large bladders from a local tanner,
each smeared with resin. He tested them one by one for air-
tightness, inflating each by mouth and submerging them in a basin.
No bubbles. He exhaled slowly, satisfied.
Next came the pulleys. Malik had acquired them from the
shipwrights' warehouse—they had once served as temporary
rigging pulleys, used to pre-stretch guys and stays. He cleaned and

tested them with a loop of rope and an amphora filled with sand,
greasing the grooves until they turned smoothly. He had only one
real chance to get it right; failure in the tomb chamber meant the
casket might never be retrieved.

Sweating despite the cooling afternoon breeze, Malik turned to the
most delicate preparation: assembling the sling.

It was the rigging of a merchant galley, repurposed for a scholar's
daring—a web of shrouds and ratlines once scaled by sailors, now
refitted into a sling wide and strong enough to cradle a king's tomb.
This too had come from the shipwrights' warehouse. It would serve
as the final safeguard: the net cast across the outflow pipe of Portus
Magna to "catch the fish," as he had told Nas'r. A strange image,
perhaps, but the principle was sound. Once snared, they could drag
it ashore with oxen, if necessary.

As the shadows lengthened, he moved back to the bundle of tools
he had laid out with care: iron rods for leverage, chisels, hammers,
waxed hempen cord for waterproof binding, a measuring rope with
knots at regular intervals. Each was oiled, tested, and laid again in
order. Lastly, he rolled up two small scrolls—his notes and
diagrams—and sealed them in a leather pouch. If anything
happened to him in the canal, someone would need to know how to
proceed.

As the sun dipped toward the western rooftops and the cries of
evening prayer began to echo from distant towers, Malik stood,
stretching his stiff back. His hands were black with soot and pitch,
his tunic stained and torn at the hem. He allowed himself a single
breath of stillness.

Then he walked to the cloister gate and looked toward the distant
road. No sign yet of Nas'r and the wagon, but they would come.
And when they did, every part must be ready. Every rope, every
knot, every pulley.

They were no longer merely caretakers of knowledge.

They were thieves of history—plotting to steal a dead king from
time itself.

Chapter 9

The sky over Alexandria had deepened to a bruised indigo.
Lamplight flickered along the parapets of the Library, and the

rustle of cloaks and distant whispers of prayer carried on the breeze like fading incense. Within the eastern cloister, Malik made one final inspection of the raft components.

To his left lay the cedar beams—six in total. Four for the raft, two for the ramp. It should be enough to support the weight of the bronze casket. Once they reached the shoreline at Portus Magna, two of the raft beams would be repurposed as skids to guide the casket up onto the wagon.

In the centre were the ropes, pulleys, and lashings. He had checked and rechecked the load-bearing strength of each component. If he had guessed the casket's weight correctly—and he was confident he had—they should hold. The only unknown was whether the ancient iron rings set into the vault's ceiling would bear the strain once the casket was freed from its resting place. That was a calculation no parchment could resolve.

To his right, the goatskin floats lay bundled and bound, each treated with resin and pitch. He had marked the central floats with additional tar—these were the ones they would manipulate for buoyancy, and to draw breath when needed. It was the trickiest part of the entire operation. It had to be done slowly and incrementally. And all of it depended on one uncertain hope: that the casket was sealed. If it wasn't, the plan would fail before it began.

At his feet lay the modified ship's rigging, reshaped into a broad net. Two long shared lines had been joined at the apex of the shrouds—this would allow several men to haul in the net and its "fish" with relative ease. If the raft retained neutral buoyancy, the weight on the lines should be no more than the rigging itself—until the final pull toward the shoreline, when the oxen would take over. Beside the rigging were the iron bars they would use to break open the canal's rusted grate. The opening had to be wide enough to allow the raft and its burden through. If the bars failed, hammers and chisels were their backup—carefully nestled alongside.

As Malik ran through the plan for the tenth time that hour, Stephanos and Nas'r arrived with the ox-wagon, drawn faithfully by two sturdy beasts. Together, they loaded the components into the cart, covering them with a large sheet of linen—soon to be used to conceal the casket during transport. In Malik's mind, there was nothing more to adjust. Every decision had been made. Every variable anticipated.

Nas'r cast his eye across the bundles, then turned to Malik.

"Is everything in readiness? We'll depart once nightfall settles. Have you chosen the men for each task?"

"Yes, Nas'r. Everything is as ready as it can be. Brother Yohanon and I will guide the raft. He's strong, capable, and steady. You and Father Athanasius will control the descent from either side of the canal—that will be easier than trying to steer from the water. When we reach the grate, you and the Father will break it open with the iron bars. That part will be harder. I'm hoping age has weakened the metal enough to yield."

He gestured toward the net. "Stephanos and Theonidas will manage the rigging. The lines are long enough to be operated from the wharf, but it must be done with care—no jerks or sudden pulls. Once the casket is at the landing point, we can guide it to shore. The oxen will do the rest."

Nas'r gave a slow nod. The plan was clear, thought-through, and precise. Malik had done all he could. The rest was with God.

He placed a firm hand on Malik's shoulder.

"The plan is sound. You've prepared for everything we can foresee. Only heaven can help or hinder us now. Let's gather the others. Darkness is almost upon us."

The six brethren led the cart toward the Domus Gravias. This time, there would be no escape into darkness if threats approached. Fortunately for the troupe, only a few looters prowled the streets. The governor's decree—and its strict curfew—was beginning to take effect. Looters and rioters were now to be executed on sight; anyone found outside after dark was assumed to be one of them. Nas'r felt reassured by the decree tucked safely into his satchel.

They pressed on until they reached the Domus. After carrying the beams, floats, pulleys, and ropes into the central courtyard, Nas'r, Father Athanasius, Malik, and Brother Yohanon bundled the remaining tools and bid Stephanos and Theonidas farewell. With luck, they'd soon be the luckiest fishermen in Alexandria.
The two groups parted: one slipping inside through the servant's entry of the Domus, the other gathering their cloaks and heading quietly for the old wharf.
Only time would tell.

Malik had already removed the central tile by the time Nas'r and Father Athanasius arrived with the remaining tools. He was practiced now, the motion almost routine. Working together, they lowered the beams down the narrow spiral stairwell, followed by the ropes, floats, and pulleys. Lighting their oil lamps, they descended into the darkness.
At the bottom of the winding stairs, the familiar damp air greeted them like a second skin. They regrouped and began hauling the gear to the antechamber. The main vault granted them room to move. Malik immediately began lashing the raft together. Meanwhile, Athanasius and Nas'r crossed the narrow wooden bridge still in place from nights before. Their oil lamps cast flickering shadows on the great sarcophagus. Nas'r paused, marveling at the intricate reliefs carved into the lid and the tomb walls—drawn especially to the remnants of bright color still painted across the stone.
After a brief inspection, Nas'r called over the canal's steady churn. "Malik, can we remove the lid? Athanasius and I should be able to manage it with the levers."
"Yes!" Malik shouted back, nearly drowned out by the roar of cascading water from the four pipes. "Try to get it off in one piece—if it lands flat on the other side, we may be able to use it as an anchor to lower the casket down the ramp. Do your best, Nas'r."

The two men set to work, inserting their iron bars into the engineered slots at the tomb's corners. The lid resisted at first, refusing to budge more than a fraction. But with careful timing and equal force, they coaxed it backward.

When the lid was a third of the way back, its weight shifted—just enough to ease their burden. At the halfway point, both men paused, panting and slick with sweat. They drank greedily from their hip flasks.

Nas'r took the opportunity to warn the others.

"Malik, we're about to tip the lid. There'll be noise. And dust." Malik simply waved a hand without looking up, absorbed in his task of tightening the raft's lashings.

Nas'r and Athanasius returned to the lid. It was delicately balanced now—another few nudges would send it toppling. Slowly, carefully, they pushed. The stone slab teetered at the brink—then, with a deafening grind, it slid off the sarcophagus and crashed onto the chamber floor. The impact shattered the corners and sent fragments skittering, but the bulk of the slab remained intact. It slammed against the far wall and came to rest in a cloud of chalky dust.

The swirling haze obscured the vaulted ceiling and the reliefs on the surrounding walls. The men coughed and waited for the air to settle.

When it did, Nas'r and Father Athanasius clambered up the tomb, using the carved reliefs as footholds. Holding their oil lamps low, they peered into the open chamber.

There it was.

Just as Malik had described it—a bronze funerary casket, green with age, coated in the solemn patina of centuries. Magnificent. Majestic.

Malik, with Brother Yohanan's help, had finished lashing the raft together. Six sturdy cedar beams had been secured to smaller but equally stout crossbeams using thick, waved hempen rope. The goatskin floats were filled to capacity and tied firmly to the underside. Malik had paid special attention to the central pair of floats, ensuring the inflation limbs were oriented outward for easy access. With Yohanan's assistance, they flipped the raft and laid it beside the canal, ready to launch when the moment came.

Malik now turned to the pulleys, laying them out on the stone floor and checking for tangles. He ensured the ropes weren't twisted and that the two matched pairs of pulleys were set to nearly identical lengths. As the group's master of numbers and geometry, he claimed this next phase as his own. The calculations were his—if it failed, so would he.

He decided to ferry the gear across in two trips. First, he slung the bundle of waxed hempen ropes over his shoulder—the bindings that would link the upper pulleys to the ceiling rings and the lower ones to the casket—and carefully crossed the narrow bridge. He deposited the bundle beside the sarcophagus, then returned for the pulleys.

Once everything was safely on the far side, Malik set to work. Climbing onto the sarcophagus, he reached as high as he could and lashed the upper pulleys to the iron rings overhead with double strands of rope, ensuring a secure bind. Once the upper pulleys were suspended in space, he looped the lower pulleys around the casket. He was grateful that the bronze box sat on stone plinths— freestanding and elevated—which allowed the ropes to pass beneath it cleanly.

He double-checked the lengths. The pulleys needed to be as symmetrical as possible; even a minor misalignment could tilt the casket and complicate the descent. They would have little clearance when sliding the cedar ramp beneath. Everything needed to work on the first attempt.

Malik clambered down and called to Yohanan, "Slide over the ramp beams." These were spare cedar planks, prepared in advance—charcoal-coated on one face for friction, with shallow notches carved to hook over the lip of the sarcophagus and prevent slippage. Huffing and grunting, Yohanan pushed them across the bridge until Malik had them positioned beside the tomb.

It was now or never.

By the light of flickering oil lamps, Nas'r and Father Athanasius collected the loose ends of the ropes and took their positions—one at the head, one at the foot of the tomb. Malik placed himself where both men could see him clearly.

"Take the strain," he called.

Nas'r and Athanasius heaved until the ropes were taut.

"Lift."

They pulled again—nothing happened.

"Lift!" Malik repeated, more urgently.

"We are lifting!" Nas'r grunted. "It's not moving!"

Malik scanned the chamber for the iron bar used earlier to shift the lid. "Keep the strain," he ordered.

Bounding up the side of the tomb, he leaned over the edge and wedged the bar between the sarcophagus wall and the casket. With every ounce of strength, he levered against the bronze.

Finally—on the third attempt—there was a groan of ancient metal. One end shifted, then the other. Suddenly, the casket lurched upward, jerking in the ropes and nearly pulling Father Athanasius off balance.

"The decay fused the casket to the stone," Malik shouted. "It's free now!"

He climbed back down and reassumed his position.

"Lift!"

The ropes tightened. Thanks to the mechanical advantage of the pulleys, the casket rose another cubit.

"Lift." Another cubit.

"Lift." A third.

On the fourth, the top of the casket rose just above the sarcophagus lip.

"Hold!" Malik turned to Yohanan, still watching from the far side of the canal. "Yohanan—we need you over here."

The young monk hurried across the bridge and joined Athanasius.
"Lift." Another cubit.

"Lift."

"Lift!"

Finally, the bronze casket hung freely in the air, swaying slightly in the lamplight. The iron rings had held.

"Yohanan, the beams," Malik instructed.

Together, he and Yohanan slid the planks into place, carefully hooking the notches over the stone lip.

"Down—gently," Malik said.

Nas'r and Athanasius eased the casket onto the ramp. The timber creaked as it accepted the weight.

The five members of the Ahl al-Khidr all exhaled at once, a collective release of tension. Malik collapsed to the ground, overwhelmed by the surge of adrenaline. They passed around their flasks in silence, each man privately marvelling at what they had achieved.

After a long moment, Malik stood. His body ached, but his voice was steady.

"That was the end of Phase One. Now comes Phase Two—the most difficult part of all."

Malik untied the pulleys from the iron rings and set them atop the casket. Using the lashings from the rings, he bound the pulleys together into a single length and looped it around the heavy stone lid leaning against the wall. "That should be enough weight to counter the descent," he murmured to himself. He then repositioned the casket pulleys to the far side, ensuring they were secure and evenly aligned.

Once satisfied, he turned to the others.

"Nas'r, Father Athanasius—you'll return to your positions. You'll guide the casket down onto the raft. With the slope and friction, it should be easier than lifting. Yohanan and I will control the start of its descent from inside the sarcophagus. Once it's balanced, we'll steady the raft. Any questions?"

There were none. They were eager—hearts quick with excitement, but also quietly aware of the stakes.

"Very well. Take your positions."

As Nas'r and Father Athanasius took the ropes, Malik and Yohanan climbed into the crypt and braced themselves between the inner wall of the sarcophagus and the casket.

"Ready—heave!"

The casket slid forward along the planks, inch by inch.

"Heave again." It crept closer to the edge.

"Prepare the ropes," Malik called out. "Yohanan—more gently now. We need it to just balance."

With cautious coordination, they eased the casket until it teetered at the tipping point. One of the cedar beams began to lift slightly off the floor, then the other.

"Take the strain!" Malik called. "Yohanan—slowly... push... slowly."

The casket tipped forward, its center of gravity shifting. The beams angled sharply now. Malik and Yohanan quickly scrambled out of the sarcophagus and steadied the casket, which now rested atop the planks like a poised predator.

"Lower, slowly," Malik ordered.

In unison, the two men let out the ropes. The casket eased down the ramp, guided and braked by the slope of the beams.

"Easy..." The planks made contact with the stone at the canal's edge.

"Lower."

Another cubit.

"Lower."

The casket continued downward without resistance. As it neared the edge of the water, Malik raised a hand.

"Halt. Tie off the ropes." He turned to Yohanan. "Now, brother—it's time for immersion."

Together, they stripped to their loincloths. Then, crossing the narrow bridge, they approached the raft. With practiced hands, they fastened the mooring lines. With delicate precision, they lifted the raft and set it onto the canal's surface, where the current instantly tugged at it. Nas'r and Athanasius quickly secured the lines to the stonework using guide ropes looped around the crypt's fixtures.

"We'll steady the raft," Malik said. "You two lower the casket. This must be slow, controlled. Once it's low enough, we'll shift it onto the raft. We may need the iron bars again to lever it in place. Understood?"

Again, silent nods.

"Lower."

The ropes creaked as the casket began its final descent—inch by inch, steady as breath. When it finally touched the stone at the canal's edge, the ropes slackened.

Nas'r and Athanasius moved in with the iron bars, levering one end of the casket onto the raft, then the other. The effort was immense, requiring all their strength and precision. Malik and Yohanan fought to keep the raft balanced, the current testing every inch of its tethered stability.

At last, it was done. The casket sat centred, its weight distributed perfectly. Malik's planning had been sound—the raft floated with mere inches of freeboard, the cedar beams just brushing the water's surface.

Malik and Yohanan slipped into the canal on either side of the raft. The freezing water stole their breath, drawing involuntary gasps from both men. They braced against the sides, shivering but steady. Nas'r and Athanasius untied the painter lines from the crypt and looped them out behind the raft—Nas'r to the left, Athanasius to the right. They would guide from the rear as the craft drifted downstream.

The oil lamps were carefully set atop the casket. Tools—iron bars, chisels, hammers—were stowed aboard. Everything was in place. They were ready.

The voyage down the canal was uneventful at first. The strain on the painter lines was light, and keeping the raft centred took only minimal effort from Malik and Yohanan. The current was gentle, the silence heavy. Shadows rippled against the low ceiling. After some time, the faint glint of iron appeared ahead — the grate. Nas'r and Father Athanasius stepped forward, grabbing chisels and hammering them into the narrow seams between the flagstones. These crude anchors would serve as tie-off points for the lines. Then, approaching the grate from opposite sides, they set to work. Leveraging their weight against the bars, they began prying the corroded metal free. Some sections snapped with ease; others resisted, groaning under each blow despite their age and decay. After over two hours of exhausting labour, the grate finally gave way with a screech of iron and stone. Both men collapsed onto the cold walkway, soaked in sweat and breathing heavily.

Meanwhile, Malik and Yohanan attacked the jagged remnants. Swinging their hammers at the broken iron teeth, they pounded the sharp edges flat against the stone to prevent them from snagging the raft during passage. The submerged parts were the most treacherous — rusted through, but hidden and hard to reach. Still, it was here that the metal was weakest. At last, they tossed their hammers aside and slumped onto the raft, every muscle aching. When their strength returned and their breaths had steadied, Malik gathered them for final instructions. This next stage wasn't the most difficult — but it was the most dangerous.

"Nas'r, Father Athanasius," Malik said, "you'll guide us gently through the opening. But before you do, light your own lamps and set them aside on the walkway. Once we're through, play out the lines slowly until we reach the descent point of the canal. That's where Yohanan and I will begin venting air from the bladders until we achieve neutral buoyancy. When the raft neither sinks nor floats, I'll give the signal. Release the ropes — and may God be with us. Hopefully the current will carry us cleanly through to the

end. If it snags, we'll try to retrieve it from the far side. Brother
Yohanan, the rest will be up to us."
Yohanan nodded, lips pale. "Understood."
"Good. I suggest you loosen the leg on the centre float now. Don't
retie it — we'll need it accessible. I think we're ready."
Each man moved with purpose. Nas'r and Father Athanasius
smoothly played out the lines, guiding the raft through the widened
grate. It caught once, jerking the ropes taut, but they freed it
quickly and maneuvered it through on the second attempt. As the
raft passed into the darkness beyond, the lamps on top of the
sarcophagus shrank into pinpricks. Then came Malik's distant
echo: "Hold there!"
The two linesmen stopped and waited.
Downstream, Malik and Yohanan bent low and untied the cords
securing the float valves. Slowly, they vented air from the central
bladders. The raft dipped, the ropes grew heavier.
"More," Malik said. Air hissed out. The casket settled, its lower
edge now brushing the water.
"Again." A soft gurgle. Half-submerged now.
"Almost there," Malik said. "Just a little more, Yohanan, and we'll
be at neutral buoyancy. Once we are, I'll call for the lines to be
released. We'll guide the raft from beside it. The current will do
the rest."
He paused. His voice dropped. "The moon will illuminate the exit.
Stay with the raft. Keep it upright. If we're moving too fast and
risk overshooting the net, dump the remaining air and let it sink. Is
that clear?"
Yohanan gave a shaky nod. "Yes, Malik."
Malik studied the casket, now just beneath the surface. No change.
No leak. He looked once more to Yohanan, then turned and
shouted upstream.
"Release!"
From above, both painter lines snaked into the water and vanished.

The men inhaled deeply and dove under with the raft. For a moment, everything was still. Then the current caught them — a surging force that sent the raft gliding forward. Too fast.

Malik jammed his feet against the canal wall, one hand gripping the raft, the other reaching blindly for the float valve. The raft bounced and rocked as the current jostled it side to side. Yohanan braced opposite him, mirroring his movements. The blackness was absolute. Malik could feel nothing, see nothing.

Yohanan took a breath from the float. Malik reached for the valve again — nothing. His sandal suddenly caught on a rough edge, twisting him violently. The jolt nearly tore him from the raft. Only his grip with the other hand saved him. He spun out of alignment, now facing backward.

Through sheer effort, Malik managed to reorient himself. Malik felt Yohanan's side dip slightly — another breath. His own lungs were burning. Still no valve.

Then — ahead — a faint circle of light. The tunnel mouth.

They were moving too fast.

Still no valve.

He slammed his feet into the slimy canal walls, kicking up clouds of silt. Yohanan did the same. Gradually, the raft's speed slowed. The pitch black began to lighten to a dull grey. They were close now.

Finally, Malik saw it — the float valve. Still sealed tight, a trickle of bubbles leaking from the seam. He seized it, pulled it to his face, and untwisted the leg.

A rush of air. Malik drank it like a man dying.

The outflow was just ahead.

Below, through the haze of silt, he saw the net — woven rope stretched wide across the canal bottom, shimmering faintly in the moonlight.

Without hesitation, Malik released the valve completely. A torrent of bubbles escaped.

Yohanan saw and followed suit. The raft dipped gently, gliding down through the water like a drifting leaf. The casket still sat upright, perfectly balanced. With a muted thump, it settled directly into the center of the net, kicking up a plume of mud.

The men kicked upward, lungs burning, limbs heavy.

When they broke the surface, gasping, the world above was silent and silver. The harbor glowed with moonlight.

On the jetty sat Stephanos and Theonidas, guide ropes in hand, as if patiently fishing.

Stephanos grinned. "Look, Theonidas — two drowned rats in our net."

Theonidas chuckled. "Drowned rats who've just delivered us a king."

Laughter broke out across the water as Malik and Yohanan swam for the rickety ladder, exhausted, shivering — but triumphant.

Stephanos and Theonidas hauled steadily on the ropes, careful to keep their movements in sync. They could feel the raft dragging along the harbor floor, scraping over gravel and weeds as it edged closer to the old timber jetty.

By the time it reached the shallows, Malik and Yohanan had climbed from the water and wrapped themselves in dry cloaks, grateful for the insulation against the cool night air. Together, the four men maneuvered the raft toward the shore.

It grounded gently, with just the top of the casket visible above the waterline. It gleamed a dull green in the moonlight, bronze fittings mottled with age and sea-salt.

Switching to the bank, the men slipped and slid in the mud as they wrestled the raft—now functioning as a sled—up onto firmer ground. The cedar beams dug into the soft earth, resisting every effort. They agreed, without needing to say it, that this part was better suited to beasts.

Stephanos braked the wagon and unhitched the oxen. Leading them down to the water's edge, he tied the ropes to the yoke ring.

With little effort, the animals hauled the raft and its heavy cargo up onto higher, drier ground.

Once clear of the mud, the men began separating the casket from the raft. It slid free easily — the slick coating of silt providing an unexpected advantage.

They lifted one end of the raft onto the wagon bed to serve as a ramp. Repositioning the net around the casket, they threaded the ropes over the wagon's frame and fastened them again to the yoke. Stephanos took the reins, ready to guide the oxen. Theonidas braced the brake lever to hold the wagon steady. Malik and Yohanan stood on either side to keep the casket aligned.

With careful, halting progress, the oxen pulled the casket up the ramp. Several times, Malik and Yohanan stopped the ascent to shift the angle, keeping it centred. The mud-caked sarcophagus resisted them at every turn, unwieldy and slick.

At last, it was aboard. They lashed it down with the same ropes that had carried it from the harbor floor.

Malik took a final look and gave his orders.

"Clean everything. No traces — not even footprints if we can help it. Then we head to the Domus. Our brothers will be just as exhausted after hauling the equipment upstairs. I think this calls for a celebration—after we're safely back at the Library. Stay sharp. Keep the wagon covered and out of sight."

Elated but drained, they draped the linen sheet over the cargo and set off into the night.

Chapter 10

For thirteen days, Amon-Sa's vessel crept steadily down the Red
Sea coast, hugging the arid shoreline like a shadow. The winds
were fair, constant in their northern push, and the boat's triangular
sail caught them with quiet efficiency. Each morning brought the
dry, brassy heat of the tropics, and by mid-journey, they had
clearly crossed into equatorial waters — the sun rode high and
punishing, and the deck planks grew too hot to stand on barefoot.
Nights were a relief, touched by cool sea breezes and blanketed
under brilliant stars.

There was little traffic on the water — a few small fishing dhows,
distant silhouettes of other coastal vessels. Amon-Sa made careful
note of each, mentally marking the shape of hulls and rigging, any
flags or features that might prove relevant later. They sailed in
deliberate anonymity, mimicking the rhythms of traders and
fishermen, their deck spars hung with fishing nets, their sails
stained with brine to dull their brightness.

The coastline itself was bleak and quiet, dotted only with
occasional palm groves, clusters of thatched huts, and the thin
smoke of fish-drying fires. No walled towns. No major harbors.
Just scattered fishing villages where curious eyes might look too
long if their vessel lingered. They did not linger.

But on the morning of the fourteenth day, the rising sun revealed a
dark smudge on the horizon — Adulis. Once the pride of the
Aksumite Empire, the port had long since slipped into a quieter
rhythm. That was precisely why Nasr had chosen it.

The harbor still held stone piers and breakwaters, weathered but intact, their foundations laid centuries earlier by skilled hands. The outer quay had partially collapsed, overtaken by barnacles and mangrove roots, but further in, where deeper water touched more stable ground, ships still docked — small coastal freighters, fishing vessels, and the occasional Red Sea trader.

The town behind the port clung to the slope like a memory. Whitewashed stone buildings with wooden shutters leaned together like gossiping elders. The larger warehouses — once filled with silks, spices, and carved ivory — now served humbler purposes: grain, salt, fish oil, goat hides. A few stood abandoned, their roofs fallen in, their interiors dark and silent, but still useful for those with reason to remain unseen.

The marketplace was modest, no longer the roaring exchange it had once been. But it lived — women bartered for dates and lentils, boys ran errands, fishermen gutted their catch beside stone troughs slick with decades of use. Arabic, Ge'ez, and old Greek mingled in the air. The Aksumite cross still crowned a cracked old chapel above the wharf. Incense drifted faintly from its door.

Amon-Sa stood at the bow as their vessel approached, eyes sweeping the port with practiced detachment. He noted the two available piers, the positions of watchful dockhands, the slope of the alleyways leading inland. This place was not dead — merely sleeping. And that made it perfect.

By the time the sail was furled and the mooring ropes cast, the sun had cleared the horizon and bathed the port in gold. Their arrival stirred no alarm. One more anonymous vessel in a harbor long accustomed to comings and goings. As Amon-Sa stepped onto the dock, his sandals clicking softly against ancient stone, he felt it clearly:

Here, no one would look too closely.

And that was exactly what they needed.

The sun rose high over the port of Adulis, casting a brilliant white glare off the bleached stone walls and dusty lanes that wound down to the harbor. Amon-Sa sat beneath the low awning of a spice merchant's shop, scroll and stylus in hand, the ink drying quickly in the heat. His script was careful and practiced, but his mind was heavy with all he had seen.

"To my brother Baruch,

 I write from Adulis. The voyage south from Berenice was without incident. Fair winds bore us swiftly along the coast, where the days were hot and close, and the nights alive with stars. We passed only a few fishing boats and coastal traders. These could be useful to our purpose. There were no Rashidun sails. The sea remains ours, for now."

He paused, wiping his brow. The memory of the journey shimmered behind his closed eyelids — the coastal villages with their clustered huts of reed and mud, smoke curling into the blue sky; the sea birds that screamed overhead in great wheeling arcs; dolphins racing the ship's bow as they rounded low capes and rocky outcrops. He resumed writing.

"I observed no signs of Arab patrols along the coast. No garrisons. Only small encampments of fishermen, traders, or shepherds. If they are watching the Red Sea, they do so further north.

The ship I send you has served us well. She is swift, low-slung, inconspicuous. I ask that her captain be placed under your service until recalled. Trust him—he is loyal and keeps his word."

He folded the parchment with reverence and sealed it with the small bronze signet he carried — an old ring of his father's, pressed into wax. Rising, he made his way back down the slope to the harbor, where the ship that had brought him was being resupplied by its crew: baskets of dried fruit, salted fish, bundles of linen.

He pulled the captain aside — a tall, weathered Nubian with deep-set eyes and sun-blackened skin — and pressed the message into his hands.

"In Berenice, find a man called Baruch. Give this to him, and only to him," he said. "No one else. Then stay with him. Lend your vessel to his purpose."

The man nodded once, solemnly, understanding the weight of the task. Without further ceremony, Amon-Sa turned from the dock and began walking into Adulis proper

.

The town was smaller than it had once been, a shadow of its glory days, but it still pulsed with a quiet resilience. The markets were lively — baskets of incense and myrrh, ropes of garlic and hanging onions, dates as dark as obsidian, copper vessels, linen bolts, and aged ceramics. Camels snorted and stamped outside the city walls while children chased chickens through the alleys. Old Greek merchants argued in a language that had mostly faded from memory, and black-robed priests moved like shadows through the crowd.

He inquired discreetly after transport, and before long, a spice-seller pointed him toward a group of traders camped just beyond the town's edge.

"They ride tonight," the merchant said. "Cooler then. Safer."

Amon-Sa followed the dusty trail to the encampment. The caravan was modest — a dozen camels, heavily laden with resin, cloth, and dried goods, and their keepers, swarthy men with curved knives at their belts and callused hands. At its centre was the ra'is — the caravan master — seated cross-legged on a woollen mat beneath a goat-hide canopy.

Amon-Sa approached with respect, offering a gift of dried figs and a handful of silver coin. "I seek passage to Aksum. I ride alone and carry only news."

The ra'is, a man named Mekonnen, looked him over with a soldier's eye, then nodded. "You'll need a camel."

There were stables just beyond the eastern gate — not much more than a corral of thorny fences and rough-hewn troughs. There,

Amon-Sa bartered for a lean but healthy dromedary with a curved
back and keen eyes. He named it Seb — after the desert wind. He
bought water skins, hard bread, dried chickpeas, and a leather pack
to carry his remaining scrolls. From the market he procured a new
set of sandals and a worn cotton robe in Aksumite style to blend in
with the others.

With his affairs settled, he sought a place to rest and found it in a
small tavern nestled in a quiet side street — a whitewashed
building with narrow windows and a low, arched door. The air
inside was cooler, scented with mint and roasting meat. He ordered
a simple meal: flatbread, lentil stew rich with garlic and coriander,
and a handful of pickled vegetables. The taste was vivid after two
weeks of dried fish and boiled grains.

As the afternoon waned, he sat in a shaded alcove, sipping warm
goat's milk from a clay bowl. Outside, the sounds of the market
drifted up — the lowing of camels, the cry of traders, the clatter of
hoof and heel on stone. But inside, all was still.

He closed his eyes and let the weariness of the past weeks settle on
his shoulders. The next part of the journey would be hard. Fourteen
days of sun, dust, and slow ascent. And no promise awaited him at
the end of it. Only the hope that the King of Aksum would listen.

As dusk crept over the town, the caravan bells began to ring in the
distance.

Amon-Sa stood, pulled his hood low over his face, and stepped
back into the fading light.

The scene at the ancient Library was one of organized chaos.
In the eastern cloister and the sun-washed central court, a slow-
moving river of carts and wagons threaded its way through the
marble colonnades. Scholars, scribes, and monks from Saint
Catherine's bustled between them, ferrying bundles of parchment,
crates of scrolls, wrapped codices, carved reliquaries, and objects

of obscure and forgotten knowledge. The Great Vesica was now being emptied to the point of echoing silence—its contents flooding outward like a breached dam into the hands of a people moving with quiet, desperate purpose.

Over it all loomed the watchful presence of Nas'r, who had slept little in two days.

Every hour, a loaded wagon was hitched to an ox or mule by Stephanos or Theonidas, and carefully driven across the city to the parade grounds of the Alexandrian Guard. There, under the protection of the Palace Phalanx, the wagons were hidden from prying eyes. Then the process began again—organizing, lifting, recording, moving. Always moving.

In the evenings, Stephanos worked alone in the old stables, tending the growing multitude of animals—oxen, donkeys, and camels— his hands raw, his tunic dusty. His duties were endless.

Malik, meanwhile, was immersed in the complexities of another journey—one far west, toward the Siwa Oasis. He charted routes, estimated distances, identified resting and watering points, and factored in the threat of brigands and the chaos rippling from the Arab invasion. The journey was immense: almost 500 Roman miles across desert and plateau. And he would be carrying the most sacred burden of all—the body of the king.

Inside the Great Vesica, two scribes—Father Athanasius and Brother Yohanan—sat hunched over long parchment sheets, meticulously annotating every item: where it was packed, what it was stored alongside, which numbered cart bore it. An evolving map of knowledge, a record of preservation.

Nas'r had returned from the Palace that morning, holding three letters: one was a royal decree from Governor Cyrus granting safe passage and protection for the caravan headed south. The other two, written by Pope Benjamin himself, was addressed to the monastic communities of the Thebaid and Upper Egypt, pleading their support and offering blessings to Nas'r and Malik and their missions.

That night, beneath the colonnade of the Vesica, Nas'r summoned the Ahl al-Khidr.

They gathered around him—dust-covered, tired, their faces drawn but determined.

"I thank you for coming," Nas'r began. "I know the days are long, and the nights even longer. Our work is not yet done, and time is no longer our ally. So please, indulge me but for a short time."

They nodded in silence.

"I bring you news. Baruch has arrived in Berenice Troglodyta and begun assembling the fleet. The local church received him warmly. The pier is being repaired, and ships are being gathered. He has sent word that Amon-Sa passed through the city only two days before—bound for Adulis. We await further word."

He paused, grim.

"On the matter of war: Pope Benjamin met with General Amr ibn al-As. He proposed a truce. It was refused. Benjamin was allowed to return to the Palace with his life, but nothing more."

Murmurs stirred the gathering.

"The Rashidun army has reached the outskirts of Damyat," Nas'r continued, using the older name for Damietta. "General Theodore will confront them with what few troops remain. Pelusium only delayed the tide—it did not break it. Word also comes from the north: Qinnasrin has fallen." He looked at them gravely. "Soon, they may take Adana. The empire trembles and may even fall."

The circle was silent, the mood grave.

"Father Athanasius," Nas'r said. "The contents?"

The old monk stood slowly. His voice was thin, but resolute. "We have worked without pause. By this time tomorrow, the loading will be complete. Everything is catalogued, inventoried, and recorded. We are ready."

Nas'r nodded. "Stephanos and Theonidas?"

The two men stood together, but it was Stephanos who spoke. "All beasts have been gathered and are housed in the old military stables. We feed them before nightfall, but our supplies are nearly depleted. We work with Father Athanasius to move the loaded wagons. The number at the barracks is growing. Space is limited—we will soon need to use the cloisters themselves."

"Well done," Nas'r said.

He turned to Malik. "And the Siwa journey?"

Malik rose, dust clinging to his robes. "It is long—nearly five hundred miles, all inland. We avoid the coast, which is now crowded with refugees and raiders. There are bandits in the interior. But I believe it is the safest path. Dhu al-Qarnayn must be returned with care."

"Thank you," Nas'r said. "I have considered this journey deeply. There is danger in every direction, but duty compels us forward. I have decided: the Palace Phalanx, while we still have them, will accompany the southern caravan. Malik…" He paused. "I'm sorry. I can offer you no protection."

Malik inclined his head, accepting his burden.

"You will not be alone," Nas'r added. "There are monks who wish to travel with you to Siwa. Provision for them as best you can. They are men of devotion and will serve you faithfully."

Nas'r stepped forward, eyes scanning the circle. "When the moon begins to wane and the last wagon is loaded—this time tomorrow—we depart, we can wait no longer. By God's will, we shall be clear of Alexandria by the second morning, and beyond the reach of those who seek to stop us."

He lifted a cup of honeyed wine. "To the journey ahead."

Each man raised his cup, lost in his own thoughts. The silence was thick with purpose and uncertainty. Somewhere in the city beyond, the distant clamour of Alexandria's streets faded into the hush of night, as if the world itself were holding its breath.

As the evening sun dipped low over the western reaches of
Alexandria, casting the city in molten hues of amber and gold.
From the high eastern cloister, the view stretched far beyond the
Library's precinct, past the rusting dome of the Serapeum and the
distant silhouettes of the unfinished towers along the Canopic
Way. But within the Library's grounds, the scene remained
frenetic.

Dozens of carts now filled the central court, their wooden frames
creaking under the weight of ancient knowledge. Scrolls bound in
waxed linen, codices sealed in leather, wooden cases filled with
pressed papyrus — all meticulously catalogued, stacked, and tied
down with cords. Torches lined the walkways, flickering against
the sandstone walls as the last light drained from the sky.

Stephanos moved like a man possessed, leading mules from the
barracks to the cloister, hitching them one by one to the loaded
carts. The beasts brayed and snorted, nervous under the tension in
the air. Father Athanasius moved beside him, checking off entries
in a long scroll, his ink-stained hands trembling with fatigue.
Beside him, Brother Yohanan darted between wagons like a
shadow, tucking fresh seals into the corners of crates.

Nas'r stood atop the steps of the Vesica, his dark cloak trailing
behind him, arms crossed. He said little, but his presence alone was
command enough. When he did speak, it was only to issue a quiet
instruction — to reinforce the load on a cart's axle, or to remove
any signs of insignia from crates that might reveal their origin.

Malik emerged from the southern gallery with a sack slung over
his shoulder, the beginnings of his desert kit packed tight. He'd
changed into travelling robes, his head wrapped in a scarf. A
waterskin hung from his belt, and a short curved dagger was
tucked into the back of his sash. He approached Nas'r silently.

"We're ready," Malik said.

Nas'r nodded, his gaze still fixed on the court. The members of the
Ahl al-Khidr had said their goodbyes earlier that evening.

"You'll leave before the city wakes. Two monks will accompany you — Brother Kallistos and Brother Mareon. Kallistos once served as a courier between Siwa and Ammon. Mareon was a hermit-monk in Wadi Natrun. They know the desert. They'll travel light and follow your command."

Nas'r removed the heavy bronze medallion from around his neck and placed it in Malik's hand, along with the letter from Pope Benjamin. Then, from a leather pouch, he gave him the remaining coins from the library treasury.

"As we discussed, use the medallion to your best advantage. If the Pope's letter cannot win you help, then bribe your way out."

Malik dipped his head in assent. "Understood."

At last, Nas'r reached beneath his robe and drew out a small glass-rolled codex, wrapped in a strip of linen. He offered it to Malik with both hands.

"When you entomb the King, this is to be entombed with him."

Malik held the codex carefully. "What is it?"

"Detailed directions to the first clue of the Library's final resting place. I'll leave markers along the journey. A second scroll, nearly identical, will travel with the collection. It will detail the first clue to the final resting place of the King. That is why you must follow the instructions precisely, Malik."

The Nubian scholar nodded, silently accepting the charge.

Nas'r placed a hand briefly on his shoulder. "Remember — this is not a race. Let the desert shape your pace."

Behind them, the great bronze gates of the eastern cloister groaned open. Theonidas strode through, breathless and flushed.

"The final wagons are being loaded now," he reported. "By the tenth hour of night, we'll be ready to move."

Nas'r stepped down from the Vesica, his boots thudding softly on the stone.

"Then tonight, we ride."

It was just before midnight, the city of Alexandria slumbered under a blanket of still, moonless dark. The distant cry of gulls and the occasional bark of a dog were all that pierced the silence. But within the bounds of the Library, the Ahl al-Kidr moved like a ghost army.

One by one, the carts rolled silently through the side gate of the eastern wall. The guards of the Palace Phalanx, now dressed in monkish robes to avoid suspicion, flanked the procession. Their short swords and shields were concealed beneath cloaks, but their eyes missed nothing. Nas'r led from the front, his lantern covered with a cloth to dim its glow. Behind him came the heart of the Library: knowledge older than kingdoms, rolling quietly through the streets like a secret reborn – one-hundred and five carts and wagons, gathered for one purpose.

At the rear, Malik watched them disappear into the veil of night. He stood beside his two companions — both already veiled and hooded — and the three of them waited for the last echoes of the caravan's wheels to fade. Only then did Malik gesture, and together they moved silently into the darkness, leading the oxen between them, heading westward toward Siwa and the burial place of kings.

By dawn, the Library was still. The cloisters lay deserted, the Great Vesica hollowed of its burden. Only faint wheel ruts traced the dust, and a broken wax seal hung at the gate — a memory already fading. Alexandria did not see what it had lost. But the world would, in time.

BOOK TWO – TO FIND A KING

Act I (Present Day) - The Lion and the Sand

Chapter 1

Alex Carey removed his wide-brimmed and heavily worn brown fedora and wiped the sweat from his brow. It was just after 9:00 a.m., and even beneath the stretched canvas awning, the Libyan sun had already begun to assert its authority. March in North Africa wasn't yet the cruelest month, but the heat still clung to every exposed surface, turning shade into mere suggestion. He had been in-country for over a week and still hadn't quite acclimated to the climate. The only reprieve came in the late afternoons, when a sea breeze whispered in off the Mediterranean before the wind shifted southward — dry, desert air sweeping up from the Sahara, brushing the dig site with a breath of ancient fire.

Before him lay the weathered bones of Leptis Magna, once the crown jewel of Rome's African provinces — a city of marble and ambition, pressed between the desert and the sea. Founded by Phoenician settlers as early as the 7th century BCE, Leptis had been folded into the Roman Empire during the reign of Augustus. But it was under the patronage of Septimius Severus, the city's most famous son and eventual emperor, that Leptis became magnificent.

Here, at its peak in the 2nd century CE, great basilicas rose beside markets, aqueducts marched over the wadi to slake the city's thirst, and marble colonnades lined the streets like ribs of a forgotten leviathan. Leptis was opulent, cosmopolitan, and powerful — a trade hub that funneled gold, ivory, and grain from the interior of Africa into the hungry maw of the Empire.

But time had turned, and the tides of empire receded.

Abandoned to encroaching sand and sea, Leptis Magna lay buried and silent for over a millennium. It wasn't until the 1920s that Italian archaeologists, emboldened by Mussolini's colonial ambitions, began systematic excavations. Their work peeled back the veil of centuries, revealing forums, baths, and triumphal arches nearly intact — as if the city had merely dozed off and forgotten to wake.

By December 1982, Leptis was enshrined on UNESCO's World Heritage List — a relic too precious to lose. Yet even that honor hadn't protected it entirely. Political instability, shifting regimes, and neglect had left it vulnerable once more.

That, Alex thought, was why they were here. Not just to uncover — but to protect.

Behind him, the rest of the dig team moved through the site like chess pieces on a sun-bleached board. Claire knelt in a shallow trench, carefully brushing sediment away from the edge of what looked like an intact mosaic. Samira was deep in conversation with a young Libyan intern, gesturing toward a series of partially exposed stone footings. And nearby, Dr. Tariq Mahfouz, their field leader, stood conferring with site engineers over the next phase of excavation.

But beneath the surface of this orderly academic endeavor lay something deeper — the reason they had all been summoned here. And summoned they had.

An invitation to join a multinational archaeological team investigating a previously unexcavated sector of Leptis Magna had stirred Alex from a life of academia and quiet, book-lined routine. While he loved teaching — and had grown fond of the red cliffs and open skies of Northern Arizona University — the rhythms of university life had become predictable. Lectures, office hours, departmental politics, and an occasional field trip to the American Southwest. But this… this was different.

This was Leptis.

And it was Harvard that had brought him here.

Late the previous year, Alex had received a formal invitation — a cream envelope, surprisingly tactile in an age of digital brevity — to attend a closed-door conference at the École Normale Supérieure in Paris, co-hosted by the German Archaeological Institute and UNESCO. The subject was tightly focused and yet tantalizingly open-ended: Preliminary LiDAR Imaging and Prospective Excavations – Eastern Leptis Magna.

It wasn't until he read the name attached — Dr. Sarah Parker —
that his curiosity flared into full-blown interest.

Parker, a space archaeologist renowned for using satellite and
LiDAR technology to uncover hidden ancient sites, had spent years
analyzing new high-resolution scans of the Libyan coastline,
focusing specifically on the periphery of the Leptis Magna ruins.
The satellite surveys, part of a broader initiative to monitor
endangered heritage sites, had revealed something unexpected — a
dense, geometric subsurface pattern extending east of the known
city boundary, just south of the Severan aqueduct's remains and
bordering the dry course of the Wadi Lebda.

It was unmistakable.

Rectilinear foundations. Domestic footprints. A consistent layout
indicative of urban planning.

She had named it tentatively in her paper — A Subsurface
Analysis of the Eastern Periphery of Leptis Magna Using Airborne
LiDAR, published in Antiquity (Vol. 97, Issue 389) — as the
Eastern Residential Quarter, or ERQ. The peer review process had
been unusually swift, driven by both the credibility of Parker's
methods and the urgency of protecting the site in Libya's volatile
political climate.

At the Paris conference, Parker herself had delivered the keynote.
With the quiet authority of someone who lets data do the speaking,
she walked the room through a stunning set of topographic
overlays. The LiDAR scans had penetrated layers of silt and
shifting dune, revealing a sprawl of possible insulae — multi-
family Roman dwellings — along with indications of paved lanes,
cisterns, and what might have been a balneum, a small public
bathhouse. The layout was distinct from the more monumental,
imperial core of Leptis, suggesting a part of the city that had
housed merchants, craftsmen, and lower-ranking civil
administrators.

And then she dropped the most tantalizing possibility of all: a
large, complex footprint that might have once been a private

domus — a villa, perhaps — built on slightly elevated ground, and untouched by prior excavations.

That domus, she posited, could hold stratified materials left intact for over a millennium.

Why had it been missed? The answer was, ironically, political. Previous excavations had been largely concentrated within the Byzantine walls — a relatively safe perimeter. Italian teams during the colonial period had focused on grand structures near the Forum and the Severan Basilica. Libyan-led teams in the 1970s and 1980s had lacked the funding or satellite tools to explore beyond the traditional grid. The ERQ had remained buried, overlooked — until the sharp, sweeping eye of a LiDAR drone caught it from 12,000 feet above.

Now, in early 2024, they were here.

The dig was backed by Harvard's Semitic Museum in partnership with the Getty Conservation Institute and France's Institut National d'Histoire de l'Art. UNESCO had formally endorsed it. Funding, permits, and political assurances had aligned with rare precision. And the presence of high-profile academics — Samira Rahani from France, Alex and Claire from NAU, and logistical direction from the esteemed Dr. Tariq Mahfouz — gave the project the aura of scholarly gravity and careful diplomacy.

To the outside world, it was just another archaeological dig.

But for Alex — standing under the withering Libyan sun, staring out at the carefully gridded trench where the foundations of that villa had begun to emerge — it felt like something else entirely.

As if history itself had been waiting for them.

Alex adjusted his hat again and turned toward the edge of the trench, where two figures stood in quiet conversation beside a foldout field table stacked with mapping documents and marked aerial prints. Dr. Samira Rahani, unmistakable even at a distance, gestured with the precision of someone trained in both excavation and diplomacy — long fingers tracing invisible gridlines in the air. She spoke with a kind of confident brevity that made people listen.

She cut a striking figure under the harsh Libyan light — tall,
poised, and dressed in light, breathable linen. Her dark curls, tied
back loosely with a scarf, caught flecks of sunlight as she moved,
and her almond eyes, sharp and thoughtful, scanned the terrain
with a practiced gaze. She had the quiet magnetism of someone
who had long ago learned how to command respect without
demanding it. She'd arrived only a day after Alex and Claire,
flown in via Marseille, and had wasted no time establishing herself
as the intellectual axis around which the field team slowly began to
turn.
French-Tunisian, with a doctorate in Classical Civilizations from
the Sorbonne, Samira was not only fluent in five languages but had
also previously worked on Roman-era North African sites in both
Carthage and Dougga. Her 2015 paper on trans-Mediterranean
trade and architectural influence under Septimius Severus was still
widely cited in university syllabi across Europe.
But that wasn't why she was here.
She had been specifically appointed to this dig by the Institut
National d'Histoire de l'Art — one of the joint funders of the
Leptis project — not just for her expertise, but for her reputation as
a quiet negotiator and field leader. Europe, still nursing political
unease over North African heritage claims and the aftermath of
colonial-era expeditions, needed a face that was both local and
global. Samira was exactly that.
She had grown up between Paris and Tunis. Leptis was not an
abstraction to her — it was part of her cultural inheritance.
Beside her stood Dr. Tariq Mahfouz, Egyptian by birth,
archaeologist by passion, and diplomatic coordinator by necessity.
Tall, silver-haired, and always dressed in a faded utility vest over a
crisp linen shirt, he bore the mark of someone who had spent
decades in the field without losing his sense of order.
Tariq had organized this dig not just as a UNESCO exercise, but as
a test case — his personal vision for how real archaeological
collaboration could unfold in politically unstable regions. He had

already led high-profile excavations at Tanis and Bubastis, had weathered military coups, ministerial reshuffles, and countless permit delays, and still carried himself with calm authority.

Leptis Magna, he believed, could be a model for how international cooperation, academic transparency, and local stewardship might work together — rather than in tension.

It was Tariq who had designed the site's operational structure: each excavation square jointly managed by rotating teams; all data mirrored across multiple university databases; Libyan antiquities officials embedded in the daily workflow. Nothing left to chance. Nothing removed without approval.

He had personally chosen Alex, Samira, and the rest not just for their academic backgrounds — but for their temperaments. Scholars who could work under pressure. People who could collaborate, not compete. Who knew when to lead, and when to listen.

And with the ERQ now revealing its first artifacts — pottery shards, bone fragments, and the unmistakable curve of a mosaic floor — it was clear his instincts had been right.

Beside Samira, Dr. Tariq Mahfouz bent over the table, peering at a magnified section of the satellite imagery. His salt-and-pepper beard, neatly trimmed, gave him a scholarly air, and the creased lines around his eyes spoke of long days in desert sun and even longer nights in libraries and war rooms.

Tariq dressed plainly: khaki trousers, a linen shirt rolled to the elbows, and always the same dusty-blue scarf draped around his neck — a quiet nod to his homeland and perhaps, to the Nile. His movements were precise, deliberate, and never wasted. Where Samira brought intellectual fire and instinct, Tariq brought discipline, strategy, and patience — qualities that had earned him respect not just in academia, but across bureaucratic and diplomatic circles from Cairo to Paris.

He glanced up as Alex approached, offering a small nod that passed for a greeting. Tariq wasn't cold — just sparing. Words, like artifacts, were valuable to him. Each one carried weight.

Just beyond the main trench, hunched over a fragment of decorated floor tile, Claire Marlowe squinted into the midday sun. Only nineteen, she already carried herself with the quiet determination of someone far older. A second-year archaeology student from Northern Arizona University, Claire had been invited by Alex as both a mentee and a peer-in-the-making—a rare privilege, and one she approached with humble seriousness.

Gifted and intuitive, Claire was particularly drawn to the hidden layers of history: obscure scripts, misinterpreted texts, the forgotten lives beneath the polished narratives of empire. Her pale linen shirt was streaked with dust, and her notebook was already half-filled with sketches and notes in tight, looping handwriting. She thrived in silence and focus, traits that made her ideally suited for the slow, patient discipline of archaeology.

Though she rarely offered her thoughts unless asked, when she did, they carried surprising weight. Both Alex and Tariq had taken notice. Samira, especially, seemed to be nurturing her with a kind of big-sister regard—sharpening her edges, challenging her softly. In the few short days since their arrival, Claire had begun to feel the shape of something stirring inside her: purpose.

Leptis Magna was doing more than revealing its secrets. It was shaping her.

Alex Carey sauntered across the packed sand toward the operations table, where Dr. Tariq Mahfouz stood beneath the shade of a canvas tarp, hunched over a large-format LiDAR printout. The Egyptian archaeologist was scrutinizing the pale green-toned elevation data with a furrowed brow, one hand clutching his reading glasses, the other tracing faint lines only he seemed to see. Despite their age difference, Alex and Tariq saw one another as peers—equals in the field, and respectful of each other's contributions. There was no posturing between them, just mutual trust.

Tariq held up the map and pointed to a clearly defined rectangle faintly outlined in the lower quadrant of the image.

"The GPS coordinates match almost exactly," he said in his deep, lightly accented English.

"Within a couple of meters," Alex agreed, stepping closer. "Claire's uncovered this corner—solid foundations. If it's a villa, it's an impressive one." He tapped along the longer side of the structure. "And this wall orients perfectly with the Byzantine fortifications. This stretch here—" he motioned with his index finger, "might have been a courtyard, likely bounded by the wall itself. If so, it's sizable."

Tariq gave a single nod, eyes flicking over the scale markers.

"We should ask Claire to trench diagonally—corner to corner. It's the fastest way to expose the full plan."

"Totally agree," Alex replied. "Then we split teams—one working north, the other south from the centerline. We'll cover more ground in less time."

Tariq gestured toward the nearest trench, where Dr. Samira Rhmani was crouched low, examining a curve of exposed foundation stones. He called her over. She stood, brushed the dust from her hands onto her light trousers, and walked with calm purpose toward them.

"We've been discussing strategy," Tariq said. "A diagonal trench—from here to here." He traced the imaginary line across the image with his finger. "Claire can lead the cut. Once that's done, we divide and expand."

Samira studied the map, then nodded. "Wonderful idea," she said in her softly accented French-English. Her pronunciation lent every syllable a lilting elegance that Alex found both captivating and mildly distracting.

He caught himself, then asked with genuine concern, "Is Claire ready for that?" He wasn't doubting her—far from it—but this was her first major international dig, and the responsibility was no small task.

Samira folded her arms, giving Alex a look of amused incredulity.

"That girl was born ready. Look at her." She nodded toward the field. "Her team listens. She's calm, precise, and documents everything. Always thinking three steps ahead. Why worry? She's learning from the best."

Alex gave a small grin. "Let's test that theory."

He waved Claire over. She jogged toward them, bounding across the trenching field with the energy of youth and sun-hardened enthusiasm.

"What's up, Prof?" she asked, brushing windblown strands of mousy hair behind her ears. The desert light glinted off her dust-speckled glasses.

Alex didn't even flinch at her casual tone—it had become part of her charm.

"The dig lead has new orders," he said, gesturing toward Tariq. Dr. Mahfouz stepped in smoothly. He held up the LiDAR map again, pointing with precision.

"Claire, I'd like you to establish this corner here, using the GPS plots to pinpoint the position. Once located, run a stringline from that corner to the one you've already uncovered. Then, excavate a narrow trench—one meter wide—along that line to full depth. From there, we'll expand north and south with two crews. Think you can handle that?"

Claire blinked in surprise, caught between pride and nerves. She looked at Alex for a beat. He simply gave her a firm nod of approval.

Her face lit up.

"Fu—"

"Nope," Alex cut her off before she could finish.

She grinned and composed herself.

"Sure thing, Dr. Mahfouz. I'll get right on it."

She dashed back to retrieve the GPS logs and began issuing instructions to her small team of Libyan workers. Watching her command the crew, clipboard in hand, boots kicking up dust, it was hard not to feel a sense of rising potential and profound pride. Alex pursed his lips and exhaled a breath.

"Sorry about that. Youthful exuberance."

Samira chuckled. "I wish I had it."

Tariq was already turning back to the map, but he allowed himself the faintest smile.

The dig was underway. And if Claire's trench revealed what they suspected, this villa—forgotten beneath centuries of sand and silence—was about to speak again.

It was late afternoon when Claire finally located the elusive northeast corner of the villa. Using the Trimble R12i GPS unit mounted on a carbon-fibre pole, she precisely marked the point where the corner was expected to be, based on overlays from the LiDAR imagery. Though the aerial scans—taken from 15,000 feet—were remarkably detailed, their resolution had limits. The data served as a guide, not gospel.

She'd been working trenches northeast and southwest from the projected location all day. Dusty, sunburned, and running on adrenaline, her patience had finally paid off. The subtle edge of a buried wall emerged from the soil, traced with her trowel and carefully brushed clean. It was unmistakably the corner she had been hunting.

Once the feature was fully exposed, she rechecked the GPS coordinates, then used the Trimble to log the point with sub-centimetre accuracy. Satisfied, she took a few steps back, drove a survey stake a few meters behind the corner, and strung a taut fluorescent green nylon line between it and the southwest corner they had uncovered earlier in the week. The string, bright under the low-angled sun, traced the diagonal line of the structure across the site.

Claire stood back to admire the symmetry. Only now, with both corners defined and connected, did the true scale of the building begin to sink in. It was large. Far larger than any other domestic structure they'd identified in the eastern quarter.

Frowning slightly, she turned and called toward the shaded tent where Alex, Samira, and Tariq were reviewing LiDAR overlays. "Hey! Come take a look at this!"

The three archaeologists walked over, intrigued. Claire pointed along the taut green line.

"We've got both corners now. If this really is a single structure—one villa—it's huge. Bigger than anything we've documented in the residential sector so far. Are we sure it's not two or three smaller buildings?"

The others examined the visible foundations, then bent over the large-format LiDAR printout that Tariq carried everywhere. The scan showed no interruption in the buried footprint—just one large rectangular mass.

"Storage perhaps?" Samira offered.

"Too far from the harbor," Tariq countered. "And no roads lead here directly. Not practical."

Alex scratched his chin as he walked the length of the line, his boots crunching softly on dry soil. "A wealthy nobleman? A trader? Someone with real money. Samira, have you seen villas this size before?"

Samira nodded slowly. "Sure. On sites in Tunisia, or coastal Hispania. But those were elite residences. Senatorial class. Governors. People we have inscriptions for. Here, nothing. Not a single reference."

"So it could be private," Alex said. "An official residence, maybe even for the governor himself."

"Probably not Governor, but potentially a Legate or Quaestor. Belisarius?" Samira suggested, a slight edge of speculation in her voice. "Or perhaps Romanus?"

"Could be," Tariq mused. "We don't even know what period this section belongs to. It might not even be Roman in the strict sense."
Alex glanced again down the line Claire had strung. The late light gave it a golden hue, slicing diagonally across the ancient earth like an arrow aimed at history itself.
"Well," he said quietly, "we're about to find out."
Claire had barely broken through the topsoil of the diagonal trench when Tariq's voice rang out across the site.
"All right, everyone—tools down! Light's fading and I don't want tired hands damaging old stone. Wrap it up!"
The collective exhale of weary diggers drifted into the golden haze of the late afternoon. It had been a productive day: Claire had begun her diagonal trench with promising early results, and two auxiliary teams had uncovered foundation outlines in adjacent plots that could belong to outbuildings or a bath complex.
Claire stood, brushed the dust from her knees, and began methodically packing up. The Trimble GPS unit was disassembled with practiced care. She unscrewed the antenna, wiped the contact surfaces clean, and tucked the receiver into its padded case. The lithium-ion batteries were clipped out and set aside—she made a mental note to get them charging as soon as she got back. A small checklist in her field notebook kept her from forgetting anything in her end-of-day routine.
At the far side of the site, Alex was kneeling beside a cross-section of the villa's exposed foundations, scribbling his last notes into a bound leather journal. The stratigraphy was clean and well-defined, and the base of the wall had confirmed what they had all hoped: crushed coral and lime mortar—typical of Leptis Magna's domestic architecture during the Roman and early Byzantine periods.
Nearby, Samira crouched over a pair of carefully labelled soil samples—one taken from directly beneath the foundation, and one just above it. She had bagged and tagged them for optically stimulated luminescence (OSL) testing. It was a newer method in

archaeological dating, but increasingly reliable, especially in sediment-rich North African sites where organic material for carbon dating could be scarce or contaminated. The samples would be sent to a lab in Tripoli—yes, Claire recalled, the University of Tripoli's Department of Geoscience had recently upgraded their OSL facilities. Cairo was always an option, but Tripoli was closer, and they had a relationship there through Tariq.

With the last notes entered and equipment stowed, the group began trickling back toward the path that led to the camp—about half a kilometer east of the site, nestled into the lee of a low, wind-polished ridge. The walk was short but welcome, a cool breeze cutting the day's residual heat as the sun dropped toward the horizon, painting the landscape in copper and ochre.

Their campsite had a comfortable permanence to it: canvas field tents, a central mess area shaded with tarpaulin, folding tables, solar-powered lanterns. A small Libyan catering crew—locals hired from nearby Khoms—had already begun preparing dinner. The aroma of spiced lamb stew with apricots, cinnamon, and cumin drifted through the air, mingling with the smell of freshly baked flatbread and grilled vegetables. Large clay water urns sweated condensation in the fading light, and a portable gas stove hissed gently under a boiling pot of sweet mint tea.

They gathered loosely around the mess table. Some sat, others stood chatting in circles. Claire leaned over a steaming bowl, ravenous. Samira and Tariq joined her, while Alex wandered over with a plate of lamb and couscous, still chewing on the last note he'd scribbled before packing up.

Dinner was informal and full of the soft hum of shared satisfaction. They discussed the trench, the clean cut of the foundation lines, the possibility of a villa this large belonging to someone of rank. There was speculation: theories tossed around between bites, laughter at Claire's retelling of nearly chasing a snake out of her trench earlier that morning.

After the meal, lanterns flickered to life one by one. Plates were cleared, tea was poured, and the evening took on a quieter tone. Tariq produced a slim bottle of Glenfiddich from his canvas chest and two enamel mugs. He handed one to Alex without a word and the two sat just outside the mess area, legs stretched toward the last embers of the sunset, sipping slowly.

"You know," Tariq said, swirling the scotch, "that coral-lime mix in the foundation—it's a signature. The same layering I saw in the villa at Sabratha."

Alex nodded. "I was thinking the same. But this one—it's too big for a merchant. No dolia, no sign of amphora racks. It's not commercial."

"So we're back to official residence," Tariq replied. "Someone important. And undocumented."

"That's what bothers me."

Meanwhile, across the fire pit, Samira and Claire shared a bottle of red wine—something French and modest that Samira had insisted on bringing from Marseille, "for morale." The two women sat cross-legged on a blanket near the edge of camp, the bottle between them, talking quietly.

"She's coming into her own," Samira said, glancing toward Alex and Tariq. "The way she handled the trench today—clear, precise, confident. She'll make a damn good field director one day."

Claire looked up mid-sip. "You're not talking about me, are you?"

Samira smirked. "Who else? You think I talk to the stars?"

Claire laughed and leaned back on her elbows, the night breeze catching her ponytail. The stars were just beginning to shimmer above the Libyan desert, brilliant and clear.

By ten, the camp was quiet. A few lanterns remained lit, casting soft pools of amber light against the tents. Most had turned in early—another day of excavation awaited them in the morning. Alex remained outside a little longer, his journal open, scotch in hand, the night cooling around him. Across the camp, Claire slept soundly, the diagonal trench already taking shape in her dreams.

Chapter 2

The sun hadn't yet cleared the distant dunes when the camp began to stir. The cool stillness of dawn hung over the dig site, the sand and stone not yet seared by the desert heat. A soft breeze whispered through the canvas tents as the team emerged from their bunks, sleep still in their eyes but anticipation stirring in their chests.

The communal mess tent, a canvas structure reinforced with scaffolding poles, smelled of fresh Arabic coffee, warm khubz flatbread, and boiled eggs. A local cook hired from the nearby town of Khoms managed their meals—a former hotel chef named Nasser, who took quiet pride in nourishing the foreign scholars and their Libyan crew.

Claire was already there, seated cross-legged on a camp stool, scribbling in her field journal with one hand while eating with the other.

"I need to get that trench going," she said between mouthfuls, her voice animated with purpose. "We're going to see the entire footprint by end of week, I swear."

Samira entered next, her curls tied back in a scarf, already in her light khaki field clothes and sunglasses. She poured herself a black coffee and joined Claire.

"The samples are packed and labelled," she said. "But I'm not going myself."

Claire looked up. "Who's taking them?"

"I'm sending Youssef," Samira said, referring to their trusted local liaison—an ex-archaeology student from Benghazi University. "He knows the customs people, knows the roads. I wouldn't trust anyone else." She sipped her coffee. "Tripoli University's lab will process the OSL and carbon runs. Cairo's backup, in case Tripoli's backlog is too heavy. I've included chain-of-custody documentation and dating context."

Claire nodded approvingly, already forming the next trench in her mind.

Tariq appeared last, laptop tucked under one arm, notebook under the other, already mid-thought. "Breakfast?" he said vaguely. "Oh. Right." He was working on a draft article for Archaeology Today, hoping to make a preliminary splash about the scope of the villa— just enough to attract additional funding and academic attention, but not enough to give away their more tantalizing hypotheses. "This place," he said, eyes flicking to the horizon, "might rewrite Leptis Magna's urban narrative. That's no small claim."

After breakfast, the team made the familiar walk to the dig—about 300 meters from camp, up over a gentle slope that offered a rising view of the crumbling ruins that spread across the coastal plateau. The sea, visible in the distance, shimmered silver-blue under the rising sun.

The morning air was still cool, a faint sea breeze brushing over the sands as Claire trudged across the shallow ridge between camp and dig site. She liked this time of day. No noise, no distractions, just her boots in the dust and the growing pulse of anticipation in her chest.

Most girls her age were obsessing over shoes or summer parties. Claire was calculating soil compaction ratios and reviewing LiDAR returns in her head. She didn't resent them—she just didn't need any of that. Here, there were no trends to follow, no curated lives to envy.

She had real things to uncover. Real puzzles to solve. And people who saw her as more than just a precocious undergrad.

Samira had noticed, of course. Samira noticed everything. The quiet encouragement, the way she handed Claire more responsibility without ceremony—it meant more than a thousand compliments.

Claire didn't want to be the best. She just wanted to belong. And here, with dust on her boots and history at her fingertips, she finally felt like she might.

To the left of the dig site, scaffolding and shade cloths had been set up over other smaller test pits. To the right stood a few stretches of surviving Byzantine wall, part of the fortified urban perimeter added to Leptis Magna in the 6th century. The wall had been partially restored during past Libyan-Italian excavations in the 20th century, but some original sections were still visible—massive stonework, pitted and sun-bleached, yet still impressive.

Alex had set up his documentation table about fifty meters away from the main trench, where the villa's long axis approached the Byzantine wall. That distance was perfectly reasonable—the villa may have backed onto the wall, with its northeast edge nestled along the boundary, typical for elite structures in defended zones. He was photographing and sketching a section of the wall that bore chisel marks and patchwork mortar consistent with a Byzantine rebuild over Roman foundations. If the villa had been built or repurposed during Byzantine control, the proximity of the wall might help date its construction.

He made notes in his journal:

'Wall construction matches Phase II Byzantine fortifications— coral-limecrete aggregate, reused marble chunks in matrix. Alignment suggests villa post-dates wall, likely mid-6th century CE or later. Pre-Islamic occupation confirmed.'

Claire reached her trench and resumed work immediately. The stringline between the two corners still held taut in the morning air, flanked by the stakes she had driven in the day before. Her team of diggers gathered around her as she outlined the next steps— excavating a full meter-wide swath along the diagonal. She handled the Trimble GPS like second nature now, verifying her markers and taking new elevation points as she expanded the trench's depth and width. Claire knelt beside the trench and pointed toward a layer of soil she wanted cleared. "Yalla, shwaya hena," she said hesitantly, her accent heavy. The workers smiled politely and obliged.

She had picked up enough Libyan Arabic to give simple instructions—dig here, be careful there, bring the tools—but anything more complex still required Samira's help. Samira, fluid and confident, moved between languages with ease, issuing commands in quick, clipped Arabic that got immediate results. Claire envied that. One day, she thought, she'd be fluent enough not to need help.

The sun had begun its climb, and already the stones were warming underfoot. But there was shade cloth, and a breeze, and they had work to do.

As the day wore on, the dig site hummed with quiet purpose under the desert sun. Samira was crouched near the suspected bathhouse complex just west of the villa site, carefully directing her team as they mapped out the subterranean layout with string lines and stakes. She moved with precision and authority, occasionally standing to reference a page of notes or call for updated photographs. Claire could hear her voice—calm, composed, confident.

Alex, some fifty meters away near the edge of the escarpment, was busy documenting the remains of the Byzantine wall. It ran like a half-buried spine behind the villa site, a fractured monument of another time. With a clipboard in one hand and camera in the other, he was mapping the relationship between the wall's remaining sections and the villa's orientation. He referenced excerpts from Procopius and Theophanes the Confessor—cross-checking measurements, attempting to reconstruct the original height and purpose of the structure. Some scholars believed it had once framed the southern border of the Byzantine quarter, but Alex suspected the villa had been purposefully built to back onto it. A defensive posture? Or status?

Tariq, ever the linchpin, paced between the base tent and his laptop, fielding calls in a mixture of Arabic, French, and English. He was updating university administrators, museum curators, and at least one Libyan government official. Claire watched him from the trench, marvelling at the way he negotiated so effortlessly—never flustered, always composed. She admired him. She admired Alex too, in a different way. There was a kind of diplomacy in both their work—just as essential as trowels and data sheets.

Claire focused her attention back to the trench. The diagonal cut she had planned was nearly a meter deep now, stretching at an angle through what they assumed was the central courtyard of the villa. The Libyan workers moved with practiced grace, lifting away baskets of soil and sediment with patience and respect for what lay beneath.

But something was wrong.

The expected tsunami layer from the great tidal wave of 365 AD—a distinctive signature of chaos and destruction in the archaeological record—was absent. Claire had read about its unmistakable markers: a band of coarse, shell-rich sand overlaying earlier occupation layers, often containing marine debris or abrupt changes in soil coloration. But here, the layers flowed uninterrupted. Continuous. Undisturbed.

Had this section of the villa been rebuilt after the tsunami? Or had it somehow escaped its fury?

Her thoughts were interrupted by a glint of colour beneath her trowel. She paused. The soil here was finer, darker—less windblown sand, more silt and organic material. As she carefully brushed the area with a soft course brush, the pattern beneath slowly came into view.

Claire stepped fully into the trench now, the sun warm on her back. She knelt low, her glasses slipping slightly down the bridge of her nose as she leaned close. Her breath caught in her throat.

A mosaic.

It began as a sliver of cobalt blue, edged in white and gold tesserae, forming a clean geometric line. As she cleared further, the floor began to bloom—radiating spirals, interlocking key patterns, and a tessellated border that shimmered in the light with unexpected vitality. Reds and greens and ochres burst to life from beneath centuries of concealment. Unlike some mosaics, which degraded under exposure or moisture, this one had been entombed in dry silt—preserved like a secret.

The workmanship was exquisite. Too exquisite, in fact.

Roman mosaics were typically more restrained in palette and geometry, especially in provincial villas. But this—the intricacy of design, the saturated colors, the stylized vegetal motifs—was unmistakably Byzantine.

Claire's brows furrowed. The villa had long been assumed Roman, perhaps from the late imperial period. But this floor told a different story. Byzantine floors often featured Christian symbology, peacocks or chalices or fish—none of which she had uncovered yet—but the style was familiar. She had seen similar patterns at Antioch, in books at least.

Something didn't add up.

She called over one of the Libyan workers and asked him to carefully help expose more of the floor, directing him with slow gestures and soft Arabic. She was learning, and he smiled, nodding in understanding.

The moment felt significant. Claire's heart was racing, but not from excitement alone. Something about this felt… off. Like the villa was hiding a second identity. A second life.

She rose slowly from the trench, brushing the sand from her knees and pulling her notebook from the back pocket of her cargo pants. Above her, the wind kicked up, tugging gently at the nylon line that marked the corner of the villa.

She looked back over her shoulder toward Samira.

"Samira!" she called, her voice carried by the wind. "You're going to want to see this."

Claire knelt at the trench's edge, her knees pressing into the warm dust, heart racing beneath her linen shirt. The mosaic lay beneath her like a secret waiting to be told—its intricate tesserae catching the sunlight in shards of cobalt, gold, and deep crimson. It was not just beautiful, it was wrong. She knew it, even if she couldn't yet articulate it.

She looked up, scanning the site. "Samira!" she called again, waving an arm sharply.

Samira, who had been conferring with another group of workers near the cluster of collapsed stone columns assumed to be remnants of a bathhouse, turned sharply. She caught the tone in Claire's voice. Urgent, but steady. Not panic—purpose. Samira trotted over, clipboard still in hand, eyes narrowing as she approached the trench.

"What is it?" she asked.

Claire stood, brushing the dust from her knees, her face flushed but lit with a raw kind of focus. She gestured to the mosaic now half-exposed at the bottom of the diagonal trench.

"This isn't Roman," Claire said. "It's glass tesserae, not stone or marble. Look at the reflectivity, the density of colour. It's Byzantine."

Samira dropped into a crouch, immediately examining the edges, drawing a gloved finger along one faint blue line. "And no sedimentary layering from the 365 tsunami?"

"None so far," Claire said. "I was expecting a telltale band of marine debris—organic material, crushed shell, salt layering. But it's clean. I don't think this site was even here when that happened. Which would date it later."

Samira frowned, leaned in closer. Her expression shifted from curiosity to intensity. She pulled out her magnifying loupe and inspected the joints, the grout, the wear patterns. Her hands moved with the precision of someone who had done this hundreds of times. Alex, from fifty meters away near the old Byzantine wall, looked up from his sketchbook and smirked at the sight of two backsides bent side-by-side in academic reverence.

Samira clicked her tongue thoughtfully.

"You're not wrong," she murmured. "This work—this technique—it's sixth century at the earliest. I'd say 540, maybe even later, based on that tessellation pattern. There's a visual grammar to it that's just... wrong for Roman Leptis. Too elaborate. Too Eastern."

"But if the tsunami was 365," Claire said quietly, "and the evidence suggests this villa wasn't here yet—"

"Then it was built after Leptis had supposedly already fallen into ruin," Samira finished. "This shouldn't exist."

They were silent a beat, both knowing that those three words—this shouldn't exist—were the heartbeat of discovery, and the first step into something much larger.

Samira stood abruptly, dusted her knees, and turned to the Libyan workers still scattered across the site. She barked a sharp command in fluent Libyan Arabic—her voice carrying over the low winds and the scrape of shovels.

وقفوا! الجميع، تعالوا إلى هنا! نحتاج إلى كشف هذا كله، اليوم!

"Stop! All of you, come here! We need this entire section uncovered—today!"

The workers, seasoned and respectful, didn't hesitate. Shovels were set down, tarps folded, and within minutes, the buzz of coordinated movement filled the air. Picks, brushes, and trowels converged on the trench like an army of careful ants.

Samira turned back to Claire, her expression unreadable for a moment. Then she allowed herself the smallest smile.

"You were right to call me."

Claire exhaled. "I wasn't sure—"

"You were sure enough. Your instincts were correct Claire, trust them – always!" Samira's eyes lingered on the mosaic. "This changes everything."

Alex approached now, sensing the shift in tone and activity. "What's going on?"

Samira pointed. "Byzantine. Sixth century. Possibly post-tsunami. It doesn't fit."

Alex whistled softly and leaned down to look. "So, we've got a major architectural anomaly sitting in the middle of a site that's supposed to be Roman."

"Or" Claire corrected gently, still absorbing it herself. "We've got a building that suggests Leptis Magna wasn't abandoned like everyone thought."

Samira nodded. "And we need to find out why."

They stood there for a moment, shoulder to shoulder, watching as the mosaic floor was revealed inch by careful inch, each tile a challenge to history itself.

The sun was beginning its slow descent beyond the far western hills, casting a golden haze across the ruins of Leptis Magna. The day's heat had softened into a gentle warmth, the air tinged with salt and distant dust. Down in the excavation trench, they had just uncovered the final section of the mosaic floor—and it was magnificent.

Laid with meticulous care by craftsmen long vanished into the sands of time, the floor sprawled out in a dazzling array of intricate inlays and bold geometry. Its tesserae—small stones no bigger than a fingernail—had been fitted together so precisely that the surface rippled like silk under the fading light. Deep reds, lapis blues, ivory whites, and rich golds interwove into floral spirals, hunting scenes, and ringed medallions. Even the Libyan workers, who had seen their share of ancient artistry, paused in reverent silence.

"Your ancestors had skill," Samira murmured to one of them in Arabic. She couldn't take her eyes off the scale of the floor— fifteen metres by ten at least, an architectural boast of opulence and permanence.

Claire was on all fours at the northern edge, tracing the curves of a procession of lions with a soft brush, calling out in bursts of excitement every time she found a new feline face. Alex was near the centre, measuring tape in hand, moving with slow, precise intent. He noted lengths, breadths, diagonals, the squareness of the room, muttering to himself, occasionally pausing to jot into his field notebook.

Tariq stood slightly apart, pacing just outside the shade of a canvas awning, his phone pressed to his ear as always. But today, he was animated—his voice more animated than usual as he spoke rapidly in English, then Arabic, describing the significance of what they'd found to the project's benefactors. His words hung in the warm air, laced with pride.

Samira gave instructions to the workers in calm, clipped tones. They had done well—very well—and she promised bonuses before reminding them that the time for shovels and baskets was over. "Soft brooms only now," she said. "We reveal, not damage."

By six o'clock, the last of the light had turned to dappled amber. The long shadows stretched across the floor like reaching fingers. There was no forecast of rain—nothing but dry skies ahead—so Tariq made the call. "We leave it uncovered," he announced, snapping his phone shut. "Let it breathe tonight. We'll continue the documentation first thing."

They packed in a quiet, reflective mood. Clipboards, GPS units, notebooks, brushes—all tucked into crates. Each one of them moved with the same unspoken reverence. What they had found wasn't just art. It was a time capsule, a ghost of prosperity rising out of the sand, a Roman echo that hadn't spoken in centuries.

That evening, they gathered for dinner at the long tables beneath the dining tent. The sky had deepened to cobalt, stars just starting to glint above. A contract chef had prepared the meal—braised lamb in a tagine spiced with cumin and cinnamon, blistered flatbread brushed with olive oil and thyme, bowls of saffron-scented couscous, and grilled eggplant soaked in garlic and lemon. The smell alone, rich and earthy, seemed to pull the fatigue from their bones.

They ate slowly, savouring each bite. A jug of cold pomegranate juice passed from hand to hand, followed by small glasses of thick, sweet mint tea.

"The floor is early Byzantine," Tariq declared, setting his fork down with finality. "Maybe around 330. Constantine I—Christian symbolism beginning to creep in. You can see it in the layout. Symmetry, iconography. Not pagan."

Samira raised an eyebrow, her tone playful but firm. "Impossible. This villa sits outside the central axis of Byzantine expansion. It's older. Two-fifty AD, perhaps earlier. Severan period. This was the prime of Leptis, and only then would a merchant or administrator build something so… indulgent."

"Could it be transitional?" Claire asked, wiping her hands. "Late Roman but anticipating Byzantine forms?"

They all looked to Alex. He hesitated, wiping his mouth slowly, setting his napkin down with care.

"It's an anomaly," he said finally. "The artistry—the refinement of the tesserae, their uniform cut and colouring—that's late Byzantine. No question. But the site, the scale, the placement… it doesn't fit. Claire may be right. It's caught between worlds. A blend. My guess is an original building, but repurposed. Possibly restored later, possibly reused."

The table fell into a thoughtful silence.

"You're not going to give us a date?" Samira asked, half-smiling.

"I'll give you a paradox," he replied.

They laughed, a soft chorus of exhausted voices beneath the stars. Conversation lingered a while longer, spiralling into details of dating techniques and stylistic markers, but weariness began to creep in. Even Alex and Tariq—who usually stayed up late with tea and satellite maps—excused themselves early.

It had been a monumental day. The kind of day that lives forever in a field journal and memory. And tomorrow, the floor would still be waiting.

Chapter 3

The sun had risen swiftly in the east, casting a honeyed glow over the rust-coloured ruins of Leptis Magna. By 7:30 a.m., the warmth had already begun to creep into the limestone, coaxing the day into motion. A light breeze carried with it the salt-kissed scent of the sea, mingling with the rich aroma of cardamom-laced Turkish coffee and the buttery flakiness of warm khubz stuffed with scrambled egg, spiced lamb, and tomatoes. On the small terrace outside the temporary dining tent, they ate quickly, seated on rickety folding chairs or crouched on the stone steps. Coffee was poured thick and black into chipped ceramic cups, and a tray of sticky dates and almonds was passed around. Conversation was minimal—everyone was eager to return to the site.

Everyone, that is, except the local Libyan Police Chief, Haroun al-Dabbas, who stood in the shade of a nearby olive tree, locked in a heated exchange with Tariq.

"I've only got five men for three checkpoints along the Coastal Road," the Chief said in clipped Arabic, his arms crossed over his sun-bleached uniform. "One of them is barely old enough to shave. I need to rotate the post near Al-Khums. It's undertrained and vulnerable."

Tariq's voice was low but seething. "Our agreement with the Department of Antiquities was clear. You provide on-site security, especially after what happened in Gharyan last month."

The Chief gave an exhausted shrug. "Then call Tripoli and tell them to send more men. I don't have enough to go around."

With that, he barked something at his two officers, both already loading up into their battered pickup. Dust billowed as the vehicle pulled away, headed southwest toward the highway. Tariq stood for a moment, jaw clenched, before snatching up his phone and retreating to the shade to make a series of terse phone calls.

By 8:00, the team was on-site at the villa. The anticipation in the air was almost electric. Today was for brushing the final veil of dust from the floor and documenting the masterpiece in full. Claire had brought the drone, packed carefully in its matte black hard case, along with extra batteries and a fold-out control unit. The Libyan workers, buoyed by yesterday's breakthrough and already chattering excitedly among themselves, moved with a rare enthusiasm. They traded out shovels and canvas baskets for soft-bristled brooms, small paintbrushes, and wide, flat sweepers. The sounds of labour shifted from the dull clatter of excavation to a soft symphony of whisking and brushing.

Claire and Alex worked in tandem to remove the small canvas tarp covering the diagonal trench that had exposed the first segment of the mosaic. It took only a few minutes to unfasten the ties and roll it back, revealing the radiant tesserae beneath. Claire wanted no visual obstructions when she flew the drone. Samira, on the opposite side of the site, was overseeing a group of labourers still tracing the outer foundation line, following the villa's footprint from corner to corner as they revealed more perimeter stones. Tariq, now divested of the Police Chief, seated beneath the shade of a hastily erected canopy, was hunched over his tablet, pecking out notes for a short abstract—likely for Antiquity or Libyan Studies—to be paired with a press release. Every so often he muttered to himself, editing and rewording.

Claire had finished assembling the drone. She unfolded the sleek graphite-coloured aircraft, clipped in the battery, and switched on the remote. The drone chirped to life with a flutter of lights. Claire watched the camera gimbal steady itself, then initiated a short test flight—hovering it a meter above the ground and panning the

camera smoothly left, then right, up, then down. Satisfied, she
brought it down to reset her image settings.

The last of the silt had been swept from the tessellated floor, and
for a moment, everyone stood back and simply stared. The mosaic
shimmered under the rising sun. Deep reds, ocean blues, and muted
golds formed swirling, concentric bands around the central tableau.
Lions—walking, sitting, resting—circled the border in a silent
parade. It was a marvel.

Claire launched the drone again, this time rising to ten meters. The
high-pitched buzz filled the air as she captured slow, cinematic
footage of the floor, then detailed 4K stills. The drone hovered,
rotated, paused, and clicked. She zoomed in on the lions, then on
the compass-like motif near the northern edge and stitched the
images into a digital mosaic on her tablet.

After several passes, she rose to twenty meters for flyovers—
capturing the broader layout of the villa, the ancient bathhouse, the
crumbling Byzantine walls to the east, and even the faint outline of
the aqueduct running toward the hills. She drifted the drone
northward toward the ghost of the old Roman harbor and then
brought it back in a wide arc.

When Claire finally killed the motors and the whine of the
propellers died down, a silence settled over the dig site—
unnaturally still. And then, in the distance, they heard it.

The low growl of engines, coming fast from the south. Multiple
vehicles. Too fast for an ordinary convoy. Too heavy to be just
tourists or shepherds.

Alex straightened. Samira turned instinctively toward the road.
Even the workers paused, brooms halfway through a sweep.

The dust trail on the southern horizon was growing, and with it, a
tension that had not been there minutes before.

Tariq looked up from his tablet, squinting into the light.

"Who the hell is that?" he asked.

No one answered.

The first sign of trouble came as a distant, rising hum—faint but unmistakable—rolling in across the desert. The morning sun, now climbing high above the limestone ruins, bathed everything in a golden warmth. The scent of dust and coffee still lingered in the air. But that sound—low, mechanical, angry—cut through it like a blade.

Three white Toyota Hilux pickups crested the rise east of the dig site, tires spitting gravel as they barrelled westward down the Coastal Road, engines snarling with urgency. Even from a distance, the way they moved told a story: too fast, too direct. These were not government vehicles. Not local contractors. Not tribal militia.

These were predators.

The moment they veered left at the Al-Khums bus stop and turned off the main road, everyone saw them clearly. Black flags fluttered from steel poles rigged in the truck beds. Gunmen in black tunics and turbans, their faces hidden behind scarves, stood braced with AK-47s raised. One had a mounted PKM machine gun, his finger already feathering the trigger.

"Get down! Take cover!" Alex shouted, his voice slicing through the rising panic.

Some of the Libyan workers, who had lived through ISIS raids before, didn't need to be told twice. They dropped tools mid-motion and bolted. Others—newer, younger—froze in place, eyes wide with disbelief. That hesitation would cost some of them dearly.

The gunfire started even before the trucks came to a full stop. Automatic fire cracked through the morning air, a hammering staccato of chaos. Dust exploded in sharp little geysers where bullets struck the sand. Tents erupted in canvas confetti as bullets tore through canvas and wood. A wheelbarrow burst into splinters, a Libyan man behind it clutching his side as he collapsed, blood already soaking through his shirt.

Alex grabbed Claire and Samira by the arms and pulled them toward the nearest wall.

"Go! Now!"

They ran—stumbling over trowels and shattered pottery, ducking low as bullets whipped past their ears, sharp as insect wings. The Byzantine retaining wall, part of the ancient bathhouse perimeter, stood only chest-high but offered the best cover in sight. Chunks of stone exploded as bullets struck it, ricocheting in furious angles. They dove behind it just as another volley tore past. Claire scraped her elbow on impact. Samira pulled a worker down beside her as he screamed in fear.

Others weren't so lucky. A young Libyan man with a bucket in hand was shot clean through the neck as he ran for a trench. He collapsed face-first, blood pumping into the sand in rhythmic surges. A Egyptian grad student, stunned and slow to react, took a round in the thigh and another in the back as she scrambled behind an overturned table. Her scream twisted into a wet, choking gasp. All around them, people were throwing themselves into trenches, pits, even shallow depressions—anywhere they could disappear. A mosaic fragment shattered under fire. Field notes and grid maps blew like leaves in a dust storm, caught in the wake of panic and rotor-like wind from the trucks.

From behind the wall, Alex peered out.

The convoy had stopped beside the main HQ tent—the command post for the dig. The fighters spilled from the trucks like wolves. One kicked over a table stacked with pottery shards. Another tore open a plastic bin, dumping out stone tablets and catalogued artifacts. A third dragged out a laptop, smashing the table it was on before jamming it into a backpack.

They weren't just here to destroy.

They were looting.

One of them, a tall man with a rifle slung over his shoulder and a black ISIS patch sewn crudely onto his vest, sprayed gunfire into a cluster of parked vehicles, shattering windshields and puncturing tires. Another walked calmly from tent to tent, shooting indiscriminately into their canvas walls, as if expecting someone to be hiding inside each one. A tent caught fire from a tracer round. Another man shot a generator, sending a hiss of gasoline vapor into the air.

Through it all, the leader stood atop the central truck, surveying the scene. When he finally raised his fist, the gunmen obeyed.

With a sudden, disciplined coordination, they leapt back into the trucks. Engines roared to life. The vehicles peeled out in reverse, wheels spitting sand and gravel. As they pulled away, one fighter emptied a final magazine into the dig site, bullets dancing across stone, tearing through banners, and hitting the side of a supply crate, which exploded in a brief fireball from stored diesel.

Then they were gone—screaming back down the access road, engines fading into the hot silence.

Only then did the survivors begin to stir.

A woman sobbed, clutching the bloodied grad student whose chest no longer moved. A worker limped into the open, dragging a man whose face had gone slack, eyes glassy and unmoving. Claire, her hands shaking, lowered the drone controller—cracked but still clutched in her fists. Samira stood, jaw clenched, eyes burning. Alex exhaled slowly and stepped out from the wall.

Smoke curled from burning canvas. Shell casings glittered like brass confetti in the dust. The mosaic floor, once pristine and glowing in the morning light, was now splattered in blood and red boot prints.

This was not an accident. This was not chaos. And this was deliberate.

The stench of blood and cordite still hung in the air like a silent affront to humanity. The gunfire was gone, but its echo still lived in the pit of everyone's chest.

The camp was unrecognizable. Canvas tents hung in tatters like flayed skin. The excavation grid had been trampled, boot prints gouged through centuries-old strata. A plume of black smoke curled lazily from the remains of the generator. Someone's hat had been caught on a shard of rebar and fluttered in the breeze like a forgotten flag.

Four bodies lay in the dirt.

One of them, face-down in the sand, still clutched a trowel in his dead hand. Another had died slumped against the trench wall, blood soaking the field notebook that rested on his lap like a confession. One of the Libyan workers—a teenager no older than sixteen—had been shot through the neck. And of course, the Egyptian grad student lay in the trench where she had been cleaning only minutes before.

Six others were wounded, scattered in pockets of shadow and shelter. A man screamed hoarsely from the shade of a ruined tent, clutching a leg bent at the wrong angle. A young woman lay moaning beside the storage crate, blood pulsing from her upper arm.

Claire was already there, her knees muddy and her hair loose, wrapping a pressure bandage over the woman's wound with trembling hands. She was speaking quietly, her faltering Libyan Arabic clipped and urgent.

"You're okay. You're going to be okay."

A few feet away, Samira had commandeered a med kit from a shattered supply box and was crouched over a Libyan worker, tying a tourniquet around his thigh, the rubber tube pulled tight with professional efficiency. She didn't speak. Her eyes were locked in a focused rage. Her linen shirt was streaked with blood. "Roll him over," she told another man. "Slowly—good—keep the pressure here. I need more bandages!"

Alex stumbled into the main tent, or what remained of it. It had been looted and gutted. The satellite phone was gone. The table smashed. He rifled through drawers, overturned crates, checked beneath a collapsed table, his hands shaking with useless urgency. "Come on… come on…" he muttered. "Where the hell is it?"

In the corner, the radio lay crumpled beneath a fallen chair, its screen spiderwebbed and dark. No signal. No power. No help.

He burst back outside, eyes scanning for anything—any sign of the Libyan police force assigned to protect the dig.

Nothing.

Just dust and sun and silence.

Finally, ten long minutes after the attack, the sound of a jeep engine came grumbling up the access road. A battered Toyota Land Cruiser, bearing the insignia of the local constabulary, pulled to a halt beside the scorched trench line. Out stepped Chief Haroun al-Dabbas, a portly man in mirrored sunglasses and a blue fatigue uniform too neat for the moment.

He took one look around—at the bodies, the burning wreckage, the grieving workers—and made a noise that was somewhere between a sigh and a grunt of disbelief.

"What happened here?" he demanded, in Arabic.

"What do you think happened?" Samira snapped, rising to her feet, her arms soaked to the elbows in someone else's blood. "They came. They killed. And you weren't here."

Haroun ignored her, already waving his arms at his two subordinates, barking questions as though the destruction might rearrange itself into a more palatable story. "Where was security? Why didn't anyone alert us sooner? Where is the camp foreman?"

"You were supposed to be here! You were supposed to be the security!" Alex barked, stepping forward, fists clenched. "They came in broad daylight. On the road your men were assigned to watch. Where the hell were you?"

Haroun didn't answer. He glanced down at one of the bodies, then turned away, muttering something under his breath.

Amidst the arguing, the sobbing, the groans of the wounded, a voice cut through the din—quiet, but sharp as glass.

"Where's Tariq?" Samira asked.

Everyone stopped.

She said it again, louder. "Tariq. Has anyone seen him?"

The name seemed to hang in the air like smoke. Claire turned, eyes widening. "He was here. He was on the trench grid—right before it started."

"I saw him," said one of the surviving workers. "He was running back to his tent to get his phone"

"Did anyone see him after the shooting started?" Alex asked.

No one spoke.

Claire looked around, scanning the faces—those present, those huddled, those injured. But not his.

Samira's expression darkened. "He's not here," she said softly. "He's not anywhere."

A heavy silence fell as the implications settled like a blanket of dust over the survivors.

They hadn't just come to kill.

They'd come to take something.

And now, Tariq was gone.

Kidnapped. Disappeared into the desert with the killers. And if he was still alive, he was somewhere beyond the reach of tents and trenches and broken radios.

The heat had returned with a vengeance, beating down like a punishment. The sun seemed angrier now, as though even the sky had borne witness to the slaughter.

Alex stood chest to chest with Chief Haroun, the two men locked in a tense verbal standoff that had already drawn the attention of everyone still standing.

"This was your jurisdiction," Alex snapped, voice low and tight, anger barely restrained. "You were supposed to be here. You were supposed to protect us."

Haroun adjusted his sunglasses and crossed his arms. "And I was told you were working under a no-risk clearance. That this site was safe. Civilian. Academic."

"Don't you dare." Alex's voice dropped to a dangerous whisper. "Don't you dare shift this on us. We filed our presence, the Libyan Department of Antiquities signed off on the schedule, the site, the local hires. You assigned two men to patrol the access road—and they weren't here when it mattered."

"You think we can afford a garrison on every archaeological dig some Westerner thinks is worth digging up?" Haroun fired back. "This is Libya, Carey. Not Luxembourg. Our forces are stretched. Our intelligence is patchy. You came knowing the risks."

"We didn't come with rifles and shoot up civilians," Alex shot back. "We didn't kidnap anyone."

That landed like a slap. Haroun took a step back, his lips tightening, but said nothing.

Disgusted, Alex turned away. The anger drained from his face, replaced with a hollow weariness. He walked past the still-smoking remnants of the headquarters tent, back toward the fallen bodies. One of the younger workers—a boy named Idris—was kneeling beside the body of his uncle, weeping quietly. Alex knelt beside him and placed a hand on his shoulder. The boy looked up, eyes red and vacant, then simply nodded and stood. He understood. Alex began helping gather the dead.

He lifted one body by the shoulders, the fabric of the man's shirt stiff with dried blood. Another worker took the legs. Together, they carried him into one of the shot-up storage tents, repurposed now as a makeshift morgue.

One by one, the four dead were moved, laid gently on canvas tarps in a row, their faces covered with cloths torn from what remained of the supply tent. No prayers were said—there wasn't time, or certainty which language to use. But the silence was enough.

None of the Libyan police helped.

They stood in small clumps by their vehicle, murmuring among themselves, casting uneasy glances at the workers and their Western colleagues. Haroun lit a cigarette and pretended not to watch. Outwardly, his hands were clean, but his inaction had already written its own guilt into the sand.

Inside Samira's tent, away from the carnage, she crouched by her travel case and unlocked a metal trunk. From beneath sealed lab samples and folders she produced a sleek black satellite phone—a French military-grade model issued to Institut National d'Histoire de l'Art field teams for exactly this kind of situation.

She punched in the number for the Institute's regional liaison in Tunis. It rang only once.

"Dubreuil."

"Gérard, it's Samira. The site at Leptis Magna has been attacked. Four dead. Six injured. One missing. Dr. Tariq Mafouz has been kidnapped. It was ISIS."

There was a sharp inhale. "Mon Dieu. Are you safe?"

"For now. But the Libyan police were absent. Locals are terrified. The entire camp is in chaos."

There was a pause. Then: "Stay exactly where you are. I'm dispatching a private security detachment now—former Foreign Legion, GIGN-trained. They'll depart from Charles De Gaul within the hour. ETA four hours. I'll start clearing their arrival with the Ministry of Antiquities and the Interior Ministry immediately."

"They'll need airspace and ground clearance and of course, transport. The local police—" she glanced outside "—are already trying to bury this under bureaucracy."

"Then I'll escalate. If the security team is blocked, we'll reflag the operation under diplomatic protection. The French Foreign Legion has a unit stationed in Faya-Largeau, northern Chad. One call to Paris, and they'll be in Libyan airspace before anyone can object. But let's hope it doesn't come to that."

Samira exhaled shakily. "Thank you."

"Are you injured?"

"No. Claire and I are doing triage. Alex is—he's holding everything together."

There was a brief pause. Then, with great sincerity:

"You have my deepest condolences. Tariq was well respected here. And well-liked."

"We need the UN notified," Samira said. "This wasn't just terrorism—it was an attack on a registered international heritage excavation."

"They'll be looped in within the hour," Gérard said. "UNESCO, the ICCROM, your insurance provider, and all partner institutions. A full investigation will be launched. Until then, you are to stand down. The site is closed. No one is to enter or leave until the security team is on-site and establishes a secure perimeter. Do you understand?"

Samira nodded. "Understood."

"I'll call back with status updates. Stay safe, Samira."

The line went dead.

Back outside, Alex stepped into the centre of the shattered dig and surveyed the carnage. Claire walked beside him, her arms still red to the elbows. Her eyes were glassy, exhausted, but resolute.

"Security team's coming," Samira announced, approaching from the tent, holding the sat phone. "Four hours, tops. Gérard is working through official channels. If they're blocked, the French military gets involved."

"About time someone took this seriously," Alex muttered.

Samira gave him a grim look. "They'll contact the UN. Everyone's going to know about this. Tariq's abduction changes everything. This is no longer an academic site. It's a war zone."

No one spoke for a long moment.

"Will they come back?" asked Claire, a little shaky.

"Doubtful," Alex suggested, "this was a smash and grab. But still, it's better to be safe than sorry."

In the distance, the sky shimmered where the desert met the horizon—still and golden and utterly, utterly indifferent.

And somewhere out there, Tariq was being held, or moved, or worse.

Alex's fists clenched at his sides.

"This isn't over," he said.

Not by a long shot.

The chartered Dassault Falcon 20 sliced through the late-morning sky, descending toward Tunis-Carthage International Airport with practiced efficiency. Its undercarriage groaned as wheels extended, and the moment it kissed the tarmac, the aircraft taxied hard and fast to a remote section of the airfield, well away from the commercial terminals. The door unsealed with a hiss.

Eight men, clad in tactical black with full combat gear and FAMAS G2 rifles slung tight to their chests, disembarked with the precision of a unit that had done this dozens of times before. They moved briskly, wordlessly, toward a waiting Leonardo AW09 helicopter. The chopper's rotors were already spinning, its skids rocking slightly from the airflow. A lean operator in the co-pilot seat signalled with a thumbs-up.

No one stopped to talk. The team climbed in, secured the doors, and within seconds the AW09 lifted from the tarmac in a storm of noise and dust, banking southward. Below, the sprawling Caserne Garde Nationale "El Aouina" military base briefly shimmered under the sun as they passed overhead.

The helicopter hugged Tunisia's shimmering Mediterranean coastline, zipping over low-slung towns and the inland salt flats near Sfax before turning east, out over the open water. They crossed into Libyan airspace just north of Misrata, clearing with Tripoli ATC on encrypted diplomatic frequencies. There were no delays. The French had made sure of that.

An hour later, they roared in low over Leptis Magna.

The ruins of the ancient Roman city stretched out beneath them—golden columns casting long shadows, the old amphitheatre worn smooth by time, the dig site now eerily quiet and scorched from the gunfight. Smoke still curled faintly from one of the tents near the kitchen area. The camp was a mess of blood-streaked dust and ruined equipment.

The pilot banked in a wide recon pass, allowing the team to perform a visual sweep. Through their visors, they scanned for hostiles, vehicles, unusual movement. None. The threat was gone—for now.

They circled once more. Then, the AW09 dipped hard, flaring just before touchdown in a cleared section beside the main encampment. The rotor wash blasted grit and loose tarpaulin into the air. One tent nearly collapsed.

Boots hit the sand. The eight men spread like clockwork, rifles up, forming a secure 360-degree perimeter.

The team leader—a tall, rugged man with close-cropped silver hair, sun-scorched skin, and the bearing of a career soldier—strode toward the heart of the camp. His rank had once been Capitaine, French Foreign Legion. The glint of a Legion insignia still rode the shoulder of his tactical vest.

He approached a cluster of workers near the edge of the site. "Je cherche Mademoiselle Rahmani," he said crisply in French.

One of the local workers silently pointed toward the ruins, where three figures stood amid broken crates and overturned field equipment.

The Capitaine jogged lightly across the sand. "Mademoiselle Rahmani!" he called out as he approached. "Je suis Capitaine Louis Delon, Sentinel Sécurité. I am here to escort you back to Tunis."

Samira turned, dust-streaked and pale but upright. Beside her stood Alex, tense and hollow-eyed, and Claire, arms crossed tight over her chest, her gaze defensive.

Samira stepped forward and extended her hand. "Monsieur, this is Alex Carey and Claire Marlowe," she said in perfect, lilting French. "Mais s'il vous plaît, anglais!"

Delon nodded, switching to heavily accented English. "Madame, Monsieur. I am here to take you back to Tunis. Immediately."

"But—what about Dr. Mahfouz?" Samira's voice caught in her throat. "He has been kidnapped. We must—must look for him."

Delon paused, choosing his words with difficulty. "Madame… if ISIS intends to ransom him, they will release a video. If not…" He gave a small, grim shake of his head. "They do not take prisoners. Not for long."

Samira clenched her fists. "We must do something! We can search the coast, the roads—they cannot have gone far."

Delon looked at her with quiet pity. "The desert is 1.3 million square kilometres. They could be anywhere—south, west, even in the empty quarter. Unless we know exactly where they went, a search is not only futile—it is suicide. My orders are to protect you, Mademoiselle Marlowe, and Professor Carey. That is my mission. Now please. We have little time."

Claire stepped in. "What about the others? The rest of the team?"

"There are buses en route to take them to Tripoli or Khoms," Delon replied. "From there, they will be flown home. My men will remain until the final evacuation. This site is now under lockdown. No entries. No exits."

Alex finally spoke. "What about our gear?"

"You have one hour to collect personal items and equipment of value. The rest stays. I suggest you do not waste time."

No further words were exchanged.

They moved quickly. Alex returned to his tent and crammed everything into his battered canvas rucksack—his laptop, field notes, passport, two changes of clothes. Claire retrieved her drone, sketchbook, phone, and laptop. Samira, meticulous even in crisis, packed her soil samples, tablet, field journal, and personal effects. None of them said much.

By the time they returned, Delon was barking instructions into his comms. His men were spreading out further, stacking up the dead under a canvas sheet near one of the larger tents. The bodies would travel on the bus. It wasn't dignified, but it was the best they could offer in the moment.

Delon gave a final nod to his men. "Secure until the last evac. When the chopper returns, you leave. Not before."

They loaded into the AW09 once more.

The flight back was silent. No one spoke. The coastline passed beneath them, golden and empty. An hour later, they touched down on the tarmac at Tunis-Carthage, where the sleek grey Dassault Falcon 20 waited, engines already warm.

A car was waiting.

Gerard Dubreuil, a trim, clean-cut man in a linen suit, approached as they stepped off the helicopter. His face was grave.

"Mademoiselle Rahmani, Monsieur Carey, Mademoiselle Marlowe. I am so deeply sorry. What happened was… unthinkable."

He handed over a folio of papers. "Your accommodation in Paris is confirmed. Park Hyatt Paris-Vendôme. The Falcon will take you there without delay. We are repatriating the bodies as soon as possible."

He looked to Samira. "We are also working discreetly with the GNS in Tobruk to open backchannels. If we receive any communication from ISIS, you will be the first to know."

Samira nodded, eyes rimmed with red but dry. "Thank you, Gérard."

The debrief was quick. Everything that could be said, had already been said.

The Falcon was buttoned up, clearance granted under diplomatic call signs. Ten minutes later, it taxied, turned into the wind, and powered up the runway—rising smoothly, elegantly into the deep blue sky, bound for Paris.

Far to the east, Leptis Magna faded into silence and memory.

The Falcon 20 climbed quickly to cruising altitude. Inside the cabin, it was just the three of them—Alex, Claire, and Samira. Alex and Samira sat opposite each other, silent. Claire was across the aisle, her head resting lightly against the window frame. Each of them was lost in their own thoughts—or simply drained after the adrenaline crash of the last twenty-four hours.

The Mediterranean slid by beneath them at 800 kilometres per hour and 20,000 feet, but no one bothered to look out the windows.

Paris beckoned. And to be honest, Alex was grateful for its warmth and the sense of safety it offered.

Hopefully, by the time they landed, there would be word of Tariq. But even as the jet hummed steadily through the darkening sky, a gnawing unease had settled in the pit of Alex's stomach—quiet, insistent, and impossible to ignore.

Chapter 5

Claire awoke to the soft, grey light of a typical March morning in Paris—damp, cool, and threaded with a veil of mist that softened the sound of early traffic below. The air was still, the sky pewter, and outside her window the rooftops of the 2nd arrondissement glistened faintly from an overnight drizzle. A cold, stubborn winter still clung to the city, despite the occasional promise of spring.

She had slept like the dead in what she could only describe as the most comfortable bed ever conceived by man. After two weeks on camp stretchers, this felt positively celestial. She let herself sink into the Egyptian cotton sheets for a moment longer, her limbs leaden with sleep, before she noticed the blinking red light on the bedside phone.

A message.

 From Alex.

She rolled over and pressed play.

'Hey. It's just past eight. I'm downstairs in the restaurant, figured I'd let you sleep a bit. Join me when you're up. No rush.'

It had been sent over thirty minutes ago. Claire smiled faintly. Another fifteen minutes wouldn't hurt.

She slipped into the ensuite and let the hot water of the rainfall shower pound away the fatigue and dust of North Africa. The sensation was euphoric—like washing off not just dirt, but memory.

Dressed and dry, she took the elevator down to the lobby of the Park Hyatt Paris-Vendôme, a hotel so discreetly luxurious that even its silence felt intentional. The foyer gleamed with cream

stone and polished brass, its atmosphere hushed, perfumed faintly
with bergamot and fresh flowers. Claire followed the elegant
black-and-gold signs to the Le Café Jeanne, the hotel's acclaimed
restaurant where breakfast was served daily.

Alex was already seated by the window, casually flipping through
Le Monde, the folded paper half-obscuring his face. He looked
rested, if slightly rumpled, and wore the same charcoal-gray jacket
from Tunisia, now free of sand and sweat.

Claire stifled a yawn and stretched languidly before sinking into
the velvet-upholstered chair across from him.

"Have you ordered breakfast yet?" she asked, reaching for the
menu.

"Waiting for you. Continental or full breakfast?"

"When in Paris…" she replied chirpily, handing the menu back
without looking.

Within minutes, a uniformed waiter arrived with a tray laden with
a quintessentially Parisian spread:

Freshly baked croissants, pains au chocolat, slices of tartine with
churned Normandy butter and three types of jam—fig, raspberry,
and orange marmalade. There were soft-boiled œufs à la coque
with soldiers of toasted brioche, a platter of charcuterie and
fromages, and delicate glasses of freshly squeezed orange juice.
Two café crèmes steamed gently beside fine china cups.

Claire took a bite of her croissant, the crust shattering flakily, and
let out a low, satisfied hum.

"Why do we always end up in France?" she mused aloud, brushing
crumbs from her chin.

Alex didn't look up. "Dunno," he said, folding the newspaper
noisily, "but what I do know is I can't read French newspapers
worth a damn." He tossed it aside with theatrical frustration.

Claire laughed, a clean, musical sound. "You'd think by now you'd
have learned."

"Cultural osmosis isn't what it used to be."

She smiled into her cup. "So, here we are. What's happening for today?"

Alex pulled out a slim, dog-eared notebook from his coat. "Well, Samira phoned very early this morning. Apparently there's a meeting with the UN Security Council rep—we've been invited, just in case they want our perspective on what happened down there. After that," he flipped to another page, "we're headed to the Bibliothèque de l'INHA. Salle Labrouste, to be exact."

Claire blinked. "So what's at this bibliothèque? What are we doing there?"

Alex sipped his coffee. "What we do best, Claire—research."

After breakfast, they regrouped in the lobby. Claire had changed into a warm navy trench coat; Alex had a satchel slung over his shoulder. The concierge, a bespectacled man with the posture of a maître d', offered them a polite nod and raised a hand for a cab. "Institut National d'Histoire de l'Art, Galerie Colbert?" he confirmed in English with a Parisian accent. "It's close—maybe eight minutes by taxi."

The cab pulled up moments later. Paris glided past their window in soft-focus: the Opéra Garnier's pale stone shimmered under the overcast light; cafés were just opening, their chairs turned toward the street like sunflowers hoping for sunlight. Claire watched as schoolchildren in navy uniforms crossed Rue de Richelieu, chattering, scarves fluttering.

The cab dropped them off at the entrance to the Galerie Colbert, a neoclassical arcade tucked discreetly near the BNF Richelieu site. Inside, under the soaring glass roof of the rotunda, the Institut felt more like a grand old museum than an academic institution. A bronze statue of Minerva stood guard at the entrance—poised, serene, eternal.

They checked in with security and were directed to the Salle Labrouste.

Claire gasped when they stepped inside.

The vast 19th-century reading room was breathtaking. Domed skylights floated above them, casting pale light onto rows of green reading lamps. The columns were pale pink and gold, the walls lined with endless bookshelves. Everything smelled faintly of parchment, beeswax, and old paper.

Alex whistled softly. "Now this is a library."

Claire nodded. "Let's find Samira."

The library attendant led them toward the rear of the grand reading room, where modern glass partitions created small, private meeting booths tucked quietly behind the towering shelves. Inside one of them, Samira sat at a sleek white table, typing briskly on her laptop. She looked up as they entered and greeted them both with a warm smile.

"You made good time," she said, closing the lid of her computer. "I wanted to brief you before we head up."

Alex and Claire sat down opposite her.

"The meeting with the UN Security Council representative is informal—just standard protocol. You're invited to sit in, but you won't be asked to speak unless they have specific questions. The INHA's legal counsel will be present, as well as the Director General, André Molineux."

She checked her watch.

"We should go. It starts in fifteen minutes—offices are up on the fifth floor."

They exited the library's quiet grandeur and took the elevator up to the administrative offices. The fifth floor was a stark contrast to the 19th-century elegance below. It was all clean lines, glass walls, brushed aluminium fixtures, and dark walnut accents. Conference rooms flanked a wide corridor, each enclosed in frosted glass with sleek signage in minimalist sans-serif font.

They were led into the Board Room, a long rectangular space with high windows and an oval glass table surrounded by leather chairs. It was already well attended: men and women in tailored suits, murmuring quietly while flipping through dossiers or consulting tablets. There were briefcases everywhere. Alex and Claire, still in their practical travel clothes, felt distinctly underdressed.

The meeting began promptly and, somewhat ironically, was conducted entirely in French. Alex raised an eyebrow at Claire, who shrugged with an amused smile—after all, English was supposed to be the official working language of the UN.

The discussion was dry but important: risk assessments, preliminary reports, legal considerations. Alex and Claire weren't called on once. They simply observed, letting the hour pass in a blur of acronyms and bureaucratic formalities.

As the meeting adjourned, Samira stood and guided them through the departing crowd toward a tall, refined man in his early sixties, with silver hair, sharp features, and a gracious air.

"André Molineux," Samira said. "May I introduce Professor Alex Carey and Miss Claire Marlowe?"

Molineux smiled warmly and extended a hand to each of them. Alex picked up on the special handshake immediately.

"A pleasure," he said, his accent tinged with the softest southern French lilt. "I've heard much about your recent work—especially your adventures in our part of the world. France owes you both a certain… cultural debt, I think. If ever you need a place to research, the Institute's doors are open to you."

Alex chuckled, exchanging a glance with Claire. "I didn't realize we were that well-known."

Samira's eyes twinkled. "Oh yes. Your reputation precedes you. Don't worry, Professor—around here, we admire academics who chase truth over prestige. You're among friends."

Claire leaned in. "So, when do we get to start digging?"

"Right now, actually," Samira replied. "I've reserved us a research suite for the day—Salle Doucet. Fully AV-equipped. We'll be able to project and analyse the drone imagery you captured at Leptis Magna."

She picked up her laptop and gestured toward the elevator.

"Shall we? I think there is more to that villa floor than meets the eye."

As they exited the boardroom, Samira led them back down a broad corridor lined with narrow glass partitions and recessed lighting. The elevator chimed softly as its doors opened, and they descended in silence.

The Bibliothèque de l'Institut National d'Histoire de l'Art was a building of contrasts—grandeur wrapped in quiet restraint. Downstairs, the architecture shifted. The entrance lobby retained its 19th-century bones—vaulted ceilings, fluted columns, and the delicate scent of aged paper and polished wood. Brass railings gleamed under pools of soft lighting. Students and researchers moved through the space with purposeful hush, leather satchels slung over shoulders, badges clipped to coats.

There was a faint smell of espresso and old stone. Somewhere near the entrance, a security guard greeted an arriving scholar with a nod. The entire building thrummed with restrained energy, a temple to knowledge.

Samira guided them past the main reading room and toward a curved staircase at the rear, leading to the second floor, where specialized research rooms were housed. Research Room 3—Salle de Recherche 3—was tucked discreetly at the end of a quiet hallway. The thick wooden door opened with a soft mechanical click.

Inside, the room was a quiet marvel of modern utility: a large central table fitted with every imaginable data and AV port—USB-C, HDMI, Lightning, Ethernet. Wireless charging pads were built seamlessly into the polished oak surface. A massive, wall-mounted 4K display dominated one end of the room, flanked by sleek acoustic wall panels that doubled as sound insulation. Plush carpet muted their footsteps, and the cool hum of air conditioning whispered in the background.

The chairs, Alex noticed, were padded, ergonomic, and upholstered in soft black Italian leather. Someone had taken care to make this space feel less like a lab and more like a sanctuary for deep thought.

Claire dropped her pack by the table and set to work. In her element, she connected her MacBook Pro, her tablet, and her phone, juggling cords and ports with quick efficiency. The screen blinked, flickered, then bloomed into color as she navigated the AV controls. A few taps later, the drone footage loaded.

Then the screen came alive.

The high-definition aerial view of the mosaic floor at Leptis Magna filled the wall. Even in the cool light of the research suite, the colors burst with startling vitality—blues as deep as lapis, ochres and reds that glowed like fire. The drone had captured every angle, every contour. There was a reverent silence in the room as all three stared.

In the center, arranged with careful symmetry, was a vivid tableau of daily life—grain harvesting, fishing, trade caravans, and scenes of sowing under the Libyan sun. The artistry was breathtaking, the perspective dynamic and playful.

Framing the outer edge of the floor were eight lions—four in each corner—stylized and muscular, captured in different poses around the border in an endless cycle. Their golden manes were rendered in radiant tesserae, their expressions vivid with a blend of ferocity and elegance.

Samira broke the silence. "Tariq..." she hesitated, her voice catching slightly. "Tariq believed it was early Byzantine. Around 330 CE. That would explain the size and splendor of the villa."

Alex tilted his head, frowning. "It doesn't gel. Look at the complexity of the inlays—the refinement of those tiny glass tesserae. The palette is too rich, the technique too mature. There's lapis lazuli in the blues, likely from Badakhshan. Those reds—possibly cinnabar. I see mother-of-pearl, serpentine, carnelian. Even Egyptian porphyry in the shadowed outlines. These materials suggest long-established trade routes. This mosaic wasn't made by a fledgling empire. There's no Roman influence left at all. This is high Byzantine—possibly even autonomous provincial."

Samira nodded slowly, absorbing it. "Claire? What's your take?"

Claire blinked. It always caught her off guard—being asked to weigh in like this. She was still just a second-year archaeology student. Sitting between two PhDs could have been intimidating. But Samira never made her feel lesser, only important. Valued. Equal.

She straightened a little. "Well… I think what bothers me most is what's missing."

Alex and Samira turned toward her.

"This villa is just inland from the Wadi Lebda floodplain," she continued. "We know the tsunami of 365 AD devastated this entire region. Every major site at Leptis Magna bears some trace— seaborne sediment, marine debris, disrupted strata. But at this site? Nothing. No mud layers. No brackish residue. No signs of marine inundation at all."

She looked up. "So if this villa existed in 330… it wouldn't have survived 365. But it did. Intact. That pushes us later. Much later."

Alex smiled slightly, and Samira gave a slow, appreciative nod. The girl was coming into her own.

Alex leaned forward again, squinting at the screen. "Claire, didn't you say you took some high-definition stills of the floor?"

"Of course," she said, already scrolling. "4K stills. You can practically see every individual stone."

"Bottom left corner. Where the lions curve around… what's that?" He gestured vaguely with his pen. "There, between the border motif."

Claire toggled quickly, then paused. "Here," she said, and with a click, the image on the screen zoomed in.

They all stood and leaned forward as the detail sharpened—stone, grout, hairline cracks—all revealed in dazzling clarity. Nestled between the paw of one lion and the tail of the next was a dark inlay that didn't belong.

"What is that?" Claire asked.

Alex narrowed his eyes. "It's… writing."

Samira stepped closer. Her voice dropped, almost reverent. "Kufic script," she said.

Claire looked up. "You can read it?"

Samira nodded. "Enough. It's early Kufic—barely formalized. This predates the diacritics we use today. But the structure is unmistakable."

She traced the text with her finger in the air.

مالك بن هارون الساحري – سنة 31 هـ

 "Malik ibn Harun al-Sahiri – Year 31 AH."

There was a pause. The weight of the revelation settled over the room.

"Year thirty-one…" Alex murmured. "That's 651 CE."

Claire let out a low whistle. "Nearly three hundred years later than Tariq suggested."

"And a name," said Samira quietly. "A signature."

Alex's voice was barely above a whisper. "Malik ibn Harun al-Sahiri. He was here."

They sat back down in silence again, staring at the screen as if the stones might speak.

Claire sat back in her chair, her brow furrowed in concentration as she stared at the magnified image on the screen.

"So... who is... how do you say his name again?"

Samira leaned forward slightly, her tone measured but certain. "Malik ibn Harun al-Sahiri."

"Right," Claire nodded. "Malik. Who is Malik is my first question. And my second is… 652 CE? That's late—seriously late in the Byzantine Empire."

"The Byzantine Empire was still technically functioning," said Alex, "but it had already lost most of its eastern territories by then. Egypt fell to the Arabs in 641. Libya followed soon after."

"The Empire basically ceased to exist in North Africa around that time, right?" Claire added, glancing at Samira.

Samira nodded. "Yes. By 652, this entire coastline was under Arab control. Leptis Magna would've been a shadow of its former self—if inhabited at all."

"So why include a date at all?" Claire asked. "I mean, most mosaic floors we've seen don't include that level of detail—definitely not a signature and a date."

"Exactly," said Alex. "It's not typical. Not for Roman mosaics. Not even for early Byzantine ones. Attribution like that was rare. Decorative inscriptions, sure—sometimes religious verses, or donor references in churches. But a personal name and an Islamic calendar date?" He shook his head slowly. "That's deliberate. That's making a statement."

"But is that even the artist's name?" Samira interjected. "You think it is?"

Alex hesitated. "Presumptive."

"Presumptive?" Claire echoed.

"I don't think that's the artist at all. I think that's the owner." He leaned forward again, pointing at the screen with his pen. "Only someone wealthy enough to commission that kind of mosaic—this level of detail, the use of rare materials, the complexity of the inlay—only he would have the authority to put his name on it. It's a declaration."

"Like a Roman titulus," Samira said. "A property mark."

"Exactly. Not an anonymous artisan's flourish. This was ownership. Identity."

"But why?" Claire asked. "Like you said—it's not normal. Not in any of the other villa sites we've studied."

"Because this isn't a normal mosaic floor," Alex said, eyes locked on the screen. "This wasn't made just to impress dinner guests. It was constructed to a design—an ideological one. Symbolic. Coded, maybe. Or simply bold. But definitely deliberate."

Samira looked back at the stylised lions marching around the edge. "Four lions. Four corners. Movement around a square. That's not just decorative—it's cyclical. Conceptual."

"And the centre motifs," added Claire, clicking back to a wide shot. "They're not imperial. No Christian iconography. No Roman gods. Just… everyday life."

"Labor. Trade. Agriculture," Alex said. "It's secular. It's civic. It's earthbound."

Samira's voice was quieter now. "Maybe it was never meant to glorify the divine or the emperor. Maybe it was about something else—ownership, legacy, survival."

"And identity," said Alex.

Claire's eyes drifted back to the inscription. "Malik ibn Harun al-Sahiri." She wrote the name into her Spirax notebook.

Samira crossed her arms, thinking. "Al-Sahiri. That nisbah suggests origin. that literal translation means Malik, son of Harun, of the desert sands,' though that might be poetic license."

Alex arched an eyebrow. "Malik, son of Harun, of the desert sands?" He smiled faintly. "Now that's a signature worth digging into."

They all stared again at the screen. The image was still—unmoving, silent—but the story it told was beginning to come alive in the space between their thoughts.

It was approaching noon, and the tension of mental exertion had begun to fray around the edges of their focus. Claire's stomach growled audibly, prompting a brief laugh from Alex.

"Pas de nourriture autorisée," Samira reminded them, tapping the placard near the door with a smile. No food allowed in the research rooms—strictly enforced by the grey-haired archivist who had given them their keys with a glare that dared them to violate protocol.

"We can leave our equipment as it is," Samira added, standing and stretching her back. "The rooms are lockable."

They gathered their notes and devices, carefully covering the mosaic projection still paused on the central monitor. Claire switched off the light board. Alex slid the door shut with a soft click, securing their temporary command post.

The cafeteria at the Institut National d'Histoire de l'Art was located on the ground floor, tucked behind a long arched hallway just off the main courtyard. Its entrance was marked by a minimalist black placard:

CAFÉTÉRIA – Personnel & Chercheurs

Inside, vaulted ceilings and stone walls framed the room with quiet elegance, softened by modern Scandinavian-style tables and warm lighting. The floor was tiled in charcoal grey, and large industrial windows overlooked a modest sculpture garden in the courtyard beyond.

The scent hit them as soon as they entered: a blend of roasted vegetables, espresso, and fresh thyme. The air was warm with the smell of baguettes just out of the oven and the subtle sweetness of tarte Tatin cooling on a rack behind the counter.

Alex ordered a plate of steak frites with peppercorn sauce and a bottle of Badoit sparkling water.

Claire chose a seasonal quiche aux poireaux—leek quiche—with a side of mixed greens and vinaigrette, along with a tall glass of jus de pomme.

Samira, always conscious of her diet and intake, selected a simple salade de chèvre chaud—warm goat cheese salad—with walnuts and honey, and an espresso, black.

She tapped her badge on the card reader at the register. "I'll put it on my l'Institut expense account," she said smoothly, before ushering them toward a table near the window.

They sat down with a collective sigh, plates steaming, hands relaxing around warm cups. For a few minutes, they ate in silence, the kind only possible among people deeply absorbed in shared thought.

"So," Alex finally said, dabbing the corner of his mouth with a napkin. "Let's state the obvious—we've never seen anything like this."

"A wealthy Roman-style villa," Claire said, "but with Byzantine-era dating, constructed in a declining Roman city... already under Arab influence and control."

"It's a dichotomy," said Samira.

"Is that the right word?" Claire asked.

Samira tilted her head. "In this case, yes. Two things that shouldn't coexist but somehow do. A contradiction... or a convergence."

They chewed that over between bites. The conversation turned speculative—hypotheses rising and falling, logic clashing with historical precedent.

"Maybe he was a transitional figure," Alex mused. "A Roman-educated Arab? Or a Christian landowner who converted to Islam but kept the aesthetic values of a past empire?"

"Maybe he wasn't Arab at all," Samira countered. "Just a local noble who adapted to survive. Kept his name Arabic to appease the new powers, but built in Roman style to maintain tradition."

"But then why the date?" Claire pressed. "Why stamp the year 652 so specifically? If he wanted to stay under the radar, he'd do what others did—say nothing."

"Unless," Alex said quietly, "he didn't want to be forgotten."

Lunch had come and gone, the café slowly emptying around them. They cleared their trays and made their way back through the echoing corridors to the secured research room. The lock clicked open again, and the world of the mosaic welcomed them back like a whisper from the past.

Alex stepped to the center of the room and turned to face the others. He was already thinking tactically.

"Alright. Let's divide and conquer."

Claire raised an eyebrow. "Did you just make a Caesarean pun?"

He gave a slight smirk. "Guilty."

"Predictable," Samira muttered, settling into her chair with a flick of her scarf.

"Samira," Alex said, "you speak Kufic, French, Arabic—you're our best shot at decoding the man. If you can find out everything

you can about Malik ibn Harun al-Sahiri. That name, that lineage, that location. Let's start with identity."
Samira gave a short nod and pulled her laptop closer. "I'll dig."
"Claire," he continued, "you're on historical context. Political control, power structures, religious influence—who ruled, who resisted, who disappeared in 652 CE. Anything that might explain how this villa came to be."
"On it," she said, already flipping open her notebook.
"And me," he said, glancing back at the mosaic projection. "I'm going to try and unravel the design itself. The geometry, the placement, the iconography. There's more to this than meets the eye. Maybe something coded. A message. A map. A warning."
With that, the room fell into quiet productivity. Only the soft tapping of keyboards and the occasional rustle of notes filled the air. The mystery of the villa, and the man who once walked its halls, lay ahead of them like a vast, ancient equation—just waiting to be solved.

It was just after 3 p.m. when they decided to reconvene. The sun had shifted position, casting warmer light through the narrow windows, gilding the edges of the table. Their trio had worked in near silence since lunch, each buried in their own research.
Claire set her laptop down with a gentle clack and reached for her notebook. She flipped back a few pages, her fingers marked with highlighter streaks and ink smudges. Then she looked up, clearing her throat dramatically.
"Alright, history class is in session," she said, half-grinning. "Let's try to make sense of what the world looked like in 652 CE."
Alex and Samira both leaned back in their chairs, ready to listen.
"So, the big picture: 652 is smack in the middle of the early Islamic expansion. The Arab armies had already swept across most of the Levant and Egypt by this point. Alexandria had fallen nearly a decade earlier, in 641. The Sassanid Empire was toast. The Umayyads hadn't quite taken over yet—that happens in 661—but

the Rashidun Caliphate was in full swing, and they were
methodically consolidating power."
She paused and flipped a page.
"Now, the Byzantines…" She exhaled and raised her brows. "They
were trying to hold on, but they were in serious decline. The
Eastern Roman Empire still technically existed—Constantinople
was still the capital—but their grip on North Africa was slipping
fast. They'd already lost Carthage, and Leptis Magna? Well…"
She looked up and softened her tone. "It wasn't even a shadow of
its former self."
Alex nodded thoughtfully. Samira kept her gaze fixed, attentive.
"Leptis had been in decline since the third century. Earthquakes,
raids, tsunami's—name a disaster. By the time the Arabs rolled in,
the city had dwindled to a small coastal community. Maybe a
thousand people still lived there, tops. Mostly subsistence farmers,
local traders, a few die-hard landowners clinging to their villas."
She tapped her pen against the edge of her notebook.
"It wasn't politically significant anymore. The port had silted up.
Commerce had mostly shifted west to Tripoli and east to
Alexandria. But there was still some trade happening—olive oil,
grain, maybe even glass. The Arabs didn't burn it to the ground.
They didn't have to. It was already fading."
Claire glanced between them to check if she was losing anyone.
She wasn't.
"And here's the interesting part," she added, leaning in.
"Culturally, the Arab influence was already beginning to seep in—
not violently, not yet. But through language, religion, trade
networks. You had Greek-speaking Christian communities
gradually being exposed to Arabic, to Islam. My guess, is that this
owner, Malik, he was an Arab from the way he wrote that date –
31 AH. I feel he was a merchant, but a very important merchant. It
put him culturally right at the crossroads of civilisation"

Samira leaned back in her chair, eyes alight with discovery, the telltale flush of someone who had struck gold in the dusty strata of historical data.

"That's interesting, Claire," she said, pointing a pen toward her. "You placed him at a crossroads—and that is exactly where history seems to have placed him too."

Alex and Claire looked up from their notes.

"I'll be honest," Samira continued, sitting straighter, a quiet excitement in her voice, "I didn't think we'd find anything on him. A name like Malik ibn Harun al-Sahiri, in a forgotten town like Leptis Magna? It felt like a dead end. But I was wrong."

She held up her tablet. "There are hundreds of references. Scattered, fragmented, obscure—but real."

Alex's brows rose. Claire blinked. "Hundreds?"

Samira nodded. "And every single one paints the picture of a man standing at the intersection of dying empires, rising powers, and clashing cultures. Even his name is symbolic. 'Malik'—Arabic for king. 'Ibn Harun'—son of Harun, or Aaron. That's a name with Judeo-Christian resonance. And 'al-Sahiri'? It roughly means of the desert, or desert-born. He wasn't just a merchant. He was the crossroads."

She paused to scroll, then flipped the tablet around. An image appeared—an illuminated manuscript, worn but legible, in Greek. "This," she said, tapping it, "is from a Christian monastery archive outside of Leptis. Dated around 644 CE. It references a man who 'walked out of the desert with gold beneath his cloak and truth upon his tongue.' A literal quote. The monks describe him as a solitary figure who arrived in Leptis Magna with nothing, and within a few years, he had a household, a trade office, and connections in every direction—Byzantine, Berber, Arab."

Claire whistled. Alex leaned forward. "So, he was a merchant."

"Not just a merchant," Samira said, almost reverently. "A money-lender. And not the kind people feared. The records consistently describe him as fair, honest, trustworthy. A sort of financial anchor in a time of massive uncertainty. The Arab accounts call him al-sarraf al-amin—the 'trustworthy exchanger.' Roman sources use a Latinised name, Mallicus de Haruno, and refer to transactions with visiting legates and consuls. There are Berber folktales—oral traditions—of a desert banker who carried scales in his cloak and never cheated a man, even in the dust storms."

Alex looked up. "That doesn't sound like a typical money-lender."

"It's not," Samira agreed. "That's what makes it so fascinating. What I'm piecing together is that he didn't just lend or trade—he created an early system. I think he may have invented one of the earliest versions of hawala."

Claire sat up straighter. "The Islamic informal transfer system?"

"Exactly." Samira's voice was rising now, animated, alive with momentum. "It wasn't codified yet, but the principle was there. He operated like a human ledger. People would come to him with coinage from one empire—solidus, dinars, drachmas, even Byzantine folles—and he would issue them a chit, a handwritten promissory note, in any currency they chose, that they could redeem elsewhere, from a contact he had in another city. Alexandria, Tripoli, even as far as Cyrene or Thebes. The note would be honoured without question."

"Like a credit system?" Alex asked.

"More like a trust system," said Samira. "It relied entirely on reputation. No central bank. No collateral. Just Malik's name—and his guarantee. If a note was dishonored, it wasn't the debtor who paid the price. It was his reputation that suffered. And there's no record of that happening, anywhere."

Claire gave a low whistle. "That's... revolutionary."

"It was," Samira agreed. "Especially in a time when currency varied wildly, and trust was in short supply. I found one fragment from a Coptic merchant in Thebes who claimed he never carried gold after trading with Malik. Just a small scroll with a stamp on it. Malik's seal."

Alex rubbed his chin, his mind clearly spinning. "So, this guy was basically running a proto-banking system across dying Roman cities, rising Islamic trade routes, and whatever else was left."

"Yes," said Samira. "And if that mosaic in the villa is his, then we're standing on top of the first bank that spanned three civilizations."

A long silence followed. Reverent. Electric.

Claire summed it up nicely, "He was linking cultures through currency."

Alex leaned forward in his Italian leather chair, his voice low with curiosity. "I never knew a moneylender could be so influential. He must have been highly educated, or extremely intelligent. Or both." He tapped a few keys and brought up a high-resolution image of the mosaic. "But I think you'll both appreciate this—it's subtle. Almost too subtle."

Claire and Samira leaned in.

"You see the lions around the outer border—four corners, four lions per corner."

"Yes," Claire said, squinting at the image. "It's a decorative frame, I assumed."

"That's what I thought too," said Alex. "But look closer."

He zoomed in on the upper-left corner until the first lion filled the screen.

"This lion here," he said, "is sleeping—curled up, young, peaceful. And the background, palm trees and the sea. Now watch."

He clicked through the others. "The next lion is walking—not hunting, just in motion, alert, with a desert background - notice the dunes. Then the third is sitting, back straight, head turned slightly, almost as if watching. And once again a different background, a fortress or tower. The final lion... look at this—he's lying down, regal, head up, forelegs crossed in the mountains. There's also age in the detail—the mane fuller, the colour darker."

Claire raised her eyebrows. "Each lion is older than the last. And the scenery has changed and it's a different location. It's a progression."

"Exactly. A visual chronology in both time and location. And now, look here." Alex zoomed in further, beneath the paw of the sleeping lion.

Samira leaned forward. "That's… a numeral?"

"A Roman numeral," Alex confirmed. "I. The first. Then, bottom left, walking lion, but the numeral is II. Bottom right, sitting lion, III. Top right, resting lion, IV."

"So it starts in the upper-left corner and moves clockwise," Claire noted.

"A sequence," said Samira. "A story told in four parts?"

"I think so. A symbolic progression—youth to age, but also four stages - sleep then to action, then to vigilance and finally to waiting. The path of the four lions. It must represent something, something in the real world perhaps – a person, an event!"

"That's definitely worth further investigation," Samira said, clearly intrigued.

Alex nodded, but his eyes didn't leave the screen. "But that's not the most interesting thing I found."

Claire blinked. "There's more?"

"Oh yes," Alex said, his voice almost gleeful. "Take a look at the scenes inside the border."

He pulled the camera back to show the full central mosaic again. "We've got, clockwise from the top left: a farmer ploughing a field. Front left: reaping the harvest. Center: two men fishing on the shoreline. Right front: market day—bartering, livestock, baskets of produce."

Samira nodded, scanning each vignette.

"And here," Alex continued, zooming in on the final panel at the top right. "This."

It was a scene dominated by a tall figure in dark robes, standing before two merchants, hands extended, exchanging coins.

Claire tilted her head. "Is that—?"

"I think it's him," Alex said. "Malik ibn Harun al-Sahiri. The man from the desert, the moneylender. Look at the way he's positioned—central, upright, respected. He's not just part of the marketplace—he is the marketplace."

"It's almost a self-portrait," Claire murmured.

"How extraordinary," Samira added.

Alex zoomed in again, focusing on the figure's chest. "Now. This." The detail sharpened. Around Malik's neck was a medallion—round, ornate, glinting.

"A merchant's badge?" Samira guessed. "Maybe a guild symbol? Or a family seal?"

"Could be," Alex said. "But now watch closely."

He zoomed in again, until the medallion filled the screen.

"It's not just part of the mosaic."

Samira's breath caught. "Wait. That's not tesserae."

"No," Alex said. "It's bronze. A mosaic of Malik… wearing an actual bronze medallion. Inset. Embedded directly into the floor."

Claire leaned forward. "Why go to such lengths unless it meant something?"

"Exactly. Why set a real object into a mosaic—and hide it so subtly—unless it was meant to draw attention only to someone who knew to look for it? I think there's something underneath that medallion. A cavity. A capsule. Something was hidden."

"Oh my God," Samira whispered. "What could it possibly be?"

"I have no idea," Alex said, already pulling up flight options on his tablet. "But you've got to get me back to Leptis Magna."

Claire shook her head, breath caught between awe and disbelief. "Fucking-A."

Chapter 6

The emergency meeting with the UN Security Council took place that evening in the same boardroom on the fifth floor.

The usual suspects were present: the Security Council representatives, their legal team, the INHA Director-General André Molineux, INHA's legal counsel, Claire, Alex, Samira, and a handful of hangers-on, secretaries, and official note-takers.

As before, the meeting was conducted in French. Claire and Alex followed only fragments of the rapid-fire dialogue, but the tone alone told them everything: this time, the mood was sharper, more urgent, the arguments louder and more animated.

Samira had her own reasons for wanting to return to Leptis Magna—most pressingly, to inquire about Tariq's whereabouts—and she pushed the point hard. "One day. That's all we need," she insisted in clipped, formal French.

But the UN's position was absolute.

"No," came the response, again and again.

The site was closed.

Too dangerous.

Too unstable.

They had already lost one academic. They weren't prepared to lose any more.

The insurance representative doubled down, calling the region "a pending war zone, if not already one," and flatly refused to underwrite a return mission.

The meeting ended in a frustrated stalemate. There would be no exceptions, no special permissions. The UNESCO site was officially off-limits. That was final.

As the delegation filed out of the boardroom in small, exhausted clusters, Molineux lingered by the door. As Samira passed, he caught her elbow lightly and said in a low voice, "Come to my office. Fifteen minutes."

Ten minutes later, Samira, Alex, and Claire were climbing the internal staircase to the sixth floor—the executive level. They walked down a corridor of polished timber and glass, its hush broken only by the faint tapping of distant keyboards and the echo of their footsteps.

At the end of the corridor, they reached the Director-General's corner office. His secretary stood to greet them, then disappeared into the outer office.

Inside, Molineux looked up from a folder and waved them in. "Come. Sit," he said.

As they sank into the overstuffed button-leather armchairs, Molineux got straight to the point.

"The UN says no. Our insurance providers say definitely no. So, tell me directly—what's so urgent that you need to return to Leptis? And what, exactly, did you find?"

The three of them took turns explaining, each reciting their part of the story as Molineux listened intently, occasionally interrupting with precise, probing questions when clarification was needed. The conversation grew animated—fragments of archaeology, ancient history, coded symbols, a hidden mosaic, a bronze medallion—all layered together into something bigger than any of them had anticipated.

Finally, Molineux raised his hand.

"Enough. Just stop. All of you."

They fell silent.

"If it were anybody else, Samira, we wouldn't be having this conversation. But since it's you—here we are. And Professor

Carey," he added, turning to Alex, "you're quite famous. Or perhaps infamous, depending on who you ask. Known, shall we say, for swimming against the tide."

Alex allowed himself a crooked smile.

Molineux continued, "If what you're saying is true, this could be a historical breakthrough. Something that might—quite literally—rewrite history. And if that's the case, then the Institut National d'Histoire de l'Art wants to be part of it."

He glanced down at his calendar, then back up.

"I have an unscheduled trip to our Tunis office tomorrow. A surprise inspection, if you will. The plane leaves Charles de Gaulle at 0700. I suggest you get there early."

There was a brief explosion of fist-pumping, back-slapping, and grateful laughter.

"Transport will be arranged from Tunis to Leptis," Molineux added. "But you'll have a security detail with you at all times. The return flight departs Tunis for Paris at precisely 1500. Do not be late."

Samira rounded the desk and threw her arms around him, hugging him tightly in genuine gratitude.

Alex stepped forward and shook Molineux's hand—recognizing, once again, the subtle tell of a Masonic grip.

Claire was practically bouncing with excitement.

As the three of them stepped into the elevator to head back down to the second floor and collect their things, Samira turned to Alex just as the doors slid shut.

"Swimming against the tide," she said. "Interesting choice of words."

Alex shrugged.

"It just means I find interesting ways to screw up."

Claire burst into raucous laughter.

The air at Charles de Gaulle Airport bit with a metallic chill that clung to skin and stung the nostrils. It was 6:30 a.m., and the grey-blue morning sky was barely peeling back the curtain of night. Sodium vapor lights cast pale halos over the deserted road leading to the private aviation terminal, tucked well away from the bustle of the main terminals. Here, on the south-eastern edge of the airport, the world felt quieter—sterile, but strangely intimate. Claire rubbed her gloved hands together as she stepped out of the INHA-supplied minivan, her breath fogging in the cold. Samira followed, scarf tight around her neck, her posture characteristically upright despite the fatigue in her eyes. Alex stepped out last, stretching his legs as he tugged his coat collar higher. His fedora, battered from field use, looked oddly at home against the elegance of the private jet apron.

They'd arrived at the Le Bourget-style VIP terminal, a dedicated facility for diplomatic, military, and private executive travel—far from the crowded halls of Terminals 1 and 2. The building itself was sleek and understated, with smoked glass windows and a minimalist steel canopy. A lone security guard in a high-visibility jacket greeted them, eyeing their temporary INHA identifications before waving them through with a nod.

The sleek silhouette of a Dassault Falcon 20 sat waiting for them on the tarmac, its polished fuselage glinting softly in the morning light. The aircraft's main door was already lowered, and a flight attendant stood poised at the top of the stairs, welcoming them with a professional, muted smile.

Inside, the cabin was warmly lit and hushed, all cream leather and mahogany accents. A small club lounge area toward the rear offered four armchairs arranged around a low table, upholstered in dove-grey. Director General André Molineux was already seated, one leg casually crossed over the other, his tailored grey pinstripe suit crisp despite the hour. His white shirt glowed faintly under the cabin lights, and his lemon-yellow tie added the only touch of color. He looked every bit the bureaucratic tactician.

He didn't stand when they entered—just motioned toward the chairs across from him.

"Come. Sit," he said briskly, voice smooth but cool. "Coffee?"
A steward in a dark vest approached, already pouring steaming espresso into small white cups.
"We've got thirty minutes before wheels up," Molineux continued, sliding three sealed envelopes across the table. "Inside are letters of designation from the INHA. They say you're part of an insurance investigation team, assessing site damage and equipment loss. You're not archaeologists. You're assessors. So—no digging."
Samira arched an eyebrow. "We're not to so much as brush off a stone?"
"No excavating," he replied, dry. "You so much as kneel in the sand with a shovel and the Libyan authorities will be all over it. And to be clear, the Department of Antiquities has already been informed—via the UN—that Leptis Magna is closed to all parties until security improves."
Claire accepted her envelope and frowned. "Then why are they letting us back at all?"
"Because I sold it as a damage assessment," Molineux said plainly. "And because we're bringing in our own security. UN-sanctioned. That was the condition."
He leaned forward slightly, clasping his hands.
"There will be a helicopter waiting when we land in Tunis. You'll be transferred to the site under escort. No exceptions. No wandering off."
Samira's jaw tightened. Her fingers, clasped around her coffee cup, were pale and bloodless. She said nothing, but the storm behind her eyes was impossible to miss.
Molineux continued, tone hardening.
"And one more thing. We're launching our own inquiry into the attack. The fact that the local police were pulled from the site hours before the ambush? Suspicious. Either someone in the government is compromised, or the police are—"
"Or both," Alex interrupted, voice low and steady.
A pause.

Molineux nodded once. "Right. Or both. For now, we don't know who had the warning. But someone did."

Silence settled for a moment. Samira's knuckles were clenched, white against the ceramic of her cup. Claire glanced at her, then back to Molineux.

"What about anything we might recover? Data, inscriptions?" she asked quietly.

"If it fits in the chopper, bring it. If it weighs more than two men can lift, leave it. No sarcophagi. No columns. No carved lions."

That last line was pointed, and Alex offered a faint, crooked smile. They all nodded.

From the cockpit, the intercom crackled.

"Ladies and gentlemen, we've received final flight clearance from ATC. Estimated time to Tunis: 2 hours, 15 minutes. Please prepare for take-off."

The stewardess—tall, composed, and wearing a tailored navy uniform—moved efficiently through the cabin, securing doors and checking seatbelts. She gestured politely.

"Seats, please. We'll be taxiing shortly."

Alex stood, tucking his envelope into his satchel. He slid into a window seat across the aisle from Molineux, adjusting the brim of his fedora as he leaned back. Claire and Samira took the facing seats beside him, continuing a quiet, excited discussion about the mosaic tiles and the information they'd analysed the day before. Alex, exhausted, tuned them out - he had obtained little sleep in the past forty-eight hours. His head tilted back, hat shading his eyes. The hum of the cabin lulled him toward a shallow, almost meditative stillness.

Outside, the Falcon taxied smoothly along the tarmac, trailing behind two lumbering Air France jets queued for take-off. From this side of CDG—Runway 08L/26R, often used as a secondary route during lighter traffic—there was a clear view across the sleeping airport: acres of concrete, streaked with lights, framed by the slow bloom of a Parisian sunrise.

Finally, the Falcon rolled into position. The twin General Electric CF700 engines spooled up with a smooth whine. The brakes released.

Alex felt the acceleration press him gently into the seat.

The jet surged forward, lifting them up and out of France, and into the deepening blue above.

The landing at Tunis-Carthage was smooth—almost imperceptible. The gentle jolt as the wheels kissed the tarmac roused Alex from a shallow sleep. His head lifted groggily from the side panel of the Falcon 20, fedora slipping slightly from his brow as the aircraft taxied quietly along taxiway 1A.

They rolled to a stop well away from the main terminal, beyond the buzz of passenger traffic and the glinting glass of arrival halls. The parking apron here was quieter, scattered with security vehicles, service carts, and a handful of military personnel. A haze of heat shimmered above the black tarmac. Twenty metres away, the Leonardo AW09 helicopter stood poised and ready, its blades still and its slender frame casting a sharp silhouette against the midday sun.

As the cabin door hissed open, a wall of heat struck like a heavyweight's punch—dry, aggressive, and unrelenting. Alex winced. The transition from the aircraft's climate-controlled cocoon to North African summer was brutal. Within seconds, his shirt clung to his back, beads of sweat forming at his temple. Samira was already fanning herself with her INHA field folder, while Claire squinted against the harsh glare off glass terminal buildings.

Waiting beside the helicopter stood ex-Capitaine Louis Delon, lean and wiry in desert fatigues, his beret tucked under one shoulder strap. He gave each of them a firm handshake and a tight-lipped nod before motioning toward the open side door of the Leonardo. "Let's move quickly. We're on the clock," he said in clipped French-accented English.

The group ducked beneath the low rotor blades and climbed into the helicopter. The interior smelled faintly of aviation fuel and vinyl, the seats worn but functional. The moment Louis pulled the doors shut with a solid thunk, the pilot up front engaged the starter. A high-pitched whine began to build, echoing through the fuselage as the rotor blades groaned into motion.

The sound rose into a rhythmic thrum, dampened somewhat by the insulated cabin but still persistent, like a heartbeat. Louis reached behind his seat and passed around aviation headsets. They adjusted their mics and plugged in.

"Check, check," Louis's voice came through the comms—tinny, metallic, underscored by a soft background hiss. "Everyone hearing me?"

Alex gave a thumbs-up. Claire and Samira did the same.

"We'll be over Leptis in about an hour," Louis continued. "Here's the situation. My orders are explicit: you are to remain together. No wandering, no splitting off. Stay as a group. We reconnoitred the site yesterday—completely deserted. But that doesn't mean it will be today. If we encounter any locals—militia, armed looters, even Libyan police—we abort immediately. The last thing we need is to get into a firefight with local militia, the police or ISIS, so we avoid them at all costs. No arguments, no cowboy nonsense. We do not engage. Understood?"

Claire gave a quick nod. Samira sat with arms folded tightly, jaw clenched. Alex simply said, "Understood."

Louis went on. "The situation in Libya is highly volatile, its changes from week to week. The Libyans are watching the site for sure, and anything even remotely suspect will get back to them. Also, we've been monitoring open radio channels, military and police. So far, there's been zero chatter about your missing professor. That could mean he's not in custody. Or it could mean someone is keeping things very quiet. We have no further intel at this time."

He scanned their faces.

"You have two hours, no more. Any questions?"

There were none. Only the muted whoosh of rotors and the building tension of unspoken possibilities.

Satisfied, Louis gave a curt nod and removed his headset. One by one, the others followed, hanging their units on the hooks above their seats. The cabin settled into silence, broken only by the deepening drone of the Leonardo as it powered east.

The helicopter carved a fast, efficient line through the air, the Mediterranean glittering below like liquid sapphire. After an hour, the edges of Tripoli came into view to the west —sun-bleached buildings, minarets, and cranes frozen above half-finished construction. Then the city fell away behind them, replaced by a dun-hued coastline and the endless, flat desolation of the North African littoral.

Five minutes out from Leptis, the pilot crackled to life on the intercom:

"Visual on Leptis. ETA five minutes."

Louis immediately leaned forward, flipping a switch on the internal console. "All right, team," he said. "Standard procedure. Weapons check."

The two French Sentinel Security personnel flanking the rear compartment snapped into motion, checking their FAMAS rifles, verifying magazine loads and safeties. Louis double-checked his sidearm and radio.

"Call signs confirmed. Evac route is the same as insertion. Pilot is Ghost One, I'm Vulture One. If I say exfil, we're wheels up in less than sixty seconds. Don't make me repeat myself."

The Sentinel team nodded. Alex's hand went instinctively to the satchel in his lap, where the INHA credentials were tucked beside his small leather-bound notebook. Claire stared out the window, her fingers tightening around the strap of her backpack. Samira said nothing, eyes scanning the horizon, as if expecting the ruins to materialize beneath them like a mirage.

Alex leaned slightly across the aisle. "Let's hope it's still empty," he said quietly.

Samira didn't look at him. "Let's hope we're not too late."

Below them, the pale limestone bones of Leptis Magna came into view—silent, sun-scorched, and sprawled across the coast like the skeleton of a forgotten empire.

They descended in a slow, wide arc. The UNESCO World Heritage site looked deserted.

The Leonardo AW09 came in hot, its rotors slicing the air with a piercing whine as it descended fast and low over the camp. At the last moment, the pilot feathered the collective, angling the blades to slow their descent, and the helicopter settled into a controlled hover before kissing down onto the sand in a whirlwind of dust and debris.

Before the rotors had fully wound down, Louis leapt out, his boots crunching into the gravel as he swept the horizon. He was quickly followed by the rest of the Sentinel team—three operators clad in desert fatigues and dark tactical gear. They moved with methodical precision, fanning out into a wide semi-circle and dropping to one knee, weapons up, eyes scanning. Fifty meters from the chopper, they held their perimeter like statues of war.

Alex, Claire, and Samira disembarked together, ducking instinctively under the rotor wash. Shielding their eyes from the sand, they moved quickly toward the encampment. Delon stood waiting, a commanding figure near the central pavilion tent, his gaze never leaving the horizon.

They regrouped beneath the shade of the dining tent—still standing, still stocked, though now ghostlike in its abandonment. The canvas flapped lazily in the breeze, sun-bleached and stained, its once-crisp lines sagging. Folding tables were set as if awaiting a dinner that would never come. Mismatched chairs, some overturned, encircled the space. Plates and coffee mugs were still stacked in bins beside a dry-water cooler. The camp was exactly as they had left it… yet something had shifted. The air was thick with unease. Memories pressed in from the canvas walls. The silence felt like an accusation.

Claire looked around slowly, her voice soft. "It feels wrong to be back here."

Samira nodded, her eyes narrowed. "Like we've come back to finish something we should have left buried."

Alex, arms crossed, exhaled deeply. "We don't have the luxury of time. This site is no longer secure. We're not here to dig—we're here to retrieve."

He laid out the plan in clipped, deliberate tones.

"We go to the villa first. We recover whatever is beneath that medallion—if anything. Then, we sweep the headquarters tent. If Tariq left journals, field notes, voice memos, anything, we take it. Finally, you can check your personal tents for anything you may have forgotten. Agreed?"

"Agreed," came the reply, unified and grim.

Alex led the way, walking side-by-side with Delon. The Frenchman's FAMAS was slung low, his fingers resting lightly near the trigger guard. His steps were silent, almost feline.

The villa lay just beyond the excavation zone, the partial Roman structure excavated and stabilized under the large protective canopy once again. Its mosaic floor gleamed beneath the filtered light—still pristine. Even after two days of neglect, a fine layer of sand had begun to settle between the tesserae, carried by the desert wind. Nature, Alex thought, was relentless. Unstoppable.

He found what he was looking for within seconds: Malik the Money-Lender. The central figure of the villa's mosaic. They dropped to their knees, brushing away sand like worshipers at an altar.

"There," Alex said, pointing.

The medallion was subtle, its presence almost invisible to the untrained eye. Crafted in bronze, it had darkened to match the hues of the surrounding stonework. Unless one was nearly prone on the ground, it vanished completely into the cloak of the mosaic figure. But now, uncovered, it gleamed faintly with age and intent.

Alex leaned closer. An intricate depiction was etched into the bronze—a falcon in flight beside the helmeted profile of Athena. The goddess of wisdom and war. The symbol was precise, elegant, purposeful.

Claire whispered, "Athena... and a falcon. That has to mean something."

"It's a seal," Alex muttered, tracing the edges with a gloved finger. "Symbolic. Protective. An Official perhaps."

The medallion had been set with surgical precision. The dark tesserae—obsidian, perhaps—representing Malik's robe, abutted it so closely there was barely a whisper of grout between them. The bronze was flush with the surrounding floor, as if born from the mosaic itself.

"I cannot believe the precision," Claire said, awed. "This isn't decorative—it's art."

"This entire floor is a masterpiece," Samira added. "The craftsmanship... I haven't seen anything like it outside of Byzantine basilicas."

Alex squinted at the circumference. "There's a fine line of grout. If we work that away, we might be able to lift it."

Claire pulled a small tool roll from her backpack. "Try this." She handed him a precision tool—larger than a dental pick, but just as sharp—used to flake sediment from bone. She also produced a brush for detailing.

They worked in silence for nearly thirty minutes, alternating between scraping, brushing, and probing the edges. The grout was stubborn, almost resinous in its hardness. But slowly, the medallion began to shift.

Then Delon's voice cut through the moment.

"Quiet."

All three froze. The only sound was the rasp of their breath.

In the distance, a faint clink of metal. Bells. And growing louder.

A boy crested the dune not ten meters away, a small herd of goats ambling behind him. His feet were bare. He blinked in surprise at the scene below—armed men, strange foreigners kneeling on an ancient floor.

Delon raised his rifle.

‏قف.

"Qif," he said flatly. Halt.

The boy froze mid-stride, wide-eyed and slack-jawed.

Delon continued, shifting to a rougher dialect.

‏خذ عنزك واغرب عن وجهي الآن.

"Take your goats and fuck off, now."

The boy backed away, uncertain. Then, with a slow turn, he began herding his goats back the way he came.

"He's a child," Samira said softly.

Delon didn't look at her. "Non. He was sent to count heads. See if we were armed. That was no shepherd."

Alex exchanged a glance with him. It made sense. There were eyes on them now.

He returned to the medallion with renewed urgency. "We don't have time."

Claire handed him a small trowel. He worked quickly, trying to pry the medallion loose without cracking it or destroying the surrounding stones.

Ten minutes later Delon's radio crackled to life.

"Vulture Two to Vulture One—be advised. We have vehicles approaching from the southwest."

"Confirmed," Delon replied calmly. Then added, "And from the east."

He turned to Alex. "Whatever it is you're looking for, Professor, you find it now."

Alex kept working, sweat streaming down his temple.

"Two hundred fifty meters," came the next radio call.

Claire cleared the last bits of grout. Samira wiped the edges clean. "Two hundred."

Alex wedged the trowel deeper.

"One fifty."

Delon stepped closer. "Professor…"

"One hundred."

"Now please." Delon instructed.

With a final heave, the medallion popped loose, flipped in the air, and landed with a soft clink in Samira's lap.

Behind it was a hollow. Roughly four inches wide, and deep, black as oil.

Alex reached in without hesitation and pulled out a tightly wrapped object. It was bound in oilcloth, sealed with wax and twine. Beneath the layers, he could feel the rigid shape of a codex—glass panels, heavy, ancient. Possibly vellum within. He didn't look. He shoved it deep into his satchel.

"Disembarking," came the voice from the helicopter.

"Exfil! Exfil! Exfil!" Delon ordered.

The Sentinel team compressed the perimeter with lethal fluidity, rifles never wavering. Samira shoved the medallion into her cargo pocket, Claire stuffed the tools away. Alex was already on his feet. Delon swept his hand forward. "To the helicopter. Now."

They moved fast—fifty meters of open terrain between them and the bird.

"Tangos advancing. Seventy-five meters."

Delon clicked his mic. "Armed?"

"Not unless concealed."

"Do not fire unless fired upon. Repeat, do not fire unless fired upon."

Twenty meters from the helicopter, the rotors screamed to life, sand erupting beneath them.

"Fifty meters and closing."

They boarded quickly, strapping in. Delon and the rest of Sentinel leapt in behind them, doors open, rifles out.

"We're clear," Delon shouted over the roar.

"Thirty meters."

"Pilot, go!" Delon ordered.

The turbine screamed. The pilot lifted the collective, and the Leonardo surged skyward, kicking up a blinding sandstorm. Figures on the ground staggered back, shielding their eyes.

"I see an AK," said Vulture Two.

But it was too late. By the time the dust settled, the AW09 was five hundred meters in the air and climbing, veering northward, the artifact safely aboard.

Below them, in the sun-baked silence, the enemy regrouped—too slow, too late. But only just.

Chapter 7

The flight back to Tunis passed in heavy silence. No one spoke. No one needed to. Alex sat rigid in his seat, his field satchel clutched tightly against his chest like a life vest in stormy seas. His arms were locked around it, as if any loosening might risk losing what was inside. Not just the object, but the meaning. The consequence. Samira stared out the window, jaw set, her mind simmering. Why had they not thought about capturing one of the militants at Leptis. She kept replaying the moment over and over, wondering why they hadn't taken just one of them alive. Interrogated him. Forced the truth out, if necessary. Even tortured. The thought made her stomach twist. Was that who she was becoming? Or always had been? The question burned hot and shameful in her chest.
Claire sat across from them, arms wrapped around her knees. She wasn't angry. Just confused. Exhausted. Why did people keep trying to kill them? They were archaeologists, for God's sake. Scholars, not soldiers. Yet this morning they'd come very close to being shot at. Again. She hugged herself tighter.

The Leonardo helicopter touched down gently at Tunis-Carthage Airport, its rotors sighing to a halt in the midday heat. The white-and-silver Dassault Falcon jet was already waiting on the tarmac, pristine and precise, like it had never moved. It was approaching 1 p.m. They still had hours to kill before their flight to Paris.
Bad choice of words, Claire thought grimly.
As the turbine noise wound down, they unbuckled and stepped out into the Tunisian sun. Delon was already on the ground, opening

the door and offering a steadying hand. He shook each of theirs in turn.

Alex gripped his with genuine gratitude.

"Thank you," he said, voice low. "For everything. For keeping us safe."

Delon gave a modest shrug.

"All in a day's work, mon ami."

To some people, risking your life seemed to be a routine part of the job.

They ambled slowly toward the Falcon. The silence remained, but it had changed—less weight, more weariness. As they climbed the short staircase into the aircraft, Alex suddenly realized how hungry he was. He hadn't eaten since half-past five that morning. His stomach gave a polite but persistent growl. He prayed the galley was stocked.

As he stepped into the cabin, he froze.

Sitting exactly where they'd left him, legs crossed and fingers steepled, was André Molineux. Immaculate as ever, not a hair out of place, not a bead of sweat on him.

"Professor," Molineux greeted warmly. "Did you get what you came for?"

Alex gave a tired nod and tapped the satchel.

"I think so."

Molineux didn't press further. He simply nodded once.

"Excellent. Since my business in Tunis is now concluded, we may depart directly."

He rose, buttoned his jacket, and slipped past them with a nod of courtesy. On the tarmac below, he met Delon with a familiar handshake and a few minutes of conversation—brief, but intimate, like men who had been in darker places together than either cared to speak about. Their gestures were animated, but their faces calm. At the end, Molineux gripped Delon's shoulder, offered a warm "merci," and returned to the jet.

There was something in the way he moved, Alex noticed—
untouchable. As if the world refused to stain him. Not heat. Not
blood. Not chaos.
Once back on board, Molineux conferred quickly with the pilot and
the uniformed flight attendant—both French, both poised and
efficient. Then he turned to address the group.
"We'll be departing momentarily. Arrival in Paris should be just
after three. Lunch will be served shortly after we level off. I
believe the chef has prepared filet mignon."
Alex nearly groaned aloud. His mouth watered at the mere
mention.
"With Professor Carey's permission," Molineux added, nodding
politely to Alex, "I recommend we deposit the—ah—relic in the
secure laboratory at our Paris facility. It's climate-controlled, of
course. Temperature and humidity monitored. Best for preservation
until we examine it in full tomorrow."
Alex nodded without hesitation.
"Of course."
"Excellent. Then, let us at least acknowledge today's small
success."
At that, the flight attendant appeared from the rear galley, pushing
a cart with slender flutes of chilled champagne. Her navy-blue
uniform was crisp, her movements flawless. She handed each of
them a glass.
Molineux raised his. "While we may toast a minor victory, let us
not forget what it has cost. Tariq—our search for you will not
end."
"Tariq," the others echoed.
The champagne was cold, dry, and sharp. It cut through the dust in
their throats like light through smoke.
As Molineux resumed his seat, the intercom buzzed. The captain's
voice, clipped and clear, filled the cabin:
"Ladies and gentlemen, we've received immediate clearance for
departure. Please fasten your seatbelts."

The Falcon taxied without delay, reached the threshold of the runway, and barely paused. The pilot throttled up the twin engines and launched them forward in a seamless roll.

The aircraft lifted off gracefully in under fifteen hundred meters—short by commercial standards, but well within the performance envelope of a Dassault Falcon 20 on light load.

They climbed steeply into the blue.

Twenty minutes later, cruising at twenty thousand feet over the Mediterranean, lunch was served.

The filet mignon was exquisite—pan-seared to a perfect medium-rare, rested in a reduction of shallots, black pepper, and red wine. It was paired with pommes purée so smooth they could've passed for silk, and haricots verts with a subtle citrus glaze. A bold Côte du Rhône was poured—earthy, deep, with hints of cherry and a finish that lingered just long enough.

Alex ate like a man reborn. Each bite tasted like civilization.

The others were no different. The silence around the table was not awkward now—it was reverent. The day's adrenaline had ebbed, and hunger had taken its rightful place. Food as medicine. Wine as balm.

Eventually, they sat back, replete and wordless.

One by one, they drifted into sleep.

Alex was the last to go. He slumped in his seat, satchel still gripped in both arms. Even unconscious, he didn't let it go.

Outside, the sky was endless and blue. Below, the land rolled on. Above them all, the jet surged north, toward Paris—and the discovery yet to come.

The descent into Paris was smooth, the afternoon sun casting long golden shadows over the city. From the jet's window, the familiar landmarks emerged from the haze—the winding Seine, the dome of Les Invalides, the spire of Sainte-Chapelle—and far in the distance, the Eiffel Tower rising like a sentinel above the rooftops.

The Dassault Falcon touched down at Le Bourget Airport, its tires whispering against the tarmac. Waiting at the edge of the private terminal was a sleek, obsidian Mercedes-Benz 500 SL, engine idling in quiet anticipation.

Andre Molineux took the driver's seat himself.

"Come," he said, motioning them in.

The four of them bundled into the plush leather interior—Alex up front, still gripping the relic satchel, with Claire and Samira in the back. The car eased onto the A1, threading into the outer arrondissements before slipping onto the Boulevard Périphérique. The familiar rhythm of Paris began to return—the chime of bicycle bells, the pastel facades, the scent of early spring rain on stone. They crossed into central Paris via Porte de la Chapelle, heading south along Boulevard de Magenta, past open-air cafés, bakeries with gold-lettered windows, and commuters weaving through traffic. The car glided smoothly past Place de la République, then turned southwest into the quieter streets of the 2nd arrondissement, where the foot traffic slowed and the architecture turned regal and understated.

At last, the Mercedes came to a halt in front of the Institut National d'Histoire de l'Art, housed inside the grand Galerie Colbert, tucked discreetly off Rue Vivienne. The glass-roofed passageway echoed softly with footsteps as they made their way inside, ascending to the third-floor laboratories.

There, a white-coated technician was already waiting by the secure lab vault. He looked no older than thirty, with sharp features and a hint of curiosity in his posture.

Alex opened the satchel and handed over the relic without a word. The technician received it carefully, locking it into the temperature- and humidity-controlled vault. Then he turned and handed a slim envelope to Andre.

"Here is the passkey, monsieur."

Andre barely glanced at it before offering it to Alex.

"After all, Professor—it was your discovery. See you all back here at 8 a.m."

With that, he excused himself, muttering about the backlog of work awaiting him in his office.

The remaining three descended to the second floor research rooms, quiet and dimly lit. The walls were lined with ancient maps, catalogued texts, and sun-bleached reference volumes. They slumped into the deep leather chairs like travellers home from a war.

"We could research our friend Malik a bit more," Alex offered after a beat.

Samira waved the suggestion away. "I'm researched-out," she said flatly, her head resting against the back of the chair.

Claire chuckled. "Let's call it a win and reconvene tomorrow."

Samira was already texting.

"There," she said a moment later. "Le Comptoir du Relais—corner of Rue de l'Odéon. Seven o'clock. Chic, but not fussy."

They agreed to meet there. Alex and Claire exited together, flagging down a cab just outside Galerie Colbert. The driver nodded at the address and pulled into traffic.

Within ten minutes, they were back at the Park Hyatt Paris-Vendôme, nestled on Rue de la Paix, only steps from Place Vendôme itself—a temple of polished stone, gilded balconies, and discreet five-star opulence. Doormen in tailored coats greeted them with practiced warmth.

Upstairs, Alex stepped into his room—high ceilings, bronze-accented wood, a marble bathroom that gleamed like a Roman spa. He let the hot shower run long, washing away the grit of travel and the weight of discovery. Then, dressed in a tailored blazer and open-collar shirt, he answered a few personal and university emails, flipped through French news channels, and checked the clock.

At 6:45 p.m., he met Claire in the marble-tiled foyer. She wore a simple black blouse and wide-legged trousers, elegant without trying. The concierge summoned a cab, which whisked them off through the golden evening.

The route wound through the 1st arrondissement, past the Palais Garnier's glowing façade, then across the river into the Latin Quarter. Paris was dressed for the evening—the streets alive with café lights and the rustle of terrace dining. The taxi glided past Saint-Sulpice, its towers pale in the dying light, before pulling onto Rue de l'Odéon. Just for fun, Claire said "Hey, I know that place!" Le Comptoir du Relais was nestled under striped awnings, ivy curling up its stone walls, candlelight flickering in the windows. Inside, it was intimate and warm, all dark wood, pressed white linens, and the quiet clink of cutlery. The maître d' recognized Samira's name and led them to a table beside the window, where the streetlamps spilled honey-coloured light onto the cobbles outside.

They ordered without hesitation.

Claire chose the duck confit, crisp-skinned and rich, served with a tangle of braised lentils and roasted root vegetables. Samira's truffle risotto arrived with theatrical flourish, steaming and heady with aroma. Alex went classic with the steak au poivre, cooked rare, the cognac pepper sauce glistening like lacquer over the meat. The sommelier paired it all with a 2015 Châteauneuf-du-Pape, robust and velvety.

Conversation was sparse at first, fatigue muting them. But the wine loosened things. They spoke of strange mentors and botched digs, of museum blunders and graduate school disasters. Laughter came slowly, then easily.

They split a tarte Tatin for dessert, still warm, the caramel just shy of burnt, the pastry flaky as ash.

"To small wins," Claire said, raising her glass.

"To peace and quiet—while it lasts," added Samira.

They clinked glasses, their eyes reflecting candlelight and something more—relief, perhaps, or the brief illusion of normalcy. Outside, Paris shimmered under the streetlamps like a city dreaming.

They convened at the Institut National d'Histoire de l'Art precisely at 08:00. Claire and Alex were the last to arrive, delayed by heavier-than-normal traffic along Rue de la Paix and Boulevard des Capucines, the morning surge washing out from the Opéra district like a slow tide.

Outside the hermetically sealed Level 2 archive lab, André Molinieux stood in quiet conversation with Samira, the two silhouetted by the soft overhead lighting. Alex was surprised to see the Director General himself present.

André noticed the look.

"You're surprised to see me here, Professor," he said, smiling faintly. "Understandable. I'm not a scientist. But I am a history buff. And whatever is in there—whether it's everything or nothing—it's priceless." He gestured subtly to the vast complex around them. "And history, after all, is what we do best."

Satisfied, Alex nodded and keyed in the security code. The door released with a pneumatic hiss, and the group stepped inside.

The room was pristine—temperature-controlled at 24°C with relative humidity held at 55%, ideal conditions for the handling and preservation of ancient documents and organic materials. The air had the sterile, ionized scent of archival spaces: filtered, dustless, anticipatory.

A young technician stood by the wall, waiting politely. Michael, in his early thirties, had a clean, academic sharpness to him—wire-rimmed glasses and a quiet confidence.

Alex removed his coat and scarf, and the others followed suit. They each donned black, powder-free nitrile gloves from the wall-mounted dispenser. Alex turned to Michael.

"Can you bring the artifact from the vault, please? The linen bundle."

Michael nodded and disappeared into the secured storage area. Samira flicked on the backlit glass inspection table, its soft glow casting a surgical light across the workspace. In moments, Michael returned, cradling the relic with practiced reverence. He placed it at the centre of the table, resting it gently.

Alex exhaled. The moment had weight.

He began unwrapping the linen shroud, careful not to tear or crease it, spreading it flat against the glowing surface. It was coarse, but surprisingly well-preserved—aged to a golden hue. The backlight revealed no visible inscriptions or markings, neither ink nor blood, nor any of the carbon ghosting sometimes left by ancient dyes.

Claire stepped forward with the lab's Nikon DSLR, snapping high-resolution shots from multiple angles.

At the centre of the linen lay the artifact: a glass container.

Alex leaned closer, visibly impressed.

The vessel was perfectly formed, a long-necked ampulla with a tapered, pointed base, clearly designed to be stored upright—though this one rested on a small wooden plinth he hadn't initially noticed.

"Blown glass," Alex murmured. "Sixth or seventh century—very possible. Alexandria was still producing high-quality glasswork well into the early Islamic period."

Claire took another series of photos.

Samira gestured to the wooden base. "Look how intact this is—for over thirteen centuries."

Alex nodded. "That chamber we found it in—under Malik's floor—it must have been hermetically sealed. Maybe lined with bitumen or bronze. Certainly watertight. Maybe airtight, too."

Claire continued photographing while Alex gently rotated the container in place. Near the base, a hairline crack split the wooden plinth. He took a pair of tweezers from the tray and carefully extracted a sliver of timber.

Michael stepped forward with a labeled Petri dish.

"Radio carbon dating, wood species, and origin, please," Alex instructed.

Michael nodded and scribbled the date and time on the dish's lid with a Sharpie.

Alex turned his attention to the vessel's neck. "Samira, what do you make of this?"

She leaned in. "Timber plug. Sealed with a wax-and-pine tar compound—fairly standard for the era, actually. Especially for high-value transport. See the rim?"

She pointed to the resinous ring lining the top of the plug.

"There's an emblem here," she continued. "Embossed into the wax."

"Claire?" Alex asked.

"On it." Claire adjusted her lens and took several close-up shots of the seal: an emblem pressed into the wax—possibly a symbol of Ahl al-Khiḍr or a monastic sigil.

Alex selected a dental pick from the tray and began to gently scrape away the wax and tar, careful not to stress the glass. Samira steadied the ampulla with both hands.

After several minutes of methodical work, the full plug was exposed. The glass neck had been reinforced, perhaps with a bronze collar, to accommodate the swelling and shrinkage of wood. It was tightly fitted.

Alex extracted a second wood sample for analysis, placing it into a second Petri dish.

He gripped the plug and gave it a cautious tug—immobile.

He tried a gentle twist—still nothing.

"This might take some force," he said quietly.

Samira nodded, adjusting her grip. "Ready when you are."

Bracing himself, Alex applied upward pressure, using both thumbs to lever around the circumference. With a soft, reluctant creak, the seal began to shift. Together, they worked in rotation, loosening the plug until finally—

—it came free.

Alex lifted it out, inspecting the underside, and set it aside for documentation. Claire stepped in and photographed it from multiple angles.

Alex peered into the container. It was dark inside, but the angled backlighting revealed the faintest silhouettes.

He leaned closer and inhaled cautiously. "No rot. No decay. No souring."

He turned the vessel slightly.

"Looks like... two, maybe three tight scrolls. Rolled tightly. Could be vellum, maybe treated papyrus. Whatever it is, it's held."

He glanced at Samira. Her expression was unreadable. Then back to Claire, who had lowered the camera.

"Let's find out what Malik left behind."

Chapter 8

Alex and Samira gently laid the scroll on the table below the linen sheet and gradually unrolled it. It was stiff with age, but the heat had not got to it under the floor to make it fragile. Gently they worked corner to corner, edge to edge until they had the velum flat on the table. The room was silent except for the low hum of the ventilation system. The overhead fluorescents had been dimmed, leaving the artifact underlit on the inspection table as the focal glow in the room. The backlight bled softly through the vellum scroll, revealing its age, its texture, and the faint, elegant lines of early Arabic script—carefully drawn by a hand that had not trembled, even in age.

Samira leaned closer, her gloved fingers carefully guiding the edge of the unrolled scroll flat against the glass. Her brows furrowed, then softened. Her voice, when it came, was hushed—barely above a whisper.

"It's Arabic. Early. Very early. Maybe Hijazi or transitional Kufic," she murmured. "The penmanship is remarkable. This wasn't written in haste."

Alex and Claire stood motionless across from her, hands resting gently on the table's edge. André had taken a respectful step back, his hands behind his back, observing with the quiet reverence of a man in the presence of something sacred.

بِسْمِ اللَّهِ الَّذِي يَرَى كُلَّ الطُّرُقِ

إلى أخي نصر، إن كنتَ أنتَ من وجد هذا — السلام عليك، يا رفيقَ شبابي.

لقد أبطأت يداي، ولكن قلبي ما زال يقظاً. أنا شيخٌ الآن، وساعتي تقترب حين أعود إلى التراب. ومع ذلك، فقد انتظرت، كما طلبتَ مني. حفظتُ كلماتك، وتبعتُ خطاك بما استطعتُ من دقّة.

كانت الرحلة طويلة ـــ أكثر من عام ونصف في البر والبحر. لكننا بلغنا الموضع. وقد أُغلِق القبر كما وصفتَ، والكهنة الذين رافقوني آثروا البقاء. وما زالوا على عهدهم، لم يبرحوا مكانهم.

أما أنا، فقد عدت، وتركتُ هذه الإشارة، كما اتفقنا. وإن لم تكن من يقرأ هذه الرسالة، فليعلم: ابحث عن المسلّة في جزيرة الملكة، ومن ظلّها، اتبع نظرة الأسد حتى تبيّن لك النجوم الطريق إلى الغرب. حيث ينكسر الأفق كوعاء من ذهب، هناك ستجد ما خُبّئ.

لم أكتب أسماء. إن كان قلبك صادقاً، فستفهم.

لعلّ هذه تبلغك مع أنفاسي الأخيرة.

مالك

الصيرفي المتواضع، وأخوك في طلب العلم

Samira began reading aloud, slowly at first, her voice steady, measured, as though each word were a stone being placed in a path they were just beginning to see:

"'In the name of the One who sees all paths...

To my brother, Abu Nas'r ibn Talib. If it is you who has found this—peace be upon you, companion of my youth.'"

A beat passed. The room seemed to breathe in.

"'My hands have slowed, but my heart remains awake. I am an old man now, and soon I will return to the dust. Still, I have waited, as you asked. I held your words close and followed where they led.'"

Alex glanced at Claire. Her expression was rapt, eyes fixed on the text, her lips parted slightly. The air between them buzzed with the weight of what they were hearing.

"'The journey was long—more than a year and a half by land. But we reached the place. The tomb was sealed, just as you described. The two priests who came with me chose to remain. They have not left their vigil of Dhu al-Qarnayn'"

Claire swallowed, her voice barely audible: "They stayed."

Samira's voice wavered slightly—not from weakness, but from reverence—as she continued.

"'I returned, as agreed, and left this sign. If it is not you who reads this, then know this: seek the obelisk on the Queen's Island. From its shadow, follow the lion's gaze, until the stars guide you westward. Where the horizon breaks like a bowl of gold—you will find what was hidden.'"

Alex exhaled slowly, feeling the ancient dust of centuries settle in his lungs. His voice was low. "The Queen's Island... in Libya?"

Claire nodded, still transfixed by the script. "The lion. Maybe it references the lions in the mosaic?"

Samira read the final lines, her voice almost tender now:

"'I have written no names. If your heart is true, you will understand.

May this reach you with my final breath.

Malik—humble moneylender, and your brother in the pursuit of knowledge.'"

Silence.

No one moved. The words hung in the space like dust motes caught in light—fragile, shimmering, ancient.

André was the first to break the stillness. "My God," he said quietly. "We are not reading history. We are being spoken to from it."

Samira gently rolled the edge of the scroll back into place and rested her hands on the glass. "This... this is the beginning."

Alex nodded slowly. "No," he said. "This is the continuation."

As before, Alex carefully reached in with the forceps and extracted the second scroll. And as before, he and Samira gently and carefully unrolled it, smoothing and gently stroking as they unfurled the edges with painstaking deliberateness. Eventually, it was laid out before them and backlit by the under-table lighting.

"Also in Arabic", noted Samira, "and definitely written by he same hand. You can see the small upticks here and flourishes there. It looks to be a short account of who Malik is, or was.

بسم الله الرحمن الرحيم
إلى من تقع هذه الرسالة في يديه:
اعلم أني كنت رجلاً فقيرًا، خرجت من صحراء الغرب لا أملك إلا اسمي وحذاءً باليًا
وثوبًا أكلته الرياح. وصلت إلى لبدة الكبرى، الأسد النائم عند البحر، مدينة منسية بين
عالمين.
ولِمَ لبدة؟ لم يكن ذلك عبثًا. فهي بين الشرق والغرب، بين الروم وأفريقيا، بين الذكرى
والنسيان. لم يسأل عنها سلطان، ولم يلتفت إليها والي. كانت خفية، وكانت مأمنًا لمن
يحمل الأسرار.
بدأت بالقرطاس والدواة، أكتب للتجار والربابنة، أحصي البضائع، أسجل الديون، أترجم
بين الألسن. ومن الحبر صرت تاجرًا، ومن التجارة أصبحت مقرضًا، ثم أمينًا للثقة
جاءني الناس لا يطلبون الذهب، بل الكلمة. وعدٌ يُرسَل من أنطاكية، ويُقبض في طنجة،
دون أن تتحرك عملة. ما كنتُ إلا الوسيط، وما كنتُ إلا النظام، دعوه الحوالة.
لم أخترعها، بل أحييت ما كان قد نُسي.
لم أتخذ زوجة، ولم أُنجب ولدًا، لكنني بنيت شيئًا أطول عمرًا من الحجر.
ما حملته من أجل نصْر، فقد حفظته بأمانة، ووضعت العلامات كما اتفقنا.
إن وصلتَ إلى هذه الكلمات، فأنت قد سرتَ الطريق، ولك المفتاح الأخير.
هداك الله كما هداني.
— مالك بن سعيد
خادم القلم، وتاجر الثقة، وساكن عند الأسد النائم على شاطئ البحر

Samira began reading and translating for the rest of the room.
"'In the name of the Most Merciful, the Knower of all Things.
To the one upon whose hands this record now rests:
Know that I was once no more than a solitary soul, who emerged
from the dust of the western desert with neither coin nor name. My
sandals were thin, my robe worn threadbare by the winds of
hardship. I came to Leptis Magna, the broken lion sleeping by the
sea.'"
"Theres that lion reference again," interjected Claire. They all
nodded, Samira continued reading.
"'Why Leptis? It was no accident.
The city lies between worlds—between Rome and Ifriqiya,
between memory and oblivion. Forgotten by kings, forsaken by

197

empire, yet watched over by the sea. It was discreet. It was hidden. And in its silence, it welcomed those who bore secrets. There, no caliph would look, no envoy would ask.'"

"Secrets," Alex said, "he must be referring to the other scroll!" Samira once again continued.

"'I began with parchment and ink, my only tools. I became a scribe to the traders and shipmasters who remained. I kept records, translated tongues, measured weights and debts. From ink, I grew into trade. From trade, into lending. Not of gold alone—but of trust.

In time, men came not for my goods, but for my word. I became the bond between cities, between caravans, between those who would never meet. A promise sent from Antioch could be redeemed in Tangier, and not a coin need travel. My name mattered little. But the system, they called hawala.

It was not invention, but revival—of ancient ways made true again by need.'"

"Does this, Malik, say that he invented, or reinvented the hawala system?" queried Molineux.

"That's what it says," offered Samira. "This would be the first evidence we have of currency exchanges and honour systems. Especially, in multiple currencies from different countries." she returned once more to the scroll.

"'I took no wife. I fathered no sons. I built no palace, but what I built stretched farther than stone. What I carried for Nas'r I carried with honour. And the clues I left, I left with care, in the pattern we agreed.

If these words find you, then you have walked the road we set, and to you I pass the final key.

May the One guide your steps as He guided mine.

— Malik ibn Haruna al-Sahiri, Servant of ink, trader in trust, watcher of the lion by the sea'"

"Well, that explains why he came to Leptis!" stated Alex.

"But who is Nas'r?" said Claire. "This is the second or third time
he has been mentioned!"
"So many questions here," said Samira, "maybe the third scroll can
shed some light?"
Once again Alex and Samira went through the motions of
extracting the vellum, unrolling and smoothing, before it too, was
ready for translating. Samira lent over the document.

الوصيّة الأخيرة لمالك الليثي
بسم الله الرحمن الرحيم
أنا مالك بن إدريس، كنتُ كاتبًا، وأنا اليوم شيخٌ كبير، أكتب هذه الكلمات الأخيرة بيدٍ
ثابتة وقلبٍ مطمئن.
قدِمتُ إلى لَبْدَة ولا شيء لي — لا مال، لا أهل، لا نسب. ما كان لي سوى حرفتي
وغبار الصحراء على قدميّ.
وبِفضل الله، وثقة الناس، ارتقيتُ: من كاتبٍ إلى تاجر، ومن تاجرٍ إلى مُقرض. ومن هنا
وُلد نظام الثقة الذي يعبر الحدود واللغات. فليحيَ دون اسمي، فهو مُلكٌ لكل من أوفى
بالعهد.
واليوم أختار أن أرحل كما أتيت — بلا شيء. أهب ثروتي، ما وُجد منها، إلى خُدّامي
الأوفياء وفقراء هذه المدينة. فلتدفئ بيوتهم، ولتملأ موائدهم.
ولأهل لَبْدَة، أُقدّم حمّامًا عامًا، ليجلب الراحة لأجسادهم وأرواحهم. أما داري، التي
ملأتها الكتب والحسابات، فأُهديها للمدينة لتكون بيتًا للعلم، مكتبةً مفتوحة لكل طالب
معرفة.
لا أحمل معي شيئًا. أعمالي تتبعني، وثقتي بالله العليّ العظيم.
مالك الليثي

"It's considerably shorter than the other two, it's his last will and
testament. He...he" she stammered, "he was certainly a pious and
generous man, listen to this." She read it in one take.
"'In the Name of the Most Merciful, the All-Wise,
I, Malik, son of Idris, once a scribe, now an old man, write these
final words with a steady hand and a quiet heart.
When I first came to Leptis, I came with nothing — no coin, no
kin, no claim. Only the skills of my trade and the dust of the desert
still on my feet.

By God's grace and the trust of men, I rose: from scribe to merchant, from merchant to lender. And thus was born a system of trust that now spans borders and tongues. Let it live on without my name, for it belongs to all who keep their word.

I choose now to leave as I arrived — with nothing. My wealth, such as it is, I give to my faithful servants and the poor of this city. Let it warm their hearths and fill their bowls.

To the people of Leptis, I gift a bathhouse, to restore body and spirit. And my home, once filled with ledgers and letters, I give to the city as a house of learning — let it become a library, open to all who seek wisdom.

I take nothing with me. My deeds will follow me, and my trust is in the Almighty.

Malik ibn Haruna al-Sahiri'"

The room was still.

A silence had settled over them since Samira finished reading Malik's will, as if no one dared to break the reverence that clung to the air like incense. Finally, Claire exhaled softly and said what they were all thinking.

"Wow," she murmured. "That's… humbling. He gave it all away."

Alex nodded slowly. "He had no family. Deliberately, I think. So, there was no one else to leave it to."

Across the table, André Molineux gestured toward the now-empty glass ampule resting in its foam cradle. "Is that everything? No hidden compartment? No trick mechanism?"

Alex gave a slow shake of his head. "No tricks. Just three scrolls. All perfectly preserved."

Samira turned to the lab technician nearby. "Once Claire finishes photographing, I want high-resolution digital scans of each scroll. Then seal them between glass plates for archival storage."

The technician nodded. Claire, crouched behind her camera, continued adjusting the lens and snapping images, the soft shutter click the only sound in the room.

Alex turned and gestured toward the vault door. "That just leaves the medallion."

Without a word, Michael stepped away and disappeared into the vault. A few moments later, he returned, carrying the object carefully cradled in felt. He laid it gently on the stainless-steel table under the inspection lights.

Alex picked it up with both hands and turned it over slowly. "It's heavy," he muttered, then pointed to the edge. "Look here—see these marks? It looks like it once had a chain or lanyard. The attachment points have been ground down."

He turned the medallion face-up. A stylized female figure dominated the design—helmeted, regal. A bird soared beside her, wings stretched mid-flight.

"The symbol on the front," Alex continued, "that's Athena, goddess of wisdom. And the bird—it looks like a falcon, or an owl. That's interesting."

He flipped it over and squinted at the back. "There's an inscription. Arabic script, but older." He passed it to Samira, who took it with reverence.

She held it to the light and scanned the engraved lines with a practiced eye. "It says: 'Official Seal, Curate of the Great Library'."

Claire leaned forward. "It looks official, no doubt. But... did Leptis ever have a great library?"

"Not that I know of," said Alex. "But we've only uncovered about a third of the city so far. There's still a lot buried beneath the sand."

"Is there a date on it?" he asked Claire.

She turned the medallion over again, checking the rim and back. "No date. Just the inscription and the front motif."

"Maybe the library refers to this villa," Claire suggested. "After all, Malik gave it to the city as a library in his will."

Samira frowned slightly. "But this medallion was embedded in the mosaic floor. That floor predates his death—it was designed while he was alive. And a title like Curate of the Great Library wouldn't refer to something that hadn't yet existed."

Alex rubbed the back of his neck. "That's a good point. If the villa became a library after he died, then that floor would've had to be added posthumously. And that would mean the mosaic wasn't Malik's design."

"But we know he designed it," Claire countered. "The visual clues in the floor correspond exactly with the references in his first scroll."

"Which suggests," Samira said slowly, "that the medallion refers to another library. Somewhere else."

The Director General leaned forward, his brow furrowed. "So… a Great Library, in another place. Or perhaps another time. And this Malik was somehow tied to it?"

Alex gave a noncommittal shrug. "Ashurbanipal's library in Nineveh, maybe. Or Constantinople. It could be either. He says in the letter the journey took him one and a half years. That's enough time to make it overland from either city."

Claire nodded. "It fits. The time, the distance… both work."

"Well," Samira said, straightening up, "whatever it is, it'll take time to unravel. Michael, scan the motif on the front, and cross-reference it with everything we have in the artifact database. Maybe we'll get a hit."

"And the embossed wax seal on the wooden plug, that might turn up something as well," instructed Alex.

Michael nodded and reached for the scanner.

"I say we store this for now," Samira added. "Until we have more information, it's too early to display it."

"Agreed," said the Director General. "This may be more important than it looks."

Alex placed the medallion back into its felt wrap, handling it like a relic.

Outside, the rain tapped gently against the tall windows of the INHA lab, the grey Parisian sky pressing low, as if the city itself were holding its breath.

Chapter 9

The team broke for lunch an hour later.

Andre Molineux bid them farewell and returned to the corporate world above, disappearing into the elevator en route to his office on the fifth floor. The atmosphere relaxed as the three scholars shared a satisfying meal in the cafeteria—a quiet interlude filled with steaming bowls of lentil soup, fresh bread, and murmured reflections on the morning's discoveries.

Afterward, Alex, Claire, and Samira made their way back up to the second-floor research suites. The soundproofed room greeted them with its cool, hushed stillness. High windows filtered the Parisian light in pale sheets. They settled into the deep Italian leather chairs, the mood contemplative.

Moments later, Samira's laptop pinged.

She leaned forward, tapped the trackpad, and scanned the message that had just landed in her inbox. A slight smile flickered at the edge of her lips. "The lab results for the OSL testing of the soil samples just came in."

Alex and Claire looked up.

"The bottom layer dated to the 6th century, and the top layer to the 7th—smack bang where we thought it would be."

"So everything correlates," Claire added. "The soil samples, the date on the mosaic, and the references in the scrolls. It all aligns!"

"One mystery solved," said Alex. "Five more to go."

"Only five?" Samira chuckled.

"Well," Alex said, sitting forward and flipping through his notebook, "let's look at what we do know. We know who Malik

204

is—or was. We know roughly when he lived and when he died. We know how he rose to notoriety. We know why he chose Leptis. And we know he was well connected—and that he started, or revived, the hawala lending system."

Both Samira and Claire nodded in agreement.

"But here's what we don't know," Alex continued, ticking them off on his fingers. "One: Who is Abu Nas'r ibn Talib? Two: What, or where, is the 'Queen's Island'? Three: What does the medallion represent? It's clearly tied to some kind of library or house of knowledge. Four: What is the actual quest—what are we meant to be looking for? Is it wealth? Is it knowledge? What's been lost that now needs to be found? And five: Who—or what—is Dhu al-Qarnayn? A person? A place? A city? What?"

"Dhu al-Qarnayn literally translates to 'Two-Horned One,'" said Samira. "It could be a person, or a place—maybe even a geographical feature."

They sat in thoughtful silence for a moment.

Then Claire spoke again. "The lions. There seems to be a recurring theme. The lion motifs on the mosaic floor. 'Following the lion's gaze.' 'Watcher of the lion by the sea.' Leptis described as 'the broken lion sleeping by the sea'... It's all interrelated. Personally, I think it's deliberately connected."

"Well spotted, Claire," said Samira. "And I think you could be right. But what is Malik referring to? Certainly not himself."

"No," Alex replied, "but I think the lion—or lions—are the key. Especially the mosaic. Four lions. Each one older than the last. Each one in a different pose. Each one in a different location. It's more than symbolic."

It was during one of those quiet, almost reverent stretches of silence—pens down, minds drifting across ancient maps and dusty glyphs—that Samira's laptop pinged again.

She glanced at the screen, her expression shifting instantly.

Without a word, she opened the email, scanned it quickly, and then snapped the laptop shut with a burst of energy that snapped Alex and Claire to attention.

"Michael's got a hit on the motif from the medallion," she said.

"That was fast," Claire blinked, surprised.

Samira gave a half-smile. "Well, he's working with a Tier-4 inference engine, cross-referenced with over sixty institutional archives. And our catalogue is partially linked to the Louvre, the British Museum, the Vatican, and most of what's been digitized from Egypt's Ministry of Antiquities."

Alex straightened in his chair. "Where?"

Samira looked directly at him. "Egypt."

"That tracks," Alex nodded. "Athena iconography wasn't uncommon in Ptolemaic Egypt. After all, Greek rulers—especially in Alexandria—tried to fuse their heritage with native symbols. The falcon of Athena wasn't just a symbol of wisdom by then; it was a mark of control over knowledge. A seal. Anywhere specifically?"

Samira's voice dropped slightly. "Specifically... Alexandria."

Alex froze. Claire looked up sharply.

"What exactly did the hit say?" Alex asked.

Samira reopened the laptop and turned it toward them. "According to the metadata, it's not just a visual match. It's an official seal. A Curate of the Great Library of Alexandria."

Claire gasped, the word catching like a breath in her throat. "But that can't be. The library was destroyed… during Caesar's siege. Or… that's what we're told."

Samira tilted her head slightly. "Maybe not all of it. Maybe history isn't as neat—or as complete—as we've been led to believe."

Claire began typing.

Then, without warning, Claire launched to her feet.

Her chair flew backward, clattering hard into the white acoustic panelling behind her. Both Alex and Samira turned, startled.

Claire's eyes were wide. Her pen dropped from her fingers and rolled off the desk unnoticed.

"No fucking way," she whispered. Then louder: "No fucking way!"

Samira raised an eyebrow, amused. "No way what?"

Claire took a breath, planted her hands on the table, and looked at them both, her voice trembling with excitement.

"Alexandria. The lion sleeping by the sea. The sea is the mediterranean." She paced now, her mind racing. "The medallion—that seal—it was found in Leptis Magna, sure, but its origin? Alexandria. The Curate's seal. The library. It's all Alexandria. Then the phrase—'Two-Horned One.' That's not just poetic language, it's a name."

She spun her laptop around. On the screen was an Arabic script entry highlighted in her notes.

"Dhu al-Qarnayn. The Two-Horned One. It was the name given to Alexander the Great in early Islamic texts. They believed he was a wise king, a traveller to the ends of the Earth, possibly even immortal – part man, part God. Some Islamic historians even thought he was a prophet—or something beyond mortal. He founded a city – Alexandria!"

Her voice sharpened now, intense. "We've been looking at this like historians. But what if these aren't just relics? What if they're guideposts? Trail markers?"

She paused.

"I think these clues are pointing us toward the final resting place of Alexander the Great."

Silence descended like a veil. Heavy. Sacred.

Then, slowly, Alex grabbed his laptop in haste, his fingers already moving across the trackpad.

"Wait… just wait a second," he muttered.

A few quick taps. A map. A reconstruction. An overlay.

He turned it around.

"Antirhodos. An island in Alexandria's eastern harbor—Portus Magnus. It was connected to the mainland by a causeway and served as a royal precinct under Cleopatra."

His eyes scanned the screen. "It housed palaces. Temples. Subterranean vaults. And it was also called…"
He didn't have to finish.
"The Queen's Island," they said in unison.
Claire lowered herself slowly back into her chair. Her hands were trembling. Her voice, when it came, was soft.
"It's not a story," she whispered. "It's a map. And according to the number one lion, the trail begins in Alexandria"

Chapter 10

The hastily convened meeting was already underway by the time the sun began slipping behind the limestone domes of Paris. On the fifth floor of the Institute's administrative wing, the Director General's private office had been cleared—appointments postponed, calls deferred. When Samira had insisted this was urgent, André Molineux hadn't hesitated.

Samira began without preamble. "André, thank you for seeing us on such short notice. We know how valuable your time is, but I promise you—this is unlike anything we've come across before."

Molineux waved her off impatiently, settling into his high-backed leather chair. "Spare me the polish. Just give me the facts. Start at the beginning."

The three archaeologists launched into a tight, focused debriefing. Samira outlined the verification of the identity Malik ibn Harun al-Sahiri, the soil sample results and the established timelines. Claire followed, linking the inscriptions in the so-called Malik Letters to the iconography on the villa mosaic floor. Then Alex brought it home, walking Molineux through the identification of the medallion itself: an official seal of a Curate of the Great Library of Alexandria, recovered from Roman soil but undeniably Egyptian-Greek in origin.

When they finished, Molineux leaned back, fingers steepled.

"So let me see if I understand," he said slowly. "You're suggesting that these clues—this medallion, the mosaic floor, these letters—all point to the final resting place of Alexander the Great? And that there are guideposts… waymarkers along the way?"

Alex nodded. "Not the final resting place, per se. That was originally Memphis, then Alexandria. But we believe that the tomb was relocated—likely in haste—prior to or shortly after the Arab invasion of Alexandria in 641 or 642 CE."

Molineux narrowed his eyes. "You're speculating."

"Partially," Alex conceded. "But look at the broader pattern. When the Rashidun Caliphate swept through the Levant and Persia—Palestine, Syria, Mesopotamia—entire cities were burned or plundered. Libraries were destroyed. Whoever protected Alexander's tomb may have seen what was coming and decided to act, pre-emptively. Hide it. Move it. Preserve it."

"That's quite a claim," Molineux said.

Alex didn't blink. "We believe the tomb was relocated before the Islamic conquest reached Egypt. Malik refers to it as already hidden in his time – The Sleeping Lion."

"And this mosaic," Molineux continued, "you believe it points to the first of several markers?"

"Yes," said Claire. "But the trail only makes sense in sequence. If someone stumbled onto the second or third marker without understanding the beginning, it would be meaningless."

"Why hasn't anyone else found this first clue until now?" Molineux asked, genuinely curious.

Samira replied, "Because the mosaic floor at the villa in Leptis Magna was buried under centuries of debris, and we're the first team to excavate that section fully. No one else had access to all the pieces—the medallion, the letters, the mosaic floor."

Claire added, "And without the medallion to pinpoint Alexandria and the references in the Malik Letters to the Obelisk and the Queens Island, it would all seem like an elaborate but isolated find."

Molineux stood and paced briefly, absorbing it all. "So… Alexandria. Antirhodos Island. There's no doubt?"

"That's where everything is pointing," Alex said. "I'm convinced."

"So am I," Samira agreed.

Claire nodded. "Me too."

Molineux looked down at the papers spread on his desk. "Very well. I have a meeting with the Board in five minutes to discuss this. Understand—this isn't just an academic question. It's a major institutional decision. High reward, but also high risk. If this turns out to be a wild goose chase, it could damage the Institute's credibility. And we'd need to reallocate funding—probably pull most of the Leptis Magna budget and dip into discretionary reserves."

"We understand," Samira said.

"Good," Molineux replied. "If the Board says no, that's the end of it. Clear?"

The three archaeologists nodded. No one spoke as they left the office and took seats in the Director's waiting room, the air thick with nerves. Claire stared at the clock. Alex bounced his knee. Samira chewed her thumbnail—something none of them had seen her do before.

Ten minutes passed.

Then the inner door opened.

"Come in," Molineux said.

They filed back inside. He closed the door behind them but didn't return to his chair. Instead, he perched on the edge of his desk, hands folded.

"The meeting with the Board has just concluded," he said, pausing. "The project is approved."

The words hit the air like an electric charge.

"Unanimously," he added, almost as an afterthought.

Alex exhaled. Samira's brows shot up in surprise. Claire gave an involuntary squeal and clamped her hand over her mouth.

"Did they approve a budget?" Alex asked.

Molineux gave a half-smile. "Yes and no."

He leaned forward. "The Chairman—Étienne Girard—was especially enthusiastic. His exact words were: 'Any legitimate chance of finding the tomb of Alexander the Great, intact or otherwise, should be considered a priority of global importance. A discovery of that magnitude would be a once-in-a-century event—priceless for the Institute, for history, and for the future of our funding.'"

Alex blinked. "So…?"

"So," Molineux continued, "he's authorized full special project status. Samira, you'll set up a secure folder—only you and I will have access. I'll assign a new cost centre under 'Special Projects – Director General.' You'll have your budget."

Samira gave a tight nod. "Understood."

"Oh," Alex added, "you'd better include a line item for scuba gear. Maybe a boat."

Molineux raised an eyebrow. "Why?"

"Because Antirhodos," Alex said, "is underwater."

That evening, the team gathered at Le Perchoir Marais, a rooftop bar-and-grill tucked above the quiet rooftops of the 4th arrondissement. It was stylish without trying too hard — mismatched lounge furniture, strings of amber bulb lights, and a view westward where the Eiffel Tower flickered in the distance like a pulse. The clink of glasses and low music formed a comforting cocoon, a welcome contrast to the intensity of their day.

André Molineux joined them for the first round, ordering a bottle of Bordeaux with a knowing smile and waving off protests. "This one's on me," he said, lifting his glass. "To the mad ones. The heretics. And to whatever you find beneath the sea."

They drank to that.

But Molineux didn't linger. Barely ten minutes in, he drained his glass, offered a warm squeeze of Samira's shoulder, and apologized with a shrug. "It's family night. My girls are waiting with popcorn and a terrible rom-com. And I've learned not to keep them waiting."

As he disappeared down the stairwell, Alex turned to Samira, puzzled. "I thought he'd stay. This is… monumental. It changes everything."

She smiled, soft and genuine. "He's always been like that. Two daughters. Worships the ground they walk on. André would rather be home on a couch with his wife and kids than drink with colleagues — even on the brink of rewriting history."

There was admiration in her voice. Not envy. Just respect.

Conversation soon shifted. The celebratory mood, while real, began to give way to the looming enormity of what came next. Plates were cleared, another round was poured, and beneath the glow of Parisian dusk, they began talking logistics.

"Tomorrow," Claire said, pulling her hair into a ponytail as if bracing herself, "we need to start breaking this thing down. Properly."

"At the Institute," Samira nodded. "Not here, not tonight. We'll need maps. Files. Dive records. And a lot of coffee."

Despite knowing where to begin — Antirhodos Island — they were no closer to knowing what they were actually looking for. A tomb? A chamber? A marker? A mechanism? They weren't even sure Malik had left anything behind.

"It could be buried," Alex said. "Scattered. Disguised. Hell, it might be a doorway no one's ever thought to open."

"And after thirteen centuries," Claire added, "it might not be there at all."

The underwater ruins of Antirhodos were now a UNESCO-protected dive site, a mecca for underwater archaeology and bucket-list divers with enough money and permits to descend into history. It was stunning, yes — but curated. Sanitized. Heavily regulated.

Tomorrow, they'd dig into what records they could find — dive footage, satellite imaging, sonar maps, anything public and everything obscure. They needed to visualize the site from above, from below, from the inside out.

And even then, they were still assembling a jigsaw puzzle without a picture on the box.

"We're chasing a shadow in a submerged palace," Alex muttered, half to himself.

Samira raised her glass. "Then let's hope Malik left us a light to follow."

They drank to that, too — to hidden obelisks, sunken islands, and the madness of chasing the impossible.

Tomorrow, the real search would begin.

Act II - The Long Reckoning

Chapter 1

It was Monday morning, mid-March, and it was Paris.
The three archaeologists had gathered in the research rooms on the
second floor of the Institut National d'Histoire de l'Art. A grey
spring light slanted through the tall windows, illuminating a clutter
of laptops, notebooks, and half-drunk coffees. The task ahead was
enormous, and Alex, as ever, believed in structure. He gestured for
them to sit.
"We've got a lot to do," he said, rubbing the back of his neck.
"And not much time. So, to avoid stepping on each other's toes,
I'm going to divide the work, if that's okay with you both."
Claire and Samira nodded immediately. They were well beyond
needing diplomatic preambles.
"Claire, you're the tech genius. We need the most sophisticated
dive gear we can get. Cameras, two-way comms, environmental
telemetry—something that can map and film underwater. And
ideally, GPS capability. If we find what we're looking for, we'll
need precise coordinates to come back."
She nodded, already scribbling in her notepad.
"Samira, I'm guessing we need permits. It's a UNESCO site—
we'll need clearance from them, plus whatever local permissions
the Egyptian government requires. Visas, INHA credentials,
anything that gets us in and keeps us legal. And see if there's a
reputable commercial dive outfit we can contract in Alexandria.
We'll need a boat and crew."

He leaned back, exhaling.

"I'll take care of the boring logistics. Flights, accommodation, tide charts, vehicle hire. We can't afford any surprises."

No one argued. They each claimed a corner of the room and got to work.

Laptops were flung open. Phones dialed. Coffee flowed. The room buzzed with quiet intensity—efficient, methodical, and quietly urgent. They only spoke when absolutely necessary, cross-checking information or updating each other on dependencies. By late afternoon, the light outside had turned golden. The whiteboards were filled with scrawled notes, and they reconvened to take stock.

Claire had made the most progress, though hers was also the most intricate.

"Okay," she began, tapping her stylus against her tablet, "here's where we're at. I narrowed our equipment suppliers to three possibilities: Blue Robotics, Sonardyne, and Kongsberg Maritime."

She pulled up a chart on her screen, rotating it toward them.

Blue Robotics is American—California-based. They do affordable, modular underwater drones and sensors. Very DIY-friendly, great for rapid setup. Their BlueROV2 is popular with universities and private researchers.

Sonardyne, out of the UK, is higher-end. Their kit is used by offshore energy and defense. They offer acoustic positioning systems, underwater modems, and real-time data telemetry. Pricier, but battle-tested.

Kongsberg, the Norwegian juggernaut, is top-tier. Military-grade stuff. High-definition multibeam sonar, subsea navigation, integrated real-time data relay systems. NASA-level overkill, but absolutely reliable.

She paused, letting that sink in.

"I've opted for Sonardyne. It's a good balance between capability and usability. Here's the layout: we'll be using a diver-mounted compact recording system tethered acoustically to a boat-mounted relay station. The relay then broadcasts to a shore-based monitoring terminal where I'll be logging and recording everything in real-time."

She swiped through a visual schematic: diver, boat, shoreline—all linked through Sonardyne's BlueComm optical/acoustic modem system.

"We'll have high-resolution video feeds, depth and orientation tracking, and full comms—Alex can talk to me directly while underwater, provided we keep line-of-sight between the boat and my relay dish."

"And GPS?" Alex asked.

"The diver won't have it directly—that doesn't work well underwater—but the boat will track relative position using Ultra-Short Baseline (USBL) systems. So long as the boat holds position, we'll have precise spatial data. And the best part? If anything goes wrong, the shore station retains the only full copy of the data. Nothing is stored locally on the diver."

Alex gave a tight nod. "Exactly what we need."

She added, "I sourced the main components from a technical dive vendor in Barcelona—they outfit scientific and salvage teams in the Balearic Sea. Gear should arrive tomorrow or Wednesday at the latest. Direct to customs in Cairo"

"Nice work," Samira said, impressed.

Claire smirked. "Just pray the customs paperwork goes through."

Samira glanced at her notes, then looked up, all business.

"Okay—permits."

She tapped the stack of papers on the table. "We're applying under the guise of conducting sediment core sampling to help validate the 'slow sink' hypothesis Frank Goddio popularized during his underwater work in the Bay. Basically, we're following up on his theory that ancient Heracleion and parts of Canopus didn't vanish overnight—but were gradually claimed by the delta's subsidence and liquefaction over centuries."

Claire gave a small nod. "Plausible, and boring enough to stay under the radar."

"Exactly," Samira said. "We've submitted our dossier to UNESCO under a research umbrella—purely geological, non-extractive, cultural heritage compliance intact. No flags. That's our cover." She flipped to the next form.

"For the Egyptian Ministry of Tourism and Antiquities , the pitch is the same. We're affiliated with the INHA, coordinating with French and Egyptian geologists. No mention of sites, ruins, or anything resembling active archaeology. I listed our core sampling coordinates as a triangle just offshore from Aboukir Bay—close enough to the ruins, but not so close that it triggers alarm bells." She paused. "The beauty of it is that Goddio's work is well-documented, so referencing it lends legitimacy. I even cited some of his 2006 findings in the application."

Alex raised an eyebrow. "We're not actually taking core samples, are we?"

"No, but we'll have the equipment on the boat—just in case we need to play the part. And if anyone asks, the cores are for sedimentation profiling to compare against Goddio's layers."

Claire grinned. "That's just devious enough to work."

Samira nodded. "I've done this dance before."

She moved to the next point. "Our visa applications are also filed under the same research classification—'marine archaeology consultants,' affiliated with the INHA. That'll get us through customs clean. And our official INHA ID badges are already in transit. They'll be here by courier tomorrow morning."

A small flicker of satisfaction crossed her face.

"We are, on paper, as legitimate as anyone else working in Egyptian waters this month."

"Now, the dive crew. I reached out to a few outfits operating out of Alexandria—most of them are geared toward recreational diving, but one stood out. They're called Aqua Nefertari."

Claire smirked. "Bit on the nose."

"Maybe, but they're solid," Samira replied. "They handle both tourist and commercial dive charters, and they've worked with university teams from Cairo and even a Canadian group two years ago. The lead operator, Omar Shoukry, speaks fluent English and has experience coordinating with archaeologists. He knows the protocols—buoyancy compensation around fragile ruins, silt disturbance, visibility thresholds, the works."

She handed over a one-sheet printout with their logo, fleet specs, and rates.

"They've put aside a RIB and a shallow-draft support vessel for us—on standby for a four-day window, starting as early as Friday. That gives us flexibility, but not luxury. They're booked after that by an Italian marine biology group doing coral sampling in the Bay."

"Why are they free now?" Alex asked.

"Because it's low season," Samira said. "Winter currents are rough and water clarity's inconsistent this time of year, so most recreational diving shuts down between January and late March. It's not ideal for tourists, but for us—if the water stabilizes—it's perfect. Fewer boats, fewer eyes."

She looked up at them both, face calm but resolute.

"So, permits are in motion, the crew is lined up, and our IDs are en-route. The only thing left is the sea."

Alex took a final sip of the now-cold espresso on the windowsill and turned back to the group. The late-afternoon sun filtered through the tall second-floor windows of the INHA reading room, casting long, golden slants across the worn parquet floor. He pulled a folded tide chart from his notebook and smoothed it across the table.

"And speaking of sea....."

Claire and Samira looked up, blinking out of their task-focused trances.

"We're in luck," Alex said, tapping the chart. "Tidal patterns this time of year in the bay off eastern Alexandria are stable. But this

Friday—March 15th—we're looking at an especially long slack
tide starting just before noon. Should last for nearly two hours.
That means minimal current, calmer waters, and the best visibility
we're likely to get."

He drew a circle on the calendar with his pen.

"That gives us about an hour of good visibility either side of the
slack. Four solid hours of dive time, assuming we coordinate
turnover and equipment smoothly."

Samira nodded, "Perfect window."

"Depth in the area around the old royal quarter—the Sunken
Palace of Cleopatra, what's believed to be the remains of the
Antirhodos Island complex—is shallow," Alex added. "Only about
4 to 8 meters, depending on exact location and tides. So
technically, we can stay down indefinitely, at those depths, as long
as we swap out tanks and follow basic safety intervals."

Claire frowned. "No decompression stops at that depth?"

"Correct," Alex said. "Within limits, obviously. But we'll be
fine—especially with how short the dives are. This isn't saturation-
level stuff. Visibility's the real wild card, not depth."

He leaned back slightly.

"Samira, if you can lock us in with the dive operator for Friday
through Sunday. Hopefully we find what we're after on Day One,
but we've got backup windows just in case." Samira nodded and
made a note.

He flipped to another page in his notebook.

"I booked us at the Steigenberger Cecil Hotel in Alexandria. Five
stars, but not flashy. Elegant, classic. It's where Churchill stayed
during the war, and it's got enough historical weight to feel right
for archaeologists—without drawing luxury-hotel suspicion."

Samira smiled. "And a good bar, if I remember."

"That too," Alex said, lips twitching into a grin.

"As for flights—we're flying commercial. I've booked three seats
on Air France 570, CDG to Cairo International Airport—CAI.
Departure Thursday morning. No private jets, no diplomatic

channels. Just a ragtag team of scientists, traveling economy with too much luggage and bad coffee. Low profile, like we're on a tight UNESCO research grant."

Samira gave an approving nod.

"Good," she said. "No one's going to look twice."

Alex continued, "I've booked us a Toyota Land Cruiser Prado through Hertz Egypt—pickup at Cairo Airport. Plenty of room for gear and crew. And—bonus—it's an automatic, so everyone can drive it."

He glanced at Claire with the faintest smirk.

Claire exchanged a glance with Samira.

She rolled her eyes. "One time I stall in a vineyard, and I never live it down."

Alex turned to Samira. "And are we basing ourselves out of the Centre for Maritime Archaeology and Underwater Cultural Heritage? Your call. What do you think?"

Samira considered it a moment. "Too public. Too close to the Antiquities Ministry. If anyone checks in on the dive, or on the permits, they'll go there first. We use it for optics—a single check-in on Friday morning to announce our activity, log the boat time, and leave a paper trail. But after that? We keep off the radar."

Alex nodded.

"Perfect. I'll schedule the Land Cruiser for one week—Thursday to Thursday. Hopefully we're done by Sunday. But if things go sideways, we've got a buffer."

A moment of silence settled between them. The plans were falling into place. Tangible now. Real.

Samira closed her laptop and stretched. "We earned a proper meal."

Claire yawned. "Somewhere with wine and no Wi-Fi."

Samira chuckled. "I know just the place—Chez Janou, in the 3rd. Provencal cooking, close enough to walk, and they do a lavender crème brûlée that's nearly spiritual."

Alex raised an eyebrow. "Sold."

They packed their things in quiet synchronicity. Laptops folded shut, papers filed, coats shrugged on. It was a satisfying kind of exhaustion—the fatigue of people who had built something from chaos, who had direction now, however uncertain the path ahead might be.

The late Paris sun was dipping behind the rooftops as they stepped out into the crisp evening air. As they walked, the city hummed around them. Tourists trickled out of galleries. Locals leaned on café railings with cigarettes and quiet laughter. Somewhere in the distance, a bell tower chimed seven times.

For now, they were just three tired archaeologists, heading to dinner.

The location was Samira's idea. After a day of unrelenting logistics at the INHA, she suggested they get out, walk off the stress, and eat something that wasn't grabbed from a vending machine or eaten over a keyboard.

Chez Janou sat quietly on a corner in the Marais, all green shutters and warm yellow glow spilling through its windows. The smell hit them before they even stepped inside—olive oil, grilled meats, lemon zest, and the comforting salt of anchovies and tapenade.

Inside, it was pure Provençal charm. The walls were plastered with vintage Ricard posters, shelves lined with dusty bottles of pastis, and the tables crowded close in that perfectly Parisian way. Waiters weaved through with armfuls of socca and bouillabaisse, laughter rising from nearly every corner. Somehow, the chaos felt cozy.

They were seated near the bar, beneath a rusted metal wall sconce shaped like a cicada. Claire looked entirely out of place, as usual—slouched in her chair in a loose NAU hoodie and black jeans that had clearly seen better days. Her hair, normally yanked into a no-nonsense ponytail, was down for once, curling in soft, unruly ringlets around her shoulders. A sleek black sweatband—half functional, half statement—kept the worst of it from her face, giving her that vaguely rebellious, science-club-chic look that only a handful of people could pull off. It suited her more than she realized—like she'd just stepped out of a server room, not an archaeological strategy meeting.

Samira, by contrast, had changed—of course she had. She wore a long, dove-grey trench coat cinched at the waist, and a fitted black top with gold-threaded cuffs. Her earrings glinted subtly under the warm overhead light. She looked like someone who knew exactly how to walk into any room and make it hers.

Alex kept things neutral in a clean, open-collar shirt and his usual blazer. Cool, unbothered, the same way he'd looked stepping off a plane in Ankara during a sandstorm. Claire often said he was either born with that calm, or he'd faked it so long it became real.

They started with a round of pastis—Samira's suggestion. Claire sipped hers tentatively, eyes narrowing. "Tastes like licorice had a baby with jet fuel."

Alex laughed. "That's the point."

Dinner followed: daube provençale for Samira, grilled sea bass and ratatouille for Alex, and for Claire, after a mild identity crisis, a mountain of truffle ravioli with shaved parmesan that she destroyed in minutes. The food was rustic, salty, perfect.

The table talk was lighter than it had been all day. The intensity of logistics, permits, dive tech, and approvals gave way to bread-breaking and eye-rolling confessions.

"I'll be honest," Samira said at one point, resting her chin on one hand, "I didn't think the Board would go for it. Too vague. Too risky."

Claire chuckled. "You didn't? I had zero faith. I mean, we're looking for…what, again? A lost underwater mystery box with no coordinates and no description? From the seventh century?"

"But we have a lead," Alex said, sipping his wine. "And sometimes that's all it takes."

Claire shook her head. "A lead based on a scroll that had been written by a money lender in the 7th century."

"And yet," Samira said, raising her glass, "UNESCO said yes. The permits are in motion. The tech is arriving. And I have a really good feeling about the tide."

They clinked glasses—Côtes de Provence for the women, a dry white Cassis for Alex.

By dessert—an absurdly generous slab of chocolate mousse that Claire swore she was "only tasting" before demolishing half—they were smiling easily, the tension loosened. The hardest part, they believed, was behind them.

Outside, the night air had turned cool. The streets were quiet, slick from an earlier rain. They walked slowly back through the Marais, the hum of Parisian nightlife in the distance.

Claire looked up at the moon and muttered, "I really hope there's something down there."

Alex didn't say anything. He just walked a step behind, his hands in his pockets, eyes scanning the horizon like a man who already knew the answer.

Chapter 2

The flight from Charles de Gaulle to Cairo was uneventful, as flights go—except for the usual grumbling over legroom and airline coffee. Samira had claimed the window, Claire had curled up with a tablet and noise-cancelling headphones, and Alex had stared through the seatback, half-asleep and half-plotting the logistics of the next 72 hours.

By the time they stepped off the plane into the thick, dusty warmth of a Cairo afternoon, March or not, the heat felt like a wall. It wasn't unbearable, but it clung to them with the subtle insistence of a thousand sun-baked bricks.

"Welcome to the oven," Alex muttered, rolling his carry-on behind him.

"Speak for yourself," Claire said. "This is practically spring in Arizona."

At the Hertz Egypt counter near the arrivals exit, Alex signed for the rental—a white Toyota Land Cruiser Prado. It gleamed like a hired mercenary: clean, capable, and expensive enough to make them look legitimate without drawing too much attention. Claire gave it a once-over and nodded approvingly.

"Automatic, right?" she asked, arching an eyebrow.

"Naturally. I'd like to keep my gearbox intact."

"Rude," she replied, tossing her backpack into the back seat.

Their dive gear had arrived on a separate freight manifest, held in customs for inspection. Samira handled the conversation in fluent Arabic while Claire and Alex waited under the flickering fluorescent lights of the cargo terminal. After a few forms, a handful of signatures, and a brief discussion with a customs officer who recognized Samira from a UNESCO panel, the crates were wheeled out on a trolley, sealed and intact.

From there, they drove across the congested sprawl of Cairo toward the portside outskirts, where they had arranged to meet their contracted dive crew. The city buzzed in every direction—horns, street vendors, minarets echoing the afternoon call to prayer. Despite the chaos, there was an unmistakable rhythm to it all.

The dive outfit was based out of a modest marina along the eastern edge of the harbor. Their contact, a sun-weathered man in his late forties named Mostafa, met them beside a sleek white dive boat named Baraka.

"Dr. Rahmani?" he asked, shaking Samira's hand with both of his. "You are right on time. We have everything ready."

"This is Alex Carey, and Claire Marlowe."

"Ah! More scientists from INHA," Mostafa said, clearly briefed. "Don't worry, we have worked with archaeologists before. We know how to stay out of the way and keep you alive."

Alex smirked. "That's all we ask."

Mostafa walked them through the dive support: a primary diver escort, a surface crew, and onboard monitoring. The boat had been retrofitted with a relay mast to handle Claire's tech specs.

By the time they arrived at the Steigenberger Cecil Hotel—its colonial charm faded but still dignified, overlooking the harbor promenade—the sun had begun to dip behind the haze. Their rooms were small but comfortable, their windows cracked open to let in the sea breeze.

Claire took over a corner of Alex's room to test the equipment. She had the gear unpacked and running in less than an hour: modular dive cameras, a two-way audio system, and a sleek custom-built console wired to her laptop. A parabolic antenna mounted on a small tripod would sync with the boat's repeater, maintaining a high-bandwidth link.

"No tethers," she explained to Alex, who stood leaning in the doorway. "We're running fully linkless comms. Cameras and audio are encoded and bounced to the boat's repeater. From there, it's relayed to my station, where I monitor, record, and log GPS coordinates in real-time."

"So, if someone finds something, you can pin it to within...?"

"About a meter. And if the boat drifts, I'll know. Which is why I need to be onshore, synced to a fixed GPS node. No lag, no dropout."

Alex nodded. "Sounds tight. You think it'll hold?"

"It better. Or I'm blaming you."

Later that night, they walked to a small Egyptian bistro tucked down a narrow side street near the hotel—all sandstone arches and mosaic-tiled floors. The scent of grilled lamb, coriander, and baked flatbread hung thick in the air. They shared a bottle of Lebanese red, and plates of mezze: baba ghanoush, ful medames, olives and labneh with mint.

As they stepped out of the café and into the warm Cairo night, Samira glanced up at the dusky sky and smiled. "Local reports say visibility's been excellent the last few days. With the tides tomorrow, we could be looking at crystal-clear water. Might be the best window we'll get."

Claire gave a confident nod, cradling her tablet under one arm. "All systems tested. Video, comms, nav—everything's talking to each other beautifully. I've set up multiple redundancy checks. I'm just hoping the satellite relay holds solid once you're offshore."

Alex stretched his arms behind his back with a faint groan. "Well, I'm ready...ish. I haven't strapped on a tank in five years, so if I don't drown, I'll consider that a win."

Samira shot him a look. "You'll be fine. Besides, you're not allowed to die. You still owe me coffee in Paris."

Claire grinned. "If he floats off into the Mediterranean, I'm not chasing him."

Alex chuckled. "You'd just track me by GPS and send a drone."

"Exactly."

They laughed—relieved, distracted, and finally, quietly excited.

They were up before the call to prayer. Cairo was still quiet, the city crouched beneath a thin haze of desert dust. Breakfast was a quick affair—thick Arabic coffee, fresh dates, and flatbread with soft cheese in the hotel's shadowed courtyard. By seven, they were en route to the Centre for Maritime Archaeology and Underwater Cultural Heritage in Alexandria, a coastal drive of several hours tracing the Mediterranean's dusty ribbon. The morning sun already pressed against the windshield of the Prado as they cut through the haze.

Once at the Centre, they lodged their dive plan with the local maritime authority. It was bureaucratic theatre, but necessary. Samira handled the permits with the practiced patience of someone who'd danced this waltz before.

By mid-morning, they met with the commercial dive team at a weatherworn dock just east of Fort Qaitbay, not far from where the island of Antirhodos had once risen above the sea. The team consisted of Mostafa—stocky, mustached, and calm as a granite block—his wiry brother Remi, who would manage the comms, and their cousin Bilal, the boatman, lean and quiet with eyes like dark glass. They knew these waters intimately and had been briefed already. Mostafa pointed out the approximate area they'd start— the southern crescent of Antirhodos, the only portion that would have remained above water in the seventh century CE.

The safety briefing was brisk but thorough: dive signals, emergency protocols, ascent rates, buddy checks. No anchors were permitted over a protected heritage site, so Bilal would have to keep the RIB in constant motion, correcting for current and wind by throttle and instinct.

Claire set off along the curve of the shoreline on foot, gear slung over one shoulder. She climbed a low bluff and found her perch—a flat outcrop high enough to catch uninterrupted satellite signals but still close enough for visual contact. She unfurled the tripod, checked the uplink, and slipped her headset on.

Back on the boat, Samira finished configuring the floating repeater rig and attached the final antenna. Alex double-checked his gear and lowered himself onto the edge of the RIB, mask around his neck. "Comms check," he said.

"Reading you five-by-five," came Claire's voice in his ear.

"Video feed clear," Samira added. "Relay stable."

Mostafa nodded. "Ready?"

"Let's go," said Alex.

Together, they rolled backward into the sea.

The water was astonishingly clear—an endless, flickering green-blue cathedral. And cool, surprisingly so, even in March. They started at the western edge of the island's submerged remains, where the depth dropped to around eight meters. There lay the crumbled southern quarters of Cleopatra's palace, sunken stone pathways, tumbled columns, and weed-choked mosaics beneath centuries of silt.

With no pressing depth concerns, they moved slowly, letting the current guide them eastward. Fish darted in streaks of silver among the ruins. Fragments of marble statues peered through layers of algae.

For the first hour, they swept a wide path. Claire monitored everything from her perch, recording and cataloging the footage on a rugged solid-state drive. Alex surfaced as his tank edged into the red, trading it out for a fresh one, while Claire reviewed the first hour of video.

"No joy so far," she said over comms. "We've got some interesting fragments, but nothing definitive."

"Copy that," Alex replied. "Heading back down."

On their second dive, they veered slightly north, gliding lazily along a corridor of tumbled stone blocks. That's when Alex saw it: a tall granite shape jutting from the seafloor at an odd angle. It stood like a miniature sentinel—four-sided, tapering upward to a soft point, about three meters tall.

He approached slowly. "Claire, are you getting this?"

"I see it. Good video. Comms are solid. Recording."

The structure was unmistakable. Not a true obelisk, perhaps, but modelled in the same tradition. Each side bore inscriptions—worn but visible—etched in deep vertical lines.

To his right, Mostafa was inspecting a partially buried statue of a lion with a paw resting atop a sphere—the iconic Ptolemaic guardian.

Alex kept circling the granite pillar. "Claire, can you make out the inscriptions?"

"They're coming through nicely. No detritus build-up. Looks recently cleared by the current."

On the final side, he paused. There it was—a carved lion, full-bodied and front-facing, its eyes narrowed in what looked like repose.

Alex's voice crackled. "Claire, how do I get a GPS coords underwater?"

"Simply ask. I am logging your GPS coords in real time."

He adjusted his body, squaring his back to the obelisk. "Okay, now."

"GPS coords logged and a geo-fix taken" said Claire.

With half a tank left, they continued east, a slow arc of exploration. Mostafa rejoined him, and both gave the OK signal.

The rhythmic slap of small waves against the hull was broken suddenly by Bilal rising to his feet, squinting toward the horizon. His hand shot out, pointing east. His voice cut through the hum of the engine.

خفر السواحل! he shouted.

"Coast Guard!"

Samira turned, following his line of sight. A white Coast Guard cutter was tearing across the open water, its bow slicing high over the waves. It was coming fast—too fast.

She stepped up beside Bilal. "This zone is restricted, right? Wake limits in place to protect the shoreline and artifacts?"

Bilal nodded sharply, eyes still locked on the oncoming vessel. "Yes. No high speed allowed here. They know that."

But the cutter wasn't slowing down. If anything, it seemed to be accelerating—bearing straight toward them.

Up on the shoreline, Claire's voice crackled into Samira's headset. "Samira, you seeing this? Have we got company? That thing is hauling ass!"

Samira frowned, her voice low but tight. "Yeah, I see them. I have no idea—but it looks like trouble."

The cutter didn't slow until it was less than a hundred meters away—its white hull knifing forward with unmistakable intent. A plume of wake fanned out behind it, the roar of its twin diesels now deafening across the water.

Samira watched it bear down on them like a missile. This wasn't routine patrol behaviour. This was an intercept.

She clicked into the dive comms. "Hey Alex, I think we've got a problem. Coast Guard's just shown up—and they're not here for tea. Stay cool."

The cutter swung broadside and coasted up alongside the RIB. Even before it stopped, figures moved along its rail—armed sailors in blue camo fanning out, rifles raised and scanning. AKM variants, Samira noted automatically. Military issue. Locked and loaded.

Bilal, Remi, and Samira all raised their hands.

A uniformed officer stepped up to the port rail, gripping a loudhailer.

اطفئ المحرك!

"Kill your engine!"

Bilal reached slowly for the ignition switch, twisting it off with a metallic cough of the outboard.

The next order cut sharper:

سيتم الصعود إلى زورقكم. لا تتحركوا أو سنطلق النار.

"You are about to be boarded. Do not move—or you may be shot."
Lines were thrown. The boats were quickly lashed together.
Moments later, five men vaulted aboard the RIB, boots thudding
onto the rubber decking. The commanding officer, a Lieutenant
Commander by his shoulder insignia, scanned the small party with
a hawk's eye.

من المسؤول هنا؟

"Who is in charge here?"
"I am," Samira said, her voice steadier than she felt. "We're
archaeologists conducting core sampling on the sunken island. We
have—"
He cut her off with a flick of his hand.

أخرجوا الغواصين فوراً.

"Bring up the divers. Now."
Samira lifted her hands slightly. "We're working under permits
from the Ministry. We're not doing anything illegal—"
The commander moved like a whip. In a flash, he yanked his
sidearm—a Beretta 92FS—and pressed it hard against Bilal's
temple. The boatman froze, jaw clenched, fear in his eyes.
"I said—bring up the divers. Now."
Samira didn't hesitate this time. She keyed the comm. "Alex. Coast
Guard's here. They want you up—now. I think we'd better do as
they say."
"I see the other boat," Alex replied. His voice was clipped but
calm. "We're coming up."
The lieutenant commander stepped back and holstered the Beretta.
His eyes didn't leave Samira. "Give me your headset," he barked
in Arabic.
Before she could respond, a bubbling surge at the stern drew
everyone's attention—Alex and Mostafa breaking the surface with
controlled precision. Air hissed from their regulators as they swam
toward the ladder, oblivious for a moment to the scene above.

Samira seized the distraction. Her gaze flicked toward the horizon, then to the coastline where Claire would be perched.

She didn't hesitate.

"Claire," she said in English, low and fast, "listen carefully. Get the fuck out of here. Run. Now."

The commander turned, catching the shift in tone—and language. His eyes narrowed.

"What did you say—?" he started.

Samira whipped off her wireless headset and hurled it high and far over the side. It arced once in the sunlight before splashing down in the waves and vanishing.

"You fucking bitch!" the officer roared, and with a brutal backhand, he struck Samira across the face. The blow cracked like a gunshot, nearly knocking her overboard. She stumbled hard into the railing, catching herself on instinct.

Bilal lunged a step forward, but a rifle barrel stopped him cold.

Alex, now halfway up the ladder, froze as he took in the tableau.

"Samira!" he shouted.

She straightened slowly, blood on her lip and defiance in her eyes. The Coast Guard wasn't here by accident.

Chapter 4

Claire stood frozen for a single, charged heartbeat, her ears ringing with Samira's voice in her headset:

"Claire, listen carefully. Get the fuck out of here. Run. Now."

The words cracked through the stillness like a rifle shot, splintering the moment. A thousand thoughts surged through her mind—calculations, risks, contingencies. Not panic. Not yet. Just focused, white-hot clarity.

Mission Impossible - *What would Ethan Hunt do now?*

The line from Rogue Nation came unbidden, a strange, steadying mantra. She muttered it aloud like a charm:

"What would Ethan Hunt do now?"

Adrenaline surged, and she snapped into action.

Her fingers moved quickly but precisely—checking the data capture first. GPS logs? Saved.

Voice comms? Archived.

Video feed? Synced and backed up.

A lifetime of academic discipline collapsed into a thirty-second triage of digital survival.

She killed the laptop with a keystroke and yanked the power cable free. The modem's antenna was unscrewed in a blur, the LiPo battery unplugged, the RKK base station powered down. The tech went dark.

Claire slid the laptop into her backpack and slung it over one shoulder. She looked around. The rest of the gear had to disappear—fast. A few metres away, behind a low limestone wall edging the footpath, some dry brush and thorny scrub clung to the escarpment.

She grabbed the tripod, collapsed it in one motion, and stuffed it into the thicket along with the base station and antenna. They vanished into the undergrowth. Unless someone climbed up and looked, no one would know it was there.

The modem and solid state hard drive, slim and rectangular, joined the laptop in the backpack. The LiPo battery pack, however, was too bulky. And Ethan's rule echoed loud in her mind: *'Move fast. Be agile.'*

She left it tucked under the base of the bushes beside the other gear.

Claire pulled the hood of her dark-blue Northern Arizona University sweatshirt up over her head and adjusted the straps of the pack. In the distance, she could just make out the faint roar of the cutter's engines echoing off the harbour. The tension gripped her chest—but she didn't freeze. She moved. *Don't look back!*

She climbed down the escarpment carefully, her Merrell hiking boots crunching against gravel. At the bottom, she stepped onto the walking path that ringed the harbour, joining the flow of early morning pedestrians.

Don't run, walk!

Running screams guilt.

Walk with purpose. Walk like you belong.

She slipped into the rhythm of the street. Her hoodie covered her hair, her gaze stayed down, and her expression was neutral. Not blank—neutral. She was just another teenager out exploring Alexandria on a cool spring morning.

Her heart hammered, but her breathing stayed even. She pushed down the fear—not gone, but managed. This wasn't just about escape. This was about the mission. About protecting what they'd found. Samira had taught her that. So had Alex. She wasn't just the intern anymore.

She moved southwest, deeper into the city. Toward the old quarter. Toward people. Toward cover.

Hide in plain sight.

Ahead, a tour group was clustering by the Citadel walls, sun hats and selfie sticks already aloft. Claire lengthened her stride, sliding effortlessly into their orbit.

Blending in. Disappearing.

Just like Ethan would.

The commandant barked clipped orders in Arabic, and his men sprang into motion. Alex and Mostafa were dragged to their feet and ordered—gestured, rather—to strip out of their scuba gear. Alex complied without a word, unbuckling the harness and peeling off the buoyancy compensator. The air tank clanked to the deck. Mostafa followed suit, glancing once at Alex with a wary frown. Samira remained where she was, leaning against the gunwale of the RIB. Her lip was split, the right side of her face swelling with a deepening bruise that shaded into purple. Blood had begun to dry at her chin, crusting at the edge of her mouth. She spat to the side and said nothing.

The commandant approached, his boots thudding against the aluminum deck. He came to a stop before Alex, eyes narrowing.

ماذا كنتم تغوصون عليه؟

"What were you diving on?"

Alex held his gaze, silent. The sea breeze tugged at his wet hair. Samira answered for him in Arabic.

هو لا يتكلم العربية. فقط الإنجليزية.

"He doesn't speak Arabic. Only English."

She kept her voice level, trying to steer attention away from him. The commandant grunted in irritation and waved a hand. More orders. Two of his men stepped forward, zip-tying Alex and Mostafa's wrists behind their backs with practiced efficiency. Just as the commandant turned to issue another command, one of his subordinates, the radio operator, called out. He was pointing toward the side of the RIB—where the repeater base station hung secured, cables still snaking back to the antenna mounted on the canopy rail above.

They exchanged words in low Arabic. The commandant climbed onto the RIB's sidewall, scanning the horizon. His gaze swept over the water—empty now save for the cutter and the RIB—and then toward the shoreline, less than two hundred metres away. He squinted.

Nothing obvious. But line-of-sight meant someone had to be close. He turned to the radio operator beside him.

اتصل بالقاعدة. هناك شخص ثالث على الشاطئ، قريب. يجب أن يكون في خط الرؤية. أرسل دوريات لتفتيش الساحل!

"Call it in. There's a third person onshore. Close by, within line of sight. Send patrols to search the coast!"

Then he gestured sharply to the RIB.

صادروا القارب! إسير افقنا. ننطلق الآن!

"Confiscate their phones and the boat! It's coming with us. We leave now!"

The cutter's crew moved with discipline, Bilal and Remi were zip tied like Alex, Samira had her hands tied in front – a woman, less of a threat. The commandant climbed back aboard the gleaming white cutter, his boots leaving damp prints behind him and the mooring lines between the two craft removed. Three men remained on the RIB—one to pilot it, and two others posted at the stern, rifles slung, eyes watchful.

Samira kept her head down, feeling the shift of motion as the rib's outboard sputtered to life. The RIB was now following along in the cutter's wake, trailing white foam in its path.

Alex shifted slightly beside her, his hands bound but his shoulders squared. He met her gaze. There was no panic, no fear—only cool composure. A message in his eyes:

Play along. For now.

Samira nodded once, subtly, then looked away as if bored.

Behind them, the cutter cut eastward, toward the naval dockyard. The city of Alexandria faded slowly into the sea haze—and with it, any trace of Claire.

It had been two hours since Claire had taken flight from the dock. She had lost herself in the tangled streets of Alexandria's old district—Al-Mansheya, just south of the Corniche, where time seemed to peel away in layers of sun-drenched sandstone and flaking colonial balconies. Here, in the maze of alleyways shadowed by faded shutters and overhead laundry lines, the smells of the city clung close: cardamom and diesel, grilled meat and salt air.

She had initially tried to blend in with a lumbering tour group of elderly American retirees, their sun hats bobbing above DSLR cameras and guidebooks clutched like talismans. But her youth and tense posture made her stand out like a discordant note in an old hymn. She slipped away casually and drifted toward a more kinetic crowd—a bevy of Japanese high school students in crisp uniforms, giggling, taking selfies, chewing on bubblegum, herding after a soft-spoken teacher waving a clipboard.

Hide in plain sight. Just like Ethan would.

The thought came unbidden, and she allowed herself a flicker of a smile. No one outside of Alexandria knew what had happened. The Coast Guard had moved fast, quietly. But if she disappeared completely, the entire mission—whatever was left of it—would die in the dark. Someone needed to know.

Who?

Her mind flipped through possibilities like index cards: The Ministry? The Embassy? The local police were out of the question. The INHA? Yes. And one man in particular.

André Molineux.

The Director General of the Institut National d'Histoire de l'Art. Her contact, her sponsor. Samira's friend. A man who had probably navigated more political landmines than most diplomats.

If anyone could act without hesitation—and without attracting too much attention—it was Molineux.

She pulled out her iPhone, casting a quick glance left and right. Still no obvious tails. Close by, a group of street vendors were arguing over sunflower seeds beside a sputtering tuk-tuk, and a mother nearby tried to keep her toddler from chasing pigeons. It all seemed innocuous. Claire tapped the screen, opened her contacts, and scrolled.

Fifth name from the top.

AAA Mum

AAA Dad

AAA University Admin

AAA Alex

Then,

André Molineux INHA

Her thumb hovered a moment. Then she pressed call.

The line rang. Once. Twice. She felt every beat in her chest. Come on, answer. Just as she was about to hang up, the voice came, clipped and formal:

"Director General André Molineux."

"Director, this is Claire Marlowe," she said in a low rush, already glancing around. "I'm in Alexandria. Listen carefully—I can't talk for long."

She pictured Ethan's voice in her head: *You've got thirty seconds before they triangulate your position. Maybe less if they're good.*

"I don't know the full details, but Alex, Samira, and the dive team were detained by the Egyptian Coast Guard—possibly under arrest. I think we found it. What we were looking for. I have all the data. Everything is on my laptop and secure. But I'm in the wind now. I'm going to head toward Cairo and disappear there."

She deliberately used the phrasing. 'In the wind.' She hoped he'd pick up on the urgency beneath the cloak of movie lingo.

"I'm going to turn off my phone now. If they're tracking me, I don't want to lead them anywhere."

"Claire! Claire, wait—tell me where you are. Let me help you!" Molineux's voice was suddenly urgent, the bureaucratic mask slipping.

"It's Alex and Samira that need help, sir. I'll be all right." Her tone softened. "You know what's at stake. I've got to go. They may already know where I am. Goodbye, Director."

She ended the call before he could say another word.

Quickly, she powered down the iPhone. She didn't remove the SIM or smash the device like they did in the films—she knew better. When off, a phone was inert. No pinging towers. No breadcrumbs. Just silent plastic and metal.

Claire drew a breath and sat down near the Japanese students again, tucking herself into the edge of their chatter. Her adrenaline still pulsed, but she let her breathing slow. She needed her mind clear.

The first step was clear: Cairo. The second… less so.

There, she could seek refuge—at the American Embassy if needed. Ethan had said once, *When in doubt, seek friendly ground.* It might be her only lifeline.

She looked up and noticed a bus stop half a block away. A lean metal sign shaded by a bent tin awning. She walked over, trying not to rush. The schedule was posted in Arabic—useless.

No Google Translate. No maps. Not without a SIM.

She needed help—from her oldest friend. The internet.

That meant a new SIM card.

Satisfied that she had, at least a semblance of a plan, Claire slung her backpack over both shoulders and started moving again—this time toward downtown Alexandria.

The city sprawled southeast along the Mediterranean, and she angled herself inland, away from the waterfront and toward Raml Station, the bustling heart of the transport grid. It was maybe three kilometres on foot. Thirty minutes if she didn't get lost.

She would find a phone shop. Buy a SIM. Get back online. Then Cairo. Then safety.

And maybe, just maybe, even Ethan Hunt would approve of the plan.

André Molineux stared at his phone in mounting frustration. The call from Claire Marlowe had come out of nowhere—brief, cryptic, and deeply unsettling. In the split second after the line went dead, he didn't just see a young archaeologist in trouble—he saw his own daughters, equally young, equally brilliant, equally vulnerable, suddenly alone in a foreign city with nothing but their instincts to keep them safe. The thought carved straight into his gut. That strange alchemy of paternal fear and professional obligation ignited at once.

Without hesitation, André jabbed at a familiar entry on his phone. It rang once—twice—before the dry, clipped voice of Louis Delon came through.

"Afternoon, Director."

"Louis, we have a situation in Egypt," André said briskly. "Our research team was detained mid-dive by the Egyptian Coast Guard—reason unknown. Claire Marlowe is on the run."

"Claire?"

"Yes. She managed to call me. She's in Alexandria for now, but she plans to make her way to Cairo and seek protection, possibly at the U.S. Embassy. I want you to drop whatever you're doing and get to Cairo immediately. Use the private jet. This is a Priority One mission."

"Just me?" Louis asked, already rising from his seat.

"Just you," André confirmed. "Land at the private airstrip at Cairo West Air Base. Use your diplomatic credentials. Carry what you need—under cloak of diplomatic privilege."

"Understood," said Louis.

"And Louis…" André paused, lowering his voice a half step.

"She's carrying sensitive data. If you can recover it, do so—but if the situation turns, forget the laptop. The girl's safety comes first. Assume she's being hunted. Use whatever means you must."

The silence that followed was brief, but heavy with understanding.
"Understood, sir," Louis replied, then ended the call.

André leaned back in his chair, exhaled once through his nose, and began scrolling his contacts again. He found the listing under 'E'—Edward Coté.

The line was picked up on the third ring by a crisp, female voice. "Office of Ambassador Coté."

"This is Director General André Molineux of the INHA. I need to speak to the ambassador immediately, please."

Moments later, the familiar, steady voice of the French Ambassador to Egypt came on the line. "Good afternoon, Director. How can I help you today?"

André's tone was direct but measured. "Good afternoon, Ambassador. I believe we may have a diplomatic issue brewing in Cairo. One of our UNESCO-sanctioned dive teams has apparently been detained off the coast of Alexandria. The circumstances are unclear, but it seems the Egyptian Coast Guard took them mid-operation. I've received no formal notice. Only a brief distress call."

"Do we know the charges?" Coté asked.

"Not yet. It may be a misunderstanding—or it may be worse. But all permits were in order."

"I see. And the detained parties?"

"One French national, and one American—consulting archaeologist with the INHA."

There was a pause on the line. Then: "In that case, it may be wise to alert the U.S. mission as well. If you catch my meaning."

"I do," André said, already scrolling. "But I'll make sure it's... properly sanctioned first."

"Keep me updated," said the ambassador. "I'll make some calls. Speak soon." The line went dead.

André found the final number he needed under 'R'—Raylan Stratten - Chargé d'Affaires ad interim, U.S. Embassy Cairo.

They'd crossed paths years ago, far from marble halls or
Mediterranean shores. In 2008, both men had been part of ISAF
rotations in Afghanistan—André embedded with French COS,
Raylan a U.S. Army colonel liaising with NATO in Kapisa
Province. It wasn't cinematic. It was austere, tactical, functional.
Two professionals running overlapping missions out of the same
mud-walled FOBs—briefings by flashlight, shared air cover, dry
rations, and dry humour. No grand heroics. Just mutual trust in a
place where that was currency.

They barely kept in touch. They didn't need to. But over the years,
they'd tracked each other's careers from afar—Raylan's transition
from uniform to suit, André's pivot from combat logistics to
cultural preservation.

And now, when André hit "Call," it wasn't nostalgia—it was a
tacit invocation of an old understanding.

This wasn't just diplomacy.

This was a call for a man who knew how to operate when the
rulebook caught fire.

The private number rang only once before it was answered.

"Afternoon, André. To what do I owe the pleasure?" came the
long, slow Kentucky drawl—loud and clear across the line.

"Good afternoon, Raylan. I take it things are good in your neck of
the woods?" André replied in his French-accented English, voice
calm but taut.

"As good as can be expected. But you're not calling to check on
my health, are you?" the American said dryly.

"Merely an icebreaker, Raylan," André allowed, then moved
swiftly on. "We've had a situation in Egypt. One of our INHA and
UNESCO-sanctioned dive teams has been detained—by the
Egyptian Coast Guard, for reasons currently unknown."

There was a slight pause. "Anyone I should be worried about?"

"Two of the team are American contractors. Consider this a
courtesy heads-up in case things… go sideways."

"I appreciate the call. When did this happen? And were they operating legally?"

"Earlier today. Around midday local time. And yes—as far as we're aware, every permit was in place and approved. This may be a case of mistaken identity, but something doesn't feel right, if you take my meaning."

"I get your drift, Director," Raylan replied. "Let me see what I can dig up on my end."

"One more thing," André added, lowering his voice slightly. "One of the Americans is a young woman. Nineteen. Her name's Claire Marlowe. She managed to escape. I believe she's heading to Cairo, possibly to your embassy. I've dispatched one of my men to try and reach her first."

"Louis?" Raylan asked, immediately understanding.

"Yes, sir. Louis."

"Good operator, that man. If anyone can find her, he can." The American's tone was resolute. "I'll keep my ear to the ground, André. I'll let you know what I find. You do the same."

"Absolutely, Raylan. Thanks for the help."

The call ended, and the room fell silent once more. André set the phone down on his desk, but his thoughts didn't follow. They turned, inevitably, to his own daughters.

What if it were one of mine?

That quiet question echoed louder than anything else in the room.

"Putain," he muttered, the word sharp and bitter in the silence.

Chapter 5

Louis rode hard through the late afternoon light to the airfield just outside Tunis.

Tunis had long served as the Institute's unofficial safe haven—low taxes, minimal oversight, and a bureaucracy uninterested in asking questions it didn't need answers to. The kind of place where things could move fast, quiet, and off-book.

He throttled down the Triumph Tiger 800, rolling it into the shadow of the hangar, and killed the engine. After a quick swipe of his access card, the security gate buzzed and opened, allowing him through the airside perimeter fence.

Inside, the pilot and copilot were already prepping the jet—heads bowed over digital briefs, glancing through airfield status updates and METARs from Tunis ATC.

"Time to go," Louis said briskly. "File for Cairo West—immediate departure. No amenities. We won't be in the air that long."

They nodded without question. The pilot moved to file the plan with air traffic control; the copilot started external checks—fuel, hydraulics, flight logs, manifests. No wasted motion.

Louis made his way to the small, windowless office at the rear of the hangar. In the back, bolted to the concrete floor, stood a drab olive-green locker—industrial, scarred, and unmarked.

He unlocked it with a thick brass key, the padlock thudding heavily into his palm. The doors opened with a mechanical groan, each one nearly the full width of the locker, reinforced steel thick enough to stop a round.

Inside, rows of weapons gleamed under fluorescent light. Ten FAMAS F1 assault rifles stood racked at the back, neatly secured. The doors themselves were lined with holsters, vests, and sidearms in foam-molded slots. Below, heavy drawers held neatly labeled boxes of ammunition.

Louis reached for a Glock 17, the standard-issue sidearm of French special forces. He slotted two spare mags into his belt pouch and clipped on a low-profile shoulder holster. With practiced ease, he shrugged off his weathered leather jacket, holstered the weapon, then slipped the jacket back over it.

Slide check. Safety on. One in the chamber.

He exhaled. This was muscle memory.

Outside, the turbine whine began to rise as the engines spooled up. In less than two hours, he'd be on the tarmac at Cairo West. And somewhere in that sprawling, watchful city, a nineteen-year-old girl was running out of time.

The hunt had already begun. But Louis wasn't the hunter.

He was the extraction.

It had taken Claire nearly an hour to find Raml Station, and by the time she stumbled onto the street that led to it, frustration burned behind her eyes. She'd gotten hopelessly lost—the signs were all in Arabic, and she didn't dare turn on her phone to use the translator app. *Ethan said no phones.*

But now she was here.

The station buzzed with chaotic life, tucked between crumbling colonial façades and gleaming new storefronts, a mismatched patchwork of Egypt's past and present. Vendors shouted, children weaved through adults with school satchels bouncing behind them, and street food carts sizzled with the rich scent of cumin, garlic, and frying oil. Car horns blared, mingling with the call to prayer echoing faintly from a distant minaret.

She wove her way through the crowd until she spotted a telecom shop, made obvious by the giant five-foot mockup of a smartphone

perched above the awning. Faded red and yellow Arabic lettering
scrawled across the windows, alongside laminated offers taped
crookedly to the glass.

Inside, the store was narrow and cluttered. Phones lay under glass
counters, sleek and spotless, glowing under harsh LED lights. The
walls were packed with accessories—colorful phone cases,
chargers in tangled bundles, earbuds in blister packs. Behind the
counter stood a single man, mid-thirties, olive-skinned, with a
neatly trimmed beard, tapping absently on a phone.

Claire stepped aside as a woman in a black ḥijāb, holding a toddler
by the wrist, finished purchasing a charging cable and shuffled past
her with a polite nod.

When it was her turn, Claire approached the counter and pulled out
her iPhone. With trembling fingers, she popped out the SIM tray
and slid the tiny card onto the glass.

The man leaned forward, squinting. He picked up the SIM and
inspected it, then smiled politely and said in Arabic,

شحن لهاتفك؟

"Top-up for your phone?"

Claire caught the word "phone," but little else. Still, she knew the
word for 'new.' She pointed at the display of SIM cards behind
him and said in halting Arabic:

جديد.

"New."

His face lit up. "Ahh," he nodded, and held up his hands—small,
medium, large?

Claire opened her arms wide. "Extra large."

Grinning, the man turned, reached for a pack, and placed it on the
counter. The package was bright orange and glossy, with bold
Arabic script, but the storage size—20GB—was mercifully in
Western numerals.

He tapped a battered calculator beside the till and showed her the
screen: 175 EGP.

Claire dug through her backpack, pulled out a few folded notes, and handed them over. The man counted them quickly, then gave a small nod and handed her the SIM pack.

She ripped it open, slid her old SIM into the wrapper for safekeeping, and inserted the new one into her phone. The device rebooted.

Apple logo. Boot screen. Welcome message.

Searching for network…

The signal bars flickered. Then—Vodafone EG – 4G. Connected.

Claire exhaled, quickly opened her translator app, toggled to English ⇄ Arabic, and spoke slowly into the mic:

"Where is the nearest bus stop to Cairo?"

She held up her phone to the attendant while the speaker spat out the translated phrase in a clipped digital voice:

أين أقرب محطة حافلات إلى القاهرة؟

The man chuckled, then launched into a rapid explanation in Arabic. Claire raised both hands. "Too fast!" she said, gesturing for him to use the phone. He took it and spoke clearly into the mic. The app translated:

"There is a bus stop three blocks away. Go back down this road, turn left, and walk three blocks. They leave every hour. The next one is at 3:30 p.m."

Claire checked her watch. 2:57.

Shit.

شكراً، she said breathlessly.

"Thank you."

She spun on her heel and burst from the shop into the street, weaving through the crowd again, eyes darting to street signs and shopfronts.

Next destination: Cairo.

And this time, she wasn't going to get lost.

As soon as the Coast Guard cutter docked at Ras el-Tin Naval Base, the detainees were separated without ceremony. Mostafa,

Rémi, and Bilal were led away by uniformed personnel and locked in a holding cell near the base's perimeter, under the watchful gaze of armed guards.

Alex and Samira, however, were treated differently.

They were handed over immediately to agents of the General Administration for the Repatriation of Antiquities and Cultural Property—commonly known as the Egyptian Antiquities Police. Two plainclothes officers escorted them across the base to an unmarked vehicle, its windows tinted against the fierce Alexandrian sun.

The car ride into the city was silent, save for the occasional squawk of radio chatter in clipped Arabic. From the naval base, the car rolled eastward along Sharia El Corniche, the sweeping coastal road that hugged the Mediterranean shoreline. The skyline of Alexandria unfolded like a faded postcard—once grand, now weathered—its crumbling neoclassical facades jostling with billboards and minarets. After passing the Bibliotheca Alexandrina, a sleek monolith of modernist ambition, they turned inland.

Twenty minutes later, they arrived at the Headquarters of the Egyptian Antiquities Police, located at 3 El-Nabih Street, Mansheya, Alexandria—a tired-looking government building squatting behind rusted iron gates, its limestone walls streaked with decades of soot and salt.

Inside, the bureaucratic indifference of the Egyptian penal system wrapped around them like smog.

Their zip-tie restraints were cut, but their freedom stopped there. They were processed, photographed, and fingerprinted, then escorted past flickering fluorescent lights and into a communal holding cell.

The air was thick with sweat and disinfectant. The cell, roughly four meters by six, was crammed with at least a dozen others— men of various ages, most in grimy clothes, with sun-darkened skin and wary eyes. Some muttered to themselves. Others dozed, curled up on the floor, using their jackets or arms as makeshift pillows. A single iron bench ran the length of the back wall, bolted into the concrete. The only window was a grilled slit near the ceiling, offering little light and no breeze.

Samira and Alex stood awkwardly for a moment before wedging themselves onto the edge of the bench, avoiding eye contact.

Despite Samira's immediate protestations—and her frequent, frustrated reminders to the guards that she was a French national, and Alex an American citizen—they were offered no special treatment. No interpreter, no phone call, no lawyer. To the guards, they were no different than the smugglers, looters, and illicit divers they'd arrested before.

Late that afternoon, their cell door clanked open.

A man entered flanked by two junior officers. He wore a dark green uniform adorned with silver braid and epaulettes. His face was lean, with pouches beneath the eyes and a permanent downturn at the corners of his mouth.

"I am Chief Commandant Ayman El-Badawi of the Egyptian Antiquities Police," he said in serviceable English. "You will remain here tonight. Tomorrow, you will be transferred to Cairo for formal questioning by the Ministry."

He had barely finished speaking when Samira stood, defiant. "But we haven't done anything wrong! We have dive permits, we're accredited researchers. We filed everything through the Centre for Maritime Archaeology and Underwater Cultural Heritage. We logged the dive. We followed protocol to the letter!"

El-Badawi switched to Arabic, his tone hardening.

من فضلك يا سيدة، إذا لم تجلسي وتصمتي، سوف يُضطرني وضعك في الحبس الانفرادي حتى تتعلمي الأدب.

"Please, madam, if you do not sit down and be quiet, I will place you in solitary confinement until you learn some manners."

Samira blinked, stunned by the blunt threat, but fury quickly flared behind her eyes.

"Wait until I get out of here," she snapped. "Your career will be over. You'll be cleaning toilets in a museum basement in Luxor."

Alex stood and placed a firm hand on her shoulder.

"Samira—stop. Before you get us both into even deeper trouble."

She hesitated, then slumped back down beside him, seething.

"They can't do this to us," she muttered.

Alex leaned in quietly. "If we don't check in soon, someone will notice. But right now, we need to buy time. Getting angry won't help."

Samira's jaw tightened, but she said nothing.

She sat still for several minutes, breathing heavily through her nose, her fingers curling into fists. She was not used to being scolded. Or restrained. Or ignored. But as the seconds dragged into minutes, her anger slowly congealed into suspicion. There was no way she had misfiled those permits. Every authorization had been properly stamped and approved. Every procedure followed.

The more she thought about it, the clearer it became:

This wasn't a mistake.

This was a setup.

And that made her even more furious.

Claire reached the bus stop at exactly 3:25 p.m., her breath short and shallow from the near-sprint through the crowded streets of Alexandria. The heat clung to her like damp linen, and her heart was still thudding from both the exertion and the pressure to stay ahead of the invisible chase she feared might not be far behind. Pulling out her iPhone, she opened the translator app and held it up to the cracked plastic timetable bolted to the shelter wall. It scanned quickly, overlaying a grainy digital translation over the faded Arabic characters. Just as the telco store owner had promised, Go Bus No. 302 was due to arrive at 3:30 p.m.—Alexandria to Cairo, with several scheduled stops along the route, including Tanta, Benha, and Shubra El-Kheima. The final destination was Cairo Gateway Bus Station, on El-Torgoman Street, right near the heart of downtown Cairo.

That gave her approximately four hours on the road—traffic willing. Google Maps confirmed her arrival time as around 7:30 p.m. Just enough daylight to get her bearings.

She quickly searched for the nearest internet café to the Cairo terminal and found one—CyberZone, just a five-minute walk east, located on 26th of July Street, wedged between a closed bookstore and a mobile phone repair kiosk. She dropped a digital pin. Next, she searched the walking distance from the station to the U.S. Embassy, which Google estimated at forty-two minutes on foot, crossing through Garden City—not ideal after dark. That would be tomorrow's mission.

For tonight, her priorities were clear: transit, internet and lodging. Before she could start a deeper search for hostels, the bus hissed into view—late by only a minute, but already trailing a thick plume of diesel exhaust. The white and blue Go Bus bore the signs of hard service: its paint was sun-bleached, its windows streaked with grime, and the engine wheezed with every stop. The side panel read "Air-Conditioned Luxury," but the stench of engine oil and sweat that seeped from the open doors told a different story.

A small crowd jostled forward as the doors groaned open. Claire took her place in line between a thin man in dusty slacks carrying a roll of rebar over one shoulder, and a teenage girl wearing a black hijab and cradling a guinea pig in a cracked plastic cage.

As passengers ahead of her tapped chipped plastic travel cards— likely subsidized regional passes—Claire stepped forward, uncertain. She hesitantly offered a crumpled fifty-pound note. The driver gave her a blank stare, sighed, and waved her through with an exasperated flick of his hand. *Allah help me with these foreigners*, his face seemed to say.

Inside, the bus was well-patronized. The overhead fans spun noisily, circulating warm air rather than cooling it. Worn brown vinyl seats were stained from years of use. Claire found an open spot beside an elderly woman who had already taken off her shoes, pulled a shawl over her face, and was gently snoring.

She slid in, cradling her backpack in her lap like a lifeline, and pulled out her phone again. Typing quickly, she scanned lodging options near the terminal. After scrolling past several high-end listings that were far outside her budget—not to mention dangerous in terms of visibility—she found a listing for Hostel Cairo Center, affiliated with the International Hostels Association. Four beds to a room, 120 Egyptian pounds per night, breakfast included. Decent reviews: 7.8 out of 10. Not great, but not bedbugs either.

She tried the listed phone number. No answer. She let it ring twice more before giving up. No voicemail. No booking confirmation. She would have to take her chances. No passport required—she hoped.

Checking into any high-end hotel would mean showing her papers, and those were her ticket into the U.S. Embassy, not onto a public registry. She'd go to the hostel first. If it didn't work out—she'd improvise. Maybe she'd linger at CyberZone until it closed. Maybe find a late-night street kitchen. Maybe she'd walk the neighborhoods, blend into the crowds, and—if it came to it—catch a few hours' rest in a well-lit plaza near a mosque.

She shifted her gaze to the window. The bus let out a mechanical groan and belched a thick ribbon of black smoke as it lurched forward, pulling into traffic on Al-Horreya Avenue, merging with the usual swarm of tuk-tuks, scooters, and honking taxis.

Beside her, the old woman was already deep into sleep, lips parted slightly, hands folded neatly on her lap. Claire envied her serenity. But there would be no rest for Claire Marlowe tonight. She was too wired. Too alert. Too hunted.

For now, though, she was just another face in a city of twenty million. A traveller among travellers. The perfect camouflage. Ethan would've approved.

By the time Major General Karim Nasser arrived at the Ras el-Tin Naval Base, the interrogation had already been underway for more than an hour. Nasser was old-school—born into a military family in Minya, he'd risen through the ranks of the Egyptian Army before transitioning into the intelligence wing of the Ministry of Defence. Now, he served as a senior liaison between the Egyptian Supreme Council of Antiquities and the security services, tasked with the "special oversight" of archaeological cases that involved foreign actors and national heritage. His formal title: Director of National Antiquities Security Operations, Egyptian Supreme Council of Antiquities. But among the Navy and Army personnel, he was simply the General.

He walked sedately across the base's cracked concrete yard, toward a disused ammunition bunker that sat partially buried at the edge of the compound. From a distance, the bunker looked forgotten—a crumbling Cold War relic surrounded by rusted barrels and sandbags eaten away by sun and salt. But it was still in use, repurposed for scenarios just like this one.

Inside, the room was raw and brutal. Bare concrete walls, no windows, no ventilation—just a single naked bulb that hung from a rusted chain in the ceiling, swaying faintly and casting fractured shadows across the stained floor. The air smelled of seawater, bleach, rusted metal, and the coppery tang of old blood and sweat. Mostafa hung by his wrists from a block-and-tackle rig bolted to a ceiling beam, his feet barely brushing the floor. His body glistened with sweat and streaks of blood, his face swollen and bruised. Nearby, Remi and Bilal sat shackled to rusted steel chairs bolted to the concrete, both stripped naked, both gagged, both shivering. Blood ran in streaks down their torsos, pooling on the floor.

As Nasser stepped inside, the three Navy personnel already in the room—one lieutenant and two enlisted sailors—snapped to attention. Their knuckles were raw and bloodied. One had a cut over his brow, probably inflicted by one of the detainees in a last burst of resistance. All three were breathing hard.

Nasser removed his uniform jacket and handed it wordlessly to the nearest sailor, who took it reverently and hung it on a bent coat hook beside the door. The General's face held a thin, almost bored smirk.

"I hate arriving late," he said, his tone low and sardonic. "Now I'll have to catch up."

He turned to the ranking officer—Lieutenant Saad, a lean, flinty-eyed man with blood on his gloves and no hint of remorse.

"Proceed, Lieutenant."

The officer nodded and walked directly to Bilal, raising a leather-gloved fist. Without hesitation, he drove it into the young man's face. The sound was like a melon splitting. Bilal's head snapped back violently, blood and spittle arcing through the air before his chin slumped to his chest, unconscious or near enough.

"No!" Mostafa screamed, hoarse and raw. "He doesn't know anything!"

Nasser tilted his head calmly. "And you do?"

"We know nothing!" Mostafa cried. "We were contracted by the INHA to provide equipment for soil and core sampling. That's it!"

Nasser gave a slow nod.

"Hit him again. Harder."

This time, Saad didn't hold back. He stepped in with a soldier's precision and delivered a brutal uppercut to Bilal's face. There was the unmistakable sound of cartilage snapping, followed by the wet crack of bone. Bilal collapsed forward, utterly limp, blood streaming from his nose and mouth.

"Fragile," Nasser muttered, glancing at the unconscious body.

"Let's try this one."

He motioned toward Remi, who was writhing against the restraints, muffled protests bubbling behind the bloodied gag.

Nasser approached Mostafa again.

"Tell me what they were diving on," he said coldly. "Give me the truth, and you all go free."

"They were scientists! Taking samples. Geological cores. That's all I know. They logged the dive at the Maritime Heritage Centre. Please, I beg you…"

Nasser's tone didn't change. "There is no please. Only the truth."
He flicked his wrist, and a nearby sailor retrieved a metal pry bar
from the workbench—a thick iron shaft with chipped yellow paint.
He handed it reverently to Nasser, who tested its weight like a
prizefighter with a familiar glove.

Still looking at Mostafa, he stepped to Remi's side.

Without warning, he brought the bar crashing down onto Remi's
left forearm. The bones shattered audibly. Remi howled behind the
gag, his legs kicking, his body twisting against the restraints.

"No!" Mostafa screamed. "We don't know anything! They're
scientists!"

Nasser raised the bar again.

"This is truth?" he said, calm and level.

"It's the truth, damn you!" Mostafa shouted. "They were there to
collect core samples. That was the dive plan! It's on file at the
Alexandria Maritime Centre. For God's sake—check the logs!"

But Nasser had already circled to Remi's other side.

One more blow. A sickening crunch as the right forearm broke, the
limb dangling at an unnatural angle. Remi's screams were cut short
by a choking spasm—then silence.

"Unfortunate," Nasser said. "Another one with a low threshold for
pain."

He turned to the lieutenant. "That leaves this one."

The lieutenant nodded grimly and retrieved a pair of bamboo canes
from the far wall—thin, springy, and cruel. The first strike across
Mostafa's back broke skin. The second tore muscle. Mostafa
howled in agony, his feet thrashing against the floor. Each cry
echoed off the concrete walls, muffled only by the heavy steel blast
door that sealed the chamber shut.

They worked him methodically. Cane strikes across the ribs,
shoulders, thighs. His breath came in sobs. Then he passed out.
When one of them regained consciousness, the beatings resumed—
rotating victims, rotating pain. A loop of agony engineered to
break the mind as well as the body. Over time, the intervals

between consciousness stretched thin. Moans replaced screams.
Then silence replaced moans.

The bus came to a halt with a sudden jolt, the hiss of compressed
air and the mechanical groan of brakes snapping Claire awake. Her
head jerked upright, disoriented. She was still clutching her
backpack tightly to her chest like a life raft, and a warm trail of
drool clung embarrassingly to the corner of her mouth. She wiped
it away quickly, blinking against the overhead fluorescents as
reality came rushing back.

Her fingers fumbled for her phone. 7:35 p.m. They'd arrived.
Through the fogged glass of the bus window, she saw the signage:
Cairo Gateway Bus Station, sprawling and chaotic, a concrete
monolith just off El-Torgoman Street. The station was buzzing
with motion—vendors hawking sweets and SIM cards, travellers
dragging bags or shouting into phones, exhaust fumes mixing with
the aroma of cumin and diesel.

Claire moved slowly, painfully, down the narrow aisle. Her legs
ached from four straight hours of immobility, and the adrenaline of
the morning had long since drained from her system. Emotional
fatigue hung heavy on her, sapping her usual bounce and replacing
it with a trudging resilience. Her body cried out for a toilet. Her
stomach, for food. Not necessarily in that order.

Outside, the desert heat had mellowed into a humid dusk. Claire
flicked open Google Maps, zoomed in, and tapped the pin she'd
dropped earlier in the day: Cyberzone Internet Café. A five-minute
walk, due east. Not far.

She walked with purpose—quickly, but not rushing. Remember
what Ethan said. *Stay aware, don't draw attention.* The sidewalk
was cracked and uneven, dust clinging to her shoes with each step.
A few wrong turns later, she reached July Street.

Cyberzone was, as the google street view suggested, wedged
between a closed bookstore and a mobile phone repair kiosk,
marked by a flickering blue neon sign in both Arabic and broken
English. The shopfront was glass, grime-streaked, and crowded

with posters advertising games, Wi-Fi speeds, and 'Fast net + Cold drink.' Inside, the light had a bluish cast—like being underwater in a fish tank—punctuated by the soft glow of monitors and LED fans spinning inside exposed gaming towers.

Claire stepped in. The air was a mix of fried oil, cheap cologne, and too many hours of unwashed teenage enthusiasm. There were rows of individual cubicles, partitioned with plastic dividers, most filled with hunched-over teens hammering at keyboards or yelling into headsets. A dull symphony of game soundtracks and rapid-fire Arabic chatter created an oddly comforting white noise.

To her relief, a counter near the back offered food—snacks, cold drinks, even hot sandwiches wrapped in paper and resting under a heat lamp. And even more importantly: a toilet sign hung above a narrow hallway.

Claire made her way to the restrooms quickly but deliberately. Ethan's voice echoed again in her mind: *Don't get lazy when you're tired. That's when mistakes happen.*

The toilet was…not ideal. The floor was slick, the fluorescent bulb above flickered like a horror movie, and the air smelled of bleach layered over something less sanitary. The cubicle had no seat, just a porcelain squat toilet and a broken door latch. Still, she entered, relieved herself, and kept her head down. She didn't have the luxury of squeamishness.

At the sink, she scrubbed her hands like a surgeon before a major operation, then emerged into the café once more, blinking against the harsh blue lights. Her stomach rumbled loudly.

She approached the food counter and surveyed the options: lukewarm chicken shawarma wraps, bags of chips, kebda (fried liver sandwiches), and a glass-front fridge with mango juice, sodas, and bottled water. She grabbed a shawarma wrap and a mango juice, paid in cash, and retreated to one of the empty cubicles.

The first bite was heaven—greasy, spicy, smoky. Real food, messy and hot and grounding. She practically inhaled it, finishing half the wrap before she even logged on.

She paid for two hours at the desk and booted up the ancient PC. It wheezed to life like an old man waking from a nap. She plugged in her phone and began charging it; she'd need every drop of battery to run her translator app.

First stop: local newspapers. She brought up Al-Ahram, Youm7, and Al-Masry Al-Youm, searching for anything related to arrests, foreigners, underwater archaeology, or anything at all about the events of the last twelve hours. But nothing. Not even a whisper. No mention of Samira. No Alex. No anonymous arrests. Not even a local police report.

Good and bad, Claire thought.

The good: she wasn't on any most-wanted list. The bad: she still had no idea where her friends were. She finished her wrap and drained the last of the warm mango juice.

Refocusing, she opened the International Hostels Association website and searched for Hostel Cairo Center. She found the listing, checked the phone number—it matched the one she'd tried earlier. She called again. Still no answer.

Frustrated but methodical, Claire next googled US Embassy visiting hours.

Embassy of the United States, Cairo
Consular Services: Sunday to Thursday, 8:00 a.m. to 11:00 a.m. by appointment only. Emergency walk-ins: 8:00 a.m. to 4:00 p.m.

That would have to do. She'd be there early. And with luck, maybe a cheeseburger from the cafeteria everyone on Reddit kept raving about.

She checked her phone again. 9:37 p.m. Her time was up.

Claire gathered her things and approached the counter, holding up her iPhone with the translator app open and ready. Before it even spoke, the attendant—a skinny teen with slicked-back hair and an earring—waved dismissively and said, "No need, I speak English good."

Relieved, she asked, "The hostel down the street—Hostel Cairo Center—do they take cash?"

He nodded. "Yes, most definitely. But you better hurry. They close the gates at 10!"

"Thanks," she said, and meant it. Slipping her pack over her shoulder, Claire followed the walking prompts on her phone, hurrying now. She needed a bed. A door she could lock. A hot shower if she was lucky, or at least a bucket and a faucet.

And best of all: no questions.

As she turned the corner and saw the faint neon sign for the hostel ahead, Claire allowed herself the smallest smile. *Cash only. No paper trail. No electronic breadcrumbs*. Ethan would be proud. It was close to 11pm!

The lieutenant approached Nasser, his face beaded with sweat beneath the glare of the overhead bulb.

"Major General," he said, saluting crisply. "If they had known anything, they would've said it by now. It's obvious. They don't know a damn thing."

Nasser's eyes scanned the room—the blood-slicked floor, the unconscious bodies slumped like discarded meat, the stink of urine, faeces, blood, and fear hanging heavy in the air. His nostrils flared with quiet fury. This wasn't the outcome he'd wanted.

"Dispose of them," he said coldly. "Leave no trace. Let the ocean claim them."

The lieutenant nodded once, without emotion. He turned away, walked to where his leather holster lay draped over a rusted chair, and retrieved his jacket. With slow precision, he buckled the belt around his waist, drew his Beretta, and racked the slide. The sound echoed through the bunker like a metallic finality.

Bilal was first.

He was barely conscious, head drooping, blood pooled beneath the chair. The lieutenant stepped forward, raised the pistol to Bilal's forehead, and pulled the trigger. The shot cracked like a whip.

Bilal's skull snapped back against the steel frame, and the back of his head exploded against the wall in a viscous bloom of blood and bone.

Remi followed.

There was no ceremony, no hesitation. A single round to the forehead. Clean. Efficient. The body twitched once, then stilled.

Mostafa wept incoherently, swaying from the block and tackle, suspended by torn wrists. He was barely lucid—more sobbing child than man. His body was a ruin of welts, blood, and lacerations. He didn't understand. He couldn't comprehend what was happening. The others were dead. But why was this happening, what had they done?

Nasser stood silent, arms folded, watching with a detached eye. He'd stopped asking questions. But he hadn't stopped the beatings. The punishment had become its own purpose. A ritual. A warning. An addiction.

The lieutenant approached slowly, the Beretta low at his side. Mostafa didn't even flinch. He had nothing left. No strength to resist, no mind to beg.

The lieutenant pressed the muzzle into Mostafa's left armpit, angled it slightly downward toward the heart, and squeezed the trigger twice.

The rounds punched through flesh and muscle, ricocheting through ribs and ventricles before tearing out through his back. Mostafa jerked once, mouth open in a final, soundless cry, then hung limp from the chain—dead before the second shell casing hit the floor.

Silence followed.

The only sound was the slow creak of the chain above and the faint drip of blood pooling beneath them. Nasser retrieved his coat from the hook behind the door, brushed off a speck of dust from the lapel, and slipped it on with care.

"Clean it," he said. "Burn their things. Get the bodies out before dawn."

He turned and walked out into the waiting dark, the sea air sharp with salt and secrets.

Chapter 6

The sun flickered through the barred, grimy window above the communal holding cell, casting slatted shadows across the concrete floor like a broken sundial. It was just past dawn, and the air was already heavy with the stench of disinfectant, urine, and human sweat.

Alex Carey lay curled on the hard bench, arms folded beneath his head, eyes open but unfocused. Across from him, Samira sat upright against the wall, knees drawn to her chest, her scarf bunched into a crude pillow behind her back. Neither had slept much—just enough to dull the sharpest edge of fatigue. They had endured the night with the quiet resignation of the wrongly accused. The only food had been a lukewarm bowl of lentil soup and a chunk of stale bread, which Alex had picked at reluctantly. Jail food, he thought grimly—just enough to keep you alive, not enough to care.

The guard appeared at 7:50 a.m. sharp, a thickset man with a permanently sour expression and keys that jingled like shackles in his hand. Without a word, he banged the cell door twice with his baton and gestured for them to stand.

Around them, other detainees stirred groggily. One groaned and turned over. Another remained motionless under a torn blanket. Alex rose, stiff and sore. Samira moved quickly but said nothing. There was no point in asking questions—not yet. These were not decision-makers. Junior guards, some barely older than Claire. Complaining to them would be like arguing with the walls.

They were marched through narrow corridors that reeked of mildew and despair, past rusted plumbing and ancient flaking walls, until they emerged into the sterile harshness of the processing room where they had been fingerprinted and photographed the day before. Nothing had changed. Same fluorescent buzz. Same bored faces behind the plexiglass.

But this time, waiting for them were two men in slightly different uniforms. Their badges were marked with the insignia of the Egyptian National Security Agency—Amn al-Dawla—not the Ministry of Antiquities. That was the first red flag.

Neither Alex nor Samira said a word. There was no point. They both understood what this meant, though for different reasons. Alex still clung to the faint hope that this was all some clerical error—a permit misfiled, an overstayed authorization. Something fixable. Something bureaucratic. He'd dealt with enough red tape in foreign digs to know that chaos and confusion were the default in these systems. Get to Cairo, straighten it out, go home.

But Samira's instincts told her otherwise.

Yes, mistakes happened. Paperwork vanished. Names were swapped. Dates were wrong. She had seen it all. But this—overnight detention, the level of force during the arrest, the refusal to contact the university or their embassy—this was beyond disorganization. This was intentional. And that chilled her.

Outside, they were momentarily blinded by the morning light. The sky was wide and indifferent, and the heat was already building. Two armed officers flanked them as they were led across the lot to a waiting vehicle.

It was an old Toyota Hilux, beige and battle-worn, its paint faded by the sun and its rear canopy rusted along the seams. Bulletproof glass had been hastily retrofitted to the windows, now hazy and scratched.

They were placed in the backseat, still cuffed, the doors locked from the outside. The guards took the front—one driving, the other fiddling with a walkie-talkie, their voices low but urgent.

Samira caught part of the exchange in Arabic. One word snapped her to attention: *Tora.*

Her blood ran cold.

Tora El-Mazraa.

The prison complex on the southern edge of Cairo. A fortress.
Officially, it was a high-security detention center for criminal
offenders. Unofficially, it housed political prisoners, foreign
nationals, journalists, and activists—people who were inconvenient
rather than dangerous. Tora had a reputation. Detainees vanished
there. Lawyers were denied access. Embassies were stonewalled.
Her breath caught in her throat.
"No one knows we're here," she whispered to Alex, barely audible.
Alex turned to her, concern blooming across his face. "What did
they say?"
"Tora El-Mazraa. That's where we're going."
He didn't reply. He didn't need to.
Both of them knew—this was no longer about a missing permit or
a lost signature. This was something else entirely.
And they were on their way to one of the darkest places in Egypt.

Raylan Stratten strode confidently into his office in the American
Embassy in Cairo's Garden City district—an imposing, sand-
colored structure that had weathered decades of diplomacy and
political storms. As the U.S. Ambassador to Egypt, Stratten
enjoyed one of the most strategically sensitive postings in the State
Department's portfolio. The stakes were always high here.
His secretary, Mary, was already waiting for him with a folder of
trade assessments and intelligence briefs on the latest round of
U.S.-imposed tariffs.
"Morning, sir," she greeted, handing over the bundle.
"Thanks, Mary," Stratten replied with a polite nod. "Hold all calls
for the next half hour."
She nodded and returned to her desk. He walked into his inner
office, closed the door, and lowered himself into the elegant
leather-bound chair behind his expansive mahogany desk. The
morning light filtered through the reinforced windows, and the
faint hum of embassy operations echoed in the background. He
glanced at his Rolex Submariner. Two minutes to nine.

Exactly at 9:00 a.m., Stratten picked up the secure line and dialed the direct number to the office of Dr. Nabil Rashwan, the Minister of Foreign Affairs of the Arab Republic of Egypt.

Late the previous night, intelligence flagged a short but alarming snippet of intercepted radio traffic: "French national, U.S. national, morning transfer and Tora." That was all Stratten needed. That was code enough. Tora El-Mazraa wasn't a place foreign citizens simply "ended up."

The line clicked, then a female voice answered in rapid Arabic.

هذا مكتب وزير الخارجية لجمهورية مصر العربية. كيف يمكنني تحويل مكالمتك؟

"This is the office of the Minister of Foreign Affairs of the Arab Republic of Egypt. How may I direct your call?"

Stratten understood none of it. But he wasn't concerned. The NSA team listening in from Fort Meade—and possibly from a field station in Germany—would take care of the translation.

He switched to English. "This is Ambassador Stratten. I need to speak with Dr. Rashwan immediately. It's urgent."

The voice came back, now in polished, neutral English.

"Minister Rashwan is not in at the moment. May I take a message?"

Stratten didn't flinch. He knew Rashwan was in his office. Intel had confirmed it twenty minutes ago.

"Please inform the Minister that I will remain by my phone for the next five minutes. If I haven't heard from him by then, I'll be forced to call around in person. The matter is sensitive."

"Yes, Ambassador. I'll inform him right away."

The line went dead.

Message sent, Stratten thought. And sure enough, before a minute had passed, the phone rang.

He picked it up. "Good morning, Minister Rashwan. So nice of you to ring me back."

"Of course, Ambassador Stratten. No problem at all. How may I help you?"

Rashwan was nothing if not diplomatic. A seasoned statesman in his early 60s, he had risen steadily through Egypt's foreign service with high-profile postings in Berlin, Geneva, and Washington. Educated at the American University in Cairo and later at Sciences Po in Paris, he spoke fluent Arabic, English, and French. A shrewd negotiator, Rashwan was known for his calm demeanor and sharp instincts. He understood nuance. He understood leverage.

"Minister, the U.S. diplomatic service has reason to believe that one of our esteemed and highly credentialed university professors is being detained under false pretences by Egyptian authorities."

There was a pause. "I have no knowledge of this. Do you have more details?"

Of course he didn't. Local law enforcement seldom ran things up the chain fast enough.

"According to our sources, early yesterday afternoon, a French national—Dr. Samira Rahmani—a U.S. citizen, Professor Alex Carey, and three Egyptian nationals were arrested while conducting a geological underwater survey for the United Nations, in conjunction with the INHA."

He let it hang.

"Now," he continued, "this may be a simple case of mistaken identity or missing paperwork. But I would like them released. Today."

Rashwan shifted slightly in his chair.

"Thank you for the information, Ambassador. I assure you, I've received no notification of such an incident. If you allow me some time to investigate—"

Stratten cut him off.

"These individuals are of high importance to the United States, Minister. Their health and well-being are of high importance. I think you get my meaning."

There was a beat of silence. Then Rashwan replied, voice still calm, but clipped.

"Yes, Ambassador. This may indeed be a case of misplaced paperwork or misfiled approvals. If you allow me one hour to inquire, I will revert with more news."

Stratten pressed again.

"Nabil, off the record, let me stress how valuable these two citizens are to the United States. The Senate Appropriations Bill for Egyptian aid goes before Congress next week. Now, it wouldn't reflect well if it were made public that a U.S. citizen is being detained in an Egyptian jail because of an administrative error. I mean, you would agree, $1.3 billion is a hell of a lot of goodwill."

Rashwan was fidgeting now, though he masked it well. Two academics did not warrant this level of pressure. They must be carrying something valuable. Or dangerous.

"Raylan, your message is not lost on me. Give me one hour. I will find out what I can and call you back."

"All right, Nabil. That's the least I can offer. I'll be here. Don't keep me waiting. Have a good day, Minister."

Stratten hung up.

Was the funding bill actually going to Congress next week? No. It was next month. And a single U.S. detainee wasn't likely to tank it anyway. But the Egyptians didn't know that. That, Stratten thought, was the whole point.

Apply pressure where pressure works.

Claire woke with a start, blinking at the unfamiliar ceiling. It took a moment to register where she was—Hostel Cairo Center, tucked down a side street away from the chaos of downtown. The bed was—well, generous to call it a bed. It was flat, stiff, and thin enough to feel the slats beneath, but after the previous day, it may as well have been a suite at the Ritz.

She rolled out of bed and padded toward the narrow en suite bathroom, claiming the lukewarm shower before anyone else in the hostel stirred. It wasn't hot, but it was clean, and it did the job. She towelled off, pulled on her jeans, laced up her shoes, and tugged her NAU sweatshirt over her head. The cotton was soft and familiar, like armor. In the shared kitchen, she helped herself to a cup of complimentary coffee—decaf, sadly, but beggars couldn't be choosers. The fridge offered little else: a half-used jar of tahini, a container of something green and furry, and a packet of eggs that looked as though they had been there since the Arab Spring.

Nope. Salmonella was not on the itinerary.

Claire slung her backpack over one shoulder, double-checked for her passport, laptop and wallet, and handed in her key at the front desk. The young man barely looked up from his phone, muttered something in Arabic, and waved her out with a sleepy smile.

Outside, Cairo hit her like a full-body slap. The sun was already high and bright, warming the dusty facades of buildings still waking to life. A cacophony of car horns, shouting vendors, and the low, persistent thrum of a city in motion engulfed her senses. Mopeds darted between cabs and buses belching diesel smoke. The scent of grilled meat wafted from a stall down the block, mingling with the sharper tang of exhaust and something sweet—baklava maybe? Or dates cooking in syrup?

She stepped onto the pavement, phone in hand, and opened Google Maps. The little blue pin marking the U.S. Embassy blinked patiently at her—just under a thirty-minute walk, cutting southeast through Garden City. If she was lucky, she'd find something edible on the way. If not, there was always the fallback plan: a double cheeseburger and fries from the cafeteria in the embassy's fortified walls.

Claire adjusted the straps on her bag, inhaled deep, and began walking with a purposeful stride. Her muscles were still tight from the bus ride the day before, but the sun on her back and the hum of the city gave her renewed vigor. She passed newsstands stacked with Arabic broadsheets, cigarette vendors perched on folding stools, and a woman selling fruit from a cart shaded by a fraying umbrella. A gaggle of schoolchildren weaved past her in matching uniforms, laughing and shouting, while a man herding three goats across the street forced traffic to halt with a surprising air of authority.

It was chaotic. Noisy. Dusty. And utterly alive.

Claire smiled despite herself. She was moving forward. She had a plan. And for now, she was still under the radar.

The drive to Tora was long, silent, and grim. The battered Hilux groaned with every jolt of the uneven asphalt as it left Cairo proper and cut southward, the sprawl of the city fading behind them in a dusty haze. The late afternoon sun turned the desert light amber-gold, washing the low hills and the smog-softened skyline in a surreal glow. Neither Alex nor Samira spoke. The two prison guards in the front seat said nothing either, their uniforms dusty and sweat-stained, their faces impassive.

Alex stared out the window. Sand and trash blurred together in the ditches lining the road. In the distance, he could make out the low concrete shapes of government buildings, industrial facilities, and squat apartment blocks—structures that looked like they'd been poured into place and left to decay.

Then he saw it.

Tora Prison.

It rose like a fortress out of the earth—flat-roofed blocks surrounded by endless walls of beige concrete topped with snarled coils of barbed wire. Guard towers stood at every corner, casting long shadows across the compound like the fingers of some sleeping giant. The entire complex was encircled by a double perimeter fence and, beyond that, an empty no-man's-land of gravel and watchful silence.

A heavy steel gate marked the main entrance. As they approached, a sentry emerged from a squat booth, his rifle slung low. The Hilux idled as the sentry checked the credentials of the driver. With a buzz and clank, the first gate opened. The truck crawled through, then stopped again at the second—this one thicker, armored, with reinforced hinges. Another moment of inspection, and then it too creaked open.

Samira leaned toward Alex, whispering, "It's like a Kafka novel with heatstroke."

The vehicle rolled forward again, passing slowly under the shadow of the inner wall. The sun disappeared behind the concrete, and the world grew colder in an instant.

Inside the compound, the Hilux turned off the main drive and pulled into a sun-scorched courtyard lined with rusted steel doors. A small platform jutted from the side of a building—the delivery dock. Two more guards emerged, one carrying a clipboard, the other with keys dangling from his belt.

The front passenger guard hopped down quickly and opened the door for Samira without a word. The driver did the same for Alex. Both of them stiffened as they climbed out. The air smelled like diesel, heat, and bleach. Somewhere nearby, a distant voice echoed over a tinny loudspeaker. A dog barked. Then silence again.

They were led briskly through a heavy steel door and into a narrow hallway painted the color of bone. A camera tracked them from above. No one explained anything. No one answered Alex's questions.

They passed through two more security doors—one operated by a guard with a biometric panel, the other buzzed open from a central console behind tinted glass. Every sound was amplified—the clack of boots on tile, the slam of steel against steel.

Their final destination was a corridor lined with cells—each one windowless, uniform, and heavy with the stench of sweat and stale air. A small placard near the door read in Arabic: High-Security Detainee Wing – Political Division.

"This is the deep end," Samira murmured. "Political dissidents. Enemies of the state. People who were inconvenient."

The guard opened the final door with a deep mechanical hiss—the latch was electronic, the locking mechanism embedded into the reinforced frame. Alex barely had time to look around before they were pushed through, the door slammed behind them, and the bolt clicked into place with a finality that made his stomach drop.

The cell was small, dimly lit by a flickering overhead bulb. Two metal cots, no sheets. A dented stainless-steel sink. A hole in the ground that served as a toilet. No windows. No clocks. No sounds but the hum of distant fluorescent lights and the buzz of their own nerves.

Alex turned slowly, still half-hoping this was a bureaucratic error—some mistake that would be corrected when someone checked a logbook or re-verified an ID. But every minute in that concrete box made the truth more certain: this was deliberate.

"This place isn't for holding," Alex muttered. "It's for disappearing."

Samira slumped onto one of the cots, face pale under the fluorescent glare. She looked around once, then leaned back against the wall, eyes closed for a long moment. "Holy shit, Alex," she said finally, her voice hoarse, "no one even knows where we are. This doesn't look good."

Alex stayed standing, fists clenched at his sides. "Someone will know we're missing. We haven't checked in with the Institute since Thursday evening. They know we were headed to the dive site. Something will trigger concern. They may already be looking."

Samira opened her eyes and looked at him—not doubtfully, but not quite hopefully either. "I hope you're right," she said, with more courage than she felt. "But people go missing in places like this."

Alex didn't answer. He simply sat down beside her, leaning forward, elbows on knees. The room was too small for pacing, too silent for shouting. The kind of silence that swallowed your voice. All they could do was wait—and hope that somewhere out there, someone was piecing it together.

At exactly 9:55 a.m., the phone on the outer desk rang—sharp, punctual, and unmistakable. Mary, Raylan Stretton's longtime executive assistant, picked it up before the second ring. Through the closed door of his office, he heard her voice—muffled, professional, precise.

A moment later, the intercom on his desk buzzed.

Stretton pressed the button.

"It's Minister Rashwan on the line for you, Mr. Ambassador."

"Thank you, Mary. Put him through."

He sat back in his chair, already knowing who it was. Right on time. Egyptian Minister Nabil Rashwan was never early, never late—always five minutes ahead of the clock when something unpleasant needed managing.

The line clicked, and a voice, warm but cautious, filtered through the speaker.

"Good morning, Mr. Ambassador," Rashwan began, his voice thick with formality. "I think I have located your citizens. It appears—how shall I say this—a small administrative oversight has occurred. There was a cancellation of their site access approvals, and they were detained for illegal diving on the protected UNESCO World Heritage site—"

Stretton cut him off mid-sentence. His tone was cool but firm, and completely devoid of patience.

"Where are they, Nabil?" he said flatly. Not a question. A demand.

There was a brief hesitation on the other end of the line. Paper shuffled. A throat cleared.

"They... they have been transferred to Tora Correctional Complex."

Stretton sat forward in his chair.

"Tora?" he repeated, voice rising slightly in disbelief. "Are you telling me two prominent archaeologists—foreign citizens—have been transferred to Tora because of an 'administrative error'?"

He made no attempt to hide the sarcasm, leaning hard on the final words.

Rashwan exhaled audibly. "I assure you, Mr. Ambassador, it's entirely procedural. Temporary. While we clarify the status of their revoked permits. They are not being charged with any crime—yet. The Ministry of Antiquities is involved. It's just—"

"Minister," Stretton interrupted again. He paused, letting the silence stretch just long enough to make the man on the other end squirm.

Then, calmly and with the clarity of a razor's edge, he laid out the terms.

"Here's what's going to happen, Nabil. And I suggest you write this down."

He waited half a beat.

"At exactly 4:00 p.m. this afternoon, I will arrive at the Tora Prison Complex, south gate entrance. At that time, I expect both Doctor Samira Rahmani and Professor Alexander Carey to have been notified of my arrival, and to be waiting, unharmed, in good health and in good spirits. They are to be brought to the visitation room without delay. I trust you understand me?"

"Yes, Mr. Ambassador," Rashwan replied, this time without hesitation. He sounded relieved it wasn't worse. "It will be as you wish."

"Good day to you, Mr. Rashwan."

"Good day, Mr. Ambassador."

Stretton ended the call with a firm press of the button.

He sat for a moment, the office silent around him, the faint hum of central air the only sound. He reached for his Montblanc pen, tapped it twice on the desk, then muttered under his breath.

"Holy shit…"

This wasn't a misunderstanding. It wasn't even bureaucratic sloppiness. Something deeper was moving beneath the surface— and he was just now seeing the shape of it.

He stood, straightened his jacket, and pressed the intercom again.

"Mary?"

"Yes, sir?"

"Clear my afternoon. I'm going to Tora."

It was just after 10:00 a.m. when Claire stepped out of the main street and crossed the dusty plaza, the sun already baking the city in a haze of shimmering light. She passed the garden compound surrounding the Qasr El-Dubara district—what locals called Garden City—and followed a narrow, winding alley between ochre-colored stone walls and rusting iron gates. At the far end, framed by the alley's tight aperture, stood her destination: the Embassy of the United States of America.

She paused.

The building was unmistakable. A massive concrete fortress draped in the iconography of her homeland—three-story, sand-colored walls punctuated by ballistic glass windows, the Stars and Stripes billowing from the rooftop in the warm breeze. The perimeter was lined with two layers of wrought iron fencing, both topped with coiled razor wire. Armed Marines stood motionless inside the gates, eyes hidden behind black sunglasses, their M4 carbines slung casually across their chests. Above them, security cameras tracked every movement.

Claire's breath caught in her throat. She was so close.

This was it. Sanctuary. A home base. American soil, in the middle of Cairo.

But then came the doubt.

What would she even say? That she was part of a team that had been arrested? That she'd fled detention and been wandering the city alone for almost twenty-four hours? Would they believe her? Would they take her in?

She was a citizen. She had rights. That had to mean something. Once inside, they could sort through the details—behind those fortified walls, someone would understand.

Just as she took a step off the curb to cross the street, a strong hand clamped around her torso and yanked her backward into the alleyway.

Her scream barely formed before another hand smothered her mouth. Panic surged through her chest. She kicked blindly, clawed

275

at the air, trying to twist free. Her instincts screamed fight! She elbowed hard, aimed for the face, for the eyes—anything.

"Claire!" a voice hissed, breathless but familiar.

She didn't stop.

"Claire! It's me!"

Still she thrashed—until the voice cut through the panic like a blade.

"Claire! It's Louis! Louis Delon!"

She froze.

Breathing hard, she blinked, trying to orient herself. The hand loosened, and she turned sharply. The man holding her stepped into the dim light of the alley.

It was him. Louis Delon. Disheveled, tired—but unmistakably the same quick-witted, sharp-eyed Sentinel Security protector from Leptis Magna.

"It's me, Louis," he said, finally letting her go. "Wherever you go, les Français are never far behind."

And just like that, the tension collapsed. Claire threw her arms around his neck, burying her face against his shoulder, her entire body shaking. The sobs came without warning—raw, uncontrollable.

From abduction to preservation.

Louis held her firmly. "You're safe now, Claire. You're alright. Just breathe, okay? Breathe with me. One. Two. Slow."

She nodded into his shirt, forcing herself to inhale deeply, then again. Ethan would have told her to get control. She wiped at her eyes with the back of her wrist.

"What... what are you doing here?"

"I'm here to find you," he said, simply.

"You... you were sent?"

Louis nodded. "André Molineux, Director-General at INHA. He asked me to come find you."

"Me?" she said, stunned. "I thought—I thought I was on my own."

"Not when it comes to the Institute," he said with a touch of pride. "We are French, and we take care of our own. And you, mademoiselle, are family."

She blinked again, this time with a shaky laugh. "Holy shit."

"Exactly."

Claire looked toward the embassy. "I almost made it to home base," she said, motioning with her chin. "I was ten seconds from the gate."

"Let me show you something," Louis said, and took her hand. They moved quietly up the alley until they reached the edge of the street that faced the embassy's main entrance—Kasr El Aini Street. Louis gestured discreetly.

"See that blue van, parked next to the yellow kiosk?"

She nodded.

"And the white sedan with tinted windows further down the street?"

"Yeah," she said. "They don't look like much."

"They've been there since six this morning," Louis said. "And they weren't parked to enjoy the view."

Her eyes widened.

"They were waiting for me?"

"They were. And they'd have taken you before your foot hit the first step of that embassy gate."

"But... the Marines—" she began.

"Can't intervene outside the perimeter," Louis said. "Only inside those gates is American soil. Outside? It's Cairo. You could've been dragged away right in front of the flagpole and all they could do is shout and radio for backup."

Claire stared at the embassy for a long moment. Then she whispered, "Oh my God... I could've been kidnapped."

"You were lucky," Louis said. "So was I. You nearly walked into a trap."

She turned to him. "How long have you been waiting for me?"

"Give or take... fourteen hours."

Her mouth dropped open. "Here? Outside the embassy? All night?"

"Oui, mademoiselle," he said, smiling faintly. "Waiting for mon chérie Claire."

She laughed again, overwhelmed by the absurdity and tenderness of it all.

After a moment, she asked the next obvious question.

"If I can't go to the U.S. Embassy… then where can we go?"

Louis grinned. "That's easy. The French Embassy. It's ten minutes' walk from here."

Claire nodded, bracing herself. "Fucking-A," she muttered. "Lead on."

And together, they slipped away from the embassy gates, back into the maze of alleys—two fugitives under the Cairo sun, heading toward a sliver of hope.

Chapter 7

The phone call between Ambassador and Minister had detonated like a small explosion in the corridors of power. Within minutes, a cascade of encrypted communications began to surge through secure lines, diplomatic channels, and military conduits.

Minister Rashwan stood stiffly in his office, sweat slick on his brow despite the heavy air conditioning. He had used the secure line to the Heliopolis Presidential Palace, The President of Egypt, seated beneath an immense oil painting of Nasser crossing the Suez, gripped the receiver in one hand and motioned for silence with the other. His eyes burned as Rashwan summarized the conversation with Ambassador Stretton, word for word.

When Rashwan finished, the President exploded.

"If this endangers the $1.3 billion in military aid and support the Americans give us every year, then it will be your head, Rashwan! Do you understand me? If this causes even a week's delay—your head! Deal with it." He slammed the receiver down and cursed the name of the Foreign Affairs Minister.

Rashwan didn't wait for a second rebuke. He pulled his cell phone from his jacket and dialled the Director of the Egyptian Supreme Council of Antiquities.

The line clicked. "Khoury."

"Dr. Khoury. This is Minster Rashwan. Listen very carefully."

There was a pause. A rustle of papers. "Go on."

Rashwan's voice dropped to a flat, controlled growl. "The American Ambassador has invoked a diplomatic clause. He is arriving at Tora Prison at exactly four o'clock today. You are to

ensure that the detained archaeologists are present in the visitors'
centre, unharmed, and ready for immediate release. No bruises, no
blood, no missing fingernails. Are we clear?"

"Ambassador, I—"

"No interruptions. If this causes an incident, the President will
have your career—and mine. I won't shield you, Khoury. Make it
happen."

Khoury's voice was tight, reluctant. "Understood. It will be as
you've instructed."

Rashwan hung up.

Dr. Samy Khoury—a grubby little man with nicotine-stained
fingers and a fondness for vintage pornography—sat alone in his
office, staring at the silent phone for a long beat. Then he opened a
secure drawer in his desk and pulled out a burner phone. He dialled
a number from memory.

The voice on the other end answered instantly. Crisp. Cold.
"Report."

Khoury cleared his throat. "The Americans are coming for the
prisoners. We have until 1600 hours. No time for extraction, no
time for leverage. The President himself has intervened."

The reply was immediate and ice-calm. "Interrogate them before
they're released. No physical violence. Use whatever
psychological means you must—threaten, intimidate, bluff, break
them down. I want to know what they were diving for, what they
found. Locations. Data."

Khoury scribbled notes furiously.

"And double your efforts to find the third operative. If this is the
same team from Leptis Magna, then the missing agent is likely the
American student—the girl. Find her. Tail her. Relieve her of any
intelligence she carries."

"Yes, sir."

The line went dead.

Khoury sat back in his chair and immediately placed another call, this time to Major General Karim Nasser, Director of National Antiquities Security Operations.

"Karim. It's Khoury. You need to get to Tora now. Interrogate the two prisoners—no physical force, understood? But you may use any other means necessary. Psychological pressure. Threats. Coercion. Just get something out of them. You have until four p.m."

"Understood," Nasser replied. No questions. Just the rustle of gear being packed.

Khoury disconnected and leaned back in his leather chair, his fingers drumming an anxious rhythm on the armrest.

This had all been so carefully orchestrated. Timelines. Intercepts. Surveillance windows. And now, thanks to one goddamn phone call, the entire operation was teetering on the edge of exposure.

The Client would not be pleased.

And Khoury knew all too well what happened to those who disappointed him.

The moment Louis spotted the two men loitering outside the American Embassy in their vehicles—arms folded, eyes restless, postures just a little too rehearsed—his instincts kicked in like muscle memory. They weren't tourists. They weren't bored civil servants. They were watchers. Predators. And they were waiting for someone.

Claire.

He'd intercepted her just in time, now he was drawing her away with a quiet word and a firm grip on her arm, slipping into the artery of Cairo's midday chaos. Deliberately, they wove a serpentine path through the city's dense urban sprawl—cutting through shaded alleys, looping around mosques, ducking into convenience stores and rejoining traffic at unpredictable angles. At every intersection, Louis checked for shadows. When the tension in his neck finally eased, they emerged onto Rue al-Ahram, directly opposite the French Embassy's eastern gate.

A white stucco wall ringed the compound like a citadel. A pair of French gendarmes stood under a canvas awning beside a motorized gate, rifles slung and gaze alert.

Louis pulled out his slim black Nokia and dialled a number from memory. It rang twice.

"André Molineux."

Louis spoke without hesitation. "Director, it's Louis. I have the girl."

He could hear the relief in Molineux's silence, though the man's voice remained dry and practiced.

"Any complications?"

"Almost. I intercepted Claire just before she reached the U.S. Embassy. They were waiting for her." Louis looked sidelong at Claire and winked. She gave him a tight smile, her nerves flickering beneath her eyes.

"Where are you now?"

"Across the street from the French Embassy. East gate."

There was a pause. "Stay put. I'll call you back in thirty seconds." The line went dead.

Louis turned to Claire. "That was the Director. He'll make a call. We should be able to walk in without trouble."

Claire nodded, but he could see the tremor in her hands. Her world had spiralled too fast for her to find footing. She wasn't in control anymore—and she knew it.

A minute later, the phone vibrated in his hand.

"Delon."

"Louis, I spoke to the Attaché. They're expecting you. The guards have orders. Walk straight in. Just you and the girl."

"Oui, mon ami. We're on our way."

He pocketed the phone and turned to Claire with a smile that barely masked his unease. "Are you ready, ma chérie Claire?"

She nodded. "Not really."

"Good. Neither am I."

Louis peeked out from the shadows of the building, scanning Rue al-Ahram up and down. No time for proper threat assessment. No time to read the angles or pick out who didn't belong. They had to move.

He took Claire's hand.

"Let's go."

They stepped into the street, waiting for a gap in the surge of honking cars and weaving scooters. Cairo traffic was its own beast—chaotic but oddly rhythmic, a tide of noise and dust. They moved briskly, trying not to run, but still moving with purpose. Invisible, but not suspicious. Swift, but not hurried.

Halfway across the road, a low growl echoed behind them.

An engine revved.

Tires shrieked against asphalt.

"Keep going," Louis said—half to Claire, half to himself.

Ten meters.

The embassy gate groaned as it began to slide open.

The car was gaining—fast. It careened down the road, horn blaring, pedestrians scattering.

Five meters.

The gate was halfway open.

"Run!" Louis snapped, and they bolted.

The embassy guards spotted them and the approaching vehicle in the same heartbeat. Both raised their FAMAS G2 bullpup rifles—standard issue for French diplomatic security—and took defensive stances just inside the threshold.

Claire and Louis burst through the half-open gate a second before the car skidded to a halt, tires screaming, just meters from the entrance.

Two men leapt from the vehicle. Unshaven, middle-aged, both in faded jeans and stretched-out T-shirts—plainclothes muscle, hired help.

The guards didn't hesitate. Weapons raised. Eyes locked. One barked in French, "Pas un pas de plus!"

The assailants froze.

The gate reversed and finished its slow, deliberate glide shut with a final clunk of reinforced steel.

Louis turned to get a good look at them. The men stared back with barely concealed rage.

He offered them a wide grin and—true to French tradition—placed his hand under his chin and flicked it outward in a sharp gesture. La barbe. A Gallic insult as old as Molière. *Screw you.*

Then he turned, caught up to Claire, and walked alongside her up the crushed-stone driveway.

The French Embassy loomed ahead—an elegant, early 20th-century villa in cream-colored limestone, shaded by jacaranda trees. It was unmistakably colonial: high-arched windows with wrought iron balconies, blue-shuttered façade, and a tricolor fluttering crisply above the portico. The main building rose three stories, flanked by manicured gardens and a courtyard with a central fountain.

As they approached the main entrance, Louis overheard one of the guards at the gate behind them spit on the pavement and muttered in clipped French:

"Dégagez, connards."

Fuck off, assholes.

Claire exhaled for the first time in minutes.

They had made it.

French soil.

Protected.

Safe—for now.

Inside, the shaded drive to the main building of the French Embassy in Cairo stretched out like a calm boulevard—a world away from the chaos and tension of the city just metres beyond the walls.

Two armed guards in dark blue GIGN uniforms approached immediately. One, a tall man with a trim beard, addressed Louis in crisp, Parisian French.

"Identité, monsieur."

Louis reached into his inner jacket pocket and produced both his INHA credentials and his diplomatic passport. Claire did the same, handing over her American passport and laminated INHA ID card. The guard studied them both for a moment, nodded silently, and passed them to a second officer who vanished into a small booth. A third security officer appeared, gesturing politely but firmly for Louis to remove his jacket and surrender his sidearm.

Louis gave a small Gallic shrug and carefully pulled out his compact Glock 17, ejecting the magazine and clearing the chamber with professional precision. He handed it over grip-first.

"Règlement est règlement," he muttered with a wry grin.

The guard patted him down with a brisk but respectful thoroughness, then gave a nod of approval.

A moment later, a door opened from the main building and a tall, silver-haired man in a tailored charcoal suit descended the short stairs with quick, practiced steps. His face was patrician, his eyes intelligent and alert behind frameless glasses. He smiled warmly as he extended his hand.

"Bienvenue. I am Étienne Moreau, Deputy Attaché and Chargé d'Affaires," he said, first to Louis, then turning to Claire with a courteous nod. "Mademoiselle, welcome to the French Embassy. We were informed of your imminent arrival by Director Molineux personally." His English was almost flawless.

Claire straightened. "Do you know him? Molineux?"

Before Moreau could answer, Louis interjected, flashing a grin.

"Bien sûr. We are all ex-COS. Nous sommes tous des frères."

Claire raised an eyebrow. "What's COS?"

"Commandement des Opérations Spéciales," Moreau said with a half-smile. "Our version of your JSOC, I believe."

Before Claire could respond, Moreau gave her a more sympathetic look.

"You must be hungry. May I offer you something to eat or drink?"

She nodded immediately, with a sheepish laugh. "Famished. I haven't had anything since last night."

"Then let's remedy that." Moreau gestured for them to follow.

They entered the main building—a stunning, early 20th-century French colonial villa with tiled floors, high ceilings, and antique brass chandeliers that cast a warm, amber light across the polished marble. The halls were quiet, the kind of quiet that comes from layers of diplomacy and protocol.

He led them through a pair of heavy wooden doors into the embassy cafeteria. To Claire's surprise, it was bright, modern, and unmistakably French. Rows of glass cases held fresh baguettes, croissants, chèvre salads, quiches, and rows of delicate pastries. A barista worked a gleaming espresso machine behind a marble counter, and a chalkboard in fluent French listed the day's specials: Boeuf bourguignon, soupe à l'oignon, tarte fine aux pommes.

Louis and Claire grabbed trays and ordered without hesitation. Louis piled his with food: a steaming bowl of bouillabaisse, a fresh baguette with pâté, and a large croque monsieur dripping with béchamel. Claire ordered more modestly: an omelette aux fines herbes, a small salade niçoise, and a slice of apricot tart. They both took tall glasses of water and Louis added a double espresso to his tray.

Moreau, ever the diplomat, settled for a black coffee and nothing more.

As they sat down, Moreau sipped his coffee and checked his watch. "Molineux has recalled the Falcon jet. He should be wheels down in Cairo around 18:00. There will be a full briefing this evening, just before his arrival. You are expected to attend."

Claire nodded, swallowing a bite of her omelette. "Any news about Alex? Or Samira?"

Moreau's expression darkened slightly. "I'm afraid we've heard nothing official. But Molineux is... resourceful. If anyone can extract them, it's him."

He placed two white keycards on the table. "These are for your rooms. Second floor. They're guest quarters, modest but private. You're free to rest, shower, or explore the compound. There's a small library, a secure internet suite, and even a garden if you need some air."

He stood. "I'll leave you to eat in peace. You'll be collected at seventeen forty-five sharp."

Moreau offered a slight bow, then turned and exited with the grace of a man used to moving between worlds.

The moment the door swung closed behind him, Claire slumped slightly in her chair, let out a long breath, and looked at Louis.

"Thank you," she said softly. "For saving my life. Again."

Louis smiled and raised a forkful of bouillabaisse. "C'est une habitude," he said with a wink. "It's becoming a habit."

Claire laughed—genuinely, for the first time in days.

Louis leaned back, savouring his food. For a fleeting moment, the world outside the embassy walls felt distant, and the war they were all caught up in faded into the background.

Alex and Samira had been in the cell for hours. Long, silent, and suffocating hours. Time had ceased to move in any meaningful way. The silence was absolute, the concrete airless. There was no sound—no footsteps in the corridor, no mechanical hums, not even the creak of plumbing. Just stillness. It felt like sensory deprivation.

"They could've put us in a vacuum," Alex muttered at one point, his voice a whisper against the concrete. "Might've been more humane."

Samira didn't reply. She had lain down on the metal bunk and stared at the ceiling for so long that the uneven patches in the plaster began to form shapes. She had seen desert gods and lions and birds that couldn't fly. And once, for a moment, a mountain she had never climbed. She had closed her eyes then.

It was just past midday when the silence shattered.

The bolt on the door clanged open with a grinding scrape, loud enough to make Alex wince. In the stillness of the high-security wing, it sounded like a scream.

The heavy steel door swung inward.

A single uniformed guard stood there, face unreadable. He gave no greeting, no orders. Just a single, silent motion with his hand—up.

Alex rose slowly from where he had been sitting cross-legged on the floor. Samira pushed herself upright and stepped forward, legs stiff, face calm. Neither of them spoke. They didn't need to.

The guard checked the handcuffs securing their wrists—still locked—and then turned, gesturing for them to follow.

Maybe food, Alex thought. A shower, Samira hoped—unless it was the kind with a firehose. Then they could keep it.

The corridor outside was just as sterile, just as soundless. They were marched in silence past blank concrete walls, through a security door, and into a secondary hallway where the light was harsher and the floors more polished. On the right-hand wall were a series of unmarked doors—each sealed, each identical.

Except for the placards.

Arabic script above each door. Alex squinted. Nonsense to him. But Samira, even in this moment, couldn't help herself. She read aloud:

غرفة الاستجواب ١

"Interrogation Room One," she translated, dryly. "Looks like someone's ready to talk."

"Swell," Alex muttered. "Let's hope they actually listen and figure out this is just one big, idiotic mistake."

The guard didn't react.

They were ushered through the door into a sparse interrogation room—bare walls, no windows, metal table bolted to the floor. Two steel chairs. One overhead light.

The guard motioned them forward. They sat.

A thick chain was pulled through the handcuff links at their wrists and looped around a metal ring embedded in the centre of the table. The guard secured it with a rusting padlock. The final click echoed like a verdict.

Then he left, the door sealing shut behind him with another groan of metal.

Alex looked at Samira.

"Comfortable?" he asked, with forced lightness.

She smiled faintly. "It's got that East Berlin charm."

He laughed softly. "All that's missing is a bare light bulb and a guy with a rubber hose."

"Give it time," she said. Then her expression shifted. "Alex… whatever happens, don't let them separate us. Promise me."

He nodded. "I won't."

And then they waited.

They sat and waited.

There was no clock in the room—part of the torture, Alex thought. No sense of time, no rhythm to anchor the nerves. Just silence, humming fluorescent lights, and tension thick enough to cut.

Five minutes passed. Or ten. Who could tell?

Then the door swung open with a metallic creak.

A man stepped through, shrugging off a crisp military jacket and handing it wordlessly to the guard behind him. The door closed with a dull thud.

"My name is Major General Karim Nasser," he began, his English clipped but confident. "I'm here to facilitate your release."

He paused—barely—and continued.

"But first, a few simple questions."

Sensible, Alex thought.

Disarming, Samira thought.

Nasser approached the table with a predator's ease. "You were caught diving in a UNESCO World Heritage site," he said. "No permits. No authorization. Why were you stealing artifacts for the black market?"

"We weren't stealing anything," Samira replied quickly, voice sharp. "We were taking core samples from the harbor floor—"

"Without permits," Nasser interrupted coldly. "Which makes your entire operation illegal." He let the words hang, then leaned in slightly. "Most illegal dives we intercept are looting antiquities. So—what were you after?"

"I told you, we had—"

"Had?" he cut in, arching an eyebrow.

"Have. We have the permits. Everything's in place. We're not looters, we're archaeologists."

"In my experience," Nasser said, casually inspecting his nails, "there's a very fine line between archaeologists and looters."

Alex's eyes narrowed. "Then you should know," he said calmly, "your own Minister of Antiquities has been accused multiple times of selling relics to the black market."

Nasser looked up slowly. "Ah. The American speaks," he said, voice dripping with derision. "And here I thought you'd hide behind a woman forever."

He took a step closer.

"Let me be clear. Black market trafficking of antiquities is a capital offense in Egypt. Life in prison... if you're lucky. Death, if you're not. Even your U.S. Ambassador can't save you."

Samira slammed a palm against the table. "We weren't stealing anything! We have permits. You saw the equipment on the boat!"

Nasser gave a mirthless chuckle. "Ah yes, the boat." He gestured vaguely in the air. "Strange... because when we boarded it, there was no coring equipment. And the crew? Known smugglers, both of them. Guilt by association... wouldn't you say?"

Samira's breath caught. Her eyes burned with fury. But Alex remained calm, his expression unreadable.

Nasser leaned forward again, his voice low and gravelly. "Tell me,
Dr. Carey. What were you diving for? What were you planning to
steal?"
Samira snapped. "We weren't stealing anything, we—"
Alex reached out and grabbed her wrist gently but firmly. She
stopped mid-sentence, still seething, and sank back in her chair.
Nasser smiled faintly, then switched tactics.
"We have the girl, you know. The young student. She's being
detained as well."
He glanced at his watch with studied disinterest. "In fact, she's
likely being interrogated right now."
Samira's chair scraped against the floor as she stood.
"She's just a girl. She knows nothing! Leave her out of this!"
"Nothing, something... or everything. Tell me what you were
diving for," Nasser said, his voice tightening, "and I'll let her go."
Alex beat Samira to the reply.
"She's a French geology student. She wasn't even on the dive
team. Let her go."
Nasser shrugged. "Student or not, she must have seen or heard
something. You want her released?" He paused, his eyes fixed on
Alex. "Tell me what you were really diving for. All of you go
free."
He emphasized the last words like an offer from the devil.
But Alex's face didn't move.
Instead, he leaned back in his chair.
"How long did they give you?"
Nasser blinked. "What are you talking about?"
Alex noticed the micro-expression—left eye twitch, jaw tightening.
A flash of something he wasn't supposed to show.
"How many days until they pull you out? Or was it hours?"
"I don't know what you're implying," Nasser said, voice
hardening.
"We'd like to return to our cell," Alex said calmly.
Samira turned to him, bewildered. "Alex...?"

"I think we're done here."

Nasser slammed his hands on the table, rising in a flash. "I decide when we're done!"

Alex stared at him, unflinching. "No," he said. "You already told me."

Nasser's face twisted with rage. In one sudden move, he lunged across the table and grabbed Alex by the throat.

"Alex!" Samira screamed.

But Alex didn't resist. He just smiled—tight-lipped, eyes steady—even as Nasser's grip tightened.

Then, just as suddenly, Nasser let go, shoving him back in disgust. He stormed to the door, snatched his jacket from the guard, and barked in Arabic.

"Take them back. No food."

The guard unshackled them and marched them wordlessly down the dim corridor, the sound of boots on tile echoing like a metronome of dread.

Once back in the cell, the door clanged shut. Silence again.

Samira turned to Alex, breathless. "What the hell was that about?"

Alex sat down on the edge of the cot.

"He slipped," he said. "Twice."

Samira frowned.

"He mentioned the U.S. Ambassador. That means they know exactly where we are—and that someone from our side is involved. But more importantly, he said they have Claire."

Samira was still confused. "So?"

"They don't," Alex said simply. "If they did, they'd have brought her in. Used her to break us. And Claire? She'd never pass as a French geology student the second she opened her mouth."

Samira's eyes widened. "So they were bluffing."

"They're stalling. Playing for time. That means our people are close. Close enough to make Nasser nervous."

She looked up at him, her voice quiet but sure.

"We just have to hold on a little longer."

Alex nodded, swallowing painfully. "Yeah. We wait. And we don't give them a damn thing."

At exactly 3:45 PM, the heavy steel door to the holding cell scraped open. The same disinterested guard from before entered, eyes blank as ever, baton swinging gently at his hip. He checked the handcuffs on Alex and Samira with mechanical precision, then wordlessly motioned for them to follow.

They rose, stiff from the bench and the stale air, and were led out into the now-familiar corridor—gleaming under harsh overhead lights, echoing with their footsteps. But instead of turning right toward the interrogation wing, they were directed left, into the administrative section of the prison.

"At least it's not another session," Alex muttered dryly.

The guard shot him a glare. "La takallam." No talking!

They passed through several turns and narrow halls before emerging into the visitor processing area—the same place they'd first entered. There, they were instructed to sit on a steel bench bolted to the wall. A second guard approached, removed their cuffs, and returned their personal effects in sealed plastic bags: phones, INHA identification cards, wallets—everything intact. Alex allowed himself the faintest grin. They'd been found. Help was at hand. Samira met Alex's gaze but said nothing. She was coiled tight—relief, anger, and caution warred beneath her otherwise calm exterior. Alex caught the signs: the rapid blinking, the clenched fists, the restless tapping of her foot against the tiled floor.

But Samira said nothing, her posture upright, her expression unreadable. But her fingers trembled slightly as she fished out her phone from the bag and then paused—almost reverently—before tucking it away. They didn't speak. They didn't need to.

At precisely 4pm, the black Chevy Suburban with tinted, bulletproof windows eased through the outer prison gates right on time. There was no escort vehicle, no diplomatic fanfare, just the

whisper-quiet arrival of a machine built for discretion and
protection.

Inside sat two armed men in the front: U.S. Secret Service, dressed
in standard-issue black suits, white shirts, and dark ties. In the
second row was Raylan Stretton, the U.S. Ambassador to Egypt,
jaw set, eyes fixed on the administrative building ahead. He had
already spent every ounce of political capital he could marshal—
calls to Washington, late-night communiqués with Cairo's foreign
ministry, and finally, a direct line to the President himself. This
was the result.

He didn't plan to exit the vehicle. Standard SOP. The scene was
still technically unsecured. The Suburban's GPS and telemetry
were being monitored in real time—both at the U.S. Embassy and
at NSA's remote command node in Wiesbaden, Germany. If
anything went wrong, a distress button was located just beside his
thigh. He didn't expect to need it.

One agent stepped out of the SUV and approached the main glass
doors, while the second remained just outside, eyes scanning, alert.
Inside, Alex and Samira looked up at the sound of the door
opening.

The agent strode in, passing through the mesh security gate with a
buzz and nod from the prison guards. He moved with calm
efficiency, eyes sweeping the room until they locked onto the two
figures seated against the far wall. They were uncuffed, dressed in
the same clothes they'd worn on arrival, and clearly exhausted.

He pressed his cuff mic. "I have eyes on the package."

As he approached, both Alex and Samira instinctively stood, but
the agent held up a hand, palms facing out.

"Dr. Samira Rahmani? Professor Alex Carey?"

"Yes," they answered in unison.

"Identification, please."

Samira fished out her INHA card and handed it over, followed by
Alex. The agent examined both IDs carefully, then pulled out a
phone and compared the photographs on file to the faces before

him. It was an extra layer of verification—one that couldn't be faked by a simple card.

He nodded once, sharply. "Confirmed," he murmured into the mic. "Package secure."

Then, to them: "Follow me."

The security gate buzzed open, then the glass doors. The second agent stepped aside to hold it open for them. As they emerged into the late afternoon light, the golden hue of the Cairo sun bathed them in warmth. Alex squinted upward, breathing deep for the first time in what felt like days. The open air, the scent of hot dust and traffic, the simple sky—he had never appreciated it more.

Samira stopped just outside the doors, blinking into the light. Her face lifted, eyes closed for a heartbeat. Then she exhaled, the tension leaving her shoulders in a visible wave.

And there it was. The black Chevy Suburban. Gleaming. Waiting. Alex almost laughed. "I never thought I'd be so happy to see a Chevy in my life."

The lead agent opened the back passenger door and gestured. "Get in, please."

They climbed in. The interior was cool, quiet, cocooned in leather and reinforced steel. The door closed with a solid thunk.

"Raylan Stretton," said the Ambassador, extending a hand across the console. "U.S. Ambassador to Egypt."

"We're… very glad to see you, sir," Alex replied, shaking it firmly.

Samira offered a quiet "Thank you," her voice catching slightly. The Suburban pulled away from the prison compound and turned onto the road that led back toward central Cairo.

Stretton leaned back slightly. "I want you to know that this will not be swept under the rug. There will be a full investigation into your detainment—conducted through diplomatic and legal channels. I'll oversee it personally. There is a 6pm meeting this evening to get a download on the events that have transpired."

He paused. "Right now, we're en-route to the U.S. Embassy. You'll have private quarters, showers, clothing, and time to rest. Secret Service agents have already gone to your hotel to retrieve your things."

Alex nodded, absorbing it all—but his thoughts were already elsewhere.

"Claire?" he asked, voice taut with emotion.

Stretton smiled faintly. "Safe. She's at the French Embassy under full protection. Quite the resourceful young lady, from what I hear."

Samira let out a quiet chuckle, the first sound of warmth in days. "Yes. She really is."

"I need to contact my Director, Mr. Ambassador," Samira said after a pause. "Let them know we're safe."

"Of course." Stretton reached into his jacket and handed her his personal cell. Andre Molineux's number was already up on the screen.

She blinked in surprise, then pressed Call.

It rang once. Twice.

"André Molineux."

"André—it's Samira." She was holding back tears now. "We're safe. We're with the American Ambassador."

"Dieu merci," came the immediate reply. "Are either of you hurt?"

"No. We're fine. Heading to the U.S. Embassy now."

"Good. I'll see you at the 6 PM joint briefing. You're safe now, Samira. Everything will be all right."

She ended the call, handed back the phone, and whispered, "Thank you."

"How far to the Embassy?" Alex asked, voice calm but hollowed by exhaustion.

"Fifteen minutes, give or take," said Stretton.

"Good," Alex exhaled. "I could use a cheeseburger. And an espresso. Please tell me you have espresso."

Stretton chuckled. "Plenty. You'll be well taken care of."

As the Suburban sped through the Cairo traffic, cradled in armoured steel and American bravado, the two passengers leaned back—safe, for now. The city flashed past, the Nile glittered in the distance, and for the first time in what felt like forever, they let themselves breathe.

Chapter 8

The 6.00pm meeting was a two-part affair.

In the small, modern conference room of the U.S. Embassy, Alex, Samira, and Ambassador Raylan Stretton sat around a sleek, oval table of matte-finished walnut. The space was compact but cutting-edge: recessed LED lighting, a wall-mounted 85-inch video display, and high-spec AV equipment built discreetly into the walls. Six high-backed leather chairs flanked the table, and a discreet camera in the ceiling tracked automatically as participants spoke.

Several kilometres away, inside the French Embassy, Louis Delon, Claire, André Molineux, and French Ambassador Étienne Moreau gathered in a near-identical room—an architectural twin to the American version. The French had made their own touches: a vase of fresh camellias on a sideboard, and dark navy upholstery instead of black. But like its counterpart, it was fully AV-equipped, and at precisely 6:00 PM, the screen on both sides chimed and burst to life.

Secure satellite communication kicked in instantly, the feed encrypted and crystal clear, with only microsecond delays between transmissions. Ambassador Stretton's image filled the screen in the French room. The four there stopped what they were doing and took their seats.

"Good evening, Ambassador," Stretton began. "Thank you for arranging this meeting. Just for clarity, this is a secure, encrypted microwave feed—point-to-point between our embassies. It's not routed through the NSA or the DGSE."

"Understood," said Moreau, gesturing open-palmed. "You have the floor."

Stretton tapped a key on his laptop, and the screen split into a full-room view of both conference rooms. Everyone could now see everyone. Claire, spotting Alex and Samira on the screen, rose instantly.

"Professor! Samira!" she exclaimed, voice cracking. "Oh my God, I'm so glad to see you two are okay!"

Samira and Alex both leaned forward instinctively, smiling with genuine warmth.

"We'll see you tomorrow, Claire," Samira said. "Ambassador Stretton's arranged for us to be transferred to the French Embassy under secure escort. I can't wait to see you in person and hear everything."

With the emotional reunification behind them, Stretton brought the meeting to order.

"Firstly and formally," he said, "I'd like to thank Ambassador Moreau and the French Republic for offering sanctuary to an American citizen in a moment of need. And André, thank you for allowing our continued involvement in what is clearly a much broader and more dangerous situation than we initially believed."

"The sentiment is reciprocated," Moreau said, nodding toward Samira.

Stretton continued. "Let's begin with the apparent accusations levelled at Professor Carey and Dr. Rahmani. We've been in touch with the UNESCO Permits Division. According to their records, the authorization to dive at the site off Alexandria—a designated World Heritage zone—was rescinded."

"Rescinded?" André Molineux interjected. "By whom?"

"The cancellation was, allegedly, submitted by the INHA," said Stretton, "and signed off under the name of Dr. Rahmani."

Samira turned sharply in her chair. "I never cancelled any permits," she said, voice firm.

"Impossible," said Molineux, turning to address Stretton directly. "I reviewed those permits myself before they were issued. They were approved for a seven-day period starting yesterday. There's no way Samira would have cancelled them—accidentally or otherwise."

"Agreed," said Alex.

Stretton raised a calming hand. "Look—I'm just telling you what came back from the Permits Division. But crucially, they couldn't produce any documentation—nothing from the INHA, and certainly nothing signed by Dr. Rahmani. No emails. No memos. Nothing."

"This is no clerical error. Are you implying the UNESCO Permits Division is compromised?" Moreau asked, leaning forward.

"Not UNESCO as a whole," Stretton said carefully, "but I believe there's a rogue element in the permitting chain. And I'll tell you why in a moment. Let's talk first about the Egyptian response." He took a breath.

"Under normal circumstances, unauthorized archaeological work at a World Heritage site results in impoundment of equipment, perhaps a local arrest, and usually a fine. At worst, a temporary ban from future work. But incarceration in a maximum-security prison? That's extraordinary."

"You better believe it," muttered Samira.

"That level of overreaction suggests to me that elements within the Egyptian Ministry of Tourism and Antiquities—or possibly the Supreme Council of Antiquities—are compromised as well."

"Surprise, surprise," Claire said dryly. Samira and Alex both smirked at the remark.

"How high up are we talking?" Étienne Moreau asked.

"To mobilize Tora Prison, the Egyptian Coast Guard, and the National Security Agency?" Stretton replied. "This has to be at the Director level at minimum."

"I agree," Étienne said without hesitation.

"So," Alex said, "the Coast Guard's actions were legitimate, technically? Intercepting an illegal dive?"

"The interception—yes," Stretton allowed. "The level of force, absolutely not."

"They held a gun to our boat driver's head!" Samira snapped.

"I'm not justifying it," said Stretton. "The Coast Guard reports to the Maritime Antiquities Department. We don't know what orders they were given. But from what we've gathered, the commandant on duty exceeded protocol."

He turned to his notes.

"You mentioned the dive boat operator," he said to Samira. "We followed up. Secret Service visited their business premises—place was locked up tight. No sign of anyone."

"This Nasser guy," Alex said, "the one who interrogated us—he claimed they were looters. Smugglers."

"There's zero evidence to support that," Stretton said. "Their dive business has been operating for twelve years. They've supported multiple legitimate archaeological teams off Alexandria. No police record, no red flags with Interpol. As far as we can tell—they're clean."

"But missing?" asked Delon.

"Yes," said Stretton. "Possibly in hiding. Possibly…"

"Dead," Delon said flatly.

Samira leaned forward. "Who is Nasser, exactly?"

A photograph flickered to life on the split screen—Karim Nasser in full military regalia, standing stiff-backed on a dais during the Revolution Day parade. The bright regalia of the Egyptian flag fluttered behind him. To his right, unmistakable in his tailored navy uniform and Ray-Bans, stood President Abdel Fattah el-Sisi. Nasser's eyes were fixed forward, unsmiling, the polished metal of his service medals catching the sun.

Stretton spoke, voice low and clipped.

"Nasser came to prominence in 2013, during the civil uprising that swept el-Sisi to power. Back then, he was still a captain in the

Republican Guard Armoured Division—" he paused and glanced at the screen, "—it was Nasser who personally led the arrest of Mohamed Morsi at the Presidential Palace."
Claire leaned forward slightly.
"For his loyalty and obedience, he has been rewarded ever since. Rapid promotions. Unchecked authority. Today, he effectively runs the mukhabarat—the Egyptian General Intelligence Directorate. But increasingly, he functions as a senior liaison between the Supreme Council of Antiquities and the state's internal security services."
Stretton adjusted his glasses. The next words came slowly.
"To say he operates with impunity is an understatement. Profiling suggests he's a cruel and sadistic operator. Some reports even point to sociopathic tendencies. If there's one man in Egypt capable of manipulating both the intelligence apparatus and the Antiquities Council—it's him."
André Moreau stared at the image on the screen with contempt, his lips curling faintly.
"Alors, c'est cette ordure qui tire les ficelles - So this bastard is pulling the strings?"
Stretton allowed himself the faintest smirk.
"No. He's the muscle. The hammer, not the hand that swings it."
He clicked the remote. Nasser's image vanished, replaced by the weathered but calculating face of a man in his early sixties. A sparse greying beard, rimless glasses, and an academic's tailored suit. The man looked like a weasel in clothing—sharp-nosed, thin-lipped, black emotionless eyes. The name in the corner read: DR. SAMY KHOURY.
Claire's eyebrows lifted. Moreau's jaw twitched.
"Khoury," Moreau muttered.
Stretton gave a small nod. "Yes. Dr. Samy Khoury. Formerly professor of Near Eastern Studies at Cairo University. Currently Director of the Egyptian Supreme Council of Antiquities.

Unofficially? We believe he gives the orders when el-Sisi isn't
watching."
"Khoury has long been whispered about in intelligence circles—
implicated in the black market trade of antiquities, illegal
excavations, racketeering, even human trafficking. But nothing has
ever stuck. Interpol has no active warrant. The Egyptian authorities
won't touch him."
"Why not?" Claire asked, incredulous. "If they know he's dirty?"
Stretton's reply came with a touch of dry sarcasm. "Because he's
married to the daughter of Hussein el-Sisi—the President's niece.
Which makes him practically untouchable."
Alex shifted in his seat, his voice low and thoughtful. "So
Khoury—he's the one in charge?"
Stretton exhaled. "Locally? Yes. He's the architect of the
Ministry's internal power plays. But remember when I told you the
UN permits would come into play?"
Heads nodded, despite being kilometres apart.
"Well, Khoury's reach doesn't extend beyond Egypt's borders. We
ran every trace we could. No links to UNESCO. No overlapping
academic appointments. No family ties to Western institutions or
NGOs. He's a big fish—but only in the Egyptian pond."
A beat of silence.
Stretton continued, voice dropping slightly.
"But there's someone else. Someone pulling the strings
internationally."
He clicked the remote again.
A new image appeared: a heavyset man climbing out of a black
Mercedes SL600. He was bearded, wearing a white linen suit and
dark aviators. Behind him, a glint of sea—some anonymous luxury
port in the Mediterranean.
"This is Andreas Soterakis."
Stretton let the name hang.
"A Greek shipping magnate. Self-made. Born into poverty on the
island of Syros. Orphaned young—his father lost at sea, his mother

consigned to textile mills. Raised by his paternal grandfather, a fisherman with old-world stories and older superstitions."

"By eighteen, he was already running contraband through the Aegean. By thirty, he had built a modest freight business. By fifty, he controlled one of the most powerful maritime logistics networks in Europe. Thalasson Global Shipping. On the surface, a success story."

He paused. Then: "But Thalasson was never just a business. For Soterakis, it's a vessel for something much darker."

The room fell silent.

"Soterakis is obsessed with the belief that he is the last living heir of the Ptolemaic dynasty. A claim without documentation, rooted in whispered family lore passed down from his grandfather. He believes the location of Alexander the Great's tomb was entrusted, through an unbroken chain of oral tradition, to his bloodline—and his bloodline alone."

Stretton's voice grew sharper now.

"To him, this isn't about archaeology. It's not about history. It's spiritual. A birthright. A divine confirmation of his claim to a forgotten throne."

He looked around at the gathered faces.

"Soterakis has been secretly funding illicit digs from Syria to Tunisia, from Macedonia to Upper Egypt. He moves stolen antiquities through Thalasson's commercial and private cargo routes—disguised in shipping manifests, redirected to collectors, hidden in private collections."

"And yes," he added, "he has the money and reach to bribe officials, embed agents in the UN and UNESCO, manipulate weak or fractured states like Libya and Egypt, and even use local militias as enforcers."

He turned to the screen, to address the French contingent directly.

"And that brings us to Libya. And to Leptis Magna."

Stretton clicked the final slide.

An aerial drone image of the dig site at Leptis—before the chaos. Neat tents, metal scaffolding, a path marked by white tarps and sun-bleached survey flags.

"We believe Soterakis paid the local ISIS militia to do three things: loot the site, gather any intelligence on the excavation findings... and kidnap Dr. Tariq Mahfouz."

The silence was total now. You could hear the faint whine of a cooling fan in the projector.

And the slow, grinding of Samira's teeth.

"So," Alex said, leaning back in his chair, brows drawn into a skeptical knot. "Let me get this straight. We have a Greek shipping tycoon—Andreas Soterakis—who believes he's descended from the Ptolemaic dynasty, has agents embedded in UNESCO, Egypt, Syria, Libya—hell, maybe half the Mediterranean—who manipulates and pays off government officials across those regions… all so he can track down the lost tomb of Alexander the Great, and he's funding the whole thing through antiquities smuggling and black market sales?"

There was a beat of silence.

"We believe so," Stretton replied, his nod curt, his tone dry as dust.

Claire looked unconvinced. "But that doesn't add up. The timeline's wrong."

All eyes turned to her.

"If Soterakis only found out about the Leptis dig through the UNESCO permit applications, then he wouldn't have known what we were looking for. Those permits didn't mention Alexander. Or Malik. Or anything even close to a tomb. They were just approvals for excavating subsurface anomalies flagged in the LiDAR scans that Sarah Parker sent from Alabama. That's all. Nothing to do with anything Byzantine or Ptolemaic."

Stretton opened his mouth, but Samira spoke first.

"Oh my God," she whispered, her hand flying to her mouth as if to stifle the words. Her voice trembled with sudden realization. "That night. The night before the attack—Tariq was on the phone with the sponsors. With the UN. He was excited, frantic almost. He was telling them what we'd uncovered, including the late Byzantine interpretation of the mosaic. He even sent out a draft press release and an abstract. I remember—it was half-finished. He was going to finalize them both the next morning…"

She trailed off. The room was silent for a heartbeat.

"And the next morning was the attack," she finished.

"Could Soterakis have been listening in?" Alex asked, his voice low.

"Entirely plausible," said Stretton with a slow nod. "A man with that much money, power, and reach doesn't need to wait for headlines. He can buy access. Surveillance. Forwarded transcripts. People. Data leaks. If Tariq's call was intercepted, or if someone on the chain passed it along—Soterakis would have known everything within hours."

"But even so," Claire pressed, not backing down, "that doesn't explain the Alexandria permits. They were strictly limited to core sampling for soil displacement and stratigraphy. Not tomb excavation. Not even burial sites. Nothing remotely suggestive of Alexander."

"I think," said André Molineux, speaking for the first time, "that he was gambling. That's what this is. He's playing a long game, but he's playing on instinct. He was simply following the breadcrumbs – INHA permits. He put two and two together—and he's betting that we're on the verge of confirming something that no one else has dared to believe."

He looked around the room.

"No one outside this team knows that this could possibly lead to the final resting place of Alexander the Great."

"Mon Dieu," Delon added softly. "I didn't even know this until now."

Moreau crossed his arms. His voice, when it came, was like gravel scraping steel.

"So this Soterakis—how dangerous is he?"

Stretton's lips twitched into something between a frown and a smirk.

"Put it this way, Étienne," he said. "Soterakis is a man who doesn't accept disappointment. He's used to getting what he wants—and he uses every means necessary to make sure he does."

There was something final in his tone. A heavy, cold truth settling over the room like a curtain drawn closed.

Chapter 9

The black Suburban SUV rolled through the wrought-iron gates of the French Embassy in Garden City at precisely 8:30 a.m.—a full thirty minutes ahead of schedule. It was supposed to be nine. But neither Alex nor Samira could bear to wait another second to see the rest of the team.

Cairo in the early morning was already awakening with a kind of chaotic grace. The low golden sun spilled across the whitewashed rooftops, throwing long shadows on the dusty streets. Minarets pierced the skyline, silhouetted against a soft salmon sky. The scent of freshly baked baladi bread mingled with exhaust fumes, diesel, and a trace of jasmine from a nearby garden. Street vendors pushed carts loaded with fruit, their calls punctuated by the metallic clatter of shutters being raised, the bray of donkeys, and the distant honking of impatient taxi drivers.

Inside the SUV, there was a quiet tension—the kind born of anticipation, not fear. Alex sat rigidly upright, his hand resting on his thigh, fingers drumming idly. Samira sat beside him, arms folded, her face still bearing the raw marks of her recent ordeal. Her split lip had scabbed slightly; one eye was darkened by a bruise. She hadn't complained once.

When the vehicle came to a stop in the embassy's circular driveway, the two DGSE security agents in the front leapt out in unison and pulled open the rear doors. A crisp wind stirred the embassy's French and European Union flags as Alex and Samira stepped out into the sun-drenched courtyard.

Waiting just beyond the glass entry doors were Claire, André Molineux, Ambassador Étienne Moreau, and of course, Louis Delon. They were all already watching—Claire most intently, shifting from foot to foot.

Before any greetings could be exchanged, two members of the Service de sécurité de la Défense—the SDG officers stationed at all French embassies worldwide—intercepted them for a quick but thorough security check. IDs were checked. Bags were scanned. Protocol was respected. The morning was not to be stained by oversight.

But the moment the formalities were over, Claire broke free. She sprinted forward, barely containing herself, and threw her arms around Alex in a hug that was equal parts relief and resolve. Then she turned to Samira, embracing her with a gentleness that betrayed her concern.

"It's so good to see you both," Claire said, stepping back to take them in. "I was so worried when they arrested you... Egypt being Egypt..."

"Yes," Samira replied with a crooked smile, her voice dry, "It's been an interesting forty-eight hours." Claire's eyes darted instinctively to the bruises on her face, but she said nothing. She only tightened her lips and nodded.

After warm greetings were exchanged with the Ambassador and Molineux—who each took turns shaking hands and offering polite words—the group turned to head inside toward coffee, comfort, and the long conference table waiting in the embassy's secure briefing room.

But Alex held back. He placed a hand gently on Louis Delon's elbow as the others drifted ahead.

"I just wanted to say—Louis," Alex began, his voice uncharacteristically raw, "what you did for Claire... it meant everything. I don't always say this kind of thing, but... she means a hell of a lot to me."

Delon stopped, the warmth in his eyes tempered by the steel beneath. He inclined his head respectfully.

"You know, Monsieur," he said, his accent thick with gravel and old-school formality, "she is a most remarkable woman. Une enfant, oui—but with remarkable force intérieure. Not many like her."

He gave a small, wistful smile, then added, "She said she had a friend in her head, guiding her after your arrest."

Alex blinked. "A friend?"

Delon's grin widened.

"Ethan Hunt," he said. "Apparently, quite well known in your parts."

Alex laughed, genuinely, the sound catching him by surprise.

"Claire Marlowe channeling Ethan Hunt," he murmured. "Now that's something I never thought I'd hear."

Together, they followed the others into the embassy.

The door clicked shut behind them, shutting out the sounds of Cairo, and with it, the uncertain world outside. For now, at least, they were together again.

They assembled in the same conference room that had hosted the ultra-high definition video call the night before. Morning light spilled through the tall windows, softened by gauzy white curtains that billowed ever so slightly from the draft of the embassy's old air-conditioning system. The table was set with light refreshments—miniature croissants, fresh dates, a silver thermos of dark coffee, and an elegant white porcelain teapot. Alex nursed a double espresso, its bitter heat sharpening his focus. Samira cradled a delicate jasmine tea, the floral aroma soothing her raw nerves. Claire, as always, had her signature mochaccino, half foam, double shot, extra cocoa powder dusted on top.

At the head of the table, Ambassador Étienne Moreau stood to speak. He was dressed impeccably in a navy blue suit, his tie a muted tricolor stripe—subtle, diplomatic.

"Mesdames et messieurs," he began, voice calm and resonant, "on behalf of the French Republic, I wish to extend our deepest support to the members of the Institut National d'Histoire de l'Art. Your work is not only culturally vital, but historically indispensable. Though my resources here in Egypt are modest, I assure you they are at your full disposal. I will do everything within my mandate to ensure your safety, your freedom of movement, and the protection of your research. What you are doing matters—to France, to Europe, to the world."

There was a respectful silence when he finished, followed by appreciative nods from the team. Then he turned toward Molineux and offered the floor with a courteous gesture.

André Molineux rose, his expression serious.

"This is the video from the dive last Friday," he said. "It's unviewed footage—raw. No one has seen it until now." He turned to Claire, who simply nodded in agreement. "We don't know what was captured, nor the condition of the video. It may show everything. It may show nothing. But we believe, based on the dive log and GPS coordinates, that this is the segment where the object—possibly the structure described in Malik's scroll—was located."

He took a slow breath, letting the gravity settle. "This footage does not leave this room. We've been compromised too many times already. This may be our first and only opportunity to get ahead. The Ambassador has generously offered the Embassy as a base of operations, but further dives in Alexandria are... improbable, at best."

He turned to Claire and gave a slight nod. "Claire, if you would."

Delon dimmed the lights. The room fell into a soft twilight. The television—an ultra-wide, embassy-issue LG panel—flickered to life, briefly blue, then black, then lit with the mirrored screen of Claire's MacBook Pro. She clicked open the video file.

"Okay," she said, a little nervously. "This is the full recording from Friday. One hour and twenty-seven minutes. For clarity and completeness, I suggest we run it straight through. Professor, you're welcome to narrate. There's audio as well—ambient, mostly, but it might help. The first few minutes could be uneventful. Just... let's see what's there."

With unanimous nods, she pressed play.

The screen came to life with startling clarity.

The sea was a luminous, almost otherworldly shade of blue-green. Shafts of sunlight pierced through the water, scattering across submerged ruins like divine rays through cathedral glass. There was almost no particulate in the water—remarkable for a harbor dive. The visibility extended at least fifteen meters, and details sprang into focus with haunting crispness.

Shattered columns and tumbled blocks appeared in the camera's field—remnants of Cleopatra's palace. Encrusted with coral and softened by algae, they nonetheless retained a silent grandeur. A lion sculpture, its paws fractured, glared out from the silt with regal defiance.

Colour bled into the scene richly: ochre sandstone, blackened granite, the emerald hue of settled sediment. Ghosts of the past made manifest in sun-dappled ruin.

For the first hour, they watched in rapt attention—Alex narrating key features, Claire occasionally pausing to enhance images—but there was nothing conclusive. Just the familiar bones of a drowned city.

Claire paused the playback at the one-hour mark.

"This is where you and Mostafa changed tanks," she said.

"Yes," Alex replied. "It's in the last twenty-seven minutes. That's where it happened."

Claire trimmed the first hour of footage and saved it into a subfolder titled: Dive_Initial_Segment.

"Ready," she said. "Let's continue."

As the footage resumed, Mostafa could be seen gliding off to the right, examining a partially buried lion statue. Then, slowly, something entered frame behind Alex's left shoulder—hazy at first.

It emerged as a monolithic structure—granite, nearly three meters tall, rising like a phantom from the harbor floor. It was long, slender, pyramidical—an obelisk, but with dimensions unlike the classic Egyptian examples. The base, roughly half a meter per side, was partially buried in thick, silty sand.

But it was the top that drew gasps.

Where one expected a pointed finial like Cleopatra's Needle, there stood instead a chiseled insignia—the seal of the Rashidun Caliphate: a six-pointed rosette encircled by Kufic script. The mark of Islam's earliest empire.

Even to the untrained eye, this was no ordinary ruin.

"It's a statement," whispered Samira, rising slightly in her chair. "A message."

"A monument," added Alex, "to the death of the Ptolemies... and the birth of the Arab era in Egypt."

As the structure drifted into full view, Samira leaned forward. "Claire, can you take stills of the inscriptions as they appear?"

"Absolutely," Claire replied, hands poised. "I'll pull full-res stills straight from the 4K master file. Not screenshots—clean digital frames. We'll be able to zoom in without losing fidelity."

Samira nodded. "Begin with this side."

The video paused. Claire extracted the first still and saved it into a new folder titled Stills_Obelisk.

"Got it."

The next twenty minutes passed with slow, reverent silence. Side by side, inscription after inscription was captured—Kufic prayers, dedications to Umar ibn al-Khattab, warnings in classical Arabic etched deep into the polished granite.

Then, near the end, the video shifted.

The footage cut to Alex surfacing and hauling himself onto the RIB. The sky was bright overhead, the sea strangely calm. Audio played from his helmet mic—voices shouting, urgency rising.

The camera angle caught the deck, the dive bag, and then—boots. The cutter was already alongside the RIB. Armed sailors onboard. The commanding officer—young, stone-faced, in starched white— strode into frame. The resolution caught the insignia on his shoulder, the sidearm at his hip.

"Is that him" inquired Delon.

Claire answered coldly. "Yes, that's him!"

Delon leaned forward saying to no-one in particular, his voice carrying a certain menace, "Oui... we will remember you, monsieur."

The video continued for another minute—Alex removing his helmet, laying it down, the screen angling to the floor. The last thing visible: the wet decking, some feet, and then—

Samira's voice over the audio, clear, panicked.

"Claire. Listen carefully. Get the fuck out of here. Run. Now."

Then static. Then nothing.

Silence fell in the conference room.

They all sat motionless, processing what they'd just seen. The sea had given up its secrets—but at a cost. The footage had confirmed the monument. Confirmed the threat.

It was not just archaeology now. It was a war over memory itself.

The team broke for an early lunch. The embassy cafeteria, tucked beside the east wing, had put on an unexpected spread — a smorgasbord of French delights that mingled decadence with diplomacy. The air was heady with aromas: buttery croissants, steaming coq au vin, and sharp mustard sauces cut through the rich meat of duck confit. Hot and cold offerings sat in polished silver trays — Nicoise salad, onion soup with golden gruyère crusts, gratin dauphinois, tartines stacked with jambon de Bayonne, and a steaming bouillabaisse laced with fennel and orange zest.

Claire, visibly delighted, was thrilled to discover that the cafeteria staff had gone out of their way to include cheeseburgers — a playful nod to a comment she'd made on her first visit about

missing "real food." The buns were toasted, the cheese
unapologetically gooey, and the patties spiced with a hint of
thyme. She didn't hesitate.

Delon, meanwhile, revelled in his plate of cassoulet de
Castelnaudary, digging into the meaty stew with relish, practically
purring at the density of duck, sausage, and white beans.

Alex, meanwhile, opted for something simpler: roast chicken with
herbs de Provence, a side of haricots verts, and just enough Dijon
to remind him that he was on French soil. He sat beside Claire,
watching the room with quiet calculation.

Conspicuously absent from the meal was Moreau, who had
excused himself to attend to urgent embassy matters. André
Molineux also slipped away immediately after eating, citing INHA
obligations. But there was something too punctual about his exit —
something a little too rehearsed.

As lunch concluded, the group reconvened in the embassy's
conference hall, its dim lighting replaced by floor-to-ceiling blinds
drawn back to flood the space with late-summer light. A large
screen dominated the far wall, where Claire was already prepping
the slides.

Samira sat cross-legged with a leather-bound notepad on her lap.
"Claire, let's begin with side one," she said, her tone sharp but
focused. Delon once more drew the blinds and dimmed the lights.
The first still appeared on screen: the weathered surface of a
sandstone stele, covered in dark, elegantly chiseled script.

Samira leaned forward. "That's Kufic," she said, almost to herself.
"Not decorative, early style — austere. Appropriate for an official
commission of this period."

Alex tilted his head. "Would that have been the Rashidun's script
of choice?"

Samira nodded. "Absolutely. For an official state commission
around 642 CE? Kufic would be the formal choice. It's early
Islamic script — the Rashidun caliphate used it for religious and
political inscriptions."

Claire scrolled downward slowly, her fingers tight on the touchpad. "Do I go left to right or…?"

"Top to bottom," Samira said. "But read right to left on each line. Kufic's spatial structure is rigid."

She read silently, mouthing words as she traced the script with her pen. After a few passes, she remained seated and looked up.

"This is a commissioned piece," she said. "Ordered by General Amr ibn al-As himself. You can see his name inscribed here." She motioned to the top right of the screen. "It's a monument — a tribute to the Rashidun victory in Egypt. It describes the caliphate as 'all-powerful, all-conquering under God.' The date is inscribed in the Islamic calendar. 17th of Safar, 21 AH. That's 17 September, 642 CE."

There was a brief silence in the room as the weight of the artifact settled on them.

"Not much to do with Alexander or Malik," Alex finally said. "Just conquest."

"Its your equivalent of a modern-day press release! Claire, if you're ready, move to the second side, please," said Samira.

The second still loaded, similar in tone and layout, though the strokes were more flowing here, the script longer and more meditative.

"This is more devotional," Samira muttered, directing Claire to zoom in and out repeatedly. "Not historical. This side is… essentially a du'ā — a supplication."

She read aloud, her voice formal and reverent:

"Praise be to Allah, the Eternal, the Most High,
 Who brings victory to the righteous
 And casts down the oppressors.
 He alone is the Light over Darkness,
 The Guide over the lost,
 And the Giver of dominion to whom He wills."

"Propaganda," Delon said bluntly.

"Religious legitimation," added Alex.

"There's nothing here about Malik, or Leptis Magna," Claire agreed. "Just more glorification."

Samira looked unfazed. "Onto the third side."

This side immediately appeared different. The script was more rounded, some glyphs unfamiliar.

"What are we looking at?" Claire asked.

Samira leaned in. "Coptic. This was written by a native hand. Possibly a church scribe."

"Is it Pope Benjamin?" Alex asked.

"It is," she confirmed. "This side is remarkable. It reads like a formal declaration. Listen to this…"

She read aloud:

"We, the servants of the True Faith,

Welcome the army of Amr ibn al-As.

 Let there be unity between us, the Copts, and the People of the Book.

The tyrant Cyrus has departed; the yoke is lifted.

In Amr, we have found justice and peace."

"This is incredible," Claire said. "He's legitimizing the Arab entry into Egypt."

"Which would make sense," Alex said, "Cyrus, the Byzantine governor, was brutal to the Copts. Benjamin was in exile for a decade."

Samira added, "There's a historical record of their meeting. Amr is said to have been so impressed by Benjamin's humility that he restored him to power immediately, giving him back the patriarchal throne."

"And Benjamin, in turn, publicly prayed for Amr's success," Claire added.

Alex folded his arms. "So, Benjamin allies with the Arabs to get rid of the Byzantines. It's not hard to see the political chess here."

"It's not chess," Claire snapped. "It's survival. The Copts were crushed under Cyrus."

The other members of the room — Ambassadors, Secretary Generals and soldiers alike — all sat awkwardly, waiting for the academic squall to pass.

Samira raised a hand. "I think that's all from that face. Let's see the fourth side Claire."

Claire advanced to the final side of the obelisk.

From the moment it appeared on screen, everyone in the room knew they were looking at something fundamentally different. The characters carved into the black stone were unlike the Arabic, Kufic, or Byzantine inscriptions they had seen so far.

Samira leaned forward, adjusting her glasses. "This language is… highly unusual."

Claire tapped keys to adjust the playback, directing the HD scan to pan slowly across the stone surface. At the very top of the obelisk, carved with solemn precision, was the unmistakable figure of a sleeping lion, curled beneath a palm tree, waves cresting in the background.

"Holy cow," said Alex, stepping toward the screen. "That's the exact same lion as on the mosaic."

Claire blinked. "Fucking-A."

Delon chuckled, but no one else moved. The weight of the moment had landed.

"You'll need to slow this right down," Samira told her. "This script… it's early Sabaic, I think. And it's not my strongest."

Alex's brow furrowed. "Early Sabaic? That's a South Arabian script. Who the hell could even read this in 642 CE?"

Samira nodded, confirming his skepticism. "Only those who had been taught it. Scholars. Priests of the old Himyarite or Sabaean traditions, maybe. But even then—probably not even a handful of people in Alexandria at the time. It was a lost tongue even then — supplanted by Arabic and Ge'ez centuries earlier."

The room fell quiet.

As Claire zoomed in, the camera passed over several clusters of inscriptions beneath the lion. Samira read slowly, carefully. "It references the lion repeatedly. On the surface, it identifies him as Amr ibn al-As… but look, she pointed to a cluster of glyphs. "He's referred to as the lion sent to sleep until the true kingdom is awakened. That's not a typical metaphor."

Alex narrowed her eyes. "You think it's Alexander?"

"It could be," responded Samira.

"Is it coded?" Claire asked.

"Not coded. Just… cryptic," Samira replied, tracing the shapes with her eyes. "This line reads: 'Though born of the sands, his blood calls to the mountains beyond the western sea — where the silver-flecked olive grows beneath snowed peaks.'

"That's not Arabia," Alex said. "That's Macedonia. That's a poetic reference to Alexander's homeland."

Samira nodded. "Agreed. It's disguised. But deliberate. This next section is even more intriguing."

She leaned in again, reading slowly:

'When the lion's rest is broken, he shall not rise toward the sun, but gaze upon the far horizon, where the last light fades. There, in the dust of the conquerors, the next seal shall lie. Let the bearing be drawn not from stars but from purpose: Two hundred and twenty, beneath the wheel of heaven.'

Alex's pulse quickened. "That's not prophetic language. That's instruction."

Claire glanced back. "You think it's a bearing?"

"Exactly. Two-two-zero degrees. A directional cue. Not east, not south—west-southwest."

Delon raised an eyebrow. "Look to the west…"

"On a very specific heading," Alex confirmed. "He's not talking metaphorically—he's guiding someone."

Samira followed the inscription further, then stopped. At the very bottom of the stele, carved in smaller, more deliberate characters, was a final line:

"Written by the hand of Malik ibn Harun al-Sahiri, in the year 21 AH."

Andre Molineux leaned forward. "Malik? As in—the same Malik who owned the villa in Leptis Magna? The one who inscribed the scrolls beneath the mosaic?"

Alex whispered, "It seems so. He left us a message… in a language almost no one could read."

Samira leaned back, her voice low. "And yet, here we are."

Chapter 10

It was late in the afternoon by the time the team finished deciphering the final face of the obelisk. The golden light slanting in through the high windows of the compound had begun to dim, casting long shadows across the conference table. Excitement lingered in the air—a strange silence had followed the last inscription, as if the past itself had taken a breath.

Ambassador Étienne Moreau, ever the practical diplomat, stood and stretched. "I suggest we break for dinner, or something like it. We'll reconvene shortly after."

As Moreau excused himself politely, murmuring something about a diplomatic communiqué requiring his attention, Molineux too slipped away, adding with a grimace that he had urgent phone calls to return—ones that could not wait.

Dinner was closer to a peasant's supper than any formal meal. With the canteen staff long since gone for the day, they found a modest spread laid out in the small galley off the hallway: a few crocks of rillettes and pâtés, a plate of chilled hard-boiled eggs, sliced saucisson sec, a wheel of goat's cheese, and several crusty baguettes cut into thick, rustic hunks. There were carafes of water, a bottle of vin rouge someone had thoughtfully uncorked, and a jar of Dijon mustard with a worn spoon sticking out.

Claire nibbled at a sliver of Comté while Samira assembled a careful tartine with cornichons and rillette. No one spoke much. The fatigue was bone-deep, and beneath it, an unease had begun to ripple.

321

At six o'clock sharp, they reconvened in the conference room. The smell of stale coffee and furniture polish, mingled with the faint mineral tang of AV equipment. A large A1 paper map of Egypt had been unrolled across the table, secured at the corners by coffee mugs and a half-filled bottle of mineral water. Delon, always resourceful, had managed to requisition it from the stationary cabinet downstairs.

Moreau and Molineux were the last to re-enter. The air changed subtly as they entered—somber, alert.

Molineux cleared his throat, his expression grave. "Before we begin again on the path of the Four Lions, Ambassador Moreau and I have something to share. This stems from a phone call I received earlier today from Ambassador Stratten at the American Embassy."

Everyone stopped.

He continued, slower now. "We've been informed by the US Embassy that the bodies of the three commercial dive operators were recovered around noon by Egyptian authorities - washed ashore approximately five miles north of Alexandria, just outside a small fishing village called El-Maks."

Gasps rippled around the room. Samira raised a hand to her mouth, as if physically stifling a cry. Claire whispered, "My God," just loud enough for the others to hear.

Molineux's voice dropped an octave. "The Egyptian Police investigators believe they were beaten—badly—and likely tortured before being executed."

The room fell into a stunned silence.

"This," he said heavily, "changes everything. We're no longer dealing with political lightweights or thieves. Whoever is after this knowledge—this object—they're organized, lethal, and absolutely determined. I cannot, in good conscience, allow this project to continue. Effective immediately, I'm ordering a full halt to the operation."

"You can't," Claire said, her voice cracking with disbelief. "We've come too far. If we stop now—then their deaths were for nothing."

"I'm sorry, Claire, I know—"

"No," Samira interrupted firmly. "You don't know, Andre. I don't think you understand what this means to us. We've been hunted, shot at, beaten and imprisoned. I won't let some rich shipping tycoon or fanatic sweep in and steal everything. Not without a fight."

Alex leaned forward, eyes intense. "I have to agree. This might be the single most important archaeological discovery of the modern era. And you want to let it vanish into a private collection? Some glass case in a private collection, never to be seen again? No. This deserves to be shared with the world. All of it."

Molineux hesitated, clearly torn. "I can't ask you to risk your lives."

"Then don't," said Delon gently. "Don't ask. Sentinel can provide the security, and I, myself will provide… protection," he added with a slight smile. "The academics—les érudits—will be under my care. And besides…" he raised a brow. "It will be fun, no?"

Molineux countered, "Since there cannot be any UN-connection, there cannot be any UN sanction. The Board would not approve this level of risk Louis, you Sentinel or to the dig team!"

"Sentinel will provide my services gratis Director, I will volunteer the protection."

Molineux sighed. "So we're clear—you are all volunteering? Of your own volition?"

The chorus was immediate. "Yep," from Claire. "Yes," from Samira. A firm "Absolutely," from Alex.

He nodded. "Very well. Louis, if you're going to provide security, I suggest you remain armed at all times. We can't know what's coming."

"Oui, Director. Of course," said Delon, tapping the side of head.

"The Embassy will support you in every way we can," added Moreau. "You won't be alone."

With the mood still taut but galvanized, Delon stepped forward and concentrated on the map again. From his bag he retrieved a metal ruler, a black pen, and his phone.

He aligned the map to true north using his compass app, then carefully drew a bearing of 220 degrees from Alexandria, starting near the old city walls.

They gathered close, eyes tracing the clean, dark line as it cut across the map—southwest, straight into the desert.

Nothing.

No ruins. No towns. No roads or ancient tracks. No wadi. No caravanserai. Just the empty expanse of the Western Desert, stretching into silence.

Delon was the first to speak. "There is nothing along this bearing, docteur. Are you certain of the translation?"

Alex nodded. "Yes. A hundred percent. He wrote: 'Follow the lion who faces the setting sun, along a bearing of 220.' It's not ambiguous."

"I have checked the map and bearing three times," said Delon. "There is rien. Nothing."

Claire leaned over the map. "Could it be a place that existed in Malik's time—642 CE—but doesn't anymore? A town, maybe, or a site lost to the desert?"

Alex rubbed the back of his neck. "That's the thing—it doesn't align with any known Roman or Arab routes from the period. Not trade, not pilgrimage, not military. It's just… dead zone. No strategic purpose, no evidence of settlement."

Samira furrowed her brow. "But Malik was precise. He etched it on stone. This bearing wasn't symbolic. It was meant to guide."

"Which means we're missing something," Alex said quietly. "Something important."

They all stared again at the black line that pointed to nowhere, slicing through history and sand.

They checked and rechecked the calculations, the inscriptions, and the translations for another hour. Still, the results defied logic—a bearing that transgressed a whole sea of... nothing. No settlement, no ruins, no trace. Just sand. Finally, Alex closed his notebook with a sigh. Frustration clung to the group like the heat outside the embassy's walls.

Molineux stood up first, straightening his tie with a sigh of resignation. "Mes amis, duty calls. I fly to Paris at dawn. The INHA won't run itself."

Moreau was close behind him, gathering his notes. "And I'm off to Riyadh," he said, with a grimace. "We're trying to convince the Saudis to purchase the Dassault Rafale—apparently, they're having second thoughts about the F-35." He chuckled wryly, though the timing of such diplomacy seemed incongruous with the mystery they were wrestling.

"Bon voyage," Alex muttered without enthusiasm.

One by one, the small congregation dispersed to their rooms, their anticipation blunted by the night's failure. Somewhere in the translation, somewhere in the centuries, the truth had been misplaced.

Morning broke bright and clear over Cairo. From the garden terraces of the French Embassy in Garden City, the city shimmered under a flawless blue sky. The jacaranda trees, just beginning to bloom, cast lilac shadows across the manicured lawns. Bougainvillaea spilled like crimson waterfalls from whitewashed walls, and the scent of hibiscus and coffee mingled with the warm, dry breeze. Below, the Nile glinted like hammered silver under the rising sun, and the low hum of traffic floated up from the Corniche—punctuated by the occasional staccato of a distant car horn or a braying donkey cart in the old quarter.

By 8:00 a.m., the embassy cafeteria was already humming with quiet activity. Though breakfast was unscheduled, the kitchen staff—under the meticulous oversight of the Embassy's head chef—had been preparing meals since six. At least forty to fifty diplomatic and administrative staff worked in the building, many of them already queueing for strong coffee and buttery viennoiseries.

Alex was the last to arrive. He ordered a traditional French breakfast: two croissants, a boiled egg, a glass of orange juice, and a double espresso—served, of course, in a demitasse cup, with the crema still swirling on top.

Samira opted for something lighter: Greek yogurt with honey and figs, a slice of rye toast, and mint tea.

Louis Delon, true to form, requested a baguette slathered in salted Normandy butter, two scrambled eggs, and a thick slice of aged Comté cheese. He washed it down with a café au lait that could wake the dead.

At their usual table, however, one chair was conspicuously empty. In Claire's place was a page torn from her Spirax notebook, the edges jagged and flecked with ink.

Scrawled in her unmistakable looping handwriting:

"Meet me in the conference room, soonest. I've uncovered the problem!!"

Alex raised a brow. "She's not serious."

Samira smirked. "Oh, she's serious."

Delon scratched his head. "So the 19-year-old archaeology student has solved what four seasoned professionals couldn't?"

Alex didn't rush. He took a measured sip of his espresso and folded his napkin neatly. "Well, let's not inflate her ego too much."

The conference room was brightly lit, its long windows flung open to let in the spring breeze. At the head of the table stood Claire, looking unexpectedly scholarly—her dark curls pulled into a ponytail, though rebellious ringlets framed her cheekbones. Her tortoiseshell glasses slid down her nose, and her oversized oatmeal-colored jumper gave her a disheveled, bookish charm. Faded jeans and scuffed sneakers completed the ensemble.

"Thanks for joining me—eventually," she said, arms folded. "Class is now in session. Today, we're studying history… and astronomy."

Alex chuckled.

Samira gave an exaggerated gasp. "Ooh, I hope there's a quiz."

Louis raised his hands in surrender. "I concede—I'm already outmatched."

They took their seats.

"Okay," Claire began, pacing in front of the whiteboard. "We made two errors last night. Don't worry—it was a collective effort."

She grinned at Louis.

"Louis, when you drew the bearing on the map, what did you use?"

"The one Malik inscribed: 220 degrees."

"And you measured that with?"

"My iPhone, chérie. The compass app."

"Exactly." Claire's eyes gleamed. "And there's our first mistake."

Alex's brow furrowed. "Of course. Magnetic versus true north."

Claire nodded. "Magnetic compasses weren't invented until the 11th century in China, and they wouldn't have reached the Islamic world until even later. Malik would've used the stars—true celestial north—not magnetic north. And the magnetic declination here in Egypt is roughly 4.75 degrees east."

Samira leaned in. "So we need to subtract that from 220?"

"Correct. That gives us 215 degrees—true bearing converted into modern magnetic terms."

Louis unfolded the map and redrew the bearing. He inspected the new area on the map. "Still desert. Just sand, sand, and more sand."

Samira looked back to Claire. "You said there were two errors?"

Claire grinned, raising both hands. "Precession," she said, motioning with her left. "And time," she added, with her right.

She grabbed the marker and made the notes and calculations on the whiteboard. "Over the last 1,300 years, the earth's axis has wobbled—a process called axial precession. The stars' positions have shifted by about one degree every 72 years. Which means Antares, the star Malik likely used, has shifted westward by roughly 18 degrees since 642 CE."

She spun to face them. "So if Malik recorded a celestial bearing of 220 degrees in 642 CE, that same star—Antares—would now sit at a bearing of… 202 degrees true or 197 degrees magnetic."

Alex sat back, stunned. "Brilliant. Absolutely brilliant."

"I've been working on it since 2 a.m.," Claire confessed, rubbing her eyes. "I couldn't sleep. It was like a splinter in my brain."

Samira reached over and touched her arm. "Claire, that's incredible logic. Your reasoning is perfect."

Even Louis whistled. "They never taught us that in military school."

Louis bent over the map once again and redrew the bearing—197 degrees, magnetic. The line extended southwest, away from the confusion of last night, cutting through a different region entirely.

"Bawiti," he said. Claire bought it up on Google Earth on the big screen, and zoomed in. Then, something appeared. Four towns. Clustered together on the digital overlay.

"Zoom in," Alex said.

Claire keyed in the commands on Google Earth. The map resolved. Bawiti. Mandisha. Al-'Uwaynah. Bahariyah Oasis.

They stared.

Samira leaned forward. "Only one of those would've existed in 642 CE."

"Bahariyah," Alex said, slowly. "It was part of the Roman desert trade route. Caravan trails from the Nile to Siwa and beyond. Used by Bedouin tribes for centuries before that."

Claire nodded. "I pulled up historical references. Bahariyah was occupied in Pharaonic times. The Romans built fortresses and temples there. And get this…"

She typed a few quick prompts into her MacBook. After a moment, her eyes widened. "Guys… you're not going to believe this."

Alex turned from the map. Louis looked up.

Claire slowly rotated her screen to face them.

"The Temple of Alexander the Great."

Alex exhaled. "We've found it."

Samira sat back in awe.

Claire whispered, "That could be the second waymarker."

A hush fell over the room. Outside, the Nile flowed as it always had. But inside, something had shifted—like the axis of the earth itself.

They were no longer chasing ghosts.

They were following a path.

A path with purpose.

A path that had waited 2,300 years to be found.

With the revelation fresh in their minds and the map of Egypt still spread across the table, the team lingered in the conference room, the air now buzzing with renewed energy.

Claire tapped at her laptop, glasses slightly slipping down her nose as she read aloud to the group. "Bahariyah Oasis is about 370 kilometers southwest of Cairo. It's part of Egypt's Western Desert and has been inhabited since ancient times. The Temple of Alexander the Great is located roughly three miles east of the old capital, al-Qasr."

She looked up at Alex and Samira before continuing. "The temple was discovered by Ahmed Fakhry in the mid-20th century. It's built from sandstone and mud brick, and—get this—it contains forty-five rooms. The structure is partially ruined, of course, thanks to centuries of desert wind and erosion, but some of the artifacts have survived."

She flipped her screen toward them briefly. "A red granite altar inscribed with Alexander's name, a scattering of coins, amulets, domestic tools—everyday objects, really—and even ostraca with Coptic and Greek writings were recovered from the site. Most of what was salvaged is now split between the Egyptian Museum in Cairo and the New Valley Museum in Kharga."

"So," Alex said, leaning forward, "if the second waymarker is anything like what we found beneath the harbor—its size, its mass—then it hasn't been found."

"Or perhaps," Samira suggested, arms crossed thoughtfully, "it's been removed by Fakhry."

"Possible," Alex conceded. "But if it had, we'd have seen some mention of it in the records."

He turned back to Claire. "We need to be sure none of those items—especially any stone fragments—fit the profile of a waymarker. Can you dig into the museum archives, cross-reference what's listed as being recovered from the site?"

Claire nodded, already pulling up her tabs. "I'll search both the Egyptian Museum's public catalogue and the New Valley Museum's holdings, and—"

"Use the INHA database too," Samira cut in. "If Fakhry or any of his team documented everything properly, the Institute's archive should have a complete list going back decades."

"Already on it," Claire replied, fingers flying over her keyboard.

Louis Delon, who had been uncharacteristically quiet, finally stood from his chair and brushed imaginary lint from his jacket. "Right. Then I'll focus on logistics."

He moved to the map, dragging a finger southwest from Cairo. "It's at least a four, maybe five-hour drive to Bahariyah. The roads aren't bad, but I'll arrange for two vehicles—four-by-fours, ideally—just in case one gives us trouble in the desert. We'll need supplies: water, food, emergency gear. And lodging."

"Do they even have hotels out there?" Claire asked, half-joking.

"There are small inns in Bawiti," Louis answered with a grin. "Basic, but sufficient. I'll reach out to the local municipality and book rooms for the night. Just in case we have to stay longer, I'll make sure we're covered for three days."

"We can't get permits?" Samira added. "We can't even look like we are going to dig, that would raise alarm bells with the Ministry of Antiquities"

"I'll handle it," Louis said. "I'll call in a few favours. We'll go in as French tourists. Nothing heavy-handed. Not yet."

Alex exhaled, standing at the head of the table. "Okay. Let's divide and conquer. Claire, stay on the museums and databases. Samira, maybe reach out to your contacts at the INHA? See if anything unusual ever got flagged at Bahariyah but never published."
She nodded. "On it."
"I'll coordinate with the embassy's attaché staff for security protocol and make sure we're not stepping on any Egyptian toes," Louis added.
They all stood, the pace of their movements more purposeful now. "Let's reconvene at ten sharp," Alex said, "and see what we've got."
As the group dispersed to their respective tasks, the earlier frustration had evaporated like morning haze over the Nile. In its place: the electric hum of possibility.
Something had survived out there—Claire was certain of it. And if it had been waiting for over a thousand years, it could wait a little longer.
But not much.

Chapter 11

The group reconvened at exactly 10:00 a.m., each of them arriving sharp, focused, and already steeped in their respective tasks. The last to enter was Louis Delon, striding in with a bulky, dust-scuffed case tucked under his arm. They all turned to look at him. It wasn't the lateness—they barely registered that. It was the gear. The case was unmistakably military-grade: reinforced corners, rubberized casing, and scuffed paint that had seen more tarmacs than desks. A Panasonic Toughbook, Claire realized. Field-ready. Desert-proof. Practically bullet-resistant. They were more used to seeing him carry a Glock, not a laptop. Louis clocked their expressions. "What?" he asked, pretending to be affronted. "Don't think for one second that you're the only ones allowed to own tech. Some of us like spreadsheets *and* suppressors." He popped the case open, revealing the computer booting up with the hum of a portable satellite modem. Claire, seated cross-legged on the worn office chair with a notebook balanced on her knee, was—as always—the first to speak. She had the same crisp urgency she brought to everything. First to hand in assignments. First to finish exams. First to volunteer. Diligent could have been her middle name.

"Okay," Claire began, flipping through her notes with a soft rustle of paper. "Here's what I've confirmed so far. I cross-referenced the artifact records from the Egyptian Museum in Cairo and the New Valley Museum in Kharga, and then compared both sets against the INHA database."

She paused, tapping her pen thoughtfully. "There's no recorded mention—none at all—of the word 'obelisk' or 'stele' associated

with any finds from Bahariya. Which, on its own, wouldn't be so surprising, except that very little seems to have come out of Bahariya at all."
She glanced up, meeting their eyes.
"In the early days, yes—some pottery, funerary items, a few statues—those were shipped to Cairo and Kharga. But in the past five to ten years? Virtually nothing. And definitely nothing large-scale. The biggest artifact ever sourced from Bahariya was a red granite altar, and even that didn't generate much academic buzz."
Alex leaned forward slightly, interest piqued.
Claire continued, "I ran a keyword sweep, just to be thorough: lion, Malik, waypoint, waymarker, stone inscription, carving—that one got a few hits, mostly in reference to the red granite altar—path, pathway, seventh century, monument. Nothing. Not a single direct or indirect reference to an obelisk."
She looked up again. "If you ask me, whatever this second waymarker is—assuming it is an obelisk—it's never been found."
Alex let out a low whistle. "Great work, Claire. As usual."
She gave him a lopsided smile. "This could be good or bad. It might mean the obelisk doesn't exist at Bahariya at all. Or—"
"—it could mean it does, but it's still buried," Samira finished for her, her voice dry with anticipation.
Claire nodded. "Exactly."
Alex sat back in his chair. "Which means digging."
Samira was already flipping back a few pages in her own notebook. "Digging, yes—but with context."
She found the page she wanted and tapped it with her finger. "The INHA doesn't hold much on Bahariya, to be honest. There's some material on Ahmed Fakhry and his work at the Temple of Alexander—but that was back in 1942, well before the United Nations was ever established."
She shot a pointed look at Alex. "That excavation, by the way, was sponsored by Harvard."
Alex raised an eyebrow but said nothing.

Samira continued, "There has never been an UN-sanctioned dig at Bahariya. A few published reports exist—two of them written by Fakhry himself. Some tourism outfits still visit the site, but there's not much to see anymore. It's become something of a backwater."

Claire nodded. "I've gone over the Temple site in detail. It was originally constructed around 332 BCE, likely during Alexander's time in Egypt. The Greeks used it through to the late Roman period—possibly up to the fifth or sixth century. After that, the Copts repurposed it for Christian worship until sometime in the twelfth century. And then—oblivion. It was forgotten for centuries until Fakhry stumbled across it, more or less by accident, while searching for the lost stela of Thutmose II."

"Which he never found," Samira added. "So no, nothing unusual has ever come out of Bahariya. At least, nothing officially recorded."

Samira closed her notebook with a soft snap. "And maybe that's exactly the point."

Louis Delon took his cue from Alex, sitting up straighter and folding his hands theatrically as if about to deliver a monologue.

"This idea of tourists," he began, his accent thickening as he warmed to his subject, "is bête. Stupid. Ridiculous. We would never get close to the site. Not without an official escort from a licensed tour operator, and certainly not without permits. There's been a marked increase in police presence across the Western Desert over the past couple of years—an effort to clamp down on the illicit artifacts trade and stop black marketeers from raiding the antiquities. Tourists are monitored, questioned. Sometimes detained."

He shook his head, lips pursed in disdain. "So non, tourists are out."

He paused for effect, and then leaned forward, a spark flickering in his eyes.

"But—I have another idea."

Something in his voice shifted. The others picked up on it immediately: that faint thread of excitement, a conspiratorial hum beneath his words.

"We go as UNESCO site inspectors."

There was a beat of silence.

"What?" Samira blinked.

"You can't be serious," Alex muttered, already half-rising from his seat.

"I'm listening," said Claire, one eyebrow raised.

Louis held up both palms to hold back the rising tide of skepticism.

"Let me finish. Please, Professeur. Just listen, because it makes perfect sense."

He began ticking points off on his fingers.

"One—we already have bonafide UN identification from the Leptis Magna excavation. You know it. I know it. Those IDs are real. They'd pass any level of scrutiny."

Alex frowned, unconvinced, but said nothing.

"Two—it gives us legitimate grounds to conduct field examinations. We're not just tourists or looters or curious academics. We're UN inspectors. We're supposed to poke around."

He shifted to his third point, warming now, the cadence of his French-accented English growing more animated.

"Three—we go to Bahariya under the pretext of initiating a World Heritage Site evaluation. It's the perfect bureaucratic smokescreen. All we need is to claim the Temple of Alexander has recently come under review for potential inscription. It's plausible—it should have been reviewed years ago anyway. That gives us carte blanche to survey the area, document the site, and conduct minor excavations. No one would question it."

Samira was watching him closely now, arms folded, but she hadn't interrupted again.

"Four—if we forge the paperwork, the permits, the letters of approval—who's going to check? We're not pretending to be rogue academics. We're from the UN. They'd assume all the documentation passed through official channels. No one questions the blue flag."

Louis paused, letting that sink in.

"And five—we know how the UN operates. The red tape, the language, the endless procedures. Between us, we've worked enough years under their umbrella to mimic it flawlessly. We are them—or close enough to play the part."

He spread his hands in conclusion. "It's the perfect cover story."

There was a long silence. The kind that sits heavy before a verdict.

"That's insane," said Alex finally, shaking his head.

"That's... believable," Samira said slowly, her eyes narrowing.

Claire let out a breath—half-laugh, half-marvel. "That's fucking brilliant."

Louis smiled modestly, brushing invisible dust from his sleeve. "I know."

The rest of the morning unravelled in colourful, looping debate. The excitement of the plan was one thing—but the logistics, the legality, and the sheer audacity of it was something else entirely. Louis paced in front of the whiteboard, hands stuffed into his pockets, the heel of his shoe squeaking with every pivot. "Think about it," he said, voice rising. "We already are affiliated with the UN through the Leptis Magna dig. We're not just random civilians. We have credentials. We have the framework. The rest is smoke and mirrors."

Claire leaned over the conference table, chin resting on her hands. "It's reckless," she said, grinning. "God, I love it."

Alex wasn't smiling. He stood near the window, arms crossed, watching Cairo traffic crawl past outside. "This is identity fraud. International fraud. We're not just talking about being denied permits—we'd be detained. Blacklisted. Possibly worse."

"But do you have a better idea?" Louis shot back, turning to face him. "Because I don't see another way into Bahariya without causing trouble. Tourists won't work. Academic permissions will just draw attention to us and take months. And we don't have months."

Samira raised a hand gently, cutting through the rising tension. "Let's stop pretending this is about legality. None of us are naïve. We've all seen how the system works here—what passes, what gets waved through, what doesn't. If we do this, we do it cleanly, quietly, and fast. We make it look official. We give them no reason to ask questions."

Alex turned from the window, finally exhaling. "It's not the execution I'm worried about. It's the fallback. If something goes wrong, we can't call in favours. Not from INHA, not from the UN, not from anyone."

Claire sat up. "Which is why we do it right. We forge the paperwork properly, we align it with precedent, we make sure everything checks out on the surface. We've seen this kind of bureaucracy before—it's bloated, overwhelmed, inconsistent. That's not a liability. It's a gift."

Louis clapped his hands once, decisive. "Merci, Claire. Exactly. We're not fighting the system—we're using its own inertia against it."

The conversation shifted, reluctantly at first, then with increasing focus, into planning. What exactly would they need to pass as UNESCO inspectors? Permits. Travel approvals. Excavation licenses. Authorizations for removal of artifacts. And the pièce de résistance—a signed letter from the United Nations addressed to the Egyptian Ministry of Tourism and Antiquities, formally recognizing their inspection mission.

Alex ran a hand through his hair. "It's all contingent on one thing," he said. "That no one actually checks. That the people manning the checkpoints, stamping the paperwork, signing off on our dig— don't take a closer look."

"They won't," said Louis, leaning back against the wall. "This is the Western Desert. People are assigned there to disappear. It's the land of demotion and disinterest. You get sent there if you're lazy, if you're incompetent, or if someone upstairs wants to make your life miserable. It's not exactly where you find Egypt's finest civil servants."

"Encouraging," Samira said dryly.

Still, it wasn't blind hope. In the INHA archives, they found what they needed—records of old excavations in the Valley of the Golden Mummies and beyond. Copies of permits issued by real Egyptian officials. Travel permissions. Equipment manifests. Every one of them a blueprint.

"Only the names and dates need to change," Louis said, scanning the top sheet.

"And the signatures," Claire added.

"And the ministry seals," said Samira.

Louis grinned. "Details."

They moved with purpose. Samira and Claire began cataloguing what tools they would need, keeping it strictly to hand tools— shovels, trowels, brushes, and sieves. No mechanical equipment. Nothing noisy. Everything could be packed discreetly in crates for ease of transport.

Louis, meanwhile, collected the forgery templates and headed down to the admin offices on the embassy's first floor. There, behind closed doors and with quiet requests, he found a sympathetic typist who could replicate official formatting, ink stamps, and even simulate weathered paper.

After lunch—flatbread, pickled onions, and tahini spread across notebooks—they regrouped in the conference room.

"Vehicles," said Alex, chewing on the end of a pencil. "Marked or unmarked?"

"Unmarked," said Claire immediately. "Too much heat with official plates. We'd stand out."

"But not too ordinary either," Samira added. "We want to look like the kind of field team that hires locally. The UN does that all the time."

They settled on two white Toyota Prados—standard fare for NGOs and UN field teams alike. One was already in their possession, rented a few days ago and still parked at the docks. But retrieving it could be a risk.

"If it's being watched," said Alex, "we don't go near it. Not directly."

"Then I'll get someone at the embassy to pick it up," Samira said. "Someone junior. Someone invisible."

"And the second vehicle?" Claire asked.

"I'll rent it," Louis offered. "Same agency. Different name. Different license. I'm not in any database."

"Which is exactly why you're our point man," said Claire, flashing him a smile.

Alex stood, stretching his back. "Alright then. Louis secures the second vehicle. Claire and Samira pack the tools. I'll arrange accommodation in Bahariya—something modest, but credible."

"And the documents will be done by tonight," Louis added, checking his watch.

Alex paused, looking at the notes, the maps, the scatter of permits and old letters arrayed across the table like the opening hand of a very dangerous game.

"It feels like a space shuttle launch," he murmured. "Everything timed to the second."

Claire looked up at him, her expression alive with adrenaline. "All systems go, Professor."

And this time, he didn't argue.

By late afternoon, the embassy compound thrummed with a quiet, purposeful energy. The golden light of a Cairo March evening streamed in low and warm across the courtyard, catching in the olive trees and casting long, amber shadows against the sandstone walls. The air was dry and cool, touched by a faint desert wind that carried with it the dusty scent of sun-baked stone and distant jasmine.

Everything was in order.

The white Toyota Prado that had been parked for the last few days at the docks had been retrieved by a junior staffer from the French embassy—an intern, forgettable and perfectly chosen—and returned without incident. It now sat gleaming beneath the carport, body recently washed, plates clean.

Louis had done what Louis did best: made things appear. He had sourced a second, identical Prado from the Hertz counter at Cairo International Airport. No questions had been asked, and the vehicle had been delivered to the embassy within hours, its documents flawless, the transaction untraceable. The two SUVs now sat side by side like matched chess pieces, quiet, unassuming, and ready.

Claire and Samira had worked efficiently, methodically. The excavation tools had been sorted and double-checked—brushes, spades, folding trowels, soft-bristle brooms, gloves, and sieves. Everything was clean, labeled, and packed into matte-black lockable storage crates. They had even remembered the tarps, sunshades, and headlamps. The boxes had been loaded into the rear compartments of both Prados with military precision.

Inside the villa, Alex sat at the long dining table, laptop open, confirmation emails open on-screen. Three nights booked at the Safari Camp Bahariya Oasis. Reserved under a placeholder "UN Technical Team" title. Paid via a ghost credit card registered to a dormant Parisian shell corporation, one that the embassy's administrative division kept warm for occasions precisely like this. There would be no trail. No name. Just the impression of legitimacy.

He looked up as Samira entered the cafeteria, holding a sheaf of documents. She laid them down in front of him with a strange smile.

"Look at these," she said. "They're perfect."

Alex flipped through the folders: excavation permits, travel authorizations, letters of introduction from the UN's Department of Cultural Heritage addressed to the Egyptian Ministry of Tourism and Antiquities. Each stamped, signed, aged just enough. The font, the language, even the tone of bureaucratic indifference—it was indistinguishable from the real thing. The folders were thick blue stock, embossed with the UN logo, slightly scuffed at the corners as if they had been in use for months.

"They even used the proper office stationery," Claire said from the doorway, brushing dust from her jeans. "Where did they get that?" Louis strolled in behind her, whistling. "You don't ask," he said with a wink. "Just be grateful Paris has a long memory and a short list of morals."

The sun dipped lower behind the embassy walls, casting the inner courtyard into a glowing copper haze. Cicadas had begun their slow, electric buzz in the garden hedges. The city beyond the gates—chaotic, endless, vibrating—felt distant now, like another world.

Louis opened the door to the first Prado and slid into the passengers seat. From a small canvas duffel, he pulled out his Glock 17, checked the magazine, and tucked it into the glove box. A spare box of ammunition followed. In the second Prado, he stashed a backup pistol beneath the drivers seat, wrapped in cloth and secured with duct tape.

"Just in case," he muttered. "Molineux would expect no less." When one of the embassy security officers spotted the preparations, he let out a theatrical sigh of envy.

"You're all going without us?" he said, raising an eyebrow. "Adventure's wasted on the academics."

Claire caught the exchange, grinned and gave him a mock salute. "Someone has to look good in a sun hat."

By twilight, it was done. Every crate was packed, every bag zipped, every document sealed in its folder. The vehicles were fueled, aligned nose-first toward the embassy gates. Inside, there was a quiet, reflective tension—no longer the frenetic energy of planning, but the calm before execution. The hush of readiness.

They would sleep tonight, or try to. And tomorrow, before Cairo's traffic boiled into its daily chaos, they would slip out—early enough to beat the bottlenecks, early enough to vanish unnoticed. The plan was fragile, dependent on inertia, indifference, and a little luck. But it was in motion.

As Claire closed the rear hatch of the second Prado and dusted her hands, she glanced around at the group—Alex, Samira, Louis— each of them caught in a moment of their own private thoughts. She smiled.

"Well," she said. "Let the adventure begin."

And so it had.

ACT III – The Serpent and the Crown

Chapter 1

Cairo's morning had already begun to swell, like a wave gathering momentum beneath the soft hush of daybreak. The city, ever restless, shimmered under a pale golden veil. Dust rose gently in the early light as street vendors began to set up battered carts, filling the air with smells of cardamom coffee, diesel fumes, and warm bread just pulled from the bellies of clay ovens. A flock of egrets skimmed low over the Nile, wings catching sunbeams like fragments of mirrors.

From the gates of the French Embassy on Charles de Gaulle Street, two white Toyota Prados emerged in silence. The wrought-iron gates creaked open with bureaucratic finality, and the vehicles rolled forward like ghosts in broad daylight, rental vehicle vanilla for anonymity's sake.

In the lead vehicle, Alex Carey adjusted his sunglasses as he steered with quiet intensity. Samira sat beside him, glancing down at the neat folder of permits in her lap.

"Still think this is going to work?" Alex asked without looking away from the road.

Samira exhaled through her nose, her answer as dry as the dawn wind. "It has to."

Behind them, the second Prado followed at a disciplined distance. Louis, gripping the wheel a little too tightly, glanced at the rearview mirror for the fourth time in as many seconds. Claire sat beside him, her face alight with anticipation and nerves, legs bouncing restlessly.

"Tell me again," she said, "how I don't look like I'm lying."

"You look...like you were born in Geneva," Louis muttered. "They'll believe you're from the UN."

They moved through the affluent suburb of Zamalek, Cairo's traffic already building into a crescendo. Honking tuk-tuks and boxy yellow taxis buzzed through open lanes, while trucks loaded with cement or vegetables clogged the intersections. The convoy weaved onto the Ring Road, the eastern sky growing sharper and more defined by the minute.

The plan was simple: exit Cairo via the Ring Road, swing past the junction near 6th of October City, and head west on the Cairo–Bahariya Road. The journey would be approximately 370 kilometers across progressively emptier terrain. But the first real test lay just ahead—the first police checkpoint, where travel into the Western Desert was controlled and catalogued.

As they approached the checkpoint—a low-slung cluster of cement barricades painted in sun-faded black and white stripes—the traffic began to funnel. There was no signage, just the dull presence of uniformed men sipping tea from tin cups under a flapping canvas tarp. A rusting steel boom gate hung lazily across the lane. A striped awning provided minimal shade, beneath which a single officer stood, AK slung over his back, radio crackling with static. He was the personification of Egyptian checkpoint fatigue: his shirt was untucked, his cap too large for his head, and he looked like he'd been standing in that exact same spot since Mubarak was president.

As the first Prado eased to a stop beside the checkpoint, the guard straightened just enough to fulfill his duty.

"Waqef, waqef," he muttered, barely raising his hand.

وقف، وقف

"Stop, stop."

He took two slow steps forward, not bothering to make eye contact.

"Awraq, min faḍlak," he said, in a voice that could have been mistaken for a yawn.

أوراق، من فضلك

"Papers, please."

Samira offered him a polite smile and leaned forward with the folder in her hand. "United Nations inspection team," she said in Arabic, voice even but firm. "Travel permit and identification."

The officer barely glanced at her. He took the papers and leafed through them with all the urgency of a man inspecting menu options he couldn't afford. He counted heads: one, two. No weapons visible. No cargo in the roof racks. The registration plate matched the travel permit. His eyes flicked once more at the crest on the front of the folder—UN blue, crisp, and laminated.

"Tafaddalu," he grunted.

تفضلوا

"Go ahead."

The boom gate was raised with a shrug, and just like that, they were through.

Inside the second vehicle, Louis's hands were sweating on the wheel. Claire glanced over at him, then at the approaching guard. Her breath quickened.

"Smile," she whispered to herself. "Act like bureaucracy bores you."

The same bored officer stepped over, already reaching for the second set of papers. Claire's hands trembled slightly as she passed them over. He scanned, nodded, and counted.

UN ID. Two people – One, two. Plates match, permits in order. Another shrug. Another lift of the boom.

They were through.

"Holy shit," Claire exhaled. "That was it? That was it?"

Louis laughed—not from amusement, but from sheer, shuddering relief. "If they're all like that, we might just make it."

Back in the lead vehicle, Alex kept his eyes on the shimmering road. "We're not in the clear yet," he said, more to himself than anyone else.

Samira gave a thin smile. "But we're in."

The convoy moved westward, the urban sprawl of Cairo gradually falling away behind them. Concrete towers gave way to open expanses of yellow-grey desert. The Cairo–Bahariya Road stretched ahead, straight as a ruler, hot air warping the horizon like a mirage. Every now and then, rusting road signs in Arabic and English offered dusty reassurance that Bahariya Oasis was somewhere out there, if they kept going.

In both vehicles, the occupants fell quiet, the silence born not of fear now, but focus. The adrenaline had faded to a steady pulse. The desert was ahead. Their story was holding. The next checkpoint would decide whether it could continue.

But for now, they drove into the morning sun—foreigners in borrowed armor, threading their way into the sands of something far older than themselves.

The Toyota Prado's drove on through the scorched Egyptian wilderness, the early adrenaline of departure long since burned off by heat and monotony. The morning sun had climbed higher, now searing down from a pitiless blue sky. The desert around them shimmered with waves of rising heat, giving the illusion that the asphalt stretched into infinity. Potholes cratered the road like an abandoned war zone—some deep enough to devour a motorcycle whole—while shifting sands crept across the bitumen like pale ghosts, blown by sudden gusts from invisible dunes. Every so often, they'd pass a forlorn fuel stop: rusted signage advertising TAQR Petroleum or Misr Petroleum, sun-bleached awnings flapping lazily in the hot breeze, and a solitary attendant dozing behind a fly-specked counter.

Hours passed like minutes, then minutes like hours. The monotony of the journey had lulled them all into a sort of heat-dulled complacency. Then, without warning, the second checkpoint emerged on the horizon.

It looked sharper, more fortified. This wasn't some sleepy rural post—it was professional, alert, and austere. A concrete guardhouse flanked the road, reinforced with sandbags, shaded observation platforms, and a steel boom gate stretching across both lanes. Soldiers milled about under canvas shelters, weapons slung lazily across their shoulders, but their eyes were anything but lazy. This was the Desert Security Directorate.

Alex slowed the lead vehicle and rolled up to the thick yellow line painted across the asphalt. There were no other vehicles in sight. They had the full attention of the guards.

A young soldier stepped out from the shadow of the guardhouse. His uniform was a sharp contrast to the police blues they'd seen earlier—dust-colored desert camo with black tactical boots, and a black balaclava rolled up to his forehead. A patch in Arabic script was sewn onto his chest.

توقف هناك! he barked. Then, more disinterestedly,

"Stop there."

Alex eased the Prado to a halt. Samira rolled down her window, presenting a calm that didn't quite reach her eyes. The guard stepped forward.

أوراقكم، من فضلك.

"Papers, please."

Samira handed over their travel permits and UN IDs with casual precision. "We are with the United Nations," she said, her voice measured. "Heading to Bahariyah Oasis. Archaeological inspection."

The guard barely glanced at her.

والموافقات للوصول إلى البحرية؟

"The approvals for Bahariyah?"

Samira reached back into the folder and produced the excavation permits and the UN introductory letter. He took them silently, nodded once, and began walking back toward the guardhouse.

Samira's facade slipped as soon as his back was turned. "He's taking too long," she muttered. "That wasn't just a glance."

Alex didn't take his eyes off the rearview mirror. "Relax. Standard protocol. He's probably just photocopying everything."

Halfway across the open stretch to the building, a second guard emerged and intercepted the first. They spoke in low voices, gesturing subtly at the two white Toyotas. Then the second man, equally young, walked toward them with a more focused expression.

"Please step out of the vehicle," he said, gesturing with one hand. "Open the back."

Alex nodded, climbing out. Samira followed, keeping her movements smooth, deliberate. Behind them, Louis and Claire were already out of the second Prado, unlocking the rear compartments. Alex flashed Louis a cheeky grin and gave a subtle nod. Louis returned it without breaking stride.

The guard examined the contents methodically—UN-marked crates, digging implements, sealed document tubes. He moved to the back seat and gestured.

هل هذه لكم؟

"Do these belong to you?"

"Yes," Samira said quickly. "They're ours."

The guard leaned forward, checked under the seats, then approached the front. Coffee cups. Folded maps. Wrappers. His hand reached toward the glovebox.

Suddenly Louis was there, eyes wide with urgency – The Glock!.

"Excuse me," he said loudly, improvising. "Do you have a toilet? I need to piss."

Samira quickly translated.

.يحتاج إلى التبول

The guard, annoyed, motioned behind the building.

.من هناك ذهب

"Go there."

Samira relayed the translation. Louis, playing dumb, blinked. The guard pointed more aggressively.

.هناك .خلف المبنى

"There. Behind the building."

Louis finally nodded, offered a clumsy smile, and turned away. As he walked, he glanced back just in time to see Alex flick open the glovebox and slide the Glock beneath the passengers seat.

The guard checked inside the glovebox. Toyota drivers manual, vehicle service records, Hertz rental documents. Nothing to see.

He straightened, waved them on. "You can repack." Then he
turned to the second Prado.
Claire greeted him with a sunny smile.
صباح الخير.
"Good morning."
The guard blinked, caught off guard, but quickly resumed his duty.
He began rifling through the cargo. Claire played helpful. Louis
returned from his performance behind the building just as the first
guard exited the office again, a sheaf of papers in hand.
He handed the originals back to Samira with a crisp nod, the
familiar blue UN folder now slightly creased.
كل شيء في نظام.
"Everything is in order."
Claire received hers as well. Copies had clearly been made, but
nothing further was said.
The boom gate lifted with a clank. Engines turned over. The
Toyotas eased forward again onto the black ribbon of road
stretching toward the western horizon.
Checkpoint two was behind them.
Two down. One to go.

The sun beat down mercilessly as the two white Toyota Prados
hummed westward, engines steady against the monotony of the
road. For the last two hours, the desert had unspooled before them
like a ribbon of heat-hazed nothingness: the same blistered asphalt,
the same skeletal acacia trees scattered along the horizon, the same
tire-mangled potholes that could ruin your day if you weren't
paying attention. Every so often, a gust of wind pushed thin veils
of sand across the road—ghosts of old dunes refusing to die
quietly.
The occasional fuel station broke the spell s it had before—if one
could call them that. They were little more than sunburnt shelters
with rusted signage: "Shell," or "ExxonMobil," slogans in faded
Arabic clinging to crumbling facades. A stray donkey wandered

behind one. Plastic chairs were stacked under broken awnings. No one was ever visible, as though the stations waited for travelers that never came.

In the second vehicle, Claire exhaled loudly and slumped into the seat.

"This is actually killing me," she muttered. "I won't even have to pretend to be bored at the next checkpoint."

Louis chuckled. "Be careful what you wish for. You never know when things get... less boring."

Claire squinted through her sunglasses. "Anything would be better than this sun-baked loop of death."

Ahead of them, the road finally widened slightly, and buildings began to pepper the landscape—low, sandy-brown structures that looked as though they'd grown from the desert itself. Satellite dishes jutted from rooftops like bent antennae searching for sanity. A battered sign welcomed them, chipped but legible: Welcome to Bawiti – Gateway to Bahariya Oasis.

A dusty pickup overtook them suddenly on the left, its bed full of watermelons and yelling children. Life was reasserting itself, and it didn't care how carefully you planned your arrival.

As they rolled deeper into town, the atmosphere shifted. Bawiti wasn't bustling exactly—it didn't have the frantic rhythm of Cairo—but it was very much awake. A donkey cart trundled past a shop selling plastic buckets and chewing gum. A woman in a bright red hijab bartered with a grocer, hands flying. An old man in a galabeya waved lazily from a café where young men sat sipping mint tea under a canopy of palm fronds.

They passed the modest post office, a corner store, and then—finally—the low, concrete building with faded Arabic lettering and a flag drooping on its pole: Police Station / Desert Security Directorate. Parked outside were a cluster of vehicles—two official Hilux trucks with roof-mounted beacons, a civilian Corolla caked in dust, and one hulking DSD Land Cruiser with blacked-out windows.

Alex pulled up slowly and turned off the ignition. "No boom gate. This is more formality than security," he said, exhaling.

Louis's voice crackled through the radio. "Looks... sleepy. I expected more fanfare."

Samira opened her door. "They'll still take it seriously. Don't relax yet."

They stepped into the thick, baked air. The police station looked like most government buildings in Egypt's small towns—drab, rectangular, and guarded more by heat than men. Its paint peeled in great sun-flayed sheets, and a line of dusty ficus trees wilted out front, planted long ago with hope but little water.

Inside, the air was marginally cooler. The tiled floor had once been white. A warped ceiling fan spun overhead with a persistent click-click-click. Behind a worn counter, a stocky local policeman in a short-sleeved khaki uniform barely looked up as they entered.

Samira stepped forward and spoke confidently in Arabic.

صباح الخير، نحن من الأمم المتحدة. هنا لتقييم معبد الإسكندر والمواقع المجاورة له

"Good morning. We are from the United Nations. We're here to assess the Temple of Alexander and the surrounding sites."

The officer blinked, then turned and called through a side door. A few moments later, a taller man entered—a Desert Security Directorate officer in desert-camouflage fatigues, sidearm holstered, sunglasses still perched on his forehead. He had heard the introduction, but looked them over like he was reading a problem written in another language.

أنت من؟ ولماذا أنتم هنا في الواحة؟

"Who are you, and what are you doing here in the oasis?"

Samira repeated herself, more formally this time.

نحن مفتشون من الأمم المتحدة. هنا لتقييم الموقع من أجل حالة التراث العالمي.

"We're UN inspectors. We're here to evaluate the site for World Heritage status."

The DSD sergeant tilted his head slightly, skeptical.

النهب؟ هل هذا بسبب النهب؟

"The looting? Is this about the looting?"

Samira hesitated only slightly before shaking her head.

لا، لا .هذا تقييم فقط .سيستغرق يومين، لا أكثر

"No, no. This is just an assessment. Two days, no more."

The sergeant seemed unconvinced but nodded.

.جوازات السفر، رخص القيادة، بطاقات الأمم المتحدة

"Passports, driver's licenses, UN ID cards."

They handed everything over. He took each set of documents, checking photo to face carefully, then moved to a battered photocopier on a side desk and began making copies. Samira handed over their travel permits, letters of introduction, and site approvals. He photocopied them all without comment.

أين ستقيمون؟

"Where will you be staying?"

Samira translated for Alex and he produced a printout. "Safari Camp, Bahariya Oasis," he said.

The sergeant glanced at it, made another photocopy, then motioned to the second pair waiting behind them.

والاثنان الآخران؟

"And the other two?"

Samira translated. Louis stepped forward. "Bonjour," he said cheerfully.

Claire smiled and said, in her passable Arabic

.صباح الخير، سيدي

"Good morning, sir."

The sergeant raised an eyebrow. "Documents."

They went through the same ritual—passport, license, ID, permits, hotel booking—all copied and filed.

At last, the sergeant returned everything, handing back the thick stack to Samira with a final, almost obligatory warning.

.لا تذهبوا بعيدًا عن المعبد .لدينا مشاكل مع بعض البدو المحليين .لا نريد مشاكل

"Don't stray far from the temple. We've had problems with some local tribespeople. We don't want any trouble."

Samira inclined her head.

بالطبع. نحن هنا للموقع فقط.

"Of course. We're here for the site only."

Outside again, squinting in the glare, they made their way back to the cars. Samira reiterated the DSD warning to Alex. Alex leaned in close to Samira as they opened the doors.

"I wonder what the problem with the locals is really about?" he said under his breath.

Samira didn't hesitate. "Probably years of being shafted by tour operators and government officials. Foreigners don't get a warm welcome in places like this."

Claire, already halfway into her seat, muttered, "Can't wait to be charmingly unwelcome."

Louis just grinned and pulled his sunglasses down. "Three checkpoints and a pile of bureaucracy later… we're in."

The two Toyotas purred to life once more and began the short drive to their accommodation—closer now to the ruins, the mystery, and the secret that had lain hidden in the desert for more than a thousand years.

The short drive from the police station into the heart of Bahariya took less than ten minutes, but it felt like entering another world. The buildings here were a blend of old and older—honey-colored mudbrick homes with rounded corners and wooden lintels sat beside low concrete shops painted in faded pastels. Palm trees lined the main road, their fronds rustling lazily in the desert breeze. A fruit vendor squatted beside crates of pomegranates and prickly pears, and the air was thick with the scent of dust, engine oil, and slowly roasting meat.

As they rounded a bend in the road, the Safari Camp Bahariya came into view. It was a low-slung, ochre-toned lodge ringed by a few domed outbuildings and date palms. The main building was an inviting structure—part Bedouin style, part colonial throwback— with arched doorways, thick adobe walls, and wide verandas shaded by bamboo slats. A series of colorful rugs flapped gently in the dry wind. The only sound was the distant buzz of cicadas and the occasional creak of wood in the heat.

The cars crunched to a halt on gravel, the engines ticking cool as they climbed out.

"I've stayed in worse," Claire said, removing her sunglasses.

"Give it time," Louis replied, eyeing the front entrance with mock suspicion.

Inside, the lobby was dim and blessedly cool. The stone floor was strewn with handwoven mats, and alcoves along the walls held old ceramic jars and faded black-and-white photos of desert expeditions. Behind a dark wood counter stood a man in his fifties with a crisp white galabeya and a weathered face, smiling beneath a thick grey mustache.

"Welcome, welcome," he said in Arabic-accented English. "You are from the UN, yes? We have your rooms ready."

Samira handled the check-in quickly, their bookings confirmed and keys handed over with small brass tags. Alex noted that there were no other guests visible—just a boy mopping the floor in silence and the scent of cumin drifting from somewhere behind the lobby.

"Lunch?" the owner asked.

"Yes please," said Alex. "We've had a long morning."

They ate beneath a canvas awning, overlooking a sparse garden where the heat shimmered in waves. The food arrived quickly— simple but aromatic dishes that made up in flavor what they lacked in presentation.

Claire opted for a vegetarian tagine: slow-cooked carrots, potatoes, and chickpeas swimming in saffron-scented broth, served with a wedge of warm khobz bread. She tore a piece and dipped it thoughtfully. "I swear this is the best thing I've eaten since we left Cairo."

Louis devoured a kofta plate—spiced lamb skewers with tahini sauce and roasted eggplant. "If they arrest us later," he said between mouthfuls, "I'll ask for this in my last meal."

Alex had grilled chicken with sumac and lemon, charred slightly, tender inside. The smokiness mingled with a dab of harissa that made his brow sweat. He sipped his hibiscus tea, cool and sour-sweet.

Samira chose a shakshuka, the eggs still bubbling in their cast-iron dish, flecked with parsley. She ate quietly, eyes on her phone, occasionally checking local headlines.

They didn't speak much after that, lulled by the full bellies, the shade, and the hour.

The sun hadn't relented, but the shadows had lengthened slightly as they rolled away from the camp, taking the small dirt road southeast toward the ruins. The town thinned quickly, replaced once again by desert—this time interspersed with groves of date palms and occasional half-buried structures.

After twenty minutes, the Temple of Alexander rose ahead of them. It didn't rise much.

"This is it?" Claire asked, leaning forward in her seat.

What remained of the temple stood hunched at the edge of a dry wadi—limestone blocks weathered into soft curves, the bare skeleton of what must once have been proud. A low surrounding wall enclosed the site, broken in places and partially buried under sand. The gate was crooked and missing its latch, held open by a large rock.

They stepped out into the heat, the dry air humming around them.

"It's not much," Claire said, circling a fallen column. "For the only temple in Egypt dedicated to Alexander the Great... you'd think they'd take better care."

"She's right," Louis muttered, kicking at a piece of pottery half-submerged in dirt.

"But it's real," Alex said softly. "Authentic. And untouched, mostly."

Samira walked toward the faded metal sign near the entrance. Once white with bold black text in Arabic and English, it was now a blistered mess—most of the paint had peeled away, and what remained was illegible.

Inside the temple grounds, they wandered quietly, taking in the layout. The structure was modest—two main rooms, crumbled columns, the base of a once-impressive pylon. The walls had eroded, but some reliefs had survived.

"There's nothing in the outbuildings," Samira said, motioning south. "Whatever we're here to find—it's not out there."

Alex nodded. "It's here. Somewhere inside."

Claire called out from near the main doorway. "Here—look at this."

On the right side of the entrance, near the base of the limestone wall, a partially visible relief had been eroded by wind and time. Only the lower half remained—feet in sandals, a folded kilt, and the unmistakable Macedonian shield.

"Could be Alexander," she said.

But it was the second room, cooler and darker, that held the most detail. On the north wall, partially intact, was a faded carving of Alexander himself—offering incense to the gods Horus and Isis, his crown unmistakably pharaonic.

"He's wearing the double crown," Claire said, almost whispering. "Upper and Lower Egypt."

"He was declared Pharaoh after Siwa," Alex replied. "This temple must've been commissioned soon after."

In the final chamber, the figures of Amun and Alexander dominated the remaining reliefs. In one scene, he poured water from a libation vessel; in another, he stood flanked by priests wearing the tall plumed headdress of Bahariya.

"Definitely local priests," Samira said. "Look at the robes. Oasis style."

Time blurred. Shadows lengthened along the temple walls. Their water bottles had long run dry, and even Louis had stopped talking.

"We've been here four hours," Alex said, squinting at the sun. "We should head back. Be fresh in the morning."

They agreed, and made their way slowly back to the vehicles.
But as the cars started down the dusty road toward the lodge, they failed to notice the figure that rose from behind a dune east of the site. A young man, barely more than a teenager, dressed in a long brown tunic and a wrapped cloth around his face—not quite a turban, more like a desert scarf—rose cautiously.
His eyes were fixed on the retreating vehicles. He had been watching for hours.
Now, he stood, tightened his scarf, and picked up his staff. Without a word, he turned southeast and began walking at speed. He had seen enough.
He had to deliver the news.

Chapter 2

The sun broke over the Bahariya hills at a little after six. A thin golden light stretched across the desert floor, catching on palm fronds and rooftops still heavy with sleep. At the Safari Camp, the team was already stirring. Alex had been the first to rise, pacing the edge of the courtyard with coffee in hand as the others filtered into the breakfast room.

The smell of cardamom and fresh flatbread filled the air. The lodge owners—an older man with wind-worn skin and his sprightly teenage daughter—served a modest but satisfying breakfast: warm baladi bread, soft cheese, fuul beans with a drizzle of olive oil, sliced tomatoes, and hard-boiled eggs with a hint of cumin. A large pot of sweet, dark tea sat in the center of the table.

"No tourists this week," the owner, a man named Yousif, had smiled to Samira. "Low season. March is the last quiet month. Soon, the heat comes, and with it the Germans."

Samira returned the smile politely. "Then we're grateful to have you all to ourselves."

By six-thirty, the two Toyotas were loaded and bouncing gently along the track out to the temple. The sky was already pale and cloudless. It would be a hot day.

They arrived ten minutes later to find the site unchanged—still windswept and lonely, with that ancient, half-forgotten air. The blackened remnants of an old tourist rope fence lay coiled near the crumbled gate. The wooden sign, once painted bright white with bold black lettering, now resting on the ground, its Arabic and

English text peeling like sunburnt skin. "Temple of Alexander the Great – Ministry of Antiquities." It was barely legible.

Alex laid out the day's plan while standing in the shade cast by the southern wall. "We split up," he said. "Samira and I will take the interior. If there are inscriptions or anything left behind by Malik, it'll be inside the walls. Claire, Louis—you work the courtyard. Start at the entrance and clear a path south, then work outward."

"Backbreaking but simple," said Louis, adjusting his hat. "My kind of archaeology."

Claire rolled her eyes. "We're not treasure hunting, Louis. Try not to get distracted."

The courtyard was shaded along its eastern edge, a blessing at this hour. They set to work immediately. The sand here wasn't compacted—light, windblown, and dry. Within an hour, Claire's shovel rang out against stone.

"Louis," she called over, brushing sweat from her brow. "Come here."

Together, they cleared more sand with careful efficiency, revealing what appeared to be cobblestone flooring—intact, perfectly aligned, laid with a craftsman's hand.

"Six inches under," Claire said, impressed. "Hard to believe it stayed so clean."

"It's not clean," Louis replied, brushing off another stone. "It's just forgotten."

By midmorning, the interior team had found little new—just the familiar reliefs of Alexander presenting offerings to Horus and Isis. Samira took detailed notes while Alex compared the layout to the rough site plans he'd seen in dusty ministry archives.

At 10 a.m., they paused. Water bottles were opened, lunchboxes unpacked early for a small snack. Dates wrapped in wax paper, hunks of cheese, and small rounds of sesame bread filled their hands.

Claire, sitting on a low stone block under the temple's long southern shadow, looked up at Alex. "We found what looks like an old well. Wide, sealed shut. Centerline of the courtyard, not far from the entrance."

"Might have been closed off recently," Alex said. "To keep tourists from tumbling in."

"Or looters," added Samira. "The ministry does things like that. Quiet, cheap interventions."

"Any inscriptions?" asked Louis.

"Nothing yet," said Alex. "But we're barely along the eastern wall. There's still plenty of temple left."

The breeze picked up slightly as they resumed. The sun was climbing, and so were the temperatures, but they worked with purpose. The temple stood silent around them—worn, wind-scoured, but watchful.

Just before noon, Claire struck something solid—again. This time near the southern edge of the courtyard, along the centreline and inline with the well and the temple doorway. She bent, brushed at it with her hands, then called over her shoulder.

"Louis! Bring the broom!"

He jogged over, stiff-bristled brush in hand. "You find a Roman bathtub?"

"Better," she murmured.

They worked quickly and carefully, brushing away the sand grain by grain. A square plinth began to emerge—three feet on a side, about six inches high. It was solid granite, meticulously carved with a master's hand, weathered, but clearly not part of the flagstones.

Claire circled it, crouched low, and squinted at the base. "Wait—there's something here."

"What is it?" Louis asked, leaning in.

Claire didn't respond. She froze for a second, then stood abruptly, letting the broom clatter to the ground.

"I need the Professor," she said.

And without another word, she turned and ran—straight toward the temple.

It was also just before midday when Captain Hafez Abdel-Rahman sauntered into the Bawiti police station, brushing dust from the shoulders of his beige uniform with the casual disdain of a man who considered himself above his posting.

Another day in this godforsaken patch of sand, he thought bitterly, trudging past the cracked tile floor and barely nodding at the handful of constables who stood from their desks as he entered. None of them saluted anymore. None dared speak, either. They knew better.

He pushed open the door to his office with his boot and slumped into the creaking chair behind his desk, sweat still drying on his temples. The desk fan spun uselessly overhead. He glanced at the dirty window. The sun was at its height. The world outside shimmered with heat.

Soon, he reminded himself. Soon, I'll be out of this desert prison. All I need is one or two big shipments, and I'm done with this filthy village and its endless heat.

His eyes fell lazily onto the cluttered in-tray — mostly unpaid traffic citations and unsigned shift rosters — but paused when he spotted a neat sheaf of papers, bound with a rusted paperclip and marked 'FOR YOUR ATTENTION.'

He tugged it free.

His gaze darkened as he read. UN observers. An official inspection of the Temple of Alexander and surrounding historical sites.

Approved by the Supreme Council of Antiquities.

"What is this?" he muttered, flipping pages.

He read it twice.

No. No, no. This will not do.

The phone on his desk slammed under his palm as he jabbed at the intercom. "Sergeant! In my office. Now."

Seconds later, the door opened and the tall, heavy-set sergeant with a neatly trimmed moustache and too much nervous energy stepped inside. "Yes, Captain?"

"When did the UN arrive in Bahariya?" Hafez growled, holding the paper up like a verdict.

"Yesterday afternoon, Captain," Youssef replied cautiously. "While you were, uh… away from the station."

"You checked their documents?"

"Yes, sir. Their paperwork was in order. Approved. Official seals from Cairo."

"And you thought it unimportant to inform me?" Hafez snapped.

Youssef flinched. "I… I was going to tell you as soon as—"

"How many of them?"

"Four. Two men, two women. They said they were just conducting a survey of the Temple of Alexander and its vicinity, to assess it for World Heritage listing. That's all."

"That's all?" Hafez leaned forward, his voice dropping to a dangerous whisper. "Do you think they're just here to count broken stones and take photographs? Do you honestly believe the UN gives a damn about some ruined temple?"

Youssef swallowed. "They… they said they weren't investigating anything."

"Oh, no," Hafez muttered. "No, they wouldn't say that. But they're here to poke around. And if they find anything, we're finished."

Youssef stood frozen, unsure whether to leave or stand at attention.

"Get out," Hafez barked. "Now."

When the door closed, Hafez dialled the secure line he rarely used — the one that rang directly to Cairo.

The call connected on the second ring.

"Dr. Samy Khoury," came the crisp voice on the other end.

"Why the hell wasn't I told?" Hafez snapped.

A pause. "Captain Hafez?" Khoury asked coolly. "Told what, exactly?"

"The UN has sent a delegation to my region. Bahariya. They're inspecting the Temple of Alexander — and your department approved it."

Another pause. Then, evenly, "What delegation?"

"Don't play games with me, Khoury," Hafez snarled. "Four foreigners. They showed up with perfectly stamped documentation — your department's seal. They said they were from the UN."

"I haven't signed off on any UN inspection," Khoury said. "Certainly nothing in Bahariya."

"Well, someone in your office did," Hafez growled. "Either you're being cut out, or you're lying to me."

"I don't like your tone, Captain."

"And I don't like being blindsided," Hafez shot back. "This smells like a setup. First I hear whispers about archaeologists sniffing around. Then tribal unrest. Now international observers showing up with golden tickets. What the hell is going on, Samy?"

"I could ask you the same," Khoury said icily. "Your last three shipments were light. Rumour in Cairo is that you've been dealing off-grid. Quietly. Perhaps trying to sidestep your arrangement with me."

Hafez laughed — a hard, bitter bark. "Don't you dare accuse me. I've kept my end of the deal. Maybe it's you trying to shift the power. Is that what this is? Get the UN involved so they can finger me which then justifies you taking over directly?"

"Don't be absurd."

"Oh, I think it's very possible," Hafez said, voice tightening. "Maybe you're tired of waiting for my pieces to come through. Maybe you want to claim the whole valley for yourself. All that golden treasure buried in those tombs. You think I don't know?"

"You're paranoid."

"I'm careful," Hafez said. "And let me remind you — we had an understanding. Bahariya was mine. You get your share, as agreed. But this?" He jabbed the papers on his desk again. "This is betrayal."

Khoury's voice went suddenly quiet. "I didn't approve the inspection, Hafez. But maybe I should send my own people. A team from Cairo. Just to see what's really happening down there." There was a heavy silence.

"Careful, Khoury," Hafez said darkly. "Send someone down, and I'll assume they're here to replace me. And I won't go quietly." Khoury chuckled, dry and amused. "You forget yourself, Captain. You're a provincial cop. Nothing more."

"And you forget who's been keeping your pockets lined with artifacts smuggled through Libya and the Gulf. I go down, and I take you with me."

"I'll look into the paperwork," Khoury said after a pause. "But do nothing for now. Don't touch them. Don't make a scene."

Hafez grunted.

"And if they are UN inspectors," Khoury added, "then you'll need to play it very, very smart."

The line clicked dead.

Captain Hafez sat back in his chair, blood pounding in his ears. He reached into the bottom drawer of his desk and pulled out a bottle of arak, still half-full. He poured himself a measure into the chipped glass and knocked it back in one gulp.

Then he reached for his private burner phone.

Time to find out exactly who these foreigners were — and whether they needed to disappear.

Dr. Samy Khoury's mind was spinning.

What the hell is Hafez playing at? A UN team? Out there?

And most importantly—why wasn't I warned?

He stood at the tall windows of his Zamalek office, overlooking the Nile's sluggish brown coils. The sunlight glared off the water, but his thoughts were murky, churning. The contact inside the UN always gave them advance notice of any permits, inspections, or special delegations involving Egypt's heritage sites. It was part of the agreement. They had a system. Nothing ever came through without my knowing.

But this… this was completely off the books.

He paced the length of his office, the air heavy with the scent of jasmine from the ornamental bowl on his desk. Either Hafez is lying, or someone else is.

Then came the darker thought. The one he had been avoiding. What if Hafez is cutting me out?

It wasn't impossible. Hafez had grown increasingly erratic in recent months—arrogant, entitled, like a man who thought he no longer needed a partner. Maybe he was testing the waters, seeing if he could sell directly to someone else.

But who? Khoury had spent two decades building his network—smugglers, couriers, shipping agents, corrupt officials, brokers, and buyers from Doha to Brussels. There was no one else in Egypt who could move the kind of product he could.

Except...

His eyes narrowed.

The Client.

Soterakis!

Andreas Soterakis. The bloated Greek devil with his oily charm and old shipping ties, his fingers in every port from Piraeus to Palermo. That fat bastard had been too quiet lately. Too patient. Was this his play?

Khoury clenched his jaw and strode to his desk. He pulled open the bottom drawer, took out the burner cellular phone, and punched in the number. It rang twice.

The voice came through, thick with irritation. "What is it, Khoury? I'm busy."

He's always busy, Khoury thought bitterly.

Time for him to be a little less busy.

"I thought your informant in the UN was reliable."

"He is."

A pause. "What are you talking about?"

"I have a UN team out in the western desert. Bahariya. Conducting some kind of official inspection at the Temple of Alexander." He tried to keep the tremor of uncertainty out of his voice.

"I don't know anything about a UN team in Egypt," Soterakis replied flatly. "Other than what I told you last time."

"Then your informant missed something. It happens. Could've slipped through the cracks."

"Impossible," Soterakis snapped. "He is the crack. Nothing gets past him. He signs off on all cultural mission movements personally. I pay him well so there are no mistakes, no omissions, no surprises. Unlike you, Khoury."

That last word came like a slap.

Khoury stiffened. "What's that meant to mean?"

"It means," the Greek said coolly, "if you had acted when I gave you the intel, we wouldn't still be talking about that dive team fiasco. You had a week's warning and still couldn't find out what they were looking for. That was your failure."

"I acted immediately," Khoury lied. "Maybe it was you who sat on the information too long."

"Don't get defensive with me, you pig-witted bureaucrat," Soterakis hissed. "Your operation is fraying at the seams. Too many leaks. Too many missed shipments. If you don't tighten it up, someone else will."

There it was.

A threat wrapped in business.

Khoury's fingers gripped the edge of the desk. "Don't you dare threaten me, Andreas. I know enough to bury you along with every buyer you ever traded with."

A pause.

Then, in a voice like dry gravel:

"A word of advice, Khoury. Dead men tell no tales."

Click.

The line went dead.

Khoury stared at the phone in his hand, heart hammering.

That bastard.

 Was this the beginning of a takeover? Was Andreas laying the groundwork to replace him? Had he already made Hafez an offer? He sat in silence for a moment longer, fury rising like bile. Then he moved. He opened his contacts list, scrolling fast until he found the name he needed:

Major General Karim Nasser.

Old friend. Military man. Quiet. Discreet. The sort of man who understood how to clean up a problem without drawing attention.

Khoury's finger hovered over the dial button.

Time to remind these dogs who owns this territory.

The four of them gathered around the plinth—staring, speculating, admiring. While it could have been any piece of dressed granite in the world, here, it had special meaning.

Around the base, clearly etched by a deft hand, were the four lions—exactly as they'd appeared in the mosaic floor: one sleeping, one walking, one watching, one resting. Identical in every way.

Alex was the first to speak.

"Well done, Claire. Like—really well done. We might have missed this altogether if we'd focused solely on the temple interior. This… this is exactly what we're looking for."

"Thanks, Prof—but what does it mean?"

Samira dropped to her hands and knees to inspect the plinth more closely. It was obvious to everyone, even Louis, that this stone had been placed long after the construction of the temple and its courtyard. It was equally obvious that the pink granite had been chosen for durability—unlike the weatherworn sandstone that surrounded it.

She ran her fingers over the surface, gently caressing the stone, almost lovingly—reading its tactile story.

"There used to be something on top of it," she murmured. "The top is much smoother than the sides."

Claire knelt down beside her and mimicked the motion.

"I can feel it," she agreed. "The sides have obviously been sandblasted over the centuries—but the top's been protected."

"The obelisk must have rested on top," said Alex.

"But, mon ami, where is it now?" Louis asked.

Instinctively, they all looked around the courtyard. Nothing. Just sandstone blocks and windblown sand.

"That," Alex muttered, "is the million-dollar question."

It was just after midday, and the heat was becoming oppressive. They agreed to retreat from the sun, eat lunch, and revisit the mystery later when their eyes were hungry, but their bellies were full.

Lunch consisted of cold kofta wraps folded into soft, spiced flatbread—each one stuffed with aromatic lamb, parsley, and finely sliced red onion. Alongside came foil packets of saffron rice, mixed with charred zucchini, eggplant, and slivers of red pepper— still warm from the morning's preparation. A tub of tangy tahini sat in the center of the fold-out table, sweating slightly in the heat. There were dates too—plump, sticky, stuffed with almonds and wrapped in wax paper.

Claire bit into one and sighed contentedly.

"God bless the Lodge," she mumbled, mouth full. "This is better than the Marriott in Luxor."

"They even packed pickled lemons," said Samira, holding one aloft with exaggerated reverence. "These are handmade. I can smell the cumin."

"Luxury in the desert," Louis added, tearing into a roll slathered with spiced cheese. "Remind me why we don't just become full-time picnic archaeologists?"

They had taken refuge in the growing patch of shade cast by the temple's southern façade. The stone wall radiated warmth but blocked the worst of the sun. A gentle breeze tugged at their napkins and fluttered the loose linen of their sleeves.

Alex sat a little apart from the others, chewing in silence, eyes still fixed on the plinth. The four lions. The obelisk. Malik. What was it trying to tell them?

"You're quiet," Samira observed, brushing windblown hair from her cheek. "Thinking?"

"Always," Alex replied. "I keep circling the same idea. It's obvious that plinth wasn't part of the original temple. It's also obvious that Malik left that here for us to find."

"But where is the rest of it" Claire asked, wiping her hands on a napkin.

"That's what we have to figure out."

Silence returned—punctuated only by the rustle of packaging and the whisper of wind through the broken colonnades. High above, a pair of vultures circled, slow and deliberate, specks against the blazing blue.

Then Claire stood and stretched.

"I'm going to go commune with nature."

"You want company?" Louis offered.

"Ahh, no," she laughed. "That means I'm going to the toilet. Alone, thank you very much!"

She took a long swig from her canteen, slung her scarf over her shoulders, and disappeared around the back of the building for privacy.

No one noticed how long she took. It was one of those quiet, in-between moments in the field where each person slips into their own rhythm—resting, sketching, noting thoughts.

Ten minutes passed.

Then fifteen.

And Claire did not return.

Chapter 3

It was just after midday in Cairo when Ambassador Raylan Stratton stepped away from his desk, closed the door to his office, and picked up his mobile phone. The air outside was already thick with heat, but in the cool silence of the Embassy's diplomatic wing, everything was still. He scrolled through his contacts, selected the Paris number, and dialed.

The line clicked twice—then rang.

On the third ring, a voice answered, smooth, measured, with that faint, deliberate polish English-speaking Frenchmen reserved for international calls.

"Raylan," said André Molineux, Director General of the Institut National d'Histoire de l'Art. "It's good to hear from you, my friend."

"André, likewise. How's everything at the Institute?"

"Busy, as you can well imagine," Molineux replied. "More grant applications than researchers to fill them. And the board is still circling the question of reopening our Syrian field office. But otherwise—holding steady. And Cairo? Things calming down?"

"A little," said Stratton. "But we're coming into the tourist season. You know how it gets—lost passports, misplaced antiquities declarations, cancelled visas. The usual circus."

Molineux chuckled softly. "Plus, the occasional rogue billionaire."

"Exactly." Stratton's tone sharpened. "Which brings me to the reason I'm calling. I wanted to share some intelligence with you— about our friend, Andreas Soterakis."

"The Greek shipping tycoon?" Molineux asked, immediately
attentive. "The one you suspect is behind the artifact trafficking?"
"That's the one. Look, we've been monitoring chatter for weeks.
Until now, nothing concrete—just vague signals and dead ends.
But recently, we've picked up increased call activity between his
people and several unregistered devices here in Cairo."
"You're sure it's him?"
"As sure as we can be. The calls are almost certainly through
burners—we can't intercept the contents—but the pattern is
unmistakable. This isn't casual. He's orchestrating something, and
it's happening now."
"You think they're coordinating a new shipment?" Molineux
asked. "Or moving assets?"
"That's one possibility. Could be he's prepping for an auction,
lining up buyers, or finalizing transit routes. But there's something
else—and this is where it gets strange. We have reason to believe
Soterakis has been diagnosed with stage four pancreatic cancer."
There was a pause.
"I see," Molineux said slowly. "And what does that mean for us?"
"Maybe nothing," Stratton admitted. "But maybe everything. A
man like Soterakis—powerful, well-connected, cornered by his
own mortality—he's no longer operating with long-term goals.
He's running out of time, which means he may act with
desperation. Boldly. Carelessly. He's already dangerous, André.
But now? He's volatile."
"Understood. But how does this relate to the Institute?"
"Not the Institute directly. But we know your team is still in-
country—still pursuing the tomb, yes?"
Molineux was silent for a beat. Then: "They are. They've gone
dark since they left the French Embassy compound. Standard
precaution while they're in the field."
"Well, if Soterakis is still hunting the tomb too—and we believe he
is—then this isn't just a race anymore. It's a knife fight. He has

money, contacts, and now, nothing to lose. I thought your people should know."

"Thank you, Ambassador. I'll get word to them somehow."

"Be careful," Stratton added. "He's not the only one becoming unpredictable."

The line went dead.

Molineux sat in the stillness of his Paris office, the phone held loosely in one hand. Outside, the soft clang of construction scaffolding echoed from a nearby restoration site, but he barely heard it.

Desperation made men do foolish things. Dead men, worse.

He reached for a secure line.

The team had to be warned.

At the temple, lunch had concluded. The team packed up the hamper and returned it to the car, refilled their water bottles, and began preparing to get back to work. The sun was still high, baking the ground into a cracked mosaic of ochre and dust.

"Where's Claire?" Alex asked, scanning the courtyard.

"She went to the loo," Samira replied casually, flicking sand from her scarf.

"Yeah, but that was fifteen minutes ago. No one pees for that long."

"I'll go have a look," Samira offered, tapping the side of her nose. "Could be… women's business."

"Right," said Alex, clearly not wanting to venture further into that topic.

Five minutes passed before Samira returned. Her expression had changed. She wasn't frowning yet—but she wasn't smiling either.

"She's not there. Not behind the temple. Not near the outcrop or the vehicle. No sign."

Alex's brow furrowed. "Maybe she wandered off?"

Samira hesitated. "Maybe…"

Alex shook his head. "This is Claire we're talking about, Samira. She doesn't just wander off. Her middle name is protocol, for God's sake."

He turned sharply and called over to Louis, who was securing the last of their gear in the Prado.

"Louis!" Alex shouted. "Claire's gone missing."

Louis looked up, puzzled. "Missing, you say? Mon Dieu—are you sure?"

"We can't find her anywhere," Alex said, already moving. "Fan out. Let's just hope she has wandered off."

The look he shot Samira wasn't accusing, but it wasn't hopeful either. They all knew Claire. She was disciplined. Predictable. Methodical. The kind of person who wouldn't leave her water bottle behind, let alone disappear without a word.

For the next thirty minutes, they scoured the surrounding area— calling her name, scanning the sand, checking behind boulders and low walls. Nothing. No footprints. No clothing. No broken brush or signs of a fall. It was as if she had evaporated into the desert air.

Louis crouched near a cluster of dry acacia and offered a grim possibility. "She may have been bitten by a snake. Desert cobra, maybe a horned viper. Disoriented. She could have wandered, maybe toward one of the villages."

Alex nodded tightly. "We split up. Samira and I will go north. Take the track toward Bawiti. Loop west if we need to. You go south, Louis—cut across toward the Farafra road and check east."

"Understood," Louis replied, already climbing into the second Prado.

They drove like demons.

Alex and Samira sped north into Bawiti, dust trailing behind them like a signal fire. They went as far as the Safari Lodge, then looped west, circled the far rim of the oasis, and cut back down south. Samira called her name from the window whenever they passed a copse or rocky depression. Nothing.

Louis pushed south through the desolate margins of the Bahariya Oasis. He crossed the Al Wahat Al Bahriya–Al Farafra road, veered east toward the escarpments, and finally arced back north, making for the rendezvous point at the temple.

By the time the two vehicles met again, the light was starting to shift—afternoon settling into its long, golden descent.

Alex jumped out of his Prado before it had even fully stopped and ran toward Louis.

"Anything?" he demanded.

Louis stepped down and shook his head slowly. "Nothing, mon ami. Not a single trace."

Alex's jaw clenched. His fists balled. He looked out over the desert and let out a sudden, visceral yell.

"Fuck!"

It echoed off the sandstone walls, sharp and desperate.

Samira said nothing. She just looked at the place where Claire had last been seen, her arms folded tightly, as if to protect herself from the reality settling over them.

Alex exhaled, trying to pull himself back under control. "We check the dig site again," he said, his voice low and rasped. "Maybe… maybe she tripped over a wall or something. Hit her head. Something."

The others nodded. They all knew it was pointless—but it gave them something to do. Something to stave off the fear that clawed at the edges of reason.

And yet, even as they walked back toward the temple, one thought hovered like the circling vultures overhead:

Claire Marlowe was gone. And something was very, very wrong.

Captain Hafez Abdel-Rahman paced the length of his cramped office like a caged tiger, each step tighter, angrier than the last. The air inside was thick with heat and dust, despite the feeble oscillating fan that clicked uselessly above him. For two hours now

he'd been waiting for a call—any call—from that spineless weasel
Khoury. Nothing.

He stared at the silent phone as though it had personally betrayed
him.

Twice he reached for it, and twice he pulled his hand back, fingers
twitching with restraint. He would not be the one to beg. He would
not give that bloated, belt-stuffing bureaucrat the satisfaction of a
second call. Let him sweat. Let him wonder if Hafez had already
taken matters into his own hands.

Back and forth he paced, bootheels striking the tiled floor like
hammer blows. Each step was a thought. Each thought, a rising
tide of fury. The more he walked, the more convinced he became:
Cairo was planning to cut him out. The Ministry wanted his turf—
the bribes, the "protection fees," the artifacts that "disappeared"
before they were ever catalogued. His turf. And the blade they
were using to carve him out of the equation was that cursed UN
inspection team.

He snarled under his breath.

If those foreigners uncovered so much as a whisper of illicit
dealings—an undocumented relic, a looted cache, even an empty
crate from some Swiss buyer—he would be finished. And Khoury
would be there, all sympathetic smiles and bureaucratic pity,
helping push him out like a dying dog. No press. No scandal. Just
gone.

No. That would not happen. Not while he drew breath.

The UN team had to go.

Disappear.

Out here, in the wide quiet of the desert, there were ways. Simple,
permanent ways. People vanished around Bahariya all the time—
into sinkholes, sandstorms, smugglers' traps. He could make it
clean. Final. And no one in Cairo would ever know for certain
what had happened. A search party might find a scrap of fabric, a
broken-down Jeep, maybe nothing at all. In time, the desert would
swallow the rest.

Hafez stopped pacing. He stood still, breathing heavily, the weight of decision anchoring his rage. Outside, the wind keened across the compound wall, and a gust of fine yellow sand hissed against the glass.

He would sleep on it. Clarity always came with the stillness of night. But already the plan was forming, hardening like stone in his mind.

And if Khoury dared to interfere—if that paunchy little bastard got in his way—well, then Khoury would be next.

Claire awoke with a sudden intake of breath. The first thing she noticed was the light: soft and filtered, the faint glow of desert sun bleeding through coarse fabric. She was in a tent. The second thing she noticed—thankfully—was that she was unrestrained. Unharmed. But utterly confused.

Her body ached as she sat up too quickly, a throb pulsing at the base of her skull. A low gasp escaped her lips, involuntary. She squinted at her surroundings: the goat-hair walls, the dust motes spinning in the light, the earthy scent of sand and smoke. There was a straw-stuffed mattress beneath her—not particularly comfortable but clean. Other than a clay water jug and a folded woollen shawl in the corner, the tent was bare.

Suddenly, the flap snapped open and a young boy peeked inside. His eyes lit up with recognition, and before she could say a word, he disappeared again—running off at full speed.

Claire blinked at the opening, adrenaline beginning to build. Had she been abducted? Drugged? But there was no pain, no bindings, no sense of immediate threat. Her instinct was to lie back down, feign unconsciousness, buy time. But the boy had already seen her awake, and besides—she was an archaeologist. Curiosity trumped caution.

She sat upright, brushing sand from her trousers. There were voices outside now—low, male, approaching.

The flap lifted again, and a young man entered. He looked to be in his twenties, his skin sun-darkened and his jawline shadowed with stubble. He wore a loose cotton shirt tucked into desert-worn jeans, a checked keffiyeh slung around his shoulders. Two elderly men followed him—stooped, wiry, and sun-leathered. Their faces were deeply lined, their teeth yellowed and sparse. They wore traditional Bedouin garb: long galabiyyas of faded indigo, wrapped headscarves, and leather sandals. Silver rings adorned their fingers; one bore an ancient-looking dagger at his belt.

They sat wordlessly, with deliberate symmetry, on either side of the tent—leaving a space between them. A space that felt expectant. Claire took note.

The younger man remained standing.

He addressed her in Arabic, his voice soft but steady:

"La takhafi... nahnu lan nadurruki."

Then in halting English:

"Do not be afraid. We mean you no harm."

Claire nodded slowly. Her Arabic was passable—she could catch the gist, but not the subtleties.

"Ismi Claire," she replied in Arabic, then switched to English. "I work for the United Nations. I'm an archaeologist. My Arabic is... not so good."

The young man gave a tight smile. "It is good enough, Claire."

She pointed toward the gap between the two elders.

"One more?" she asked, intuitively.

"Yes," the young man replied. "The village elder. Our sheikh. He will come soon."

Claire nodded. That was enough for now. She crossed her legs and sat properly on the mattress, spine straight, trying to remain composed despite the pounding of her heart.

Moments later, two more men entered the tent, carrying a third between them. The sight of him made Claire gasp softly. He wasn't just old—he was ancient. His skin was ashen and thin, his frame skeletal beneath his robe. His eyes, when they turned toward her, were pale and milky, clouded by cataracts. He looked directly at her, and she felt the weight of a thousand desert suns pressing through his gaze.

The carriers gently lowered him into the centre space between the elders and withdrew, leaving five people inside the tent. Silence fell.

The old man began to speak, low and rasping. Claire caught none of it. The dialect was strange—guttural, old, something Bedouin but archaic, almost pre-Islamic in tone. The three elders spoke amongst themselves, occasionally clicking tongues or using sounds she didn't even recognise as part of any formal language.

Claire remained silent, respectful. She noticed the young man remained silent too—letting the exchange unfold without interruption.

Eventually, the old sheikh raised a gnarled hand, signalling the others to stop. He pointed at Claire, then addressed her directly with surprising force. His hand trembled, but his intent was clear. The younger man leaned in.

"They wish to ask you some questions," he said carefully. "I will try to translate, but my Bedu is not perfect."

"Nor is my Arabic," Claire offered with a smile. "But we'll manage."

"Between your Arabic and my English," he said, "we will find a way."

The elder's eyes did not leave hers. He muttered something again, and the young man translated.

"He wants to know—who sent you?"

Claire hesitated.

"The United Nations sent us," she said, lying gently. "To survey the ruins. We're archaeologists. The site is being considered for World Heritage status."

He translated. The elder nodded slowly, though his expression betrayed nothing. The three conferred once more.

Then another question came—voiced slightly differently this time.
The elder lifted his hand to the sky, gestured in a slow arc, as
though drawing a constellation.
The young man tried again:
"He asks... why you are at the temple of Setep-en-Ma'at-Mery-
Amun?"
Claire stiffened. That name. Alexander's pharaonic title—*Setep-
en-Ma'at-Mery-Amun*, Chosen of Truth, Beloved of Amun.
She paused, recalculating. Why repeat the question?
It wasn't about archaeology.
It was about intent.
She swallowed. Then decided – she would be truthful; it was the
only way.
"We are here to find the second waymarker," she said. "It will lead
us to Dhu al-Qarnayn."
The reaction was immediate. The elders' eyes widened. The
younger man let out a breath. Animated murmurs broke out
between them—words she couldn't understand, but the tone
unmistakable.
They were startled. Perhaps amazed. One of the old men repeated
the phrase:
"Dhu al-Qarnayn... al-Maqdouni."
The Macedonian God-King.
She knew.
They knew she knew.
Then the sheikh lifted his skeletal hand and pointed it straight at
her, trembling but insistent. He said something with intensity,
tapping the air toward her as if trying to reach through the decades.
The young man turned to her, solemn.
"They ask again—who sent you? Who sent you here... to us?"
Claire faltered. She glanced around the room instinctively, as if an
answer might present itself. Not the UN. Not the Institute. Not
even Director Molineux.
Who?

The truth dropped into her like a stone in water.

Malik.

Malik had set them on this path. It was Malik who gave them the direction – 197 degrees celestial. Malik who—somehow—had known what they were meant to find.

She looked the sheikh directly in the eyes, sat taller, and spoke with quiet certainty, in perfect Arabic.

"Malik ibn Harun al-Sahiri sent us."

The tent fell utterly still.

No one moved. The sheikh bowed his head and nodded. One of the elders whispered something that sounded like a prayer. The young man turned to her with something like awe in his eyes.

"Then," he said softly, "you are truly meant to be here."

The fading light painted the desert in long streaks of orange and rust as the two vehicles pulled into the makeshift car park behind the Safari Lodge. Their engines sputtered to silence, pinging softly as they cooled beneath the weight of the day. Dust hovered around them like smoke from a dying fire.

Alex climbed out of the Toyota with a heavy thud, the sound of his boots grinding against gravel oddly final. He didn't speak. He just stood there, hands planted on the roof, his head bowed, his shoulders tight with the frustration he couldn't voice.

Samira joined him, wordless, the strain of worry etched deep into her features. Louis followed soon after, his shirt plastered to his back with sweat, face drawn, eyes scanning the horizon one last time before giving up.

No one said a word.

Inside, the lobby of the Safari Lodge was hushed. A few staff lingered at a respectful distance, sensing something was wrong but offering only quiet glances and lowered eyes. The team had returned one person short.

Samira stepped to the front desk and spoke softly in Arabic. Within moments, a porter appeared and guided them to a private salon at the rear of the building—a shaded room with low ceilings, thick adobe walls, and a tired ceiling fan that ticked and turned overhead. It smelled faintly of sandalwood and the dry breath of the desert.

They sank into the wicker chairs, the silence between them heavy as stone.

"She didn't just vanish," Samira said finally, her voice sharp with disbelief, fear still lingering beneath the words. "People don't just disappear."

Alex stared into the middle distance, eyes unfocused. "No. They don't."

"We've scoured everything within ten kilometers of the site. There's nothing. No footprints. No trail. It's like the earth swallowed her whole."

Louis leaned forward, elbows on his knees, rubbing his face with both hands. "No signs of a struggle. No drag marks. No blood. Just... nothing. It was clean. Too clean. Not an animal. Not random. Deliberate."

"There's not much we can do," Alex muttered.

"We could go to the authorities," Samira suggested, though without conviction. "If Claire was abducted, we need help. Real help."

Alex turned to her slowly, voice low and measured. "We can't. If they find out who we really are—what we're really doing—we won't just lose the dig. We'll lose everything. We'll be in jail. And it's hard to find someone when you're locked in a cell."

Samira clenched her jaw and looked away. Louis had nothing left to say.

The door opened, and Yousif, the lodge's proprietor, stepped inside. He took one look at their faces and shook his head gently. "You need food," he said, kindly but firmly. "You've been in the sun too long. You must keep your strength up."

No one objected. He disappeared into the kitchen without waiting for their reply.

"I need a drink," Alex said flatly.

"Same," Louis murmured.

"Absolutely," Samira added.

A few minutes later, the drinks arrived on a polished silver tray. Heineken for Louis. A crisp Chablis for Samira. A scotch on the rocks for Alex.

The young waitress—a local girl, maybe fourteen—placed the tray gently beside Alex's chair. As he reached for his glass, he noticed something out of place. A folded piece of paper, creased once down the middle, tucked beside the tumbler. He picked it up and turned it over. Arabic script, hastily scrawled.

Frowning, he passed it to Samira.

She read it. Her breath caught audibly in her throat.

Alex looked up sharply. "What? What does it say?"

Louis leaned forward. "Claire—does it mention Claire?"

Samira nodded slowly, still staring at the note. Then she read aloud:

"كلير بخير — Claire is fine."

"That's it?" Alex asked.

"Nothing else," Samira said, flipping the paper over. "No signature. No explanation."

Louis bolted up from his chair and chased after the waitress, catching her just before she slipped back through the door. "Who gave you the note?" he asked urgently. She blinked, not understanding.

Samira stepped in and translated into Arabic. The girl tilted her head thoughtfully.

"A man," she said at last. "From outside. He gave it to me and left."

Louis burst through the front entrance and sprinted into the carpark, but it was empty. The sun had dipped below the horizon. The last light of day revealed only sand, shadow, and silence. Whoever had delivered the note was gone.

The three of them stood there for some time, staring out into the darkening desert, the silence between them thick with questions.
"At least she's alive," Samira offered, her voice fragile.
Alex turned back toward the lodge, the note still clenched in his fist. "But is she safe?"

Chapter 4

Alex had only succumbed to sleep when exhaustion finally overpowered his thoughts, the scotch dulling the edge of guilt just enough to knock him under. But even rest brought no real relief—he awoke groggy, clothes still clinging with desert sweat, his mind already racing the moment his eyes opened.

By ten minutes to seven, they were outside in the rising heat, gathering silently near their vehicles. No one said much. Louis stood off to one side, leaning against the hood of the second Prado, arms folded, eyes on the gravel. He looked particularly hollow without his usual passenger. Her absence made the group feel unbalanced, like a compass without its needle.

They took faint comfort in the note from the night before—Claire is fine. But it wasn't enough. Too vague. Too hollow. It offered no answers—only more questions. Where was she? Who had taken her? Why?

Alex had said it over breakfast, quietly and to no one in particular: "The definition of 'fine' is not exactly universal."

Breakfast had been subdued. The usual spread Yousif prepared with local pride felt heavy with tension this morning—flatbreads still warm from the griddle, soft-boiled eggs, tomato and cucumber salad dusted with sumac, olives soaked in oil and lemon, and a pot of thick, black Arabic coffee that steamed between them. They ate in near silence. Samira picked at her food. Louis barely touched his. Only Alex forced himself to chew with the mechanical discipline of a soldier—it was the only part of him that didn't feel like it was unravelling.

They debated briefly—search again or wait. Samira argued they
should head back out, retrace their steps, speak to the villagers. But
in the end, they agreed. Everything they could do, they had done.
The ball wasn't in their court anymore. Someone had taken Claire,
and that someone had made contact. That meant, at the very least,
that she wasn't gone without trace.
They would continue with the dig today, as much out of grim
necessity as hope. They needed to stay visible. To show they
weren't rattled. Perhaps the message they waited for next would
only come if things appeared to proceed as normal.
They climbed into the trucks without further discussion. Samira sat
beside Alex, the window down, a scarf tied over her hair. The
Prado rattled to life, the rising sun casting long shadows through
the dust that hung over the desert like a veil.
Alex's hands tightened around the steering wheel.
Please, he thought. Let her be alive. Let her be safe. Let her forgive
me for not stopping this.
The engine grumbled as they pulled out from the lodge, gravel
crunching beneath the tires. They drove toward the ruins under a
sky that was already warming fast, gold bleeding into white.
They hoped it would be just another day.
But for the rest of the team, unfortunately—it would be anything
but.

Claire awoke to familiar surroundings.
The muted light filtering through the fabric of the tent painted
everything in a soft amber hue. It was still early—calm, quiet. The
same jug of water sat just within reach. The same rough straw-
stuffed mattress crinkled beneath her as she shifted. Her joints
ached. Her feet were sore. But she smiled to herself.
Last night, she thought.
Everything had changed.
What began as a strange, surreal interrogation had transformed into
something mystical—almost sacred. After she'd spoken Malik's

name, the entire village seemed to exhale at once. Fear vanished. Suspicion melted. She had not just earned their trust; she had been exalted. Not as a guest. Not even as a protector.

As something more.

She had been lifted onto shoulders, paraded through the makeshift paths of the camp beneath strings of flickering oil lanterns. Music filled the night—pipes and hand drums, rhythmic and hypnotic. The Bedouins had danced for hours, whirling barefoot in the sand, hands raised to the stars. Claire had danced too. Like a schoolgirl at prom, twirling with abandon, barefoot and laughing, unsure of how she'd become the center of it all but unwilling to question the joy of the moment. She had sipped thick sweet tea, something spiced and milky, and later something stronger from a worn goatskin flask. Names had blurred. Faces had spun. The stars had stretched across the sky in endless rivers of light.

Eventually, the weight of the day—and the wine—had caught up to her. She remembered collapsing in a heap of giggles and exhaustion, someone covering her with a woven shawl as she drifted off to the sound of distant singing.

Now, the silence felt oddly sacred.

Her legs ached. Her feet throbbed. But she couldn't stop smiling. Even her hair smelled like smoke and cumin.

The tent flap rustled. A familiar face peeked through.

It was the young man from yesterday—kind eyes, calm smile. She still wasn't sure of his name. Ibrahim, she thought. Yes, he looks like an Ibrahim.

"Ahh," he said brightly in Arabic, grinning, "glad you are up. It's time for breakfast… and then we return you to your friends."

Claire sat up straighter at once. Breakfast sounded like heaven, but the promise of reunion lit a fire in her chest. Alex. Samira. Louis. They'd be worried sick.

She fumbled quickly into her Merrells and tied her hair back into a rough bun. Her body was sore, but she moved with the urgency of purpose. She wasn't about to lose sight of Ibrahim—he was her ticket back to the team, and she wasn't letting him out of her sight.

Outside, the sun was low and golden, casting long shadows across the camp. Smoke curled gently from a small cooking fire, around which several elders sat, cross-legged and quietly chatting.

Breakfast was already under way.

Over the open coals, thin rounds of bread—khubz—were being slapped onto a convex iron griddle set over glowing embers.

Nearby, a blackened pot of tea steamed fragrantly, the scent of cardamom and sage mingling with the smoke. Bowls of labneh—thick strained yogurt drizzled with olive oil—were passed around alongside soft cheese, honey, and plates of foul medames—stewed fava beans laced with garlic, lemon, and cumin.

Dates sat piled in a wooden bowl. Hard-boiled eggs, still warm, were being peeled by hand and sprinkled with coarse salt.

Someone handed Claire a piece of warm bread, folded around a scoop of beans and yogurt. She took it eagerly.

It was simple. It was perfect.

She sat beside the fire, cross-legged like the rest, and let herself sink into the warmth of the food and the community. They had taken her in, trusted her, celebrated her—and now they were feeding her like family.

She was halfway through her second piece of bread when she caught sight of Ibrahim on the far side of the camp, deep in conversation with a group of older men. He glanced back and caught her eye.

She gave a small wave. He nodded.

Don't lose him, she reminded herself. *He's your ride home.*

Still chewing, still sore, and still filled with questions—Claire smiled.

Last night had changed everything.

And today, she was going back.

Captain Hafez Abdel-Rahman stormed into the Bawiti Police Station just before 8:30 a.m.

The station, already sluggish in the morning heat, snapped to uneasy attention. Conversations faltered. Coffee mugs froze midway to lips. The few officers at their desks lowered their eyes. Captain Hafez was not a man to arrive early unless something was brewing—and this morning, his presence crackled with intent.

He didn't remove his sunglasses. His boots echoed sharply on the chipped tile floor as he passed through the lobby like a bullet through fabric.

"Sergeant!" he barked.

The station sergeant, big and broad-shouldered with a clipboard and a perpetually furrowed brow, looked up from a roster that had already defeated him twice today. More absences. More reshuffles. More pathetic excuses from his thinning ranks. He scurried over, still clutching the clipboard like a shield.

"Yes, Captain!"

Hafez didn't slow. He kept walking.

"I want you to assemble two of the older corporals. Trusted ones. Meet me outside in the motor pool in fifteen minutes. Make sure they're armed. Full kit."

The sergeant blinked. "Armed, sir? Where are we headed? There've been no reports of riots or looting in Bawiti. Nothing out of Mandishah either."

Hafez stopped then—slowly, deliberately. He turned to face the sergeant, his expression unreadable beneath the mirrored lenses. His voice was lower now, more dangerous.

"We're not going to rough-up some local, Sergeant."

He leaned in slightly, just enough to make the sergeant stiffen.

"We're going to arrest those UN archaeologists."

The sergeant's eyebrows twitched upward, his mouth starting to form the beginnings of protest.

"And then," Hafez added, voice cool as iron, "we're going to make sure they disappear—before we do."

He turned on his heel and walked out, leaving the sergeant standing alone, heart thudding against his ribs, clipboard limp in his hand.

Outside, the morning sun was rising fast over the oasis, sharp and unforgiving. In the motor pool, the dust was already beginning to dance. Hafez lit a cigarette with steady fingers and exhaled slowly, eyes on the horizon.

Today, order would be restored.

And there would be no paperwork.

Alex, Samira, and Louis worked steadily through the heat. They widened the courtyard excavation, brushing and shoveling away the sand until nearly all the courtyard was exposed. Along the eastern and western sides were edge blocks of sandstone, each with a drainage channel etched into the flagstones directly beneath. As Claire had surmised, the courtyard dipped gently to the south with a drainage camber channeling east and west and eventually south with the slope. It was well-engineered, Alex thought. They had given much thought to keeping it dry and usable, no matter what the weather. While barren desert now, back in the 331 BCE, this area was much lusher and more prone to sub-tropical thunderstorms during the wet season. Now, just sand, desert, and more oppressive heat.

Surveying the courtyard, now fully uncovered, Alex realized that the next part of the puzzle wasn't where he had hoped it would be—no shards of granite with inscriptions, no markers pointing the way, not another lion in sight, walking or otherwise. Whatever had been on that plinth, wasn't on there now, and he had no idea where to start looking for it.

Samira sauntered over, equally out of answers. "We could take some measurements," she offered. "Of what?" asked Alex, slightly disinterested. "Well, I can get a good understanding using feel how big the obelisk base might have been, and we can compare that to the one from Alexandria, to get an understanding if they were the same height, or different, to get a feel for what it is we are looking for?" "Sounds good, let's do that!"

Just as Samira and Alex were down on all fours, taking measurements of the plinth, Louis came running over from the southern end of the courtyard.

"Vehicle, coming this way, from the south!"

Both Alex and Samira stood, shielding their eyes from the mid-morning sun. There off to the south, perhaps just over a kilometre away, was a dust plume rising steadily and getting closer. Alex's gaze lingered a little longer. Two vehicles were identifiable now, racing towards them. Fast. Too fast.

"Louis," he said, "Is this normal?"

Louis once again peered to the south and made the decision. "I think, mon ami, that it is better to be safe than sorry. I suggest we find some concealment in the temple until we know who these people are, monsieur."

Alex, Samira, and Louis picked up their instruments and tools and headed for the relative safety of the temple.

"What about the vehicles?" Samira asked. "They have our personal items in there, our equipment."

"Leave it," said Alex. "If they are harmless, it will be safe."

They raced back toward the temple and scrambled through the southern opening, hiding just far enough inside to be concealed by shadows but still able to see the southern approach as the dust cloud drew nearer. A minute passed, and two battered Hiluxes came to a halt a short distance away from the southernmost ruins. Four men got out—police, but not exactly police.

"Desert Security Directorate," Louis said, almost matter-of-factly. The four DSD men leaned back into their vehicles and retrieved their automatic weapons—Russian AKs or Chinese copies. Louis wasn't sure which. It didn't really matter, he thought. They were outgunned either way.

From where they were hiding, they could hear the voices on the wind, which was in their favor.

‏إانتشروا إفتشوا السيارات!

"Fan out! Check their vehicles!" came the voice, clearly from the one wearing the dark glasses.

Two of the men went over to the two white Prados parked side by side and went through them superficially.

‏إليسوا هنا يا قائد!

"They aren't here, Captain!" came the response from one.

They regathered near the southern edge of the ruins.

‏إأنتما اذهبا شرقاً .نحن سنذهب غرباً .كونوا متيقظين .إنهم هنا في مكان ما

"You two go east, we'll go west. Stay alert—they're here somewhere!"

They split up, two to the east, two to the west—hunting UN archaeologists.

"What are we going to do?" asked Samira, her voice whispery and trembling.

Louis took charge. It wasn't the first time he'd been outmanned and outgunned.

"They're circling the perimeter first. Then they'll move through the buildings. They're testing if we run like scared rabbits or hide like them. Once they reach the far northern edge of the ruins, we run. Straight to the vehicles. They should offer some cover. If we time it right, we'll have a head start."

"And run like scared rabbits," said Alex.

"Oui, Professor. The more scared, the better."

The DSD men passed uncomfortably close to the temple entrance. Louis peered from the shadows.

"Get ready. Soon," he whispered. "Make sure you have your keys."

Alex checked his pocket. Check.

Louis raised his hand like a starter at a race meet, then brought it down. "Go," he hissed.

All three darted from the shade of the southern entrance and bolted across the courtyard. Alex was impressed by how fast Samira could run, easily keeping up with him. Louis was already meters ahead.

Voices rang out behind them—angry voices.

إتوقفوا !لا تتحركوا!

"Stop! Don't move!"

They didn't wait for translation. AKs barked in short bursts.
Bullets cracked overhead and chewed into the sand.

!استهدفوا السيارات !اضربوا الإطارات

"Target the vehicles! Shoot out the tires!"

The focus shifted. Bullets slammed into the white bodywork of the Prados. Glass shattered. A tire exploded with a hiss. The team slid behind the SUVs. The Toyotas took the beating, shielding them.

"What now?!" Samira half-screamed.

"They're undisciplined. Soon they'll need to reload. That's our chance."

As Louis said the words, the gunfire stopped.

In one motion, Louis ran to the driver's side, yanked open the door, and retrieved his Glock 17 from beneath the seat. He flipped the safety and peered out. The DSD men were reloading.

He fired. One shot struck the corporal in the shoulder. He spun, dropped his AK. The others scattered. The wounded man got up, spraying wildly from the hip. Louis sprinted to the rear of the car and joined the others.

"One down, three to go," Louis muttered.

"What now?" asked Alex.

"They're flanking us, mon ami. If they close in, we're out of options. Unless they run dry."

Three-round bursts continued to pound the vehicles. Glass exploded, metal caved.

"Stay here, stay down," Louis barked.

He crawled under Alex's Prado. Mr. Sunglasses and the gorilla-sized man flanked left, creeping in a crouch.

Time to even the odds.

At thirty-five meters, the gorilla popped up to fire. Louis waited. Aimed. Fired three times. One round struck the man in the thigh. He went down, screaming.

Then Louis heard it, the sound of shooting. But it wasn't coming from the DSD men, it was coming from somewhere else.

Chapter 6

Louis rejoined Alex and Samira, crouching low between the two vehicles as the *whump, twang, ping* of bullets continued to strike their convoy. The sound was closer now, more deliberate. Most of the tyres had been shot out. No pane of glass remained intact. Fluids and oils dripped steadily from ruined engine bays where radiators had burst and cylinders had been torn apart by gunfire. Inside, the upholstery was shredded, plastic and fabric scattered everywhere like the aftermath of a storm.

Louis opened his mouth, ready to boast that he'd clipped the big DSD man—maybe even taken him down—when the gunfire stopped as abruptly as it had begun.

Alex and Samira turned to him, alert and tense.

"Reloading?" Alex asked, voice low.

Louis shrugged. "If they are, they're taking their sweet time about it."

Or they'd run out of ammunition altogether.

The silence that followed was eerie. There was no shouting. No gunfire. Just the soft tick of dripping coolants and the distant whisper of desert wind.

"I'm going to check," Louis said.

He slid out from cover, belly-crawling to the edge of the vehicle and slowly lifted his head over the hood. His eyes widened.

Thirty metres away, the DSD men were on their knees, arms laced behind their heads. Behind them stood six men, cloaked in flowing garments the colour of sand and shadow—traditional Bedouin garb. Each one carried an AK-47 with the easy confidence of those who'd known violence all their lives.

Louis shifted his gaze eastward—same scene. The two armed corporals, once ready to kill, now knelt disarmed, ringed by Bedouin warriors.

He scrambled back to Alex and Samira, wide-eyed.

"I think we've just been saved," he said breathlessly. "Locals!"

The three emerged from their hiding place, rising to their feet to take in the scene. The Bedouins—nomadic lions of the desert, fierce and regal—had completely subdued their attackers. Their presence was commanding, their intervention both sudden and absolute.

Alex stared in wonder. Samira blinked in disbelief. Louis just looked grateful.

Then, cutting through the surreal quiet, came a familiar voice— clear, confident, and tinged with relief.

"Looks like we arrived in the nick of time. Fancy a rescue, anyone?"

Claire!

Alex and Samira turned in unison and rushed to her. They embraced her simultaneously, holding tight as if to confirm she was real. Claire hugged them both back, grinning.

Louis safetied his Glock and simply watched, admiration in his eyes. He didn't want to interrupt the moment. It was too perfect.

A barrage of questions followed—how, when, who, why—but Claire held up her hands.

"I know, I know. A million questions. But it's easier if I tell the whole story. And let me tell you—it's a doozy."

One of the young Bedouin men approached—tall, lean, with intelligent eyes. He wore a desert robe of deep indigo and tan and walked with the quiet assurance of someone respected. Two elder Bedouin followed behind him.

"I am Ibrahim," the young man said in halting but serviceable English. "Blessings of Allah upon you. We welcome you to our lands. Claire has told us much. There is more to say. But first—eat, drink. Then we talk."

They followed Claire and Ibrahim to where the Bedouins had formed a seated circle in the courtyard, shaded by the southern wall of the temple. The prisoners—the four DSD men —remained kneeling in the full sun, under close guard. Punishment had already begun.

A goatskin water bag was passed around. The guests drank first—Claire included—then the Bedouin, in descending order of age and status. The ritual was wordless, dignified, and deliberate.

Then came the elder.

He was ancient—gnarled, withered, and carried by two younger men. His eyes were clouded with cataracts, but there was something unsettlingly sharp behind the veil of age. He took his place at the center of the circle, cross-legged and unmoving, flanked by the other tribal leaders.

He began to speak—a prayer, melodic and low.

"Is that Arabic?" Alex whispered.

Samira shook her head. "No. It's Bedu. Very old Bedu. This might be the original tongue—from before the Arab conquests. It's... primal. I can't understand a word."

The guttural tones, tongue-clicks, and rhythmic vocalizations flowed like song and shadow. The others listened in respectful silence.

Finally, the old man stopped. Ibrahim nodded.

"He welcomes you. Formal greetings are extended."

The elder turned to Alex. Though his eyes were clouded, Alex felt as though the man could see straight through him. The sheikh raised a skeletal hand and pointed directly at Alex's chest.

Ibrahim translated: "The girl says Malik sent you. Is it true?"

Girl? Alex blinked. Of course, Claire!

He hesitated. This wasn't a question of allegiances—it was a test. Names, events, places—this was oral tradition. Not through years or even generations. Through millennia.

"Yes," Alex said. "Malik ibn Harun al-Sahiri sent us."
Gasps rippled through the Bedouins. Low murmurs followed.
Heads nodded.
The elder leaned forward, speaking again. Ibrahim listened, then
asked: "What path are you on?"
Path? Alex thought. For a moment he didn't comprehend. Then it
clicked. This too was a test—a confirmation that they were worthy,
righteous, seekers. Holders of knowledge. Bearers of the light.
He answered clearly: "The path of the four lions."
More murmurs. More nods. The energy shifted.
The sheikh asked again, voice frail but firm: "What message do
you carry?"
Alex froze. Message? Had Malik given them a message? There had
been scrolls, warnings, philosophy—but nothing he remembered
framed as a message.
"I... I don't know," he admitted. "I don't think we were given one."
The old man seemed unsurprised. He waved his fragile hand in the
air, gesturing to each of them—Claire, Alex, Samira, Louis—then
spoke again. Ibrahim translated, his voice slow with care:
"He says Malik did give you a message—something to carry.
Something that would last. That would endure—"
He paused. "When your message and our message come together,
it becomes *the* message. Ours has been passed down, unchanged,
generation after generation. The two halves form one whole. Only
the true seeker will understand. Malik said, 'I will show them the
symbols.'"
Alex was baffled. But Samira's eyes widened.
"In Arabic, the word for 'message' can also mean symbol," she
whispered. "Or sign. Or token."
She leapt to her feet and sprinted across the courtyard to the
wreckage of their vehicles. A few minutes later, she returned
carrying her backpack – luckily untouched by the hail of lead and
copper. From inside, she produced a cloth-wrapped object and laid
it gently at the sheikh's feet.

She unwrapped it slowly: the Great Seal of the Library of Alexandria—the brass plaque they had recovered from the mosaic floor in Leptis Magna.

A collective gasp rippled through the gathered Bedouins.

The elder called out in excited Bedu. One of the other tribal leaders came forward, bearing his own goatskin-wrapped bundle. He laid it beside Samira's seal and opened it.

An identical seal.

Two parts. Now, finally, one.

The elder raised his hand, and silence fell again.

He spoke at length, arms moving with surprising energy. Ibrahim translated as the words poured forth like the release of centuries. "He says you bring great joy to his people. That long ago, Malik foretold the coming of those from the North—bearers of knowledge, seekers of truth. He said they would carry a token, and that when they arrived, the truth could be spoken. The secret they carry—the resting place of Dhu al-Qarnayn al-Maqdouni—could at last be revealed. The Bedouin have held this trust for over thirteen hundred years, waiting for this moment."

"Oh my God," Samira whispered. "They've kept this secret for over a thousand years."

"And preserved it perfectly," Claire added. "Orally. Word for word. Symbol for symbol."

Alex turned to Ibrahim, heart pounding. "I have a question. The obelisk—it was once in the temple. Now it's missing. Do your people know where it is?" Ibrahim translated.

The sheikh waved a crooked finger toward the southern end of the courtyard.

"It is there," Ibrahim translated. "As it has always been."

Alex frowned. "What? But... there's nothing there but the plinth. No inscriptions. No directions. Just a slab of stone."

He paused, trying not to sound disrespectful. "I don't understand. We're looking for an obelisk—about six feet tall, with writing on it."

After another exchange in Bedu, Ibrahim repeated calmly, "Yes.
He has seen it. It is in the courtyard."
Alex turned in a slow circle. Everyone looked. There was no
obelisk.
"Where?" he asked. "I see nothing."
The sheikh didn't wait for translation. He chuckled—a deep,
rattling sound that shook his narrow frame—and said something
long and poetic in Bedu. Ibrahim smiled as he translated.
"He says... it is in the courtyard. You just can't see it."
Alex stared, baffled. "Am I blind?"
The sheikh burst into raucous laughter, doubling over, waving his
hands in the air until he had to be helped upright again. Finally, he
spoke once more.
And Ibrahim, now grinning, translated:
"Simple. It's down the well."
The throng gathered around the well in reverent silence.
Ibrahim, kneeling beside the old sheikh, translated carefully. "The
obelisk was lowered into the well and sealed away long before
Ahmed Fakhry's team ever laid eyes on this place. Before 1938,
the courtyard was smoothed with sand, the well hidden beneath a
thin sandstone cap. The deception was perfect."
The Bedouin had preserved the truth not in books or stones, but in
memory—unbroken for generations.
Now, with the secret revealed, the well needed to be opened once
more. Picks and shovels were fetched from the wrecked Prado.
Several Bedouin men joined Louis and Alex, and work began in
earnest. After less than an hour, the sandstone cracked, revealing a
dark aperture beneath. A dry gust from the desert swept through
the courtyard as the capstone fell inward with a low echoing thud.
The well was open.
Samira and Louis leaned over the edge, torches in hand. The beams
of light struck something grey and geometric—just a point at first,
protruding from the darkness below.

"It's there," Louis whispered. "Granite. Just the top… maybe ten feet down."

"We'll need ropes," said Samira.

By mid-afternoon, with the help of a simple A-frame rigged between two of the DSD Toyota Hilux's, the obelisk rose into view. Sunlight slid along its faces, catching the glint of its carvings. After almost ninety years entombed in an airless well, it had emerged in near-perfect condition—smooth, clean, unweathered. A silent sentinel from another age.

It was, to Alex's eye, identical to the Alexandrian obelisk in form and proportion. All four sides bore inscriptions. The first three were commemorative texts—Arabic, Greek, and Coptic—glorifying the early Caliphate and the conquest of Egypt.

But it was the fourth face that drew everyone's attention.

There, carved deep in the polished granite, was the lion.

Unlike the sleeping lion from the Leptis Magna mosaic, this one walked. Its body was taut with purpose. The mane, longer now, suggested age and wisdom. Behind it were stylized sand dunes, etched in sweeping strokes, almost windblown in appearance. And beside the lion: a line of ancient Sabaic script.

Samira dropped to her knees, notebook in hand. She began cross-referencing, scribbling quickly as she translated aloud, haltingly at first.

"This line," she said, running a finger along the top of the inscription, "is nearly identical to what we saw on the Alexandrian obelisk. It reads: 'Though born of the sands, his blood calls to the mountains beyond the western sea—where the silver-flecked olive grows beneath snowed peaks.'"

She paused, lips moving silently as she worked her way down. Her brow furrowed.

"But this line… here. This is new. The final line. This must be the instruction."

Everyone gathered around her as she stood and read it aloud in English, the rhythm unmistakably Malik's:

"Let the lion walk toward the light that falls from the Plowman's
gaze—
That steadfast flame who watches from the west,
Whose fire dips low when the sands drink the dying sun.
Follow the lion's gaze to where Simāk al-Rāmiḥ, the red spear of
heaven, sinks beyond the sands. Let the seeker walk where its light
touches last — there shall the next lion rise."
Claire let out a breath. "He encoded a bearing."
Samira nodded. "Simāk al-Rāmiḥ — that's Arcturus in Arabic.
That's our starting point."
"Bearing 287 degrees," said Louis. "West by northwest. That's
incredibly precise."
Claire looked down at the lion again. "He's no longer sleeping.
He's walking."
Samira frowned. "Do we need to adjust for precession? Like we
did with the solar alignment in Alexandria?"
"Not in this case," Claire replied. "This is a star — not the Sun.
Arcturus still sets close to the same azimuth today as it did in
Malik's time. Maybe a degree or so off at most, but nothing that
would throw off a bearing like 287."
"Then that's where we go," said Alex, his voice low.
For a long moment, no one spoke. The obelisk, warm in the
afternoon sun, seemed almost alive—its message now complete,
passed down across continents and centuries.
The second lion had revealed its truth. The path to the third—the
watchful lion—was now set.

It was late afternoon when they lowered the obelisk back into the
well.
 Its secrets had been revealed—its message heard, its path set.
Whether it would ever be needed again, no one could say. But
now, as before, the Bedouins would guard it. Keepers of truth
across generations, they closed the sandstone lid and buried it

beneath sand and silence. Malik's lion would sleep again, until the world was ready.

From the wrecks of the Prados they salvaged what they could. It wasn't much. A few bags, some torches, tools, maps, a pair of compasses, and one bent field tablet. Samira found her laptop intact, scratched but still usable. Claire retrieved her father's old Leica camera, her own laptop and the drone, miraculously unbroken. They packed it all into the two surviving Hilux's, the rest left to the desert.

Before departure, the Bedouins prepared a final meal—a traditional gesture of parting and respect. This was a once in a millennia event – they had kept the secret, and Malik's prophecy had come true. Under the shade of the Temple of Alexander, low tables were arranged in a semicircle on carpets faded from generations of use. By now the whole tribe had assembled, the women brought dishes steaming with aroma: lamb slow-cooked in earthen ovens, marinated with garlic, cumin, coriander, and cloves. There were platters of spiced rice freckled with raisins and almonds, flatbreads pulled fresh from coals and brushed with olive oil. Bowls of labneh and dates were passed around, followed by sweet mint tea poured from dented silver kettles into glass cups the size of thimbles. Alex sat beside Ibrahim as they dipped flatbread into the lamb stew, rich and tender. The smell alone made it feel like a sacrament.

Over the meal, he leaned in.

"What will you do with the DSD men?" he asked quietly.

Ibrahim exchanged a glance with the elders, then replied.

"We've known of Captain Hafez and his sergeant for many years," he said. "They stole from tombs, sold relics to dealers in Cairo and Europe. Always cloaked in authority. Always just beyond reach." He tore a piece of bread, thoughtfully. "Now they are not."

One of the elders, the chief himself—his face like sun-dried leather, eyes dark and steady—spoke in Arabic. Ibrahim translated solemnly.

"They are under Bedouin law now. The crime is theft. In our tradition, such men are judged by the tribe."

"And the punishment?" Claire asked.

Ibrahim's expression was unreadable.

"Justice must be seen, so others remember. In old ways, the hand that steals is marked, or taken. And this may come to pass. Or, they will be left in the desert—on foot, unarmed, with only their shame and the sun. If they are men of any worth, they may find their way back to civilisation."

There was no judgment in his voice. Only finality.

The conversation shifted. Laughter rose around the fire. Plates were scraped clean. Someone brought out a drum, its beat slow and rhythmic.

Suddenly, one of the younger chieftains stood and raised his cup toward Claire.

"This one," he said in Arabic, eyes warm, "this girl is brave. She has the soul of the desert and the wisdom of the stars. She should return with us. She would make a fine wife for Ibrahim."

Claire, mid-sip of tea, choked and flushed crimson.

Ibrahim nearly dropped his bowl.

"I—ah—no," he stammered. "I mean—thank you, but—she is a scholar! She has a destiny elsewhere."

The chief laughed heartily and waved a hand. "Perhaps. But the desert remembers its friends."

The laughter was still echoing when another chieftain turned toward Louis, nodding solemnly.

"You, lion-hearted one. You too are welcome among us. We have seen your fire."

Louis, grinning, raised a hand in thanks. "I might consider it," he said. "But first I must protect my friends. We seek Dhu al-Qarnayn. The road calls."

The men around the fire murmured approval.

"You have a place among the men, should you return," the elder replied.

As the sky dimmed to violet and the stars began to show, they loaded the Hilux's with what remained. Hugs were exchanged, hands shaken, words passed between friends whose languages barely overlapped. Then, with the golden light of the setting sun gleaming on the horizon, Alex climbed behind the wheel.
Samira turned once to wave. The tribal chief raised his hand in farewell.
Claire settled beside Louis in the second truck and waved goodbye to Ibrahim, who returned the gesture in pure Arabic style – touching his forehead, lips and heart. The engines rumbled to life. And with the last rays of sunlight kissing the top of the temple, they drove back to the Safari Camp. But tomorrow they would head west, toward the line of mountains where the red spear of heaven—Arcturus—was just beginning its long descent.
They were still on Malik's path.
The path of the four lions.

Chapter 7

Breakfast the next morning was almost a jubilant affair.

Alex had been the first to rise, requesting something light and early so they could leave with the dawn behind them. But by the time the others filtered in—still bleary-eyed, but buoyed by purpose—it was clear no one wanted the moment to pass unmarked. As Alex said, with a grin: "The band's back together." And it showed.

Even Yousif, the normally reserved owner of the lodge, joined in the celebration. He greeted Claire with a deep, respectful nod and a broad smile. "Miss Claire," he said warmly, "Alhamdulillah you are safe. You were missed."

Alex tried to wave off any fanfare, but Yousif would not hear of it. "Today," he declared, "you are not just guests. You are family."

Then breakfast arrived—a celebration in its own right.

Yousif's wife and two daughters carried out polished trays and clay platters that steamed in the golden light. There were warm baladi breads, still puffed from the oven, their crusts blistered and perfect for tearing. Bowls of labneh glistened with olive oil and za'atar, set beside small plates of fava beans in garlic and lemon, and shakshuka bubbling with tomato and egg. Dates, honeycomb, and slices of mild white cheese were laid out next to steaming cups of cardamom coffee and mint tea served in delicate glasses that clinked softly as they were passed.

Yousif, against his own rule, sat with them for the meal—his daughters shy but smiling, his wife quietly beaming as they all ate beneath the lodge's shaded courtyard. There was laughter. The kind of laughter that came not just from joy, but relief.

After breakfast, Louis had unfurled the map across the wooden table. He pulled out his Suunto A30 compass, calibrated it carefully, and aligned the map to magnetic north. Then, using a pencil and steady hand, he compensated for the difference between true and magnetic north, and drew the bearing.

A perfect line—287 degrees—cut west-northwest, almost directly through Siwa.

Samira leaned in, astonished. "Malik was that precise? He knew which star to use... and what its bearing would be from Bahariya?"

Alex nodded. "He was more than a guide. He was a scholar. A polymath."

"Siwa," Claire mused aloud. "Didn't Alexander ask to be buried there, at the end?"

Alex glanced up at her. "More than that. When he visited the Oracle of Amun, he asked to be recognized as Pharaoh. As divine. And I believe, yes—he asked to be laid to rest there. Whether that was honored, or not... well, history leaves us only hints."

Samira was already flipping through her notes. "The Temple of the Oracle is still standing. It existed in Malik's time and ours. That must be the next marker."

Alex gave a thoughtful nod. "I can't think of a better place. Symbolically, historically—it would have made perfect sense to Malik."

Claire let out a quiet breath. "Let's just hope whatever he left... is still there."

"What about checkpoints?" Louis asked, flipping closed his field notebook. "Roadblocks? Permits? Can we just walk into a 2,600-year-old temple without clearance?"

He looked around the breakfast table, now strewn with the remnants of pomegranate juice, dates, and warm flatbread. "I suggest we take the Marsa Matruh route—safe, paved, mostly guarded, yes, but passable."

Alex gave a resigned shrug, sipping the last of his thick Arabic coffee. "Not a bad suggestion. But that highway will have multiple military posts. And if they decide we're not supposed to be there…"

"Then we're done," Samira finished, nodding. "The temple will be sealed behind red tape before we even get our boots off."

Louis leaned back in his chair, chewing the thought. Then he reached into the old leather satchel slung across his chair and pulled out something wrapped in linen cloth. He unwrapped it carefully—a worn brass compass, dull with age but still gleaming where his thumb had polished the edges.

"This belonged to my father," he said. "8th Army. Desert Rats. He carried it from El Alamein to Tobruk and back again. I keep it with me. For luck."

He flicked it open. The needle quivered, settled.

"There's another way to Siwa," Louis continued, his voice lower now, almost reverent. "Off the books. The old LRDG trail. Ran northwest from Bahariya during the Western Desert Campaign. It skirts the Qattara Depression, passes through high gravel ridges and dry wadis. Used by recon patrols to avoid detection. It's not on modern maps."

Claire leaned forward. "And you know where it is?"

"I copied it from a hand-drawn sketch in a memoir—Charlie Turner, sergeant in the Long Range Desert Group. Found it in a secondhand bookshop in Tunis years ago." He tapped the compass. "It's rough terrain, but it'll get us to Siwa without being stopped. No checkpoints. No questions."

Samira raised a skeptical eyebrow. "And what are the chances the trail still exists?"

"Same chances the temple still does," Louis replied, grinning. "Sand hides, but it doesn't forget."

Alex nodded slowly. "We'll need to hug the escarpments. Keep off the sabkhas. The Hilux's can handle it if we ration the fuel."

Claire looked at the compass in Louis's hand. "That's the right kind of madness."

Louis stood, wrapping the compass again. "Then let's be mad. Malik's path isn't meant to be easy."

"Fucking-A" said a jubilant Claire.

By 7 a.m., they were packed and ready. Alex settled the bill with a thick wad of crisp cash and left a little extra on the side. "For the family," he said softly. Yousif shook hands with Alex one last time, pressing a cloth-wrapped bundle into his hands—flatbread still warm, brined olives, salted goat cheese, and thin slices of smoked lamb. "For strength on the road," he said. His wife added a flask of sweet tea and a folded napkin of honeyed dates.

The team climbed into the battered Hilux's, gear secured, maps and compasses ready. Louis took the lead, the old brass compass nestled beside the dash-mounted GPS—two guides from different centuries, both pointing west.

The engines growled to life.

They rolled out of the lodge courtyard, tyres crunching over gravel before gripping the tarmac road. The sun, just cresting the eastern ridge, caught their dust and framed them in gold.

Ahead lay the long road through broken asphalt and into open sand—into the forgotten tracks of war and the fading trail of a vanished scholar.

And behind them, the rising sun gave no answers—only light.

The lion was still walking.

And they were still on Malik's path.

Director Samy Khoury's office was a claustrophobic cell of smoke and stale air, the heavy curtains drawn tight against the unforgiving desert sun. His fingers trembled with barely restrained fury as he snatched up his battered mobile, the cracked screen a testament to years of silent threats and brutal negotiations. He punched in Major General Karim Nasser's number, the cold plastic biting into his skin like a promise of retribution.

Captain Hafez Abdel-Rahman had vanished into the arid wastes of the Bahariya, unreachable since yesterday. Khoury's mind churned dark possibilities. Had the fool finally lost his grip—gone rogue with secrets that could topple their fragile dominion? Or worse: was he already a shadow trader, cutting deals with the serpent Soterakis behind Khoury's back? That thought ignited a slow-burning rage, suffocating and relentless.

The phone rang sharply, cutting through the heavy air of Khoury's cramped office. On the third ring, a gravelly voice answered.

The phone rang sharply, each chime a reminder of time slipping away. On the third ring, a voice answered—gravelly, controlled, as cold as the desert night.

"Yes, Khoury. What do you want?"

Khoury's voice was a low growl, edged with steel. "General, I need you in Bawiti. Now. No delays. There's unrest brewing, and I fear it's about to ignite."

Nasser's response was calm, almost too calm. "I'm already moving. Three hours out. And what of that insolent dog, Hafez? Heard from him?"

Khoury spat the words with venom. "Nothing. Silent as the grave. I believe he's betraying us—playing Soterakis and cutting me out like a fool."

A dark chuckle rumbled through the line. "If he's dancing on the edge of the knife, we'll make sure he learns which side cuts deepest."

Khoury's tone dropped to a chilling whisper, icy and unforgiving. "No mercy for him. I don't want him healed or pardoned—I want him broken. Taught a lesson carved into his bones that he'll carry to his grave. And if he resists… then he must disappear. Erased. Vanished without a trace. Do you understand?"

"Oh, perfectly," Nasser breathed, a twisted smile lingering in his words. "Disappearance is a specialty of mine."

Khoury's eyes narrowed as he stared into the dim room, the shadows growing long and cold. "Report when you arrive. I want answers, and I want control. This chaos ends on our terms."

"Leave it to me, Khoury," Nasser promised smoothly. "You know who to trust!"

The line went dead. Khoury sat back, staring at the silent phone, the word 'trust' bitter on his tongue. Trust was a luxury long lost in these desperate times. Everyone was out to undermine him, to cut him out. His empire — painstakingly built with sweat and blood — would not be taken from him, not by Hafez, not by Soterakis, not by anyone.

The two Hilux's barreled out of Bahariya Oasis in a trail of dust, their suspensions groaning as they took on the pockmarked excuse for blacktop that stretched northward. The old desert road—never officially maintained and long since forgotten—offered little more than a cracked, faded ribbon of tarmac before it vanished into windblown sands.

Samira sat in the passenger seat of the lead vehicle, watching signal bars flicker and disappear on her mobile. The reception was too patchy for a voice call, but she managed to tap out a brief message to André Molineux before the signal cut out entirely: Heading from Bahariya to Siwa by the old LRDG route. Louis leading. Will make contact when in Siwa, perhaps tonight. Trouble with DSD, but locals came to our rescue. No service from here until Siwa. —Samira

She hit send just as the Hilux jolted off the last remnants of tarmac and rolled onto the soft, golden cushion of desert sand. The old road was gone. Before them stretched the open Sahara—undulating dunes, gravel flats, and the distant shimmer of mirages. No markers, no signposts, only sun and sand and silence.

For the next several hours, the convoy snaked westward along a barely perceptible trail. Sometimes it was there—a suggestion of tire ruts, a hardened strip of gravel. Sometimes it wasn't. Mostly, it wasn't.

Louis drove with jaw set and eyes squinting into the glare. He was navigating by dead reckoning and dusty memory, relying on faded wartime maps burned into his mind from his Foreign Legion days. It had been years, but the instincts hadn't left him. He was rusty— but focused.

Around noon, they pulled up beside a gravel ridge where a few stubby desert acacias clung to life. The vehicles groaned to a halt in the sliver of shade, and the team climbed out, already sticky with sweat. The heat was punishing—dry, suffocating, and absolute. Even in the shade, they simmered.

Lunch was simple, but glorious in its own way: soft flatbread still warm from the lodge, briny olives, salted goat cheese that crumbled at the touch, smoked slices of lamb, and a handful of dried apricots—all lovingly packed by Yousif's family. They ate in relative silence, drinking greedily from metal canteens and wiping their faces with damp cloths. After a brief rest and a routine check of the vehicles, they pushed on.

Not twenty minutes later, Claire pointed out of the passenger window. "What's that—at ten o'clock, near the base of that dune?" Louis slowed, swerved left, and cut the engine. The second Hilux pulled up behind them. Silence returned to the desert as the team dismounted and approached the strange shape in the sand.

It was a skeleton of metal.

An old Chevrolet WB 30-hundredweight truck lay half-buried in the dune, bleached and rusted by sun and time. Its paint had long since blistered off, and its tires were nothing more than cracked, blackened husks. Nearby, a stack of rusted jerry cans lay in a loose pile. The faint glint of spent shell casings littered the sand. An ammo box—British issue, World War II vintage—sat open beside the rear wheel.

"Bloody hell," whispered Louis, kneeling beside the vehicle. "This is LRDG—Long Range Desert Group. Original. She's been here eighty years, at least."

Alex crouched down beside him. "Doesn't look shot up. No bullet holes, no burn marks."

"Must've broken down," said Samira, brushing sand away from a rusted headlamp. "Or got stuck in a dune and the crew walked out."

Claire ran her fingers over the weathered hood. "They were ghosts in the desert. The LRDG operated alone, didn't they?"

"Behind enemy lines," said Louis. "Used old Bedouin caravan trails, stayed off-grid. Like us right now, and Malik before them." He stood and looked at Claire. "Would you mind photographing it?"

Alex raised an eyebrow. "It's getting late, I am not sure we have time for that. This isn't our mission!"

Louis turned slowly, his expression unreadable. "No, it's not. But this is history, too. This is archaeology. What we do isn't just about the ancients—it's about memory. About preserving what time tries to erase. If we don't record this, who will?"

Claire met his gaze, then nodded. "He's right, Alex. This is someone's story."

Samira joined her. "Someone who came before. We honor them by remembering."

Alex sighed, but relented with a wave. "Alright. Half an hour, no more."

Claire got to work. She moved deliberately, photographing every angle: the fractured axles, the scorched canvas straps still tied to the rear panel, the faded unit number barely visible on the tailgate. She took wide shots of the area, close-ups of the ammo box, the fuel cans, the pattern of wind-swept sand. She noted it all, voice-recording details into her phone and logging coordinates with her GPS unit.

"We can come back someday," she said softly, "with real preservation teams. If it's still here."

Louis watched in silence, hands on his hips. The wind whispered across the dunes, lifting a small flurry of sand through the open chassis of the wrecked Chevrolet, as if it were breathing.

At last, Claire packed her camera and nodded. "I'm done."

They returned to the Hilux's, the engines groaning reluctantly back to life. With one last glance at the forgotten ghost of war behind them, they turned westward again, deeper into the sun-soaked emptiness.

More desert. More sand.

But more determined than ever.

André Molineux sat at his desk in the old limestone building on Rue de Lille, the Seine glinting just beyond the window behind him. The spring breeze carried the faint scent of cherry blossoms, but his mind was far from Paris.

With a sigh, he picked up his encrypted line and dialed a number he'd used far too frequently of late: the secure channel for the French Embassy in Cairo. It rang three times, then clicked through with a hiss of static.

"Allô?" came the voice, tinged with heat and exhaustion. "André, mon vieux, I trust Paris is treating you better than this oven we call Cairo. It's damn near unbearable down here—feels like the air itself is plotting against us."

André smiled faintly despite the knot in his stomach. "Bonjour Étienne, it's good to hear your voice, old friend. Yes, Paris is behaving—March is kind, as always. The city's waking up after winter."

"Ahh, March in Paris. The chestnuts in bloom, the terraces filling again… Je m'en souviens. But you didn't call to talk about the weather, did you?"

"Unfortunately not. I'm calling about our team in Bahariya."

There was a pause on the line. The faint buzz of a ceiling fan could be heard on Étienne Moreau's end.

"I haven't heard from them since the day before yesterday. Last message said they were excavating near the Temple of Alexander. Said the site was sterile—no artifacts of note. Nothing more since then."

"I received a text this morning," André said, his tone quiet. "From Dr. Samira Rahmani. Short message. She said they were heading from Bahariya to Siwa—by the old Long Range Desert Group track."

"Le LRDG?" Étienne said, the fatigue in his voice replaced by a sudden spark of memory. "Oh, it exists, alright. I remember it. We used parts of it in my Legion days—originally caravan routes used by traders, then by smugglers and rebels. The British and Commonwealth patrols took advantage of it during the war. Rough country. Remote. No one goes that way anymore."

André let the silence linger for a beat. "That's what worries me. If they're using that route, they're going off the grid. No signals, no surveillance, no backup."

Moreau grunted. "Which means they either found something, or they're running from something."

"Raylan Stretton flagged something disturbing," André continued. "There's been a spike in encrypted chatter between Director Samy Khoury and Bahariya. And worse—communications with a certain Major General Karim Nasser."

Étienne made a low sound. "Nasser? That bastard still in uniform? I thought he was neck-deep in scandals three years ago."

"He was. But like many of their kind, scandal only polished his boots. If he's in play, things are more dangerous than I thought. Samira's message said they hoped to reach Siwa by tonight, but if Nasser is mobilizing assets... they may be walking into a trap."

Étienne exhaled sharply. "Merde." Then after a pause: "Do we have anything out there? Eyes, ears—anything?"

"In Siwa, no. Not officially. No embassy presence, no consulate. But…" he trailed off.

"But what?" asked André.

"We might have some friends not too far west—Libyan side. Old network, kept warm for other reasons." There was a hint of old intelligence games in his voice, the kind spoken in code and half-memories. "Let me make a call. If they're still in-country and not entirely insane, they may be able to help."

André nodded slowly, even though Moreau couldn't see him.

"That would be appreciated, Étienne. I have a terrible feeling… that la merde est sur le point de frapper le ventilateur."

Moreau chuckled, grim and knowing. "That's one way of putting it."

Then he dropped his voice, turning grave again. "I'll get back to you within the hour. In the meantime—if you get anything else from the team, even a whisper, you call me. No filters, no delays."

"Of course."

The line clicked dead.

André sat back, the phone still in his hand. The spring breeze had turned colder, or perhaps it only felt that way.

Somewhere in the great silence of the desert, his people were chasing ghosts. And something—someone—was waiting.

Major General Hassan arrived in Bahariya just before midday, the desert sun already high and cruel. Dust clung to the sides of the army-green Land Cruiser as it rolled to a halt outside the local DSD outpost—a squat, crumbling structure of whitewashed concrete and rust-stained shutters that stank of sweat, cigarettes, and fear. Hassan stepped out, brushing the sand from his uniform with deliberate precision. He needed a shower, and he needed a stiff drink. Something dark. Arak, maybe. Or whiskey, if he could get it—his private sin, sealed in glass and tucked beneath the floorboards of his Giza villa.

He pushed through the warped front doors with the confidence of a man used to command. Inside, chaos reigned. Radios crackled unintelligibly, junior officers barked at each other, and tension hung thick in the air. At his entrance, everything stopped. Men snapped to attention like puppets on taut strings.

He zeroed in on the closest uniform. A skinny corporal with frightened eyes and an oil-smudged cheek.

"Where is Captain Hafez?" Hassan asked, his voice like sandpaper and steel.

"I cannot say, General," the corporal stammered, standing rigid.

Hassan's eyes narrowed. "You cannot say, or you do not know?"

"We haven't heard from him in over twenty-four hours, sir. Neither him nor the Sergeant . They—"

"Where was he last seen?"

"He left for the Temple ruins, General. But we searched the site. There was nothing."

"Nothing?" Hassan echoed, disdain curling the word like smoke. "Surely you found something. Where is his vehicle?"

"Gone, sir. No sign of it. No tracks we could follow. Nothing."

From across the room, another corporal called out. His voice was muffled, indistinct.

"Speak up, for the sake of Allah," Hassan snapped.

The second corporal cleared his throat. "Shell casings, General. We found shell casings. A lot of them."

Hassan turned sharply. "You're telling me Hafez and his men were in a firefight—and then vanished?"

"We can't confirm, sir. But the casings were scattered over a wide area. Something happened. We just don't know what."

"Then take me there. Now."

The convoy sped across the broken trail that led to the ruins, a choking tail of dust in its wake. Twenty minutes later, they arrived. The site was still and unnerving. No vehicles. No bodies. Just ancient columns half-swallowed by sand and sun, and the spent brass glinting dully like relics of violence. Hassan stepped out, crouched, and picked one up.

7.62x39. Kalashnikov.

He pulled out his phone and hit Khoury's number. The call connected on the first ring.

"Hassan, have you found that pig Hafez yet?"

"No, Director. But there's trouble."

Khoury's voice sharpened. "Trouble? What kind of trouble? Is he dealing us out?"

Hassan turned the shell casing between his fingers. "Either your man picked a fight with the local militia, or he has double-crossed his supply network. But something went wrong. Badly."

Khoury cursed under his breath. "That dog. He's trying to cut a new deal, isn't he? A new network. The old suppliers rebelled, and now he's cleaning house."

"That's one explanation. But no bodies, no wreckage—only shell casings. Maybe someone cleaned it up. Maybe he's on the run."

At that moment, a young soldier ran up, dust streaming behind him. He stopped short, panting.

"Sir! The white Hilux's—they were seen heading west. Toward Siwa."

Hassan raised an eyebrow. "Siwa? Interesting."

He brought the phone back to his ear. "Director, seems your rogue is heading west. Perhaps to strong-arm new allies. Or perhaps develop a new network in Siwa."

"Stop him, Hassan," Khoury hissed. "Intercept that treacherous bastard before he reaches Siwa. I want him dead. Tortured and dead. I want him to understand that no one betrays me. Do you hear me? No one!"

There was a pause.

"And what do I get in return, Director?" Hassan asked coolly.

Khoury was quiet for a moment, calculating. Nothing came free in his world.

"You can have the western provinces. Full control. But everything moves through me. All of it. Understood?"

"Perfectly," Hassan said, a thin smile on his lips. "I'll call you when I have something more."

He hung up. Silence settled over the ruins. He pocketed the shell casing.

Hafez was a ghost now, but not for long.

Khoury's voice still rang in his ears. Tortured and dead.

Hassan looked west, toward the endless desert.

Siwa.

It would not hide them for long.

Chapter 8

The two Hilux's rumbled over the last shallow rise, their engines coughing with fatigue, headlights dulled by the veil of dust that clung to every surface. The smugglers route, if it could still be called that, had faded hours ago into a phantom trail—barely perceptible tire-ruts interrupted by yawning troughs of sand and gravel.

In the lead vehicle, Louis hunched over the wheel, jaw tight, eyes bloodshot but focused. Beside him, Claire sat alert, cradling a map she hadn't consulted in hours. There was no signal. No GPS. Only the stars above and Louis's battered brass compass ticking like a heartbeat on the dash.

Behind them, in the second Hilux, Samira rubbed at her temples, dry lips cracked from the heat. Alex drove in silence, scanning the terrain ahead with a grim intensity. Both vehicles had run dangerously low on fuel—one needle trembling below a quarter tank, the other kissing the red line. They'd been running on willpower and stubborn hope for the last hour.

And the water was gone.

They'd rationed it carefully through the day, but the desert didn't bargain. It took what it wanted. Even now, at night, the heat clung like a fever.

Claire leaned forward suddenly, pointing ahead. "There. Palm trees. I see palm trees!"

Louis nodded, shifting in his seat. "C'est Siwa," he murmured. "We made it."

"Praise God," Claire breathed.

Over the radio, Samira's voice crackled. "Confirm—are we seeing date palms and lights? Is that the oasis?"

Claire responded from the first Hilux. "Looks like it. We're holding together but running on fumes. Let's just pray we find fuel, water, and beds."

They descended slowly now, following the soft contours of the land as it sloped toward the basin of Siwa. The silhouettes of clustered palms swayed under the stars, and the faint glow of oil lamps flickered ahead like will-o'-the-wisps.

As they approached the edge of the village, Claire caught sight of a mudbrick guesthouse, barely visible in the moonlight. There was a hand-painted wooden sign above the archway—Arabic script, beautifully calligraphed. She pointed it out to Samira.

"Bayt al-Rimāl," Samira translated over the radio. "House of Sands. Looks like we found somewhere to rest."

Louis brought the lead Hilux to a shuddering halt, the engine ticking in protest as it cooled. Alex followed, pulling up behind them just as his fuel light blinked insistently.

The four climbed out into the cool desert night, stiff, coated in sand, lips dry, clothes crusted in salt and dust. Claire opened the rear tray and rummaged through their gear. Nothing left to drink. The last water had been finished two hours ago. Even the canteens were dry.

An elderly man stepped from the shadows near the doorway, dressed in a long white galabeya, a red keffiyeh wound loosely around his neck. His eyes, dark and cautious, swept over the team. Samira stepped forward, switching to Arabic. "We're travelers from Bahariya. We've crossed the desert. We need rooms… and water. Please."

The man studied them a moment longer, then gave a single nod. "You are welcome in Siwa. This is not Cairo. There are no questions here. But stay inside tonight. After midnight, the desert spirits walk."

Claire raised an eyebrow at Samira, who merely gave a subtle shake of her head.

"I've missed hospitality like that," Alex muttered as they began unloading gear. "Short on words. Long on meaning."

Louis didn't respond. He stood at the front of the Hilux, staring up at the stars. His fingers brushed the rim of the compass on the dash.

"Arcturus," he said quietly, "guided us the last four hours. Just like it did in ancient times"

Samira came beside him. "You did well, Louis. We made it."

"Barely," he muttered. "We have no fuel. No water. And the way back? It's closed now. Only forward from here."

Alex glanced around the quiet village perimeter. The oasis felt untouched by time. Crumbling walls, mudbrick arches, and domed roofs sat under the same stars that had guided Malik and his caravan over a thousand years before.

Claire stepped back from the guesthouse, eyes wide. "This place… it feels old. Older than Egypt, somehow."

Samira exhaled slowly. "It's not just a town. Siwa was once the seat of oracles. Alexander himself came here to ask if he was a god."

"And now we're here," said Alex, slinging his pack over his shoulder. "To find what he left behind."

The four of them entered Bayt al-Rimāl as the wind picked up gently through the palms. The desert had released them—for now. But the night was far from over.

They would sleep lightly.

Tomorrow, the Oracle of Amun would rise again.

It was early morning at the Siwa Police Station, a squat, sun-bleached building of yellowed stucco and fading green shutters that stood watch along Al-Matar Street, just off the road that led east toward Bahariyah. The structure bore the marks of both heat and neglect—cracks like spiderwebs in the plaster, and rust bleeding down from warped metal awnings.

Inside, the atmosphere was stifling, despite the sluggish ceiling fans overhead. Major General Karim Nasser paced the tiled floor like a caged tiger, bootheels tapping a rhythm of controlled fury. Dust floated in slanted bars of light through the grimy windows, as if afraid to settle in his presence.

They had arrived the afternoon prior, making no small impression on the sleepy outpost. Since then—nothing. Not a whisper, not a rumour. Captain Hafez had simply vanished.

Or, Nasser thought grimly, taken another route.

The sickly dog might have gone north, through Marsa Matruh— doubling his travel time to Siwa. But for what? To buy time? To rally support among the northern networks ahead of the inevitable turf war?

Let him try, Nasser mused. The more rats that fled the nest, the easier they were to kill in the open.

But he wouldn't leave anything to chance.

"Sergeant!" he barked.

A wiry man with a waxed mustache and the unfortunate look of someone already halfway to a heart attack snapped to his feet. He had spent most of the morning trying to remain invisible in the corner, but now stood rigid, trembling slightly under Nasser's gaze.

"Yes, General!"

"I want every available man pulled off whatever nonsense you've assigned them to. I want roadblocks on every road, every trail, every damn goat track that leads to or from this town. Armed patrols. Full kit. No excuses. Anyone heading east gets stopped, questioned, documented."

"Understood, General."

"And Hafez…I want him in custody by nightfall. Drag him back by the ankles if you have to. Do I make myself clear?"

"Perfectly, General."

The sergeant bolted from the room like his boots were on fire, leaving Nasser alone again in the echoing silence.

He moved to the open window, inhaling the brittle desert air.
Somewhere out there, the Captain was running. Perhaps making
deals, perhaps begging favours. But it didn't matter.
He would be found.
And when he was, Nasser would make a spectacle of him—
something that would etch itself into the memory of men for
generations.
He reached into his pocket, produced his mobile phone, and
unlocked the screen with one fluid motion.
Time to call Khoury.
 He had to keep the Director informed—or that spineless dog might
turn rabid too.

Alex, Samira, and Louis all woke late.
Their bodies ached, their mouths were dry, and their dreams—
when they had managed to sleep—had been fractured, restless. The
Hilux convoy had rolled into Siwa just after midnight, silent and
spent, like some ghost caravan arriving from another time. They'd
barely managed to find a place to stay—an old, mudbrick
guesthouse on the edge of the oasis—before collapsing into their
beds.
The trek had taken its toll.
Even the eternally composed Samira Rahmani looked worn, her
dark curls tousled and eyes shadowed with fatigue. She sipped
slowly from a tin cup of warm water, trying to rehydrate, her gaze
distant as she watched the morning light slide across the window's
woven shade.
"My mouth tastes like sand and diesel," muttered Alex, sitting up
and rubbing his neck. His shirt clung to him, still damp from the
previous day's sweat. "We must've lost ten pounds of water out
there."
"It's a miracle we didn't lose a kidney," Samira replied dryly.
From the next room came the sound of coughing, cursing in
French, and the metallic rattle of gear being checked. A moment

later, Louis emerged, pulling on a fresh shirt and blinking at the light.

He looked at them both, bleary-eyed but smiling. "Bon Dieu, that was not a drive. That was a war of attrition."

Alex gave a tired chuckle. "You said it last night. Now you know what the Long Range Desert Group went through."

Louis nodded, his expression sobering. "Oui. They were madmen, but glorious ones. Imagine—driving open-top trucks through this endless hell, at night, under blackout, navigating by compass and Arcturus... and then arriving just in time to blow up an airfield or ambush a supply column."

He shook his head, eyes distant with respect. "A special kind of madness."

Samira gave a faint smile. "They were ghosts in the sand. And now we've followed in their tire tracks."

Alex stood slowly, stretching his back with a groan. "Well, ghosts or not, we're not quite dead yet. We should check the trucks— make sure the suspension's still holding. And refill whatever we can. Water, diesel, food."

Louis sighed. "Water will be easy. Fuel, maybe. Decent food? We are in the hands of fate."

Samira rose and adjusted her headscarf. "Let's not forget—we're not just tourists anymore. Someone's going to notice we've arrived. If Khoury or Nasser is anywhere near here, we need to move quickly."

Alex nodded. "Agreed. Let's grab what we can and be on the road again before noon. We'll have to keep a low profile."

Louis muttered under his breath in French. "The only thing lower than our profile is our blood sugar."

They all laughed, tired but alive.

Outside, the Siwa morning was already heating up, golden light catching on the palm fronds and crumbling mudbrick walls. The oasis shimmered, deceptively calm. Somewhere beyond it, danger still hunted them.

But for now, they had survived the night.

They ate breakfast at 8 a.m., bleary-eyed but a touch more human after showers and fresh clothes. The innkeeper, a wiry old Siwan named Hamid, had taken pity on them and prepared a simple but satisfying meal. They sat under a shaded pergola in the courtyard, palm fronds rustling softly above.

The breakfast was traditional—fresh flatbread, still warm from the taboon oven; black olives, slick with brine; crumbled mish, a sharp fermented cheese that Samira claimed was "an acquired taste," though Louis had taken to it immediately; honey and date syrup drizzled in clay bowls; and boiled eggs, their yolks rich and golden. There was strong, bitter tea, steeped with sage and mint, and a jug of tepid but life-giving water beside them.

Alex ate quietly, chewing and thinking at once. The weariness from the desert still clung to his bones, but the meal steadied him. Louis polished off the last of the eggs and wiped his mouth with the back of his hand. "That, my friends, was divine. You don't know what you've got until you've crossed an ocean of sand to get to it."

Samira raised an eyebrow. "Let's just hope we don't have to do it again anytime soon."

They repacked the Hilux's by 8:45, working in quick, practiced silence. The heat was already climbing. The first order of business was water—they topped off every available container from a hand-pump well in the alley behind the inn, nodding to a curious old woman who watched them from a nearby rooftop.

Diesel was trickier. There were no major stations in the oasis itself, but the innkeeper had directed them to a small fuel depot on the eastern edge of town, just off Route 19, called Mahmoud Fuels & Lubricants. It served mostly agricultural vehicles and desert transporters, and more importantly—it had diesel.

They drove there in a tight convoy, keeping their heads down, paid in cash, and filled their tanks to the brim. The station attendant, a teenager with sun-scorched skin and Bluetooth headphones, barely looked up from his phone.

It was only then, as they returned to the quiet perimeter of the town, that Hamid's final remark came back to them—casually tossed over his shoulder as he'd seen them off.

"You all slept through the noise this morning," he'd said, adjusting his turban. "DSD and local police—everywhere. They cleared out of town just after dawn, trucks and patrol cars heading east, west, south. Even some back streets. Looking for someone. You missed the chaos by a hair."

Samira had exchanged a quick glance with Louis. That wasn't good news.

Or maybe… it was.

If the security forces had emptied out of Siwa—then the Temple of the Oracle might be completely unguarded.

By 9:20am, both trucks were loaded and ready. Alex double-checked their gear: cameras, notebooks, measuring tools, Claire's GPS, a small drone, and their hidden dossiers. Everything was accounted for. Louis checked the Glocks.

They took a winding, indirect route—avoiding Route 17 and the center of town, cutting instead through dusty alleyways and unnamed backroads used mostly by donkey carts and date farmers. Louis led the way in the first Hilux, navigating by instinct and memory, while Claire rode shotgun, with Alex and Samira behind. No one gave them a second glance, just two beat-up white DSD vehicles going about their business.

"Twenty minutes, if the roads stay quiet," Samira said, peering at the map folded in her lap. "We'll approach from the south. The access track is still there, according to satellite images."

Claire, sitting beside Louis, held the GPS up to the windshield. "No checkpoints so far."

Alex's voice crackled over the radio. "With the luck of the gods, we'll get in, find what we need, and be out before anyone even knows we were here."

Louis didn't look back, eyes on the road ahead. But his voice was steady.

"Let's just pray the gods are still awake." he said into the radio mike.

The desert stretched ahead again—familiar, unforgiving, and full of secrets yet to be unearthed.

The two Hiluxes wound their way along a narrow dirt path barely etched into the southern edge of the Siwa Oasis. With Louis and Claire leading the way in the front vehicle, and Alex and Samira close behind, the tires crunched over loose sand and dry stone. Here and there, old wheel ruts had been swallowed by drifting dunes. Overhead, the sun was still low and casting long golden blades across the palms, but already the heat was beginning to rise again, pressing against the glass.

The scent of desert dust and sweet date palms drifted in through the cracked windows. Insects buzzed somewhere nearby, and the occasional croak of a desert raven cut the silence. They had taken the back tracks on purpose, avoiding paved roads and police checkpoints, trusting instead in Samira's intimate knowledge of the terrain and Louis's steady compass work.

Then Claire saw it first.

She leaned forward in her seat and pointed through the windshield. "There," she said, breathless. "Oh my God…"

The desert opened up before them like a revelation.

The Temple of Amun stood on a sandstone rise, lifted above the palms like a throne carved by gods. It was not a ruin so much as a citadel—a crumbling crown of ochre-colored stone rising from the sea of green that surrounded it. The morning haze gave the entire scene a surreal quality, as if it were a mirage or some colossal ship rising from the tide of palms.

Its towers and battered walls glowed in the dawn light, burnished gold by the desert air. The architecture was irregular, eroded and majestic, an ancient fist thrusting up through time itself. The vast field of palms below stirred with the breeze, a living moat of rustling fronds. A hawk circled silently above the structure, as if drawn by memory.

The Hiluxes crawled to a halt. No one spoke.

Even Alex, who had seen the Parthenon at sunrise and knelt alone in the ruins of Ur, was silenced.

Samira stepped out, the sand crunching softly beneath her boots. "This," she said quietly, "is not what I expected."

Alex came around to her side, staring upward. "No. It's… it's not a temple. It's a testament."

Louis stood with both hands on his hips, shaking his head in awe. "And to think... Alexander the Great came here. To this exact place. To hear the voice of Amun."

Claire stepped beside him. "It's not modest at all. It's glorious."

The team stood there a moment longer, letting the gravity of it settle over them. They had crossed the desert by starlight, nearly out of water, their fuel gauges kissing empty. And now, they were here—at one of the most sacred, secret, and storied places in the ancient world.

And it was waiting for them.

They parked in the designated area just southeast of the temple mound—a sliver of gravel cleared of palm undergrowth, sun-bleached and mostly empty. It was low season for tourists, and it showed. Only one other vehicle was present: a dusty silver Toyota Prius with local Siwan plates. Rental agencies were rare in Siwa, almost nonexistent, but it wasn't impossible to arrange a lease from Marsa Matruh or even Cairo and have it delivered this far out—especially if one knew the right people. But these were locals. Either way, the presence of the car made Alex uneasy.

Still, time was pressing. They moved efficiently.

Samira and Claire distributed gear into their backpacks—LED torches, a collapsible drone, their laptops, camera gear, water bottles, and notebooks. Alex slung his worn leather satchel over one shoulder, the same one that had carried heretical scrolls and letters in France. Louis, ever the minimalist, carried nothing but his calm demeanor and the Glock tucked neatly into the deep side pocket of his cream linen trousers. If he needed to act fast, he didn't want to be encumbered.

The group stepped away from the vehicles and began the slow, rising climb.

The staircase wasn't straight. Instead, it spiraled gently around the circumference of the sandstone mound, worn smooth by centuries of use. To the south and west, the oasis rolled away in waves of green—date palms swaying rhythmically, rustling like whispers. The air was thick with their scent: earthy, sun-warmed, and ancient. Somewhere below, a donkey brayed once, briefly, then silence returned.

As they ascended, the Temple of Amun emerged into full view— serene, stoic, and somehow surreal, its fractured towers and angled walls worn by centuries of desert sun. The complex had grown like coral—added to, adapted, and fortified over time. Sections had been repurposed, others left to crumble, and some walls had clearly once led to rooms that no longer existed. It was a labyrinth. And in that, there was opportunity.

At the summit, they found themselves in a broad open courtyard, flanked by what was unmistakably the main temple building to the north. It was the tallest and most impressive structure on the rise, its upper edges jagged but proud. To its west stood the newer minaret—a later addition from the Islamic centuries, a slender tower of mudbrick and stone used to summon the faithful to prayer. The juxtaposition was striking: the old god and the new, side by side in the sun.

The central temple itself was divided into four large rooms, each one echoing a different phase of its long, evolving life. Even in ruin, there was power in its symmetry. The carved reliefs had weathered badly, but in places they were still readable—images of Amun crowned with feathers, pharaohs in supplication, papyrus bundles, offering tables, bulls, and cobras.

Alex gathered them quickly. His tone was calm, but clipped. "Alright. Let's split up. Looks like we have the place to ourselves—for now. Louis and Claire, you take the two southern rooms. Samira and I will check the northern ones. Now…" he gestured toward the worn façade, "…as Samira's pointed out, this temple—this building—would have been here in Alexander's time. Malik may have chosen to mark it, or use it, in some way. Just like Bahariya. It could be an obelisk, a carved niche, or something right under our feet."

"Also, don't get lost!" He looked around reflexively—and his eyes landed briefly, unintentionally, on Claire. She arched an eyebrow and rolled her eyes but said nothing.

"Be thorough," Alex added, "and keep in voice contact. Let's get to it."

They broke into pairs.

Samira led Alex into the first northern chamber—a broad, cool room roughly seven metres square. The stone beneath their boots echoed faintly, the walls still carrying ghostly carvings of lotus flowers and ibis-headed gods. Across the complex, Claire and Louis dipped into their first room, slightly smaller but similar in form and construction.

The rooms were built from carefully dressed sandstone blocks, interlocked like an ancient puzzle. In some places, it felt as though the rooms had been hollowed directly from the living rock of the mound itself. Carvings adorned every surface: some faded beyond recognition, others surprisingly clear despite the centuries.

The air was dry, still, and fragrant with old stone and the ever-present perfume of dust. The light inside was soft and indirect—filtered through the narrow slits and doorways that marked each room's entrance.

An hour passed. Nothing.

The teams rotated. Alex and Samira moved into the second northern chamber. Louis and Claire explored their second to the south. The rhythm of quiet boots, soft voices, and distant birdsong became the backdrop to their methodical search. Alex paid particular attention to the floors this time—after Bahariya, he wasn't going to be caught overlooking something right under his nose. But this place was different. There was no plinth. No well. No central altar. Just stone, sand, and silence.

Outside, a small cluster of tourists—locals, by the sound of it— came and went. Claire had spotted them through a crack in the wall. "Egyptian Arabic," she whispered to Louis. "Probably just day-trippers." They stayed five minutes and left. The site was too quiet, too empty for their liking. No photo ops. No cafés. Just ruins.

By the time the four of them reconvened in the sunlit southern courtyard, the mood was growing heavy.

Claire wiped sweat from her brow with the edge of her shirt. Louis squinted toward the horizon. Samira leaned against a pillar, frowning in thought.

"You didn't think Malik would make it easy, did you?" she said. "We dove into the Mediterranean Sea for the first one. Had to climb down into a death trap in Bahariya for the second. If it were simple, it would have been found already."

Alex nodded. She was right. But the clock was ticking. The longer they stayed, the higher the risk.

It was then, absentmindedly, that Claire sat.

A sandstone block had tumbled from the outer wall, half buried near the edge of the courtyard. She settled onto it to rest, looking up at the wall it must have once belonged to.

Then she saw it.

Not all at once—but gradually.

At first, it was just a pattern—something half-familiar.

Then the curve of a nose.

An eye.
A second eye.
An ear.
A mane.
Her heart skipped. She stood slowly, took a step closer. Blinked.
A lion.
Carved in relief—worn almost smooth in places, but unmistakable.
A lion, seated proudly, carved into the wall, staring directly at
them.

Chapter 9

The heat inside the police station had grown oppressive, but the temperature beneath Major General Karim Nasser's collar was hotter still.

The single air conditioning unit—ancient and coughing—had long given up the fight against the North African sun. The walls of the cramped main office radiated stored heat like kiln-fired bricks, and every surface, every breath, felt like it was trying to suffocate him. Sweat clung to his undershirt, dampened the inside of his collar, and turned the gold trim of his epaulets into hot wire.

He paced like a caged predator, slow, deliberate steps across the cracked tiles of the floor, his polished boots tapping like a metronome of barely-contained rage. Each pass took him by the barred window overlooking the dusty courtyard, then back toward the radio desk where a corporal—young, scrawny, and visibly afraid—sat with a trembling hand resting on the transceiver mic.

They had nothing.

No sign. No whisper. No shadow.

Captain Hafez, the bastard, had simply disappeared.

Or worse—outmaneuvered them.

Nasser clenched his jaw as he passed the radio desk again. He stopped abruptly.

"Again," he barked, gesturing to the mic. "I want every roadblock and every checkpoint called. I don't care if it's the tenth time— they answer, and they report."

The corporal nodded hastily and began the drill. One by one, the voices crackled over the radio, all reporting the same useless nothing:

No sightings. No incidents. No unidentified vehicles.

No Hafez.

He's playing us, Nasser thought.

The little snake had probably peeled off north during the night, toward Matruh or even as far as Alamein. Trying to raise support. Whispering poison into the ears of disloyal men. A coup in slow motion. A turf war in embryonic form.

And worse: a direct challenge to Khoury's rule.

Which meant a direct threat to Nasser's own position.

The general exhaled hard through his nose. His temples throbbed. He reached for a glass of water—lukewarm, slightly dusty—and drained it. The corporal looked over his shoulder, pale and hesitant.

"Sir… same report. No contact. No leads."

Nasser didn't respond immediately. He turned back toward the window, fingers drumming against the sill, his eyes scanning the sun-bleached courtyard and the swaying palms beyond.

Think. Don't react. Hafez wants you impatient. Wants you exposed.

He would not give him the satisfaction.

No, this was a war of attrition now. A contest of endurance.

The cat always gets the mouse, he reminded himself.

As long as he waited. As long as he watched.

Eventually, the mouse slips.

And when that moment came, Nasser would strike—not with strategy, not with negotiation—but with finality.

His mind drifted for a moment to what that would look like.

A public arrest. A broken body. An execution so brutal it would echo through the ranks for a decade. A message in blood.

The thought soothed him. A little.

He turned back toward the corporal. "Keep calling. Every hour. Report anything—suspicious vehicles, missing locals, power outages, anything."

"Yes, General."

Nasser nodded once and moved to his desk, sitting at last. He rolled his shoulders, exhaled through gritted teeth, and stared at the map of the region splayed across the surface. A maze of tracks, trails, wadis, and nothingness. Somewhere in that spiderweb, Hafez was crawling.

A sneaky bastard.

But every rat comes up for air eventually.

And when he does?

Nasser would be waiting—with his jaws wide open.

Claire slowly rose from the sandstone block she'd been resting on, brushing grit from the back of her pants. She blinked twice, tilted her head to the left, then to the right. Her hands went to her hips as she stared in contemplation at the outer temple wall. Something was there—she was sure of it.

She took ten steps to the left, then ten back to the right, then another ten steps to the right, then back to centre, returning to stand directly in front of the block. Her voice broke the silence.

"Are you guys seeing what I'm seeing?" she asked, not turning around.

Alex and Samira both looked up from their notes and gear.

"What are you talking about, Claire?" Alex called out.

"This," she said, pointing toward the wall, defiant and unwavering. "This lion. Carved into the wall. Can't you see it?"

Samira squinted. "I don't see anything."

"I think you need to be standing here," Claire said, beckoning them closer. "Exactly here. Right in front of this rock. You can't see it from anywhere else."

Alex approached skeptically, coming within a few feet of her, his brow furrowed. "Just what are we supposed to be looking at?"

"There," she pointed at a worn patch of stone. "That's an ear. And just below it, see that faint arc? That's an eye. Another there. And look at the curvature—doesn't it look like a mane?"

Alex shook his head. "Nothing. I think the sun's cooked your brain."

"No," Claire insisted. "Stand right here." She marked the ground with hiking boot and nudged him into her exact footprint and stepped aside. Then, leaning over his shoulder, she traced the outline in the air. "There's the eye... now look to the right—see it?"

Alex's eyes widened. "Wait... wait, yes. That's an eye. That's definitely an eye." He stepped forward slightly, and the illusion vanished. "Incredible. I was only a few feet off and didn't see it at all."

"I think it's deliberate," Claire murmured. "The chiselling... it's so shallow, so subtle. It only catches the light when you're standing in the right spot, at the right time of day."

She stepped back, watching the wall as the second eye appeared with the sun's shifting angle. She moved to the left and scuffed the dusty ground with her Merrell boot. "Here," she said to Samira. "Stand on this mark and look straight ahead."

Samira did so—and gasped. "My God," she whispered. "I see it. The second eye. And... the brow ridge. It's so lifelike."

Claire moved right, tracking the wall with hawk-like focus. Another scuff mark. "Louis, come here." He ambled over, raising an eyebrow.

"Stand where I'm standing now," Claire instructed. "Right here. Now look—up and a little to the left."

Louis's eyes narrowed. Then suddenly: "Mon Dieu," he said aloud. "The nose... and the whiskers. C'est magnifique."

"I've got the right eye," said Alex, still frozen in place.

"And I've got the left," added Samira.

"It's looking at us," Claire murmured, stepping back to take it all in. "This wasn't an accident. She stared in awe as the three separate perspectives coalesced into one massive lion's face— silent, eternal, and regal, carved into the temple wall and only visible to those standing precisely where they were meant to.

And then, softly, like a memory drifting in from far away, Claire said:

"Follow the lion's gaze, and you shall find the resting place of kings."

Alex nodded, the words anchoring in his mind like a cipher clicking into place. "Malik wrote that in the margin of the codex we found in Alexandria," he recalled. "We thought it was metaphorical."

"But it's literal," Claire said. "The lion is looking at something. That's the next clue."

All four of them turned and traced the lion's carved eyes across the temple grounds—northwest, toward the ridge just beyond the temple walls, where jagged stone broke through the sand like old bones. Somewhere in that direction, something ancient waited to be uncovered.

Claire knew there was more to be done. "What's the time, quickly."

"Its just on midday," said Alex, enlightened.

And the lion—centuries old, forgotten by time—was still watching.

Claire moved with purpose and precision, like a dancer in rehearsal or a general coordinating a battlefield. She mapped the contours of the lion with quick scuffs of her boot, first marking the eyes—one here, the other just there—then the nose, the proud arc of the mane, the suggestion of a paw, the curved tail disappearing into the lower corner of the wall. Each position required a shift in stance, a turn of the head, a brief call to one of the others to step in, verify, confirm. She was the conductor, and the others—Louis, Samira, Alex—her obedient orchestra, moving into place as she instructed.

"Hold there, Samira—good. That's the ear. Alex, two steps left. Do you see it now? The edge of the mane?"

Five minutes passed like seconds. Breathless, her cheeks flushed from the sun and the intensity, Claire stood back, arms crossed as she surveyed the pattern they had summoned from the stone.

"It's not visible from one place alone," she murmured. "But it's there—clear as anything—if you're looking from the right angles, at the right time."

The lion's form now lay fully revealed—just not to the eye all at once, but mapped through triangulated sightlines. From various scuffed positions on the temple floor, the sculpture's face, form, and power came together.

"It's staring right at us," Claire said, her voice tinged with awe. "South-southeast. Almost like it's judging us."

The sun had shifted now, past its zenith. Shadows lengthened. The hard angles of the lion's features began to soften. Within seconds, the illusion vanished completely.

Claire shuffled side to side, tried new angles, leaned and squinted—but it was gone.

"That was it," she whispered, exasperated. "That tiny window at midday. If I hadn't sat down, at that exact moment…"

She shook her head, stunned by the razor-thin margin of chance.

"Mon amis," said Louis, stepping up beside her with a low whistle, "this Malik—he is a génie, yes, but also…" he grinned, shaking his head, "a farceur. A trickster. He plans with such cunning. It is—how do you say—deliciously maddening."

"So what now?" Samira asked, arms folded as she eyed the wall again. "We know where he's pointing. Do we come back tomorrow, at exactly the same time, and try again? Because I'm not seeing any inscription. No annotations. Nothing left behind."

"We don't need to," said Alex. "We have what Malik gave us. 'Follow the lion's gaze, and you will find the resting place of kings.' That's what the obelisk said. That's what he wanted us to do."

He turned to Louis. "Can you get a bearing?"

"Easy," Louis replied. He dropped to one knee, pulled out his Suunto compass and laid it flush along the edge of the wall, aligning it carefully. "The wall runs 65 degrees," he said, "so if the lion is looking directly out from it, we add 90 degrees. That gives us 155.”

“South-southeast,” Claire echoed, eyes narrowing.

Alex climbed up onto the large block where she had been sitting. The elevation gave him a clearer line of sight. He shielded his eyes with his hand and looked into the distance. Heat shimmered on the horizon, but beyond it—hazy, faint, and alluring—rose the faint outline of low, rugged hills.

“There,” he said, pointing. “Mountains. Or at least a ridge. That’s the direction the lion is staring.”

He was about to jump down when he froze.

Something was wrong… or rather, something was right, but unexpected.

Below him, the temple floor was no longer just a mess of footprints and scuff marks. As Claire had darted back and forth marking the points of the lion’s features, a secondary shape had taken form in the dust.

He stared at it, heart beginning to race. It wasn’t random. It was precise. It was geometric.

From above, he saw them clearly: arcs, intersections, proportions—almost like a mandala or the sacred geometry used in Ptolemaic mapmaking. It was a design, made entirely from Claire’s scuff marks. But it hadn’t emerged until he’d looked down from above.

“Claire,” he said, voice low and urgent, “I think you’ve mapped more than just a lion.”

She blinked up at him. “What do you mean?”

“You didn’t just mark its features,” he said. “You followed instructions you didn’t know you were following. From up here… it’s not just a shape. It’s a symbol. Some kind of layout. It might be a map.”

Samira stepped up beside him. “Could it be coordinates? Or a direction overlay?”

Alex jumped down and landed beside them, eyes scanning the dust with new intensity. "It could be a projection," he said. "A miniature layout of the path. Malik didn't just leave us one clue. He left us two. The lion's gaze gave us the direction. But this—this could give us the location."

Claire stood quietly, letting it all sink in. Her earlier frustration gave way to dawning awe. "That sneaky bastard," she muttered with a grin. "He used me like a compass."

Louis chuckled. "Farceur, I told you."

Alex crouched beside the pattern, now slowly fading as the light changed and footsteps disturbed the dust.

"Photograph everything," he said. "Get the drone up. We may not have this again."

Claire already had her camera out. "On it," she said. "Let's make sure Malik doesn't get the last laugh."

They moved with a quiet reverence now, careful not to disturb the scuff marks Claire had drawn in the dust—marks that, by chance and design, had revealed so much more than they'd ever expected. Every footstep was deliberate. Every breath felt shallow, as if even exhaling too hard might erase the fragile map they'd summoned from the earth.

Claire had already set to work, assembling her drone on a flat stone at the far end of the courtyard, well clear of the geometric pattern they had uncovered. She ran a quick pre-flight check, her fingers gliding with practiced ease over the controls, synching the controller, checking battery life, ensuring camera feed and signal strength were solid.

The drone hummed softly as it rose into the midday sky, blades slicing the still air. She kept it low at first—ten feet—click, a still photo. Then fifteen—click. Then again, this time recording smooth 4K video as she slowly orbited the site, capturing the map from every possible angle.

While it hovered, she guided it carefully to the wall where the lion had appeared earlier. The sun was now slightly past its high point, but Claire hoped the ultra-high-definition footage might still capture some lingering trace—perhaps enough to isolate the lion's outline in post-production.

"Get every inch," Alex said quietly, watching her work. "We may never get another shot like this."

"I am," she replied without taking her eyes from the screen. "We'll pull the data into DaVinci Resolve or Adobe tonight. Boost the contrast, mask the shadows, colour-pick the light. We'll get it."

When the flight was done, Claire landed the drone softly, detached the SD card, and slotted it into her MacBook Pro. They all crowded around the screen as the files loaded—Claire scrubbing through stills and video alike with the quick precision of someone who lived between fieldwork and post-production.

"There," she said, pointing at one still captured from a height of twenty feet. "This one shows the whole thing."

The image on the screen was clearer than any of them expected. Against the sandy temple floor, the scuff marks took on the appearance of a crude but deliberate shape—an abstract form, jagged in places, flowing in others.

"It looks like… a pyramid," Samira said, squinting, "but melted. A step-pyramid, maybe—but the angles aren't right. It's too—organic."

Claire nodded. "I don't think it's a pyramid at all. Look at these curves. The asymmetry. It's a landform—natural, not constructed."

"Oui," Louis chimed in. "This is a mountain, I think. Cartographes—how you say in English?"

"Cartographers," Alex offered.

"Oui, yes. Cartographers, they draw mountains like this in the old maps. And today, even—they do it the same. Stylised, like a thumbprint on the land. If we match the shape—we find our destination."

Alex stared at the image, then slowly raised the MacBook, turning south-southeast, letting his eyes trace the line from the drone's perspective to the real horizon. He squinted into the haze. There, rising above the shimmer of heat, was a mountain. Not tall, but broad and craggy—etched into the sky with a slow, weathered grace.

"Gabral Dakrur," he said aloud. "That's it."

"Louis," he called over his shoulder, still pointing. "Get a bearing on that peak."

Louis already had his Suunto out. He dropped to one knee, spun the bezel, waited a moment, and read off the result with a flick of his wrist.

"Exactly 155 degrees, monsieur professeur. It aligns exactement."

Alex turned back to the laptop, now brimming with certainty.

"Claire," he said, tapping the screen, "this point here—this lone dot near the centre. Do you remember what that represented on the lion?"

Claire stood and began retracing her steps. She repeated the strange, intuitive choreography she had done earlier—left, back, side-shuffle, pivot, lean. She landed on the same scuff mark, planted her feet, and looked up at the wall with narrowed eyes.

"This is it," she said finally, turning to Alex. "This was the nose."

"Then that's our key," Alex said, eyes blazing now. "The nose—on the lion—is this dot. It's the tip. The marker. The exact location we're meant to go. Everything leads to this."

Louis let out a low whistle, then exhaled deeply. "Putain de merde," he said with a slow grin. "I cannot believe we are this close."

"Indeed, we are," Alex replied, eyes still locked on the image. "And Malik… Malik has led us here every step of the way."

Claire folded her arms and looked out across the desert. The wind had picked up slightly, and the lion had long since vanished from the wall, but its purpose remained—etched now in memory, in pixels, and in destiny.

"Let's get packed," she said. "We've got a lion to follow."

Chapter 10

Major General Hassan Nasser was still pacing the sweltering confines of the police outpost office, the arid afternoon air doing nothing to calm his nerves. His uniform was damp under the collar, and the sweat ran in steady rivulets down his back. The ceiling fan above him squeaked and groaned as it turned, moving the heat around but offering little relief. His boots echoed on the tiled floor with each frustrated step, a slow, deliberate rhythm of impatience. Then his cell phone buzzed in his pocket.

He didn't need to look. He knew exactly who it was.

"Khoury," he said flatly, lifting the phone to his ear even before answering properly.

"Have you found that traitorous snake Hafez yet?" barked Dr. Samy Khoury on the other end, his voice sharp with tension.

"No, Director. Not yet," Nasser said, calm but tired. "But it is only a matter of time before he reveals himself. And then—I shall have him."

There was a pause. The line crackled slightly.

"Maybe I should send someone else," Khoury said coldly. "Someone who can guarantee results..."

"Don't be a fool," Nasser snapped, cutting him off. "We both know you have no one else. That's why you called on me in the first place—to clean up this delicate situation of yours."

Khoury's silence was telling. A small victory for Nasser.

"Just get it done, Hassan," Khoury hissed, trying to reclaim control. "Every hour he remains at large, he gains ground. He has contacts. Influence. You know as well as I do, if he's not stopped,

he will use that to build support—for a coup, for whatever lunacy he's planning—"
"He's not building support," Nasser interrupted again, voice low, assured. "He's running. He knows we're watching. He's scared. Like a mouse."
He smiled grimly to himself.
"And the mouse never hides forever. He'll slip. And when he does, I'll be there."
Khoury said nothing. Just the faint sound of breathing on the other end.
"I'll call you when I have something," Nasser said coolly.
Then he hung up.
Khoury stared at the darkened phone screen for a moment, then dropped it onto his desk with a heavy sigh. He leaned back in his leather chair, the faint whir of the air conditioning the only sound in his luxurious Cairo office.
He was swimming against the current now—fighting a tide he no longer understood.
Hafez was missing, perhaps gathering allies. Hassan was becoming insufferably arrogant—useful, but dangerous. And now Soterakis, that bloated Greek pig, was pressing him for a bigger slice of the market and hinting at outside investors. The whole board was shifting beneath him.
Khoury reached for his glass of whisky and stared out over the city skyline.
Maybe I should take matters into my own hands.
But the thought vanished just as quickly. He had no more pieces left to move—not yet.
For now, all he could do was wait.
And Khoury hated waiting.

As they packed up their gear on the summit of the crumbling temple, Samira pulled out her cellphone and checked for reception. Vodafone flickered to life—two bars. Just enough.

She tapped in the number for André Molineux and held it to her ear. It rang three times before diverting to voicemail.

"Hi André, it's Samira. We're in Siwa. We think we've found the final waymarker—it's pointing us toward a series of small hills called Gabal Dakrur. We believe this could be it. The last step. The final resting place. We're so close, we can almost feel it in the air." She paused for a second. "Anyway, if you get this message, feel free to call back. Reception's spotty out here. I'll call again soon. Au revoir!"

She ended the call, slipped the phone into her side pocket, and joined the others as they descended the circular stone pathway. Dust rose around their boots as they spiraled down to the carpark below. Once at the base, they moved quickly, stowing their equipment in the trays and footwells of the two Hilux's. Years of fieldwork made packing second nature now—precise, silent, efficient.

Claire climbed into the passenger seat of the lead vehicle and opened Google Maps. "It's all coming up as via unnamed road," she muttered, frowning at the screen.

"Bien," Louis said, glancing her way as he started the engine. "We'll just drive by feel."

She gave a nod, eyes still scanning the route. "Take the next left, then another left through the date groves. It should be about two kilometres south-west."

The convoy rolled forward, crunching over loose stones and drifting sand. As they left the ruins behind, the palm forests of Siwa swallowed them. The narrow, twisting tracks wove like veins through the dense date plantations. The trees hung thick overhead, a lush canopy in stark contrast to the surrounding desert, obscuring every sense of direction. Even the sun was filtered, refracted through fronds and dust.

"Feels like a maze," muttered Alex from the rear seat. "A green labyrinth."

After ten minutes of slow winding, the grove broke open—and
there it was.

Gabal Dakrur.

They pulled up just outside a rustic compound labelled Mountain
Camp Ali Khaled, an unassuming collection of mudbrick structures
shaded by a few sparse palms. Tourists would think they were just
another group of dusty visitors. And that was exactly what they
wanted.

The hills themselves rose gently before them—low ridges of pale,
weather-worn sandstone, shaped by centuries of wind and sun. In a
land defined by its flatness, Gabal Dakrur stood out like islands in
a golden sea. There were two prominent peaks, and a smaller third
one nestled between them. The tallest stood perhaps thirty, maybe
forty metres above the surrounding plain—not much in height, but
commanding nonetheless.

The team disembarked and began gathering their usual kit: Claire's
drone, Alex's notebooks, Samira's laptop, Louis's compass.
Canteens sloshed. Hats were adjusted. Boots were tightened.

The air here had a different quality—still dry, still hot, but
somehow heavier. As if history itself lingered in the dust.

Without a word, they set off toward the nearest summit, trudging
single file across the drifted sand. Their footsteps left narrow trails
behind them. The silence between them wasn't awkward—it was
charged. Full of unspoken anticipation.

They were close now.

They could feel it in their bones.

The end was no longer a vague promise—it was a direction, a hill,
a dot on a screen. And they marched toward it with purpose.

Determined.

Resolute.

André Molineux grabbed his phone the moment MESSAGEBANK
1 flashed across the screen. His gut clenched. He flipped the
device, tapped to dial 101, and brought it to his ear.

Samira's voice crackled through the speaker—clear, confident, laced with excitement. She was in Siwa. They had found something. Gabal Dakrur. He listened carefully, already calculating timelines, risk factors, and possible contingencies. When the message ended, he exhaled slowly.

Things were moving fast.

Too fast.

And the team was nearly three thousand kilometres away from him—isolated, exposed, far from support.

André didn't hesitate. He tapped his speed dial—number two now, just after Samira—and the line to the Cairo Embassy connected almost immediately.

"André," came the smooth, diplomatic voice on the other end, "I trust this call finds you well."

"I'm fine, Etienne. And you? Still charming the sand out of the Sahara?"

A low chuckle. "Busy as always, but that is every French embassy, mon ami!"

"I need to ask you," André continued, the smile fading from his voice, "whether our ace of spades is still in place. Ready."

There was a brief pause, a shift in tone. "Yes. Ready. Standing by at a moment's notice. Are we saying the moment is now?"

"Not yet," André replied carefully. "But very soon. We need to be prepared. Everything depends on that."

"Oui, we will be ready, Director. You have my word. Just say the word, and we will be there."

"I'm grateful, Etienne. Truly."

"Au revoir, mon ami."

"Au revoir."

André ended the call and lowered the phone into his lap. The stillness in the room settled like dust after a storm. He stared out the narrow window of his office, watching the sun sink into the desert haze beyond the rooftops of Tripoli. A world away, in the scorched silence of Siwa, something extraordinary was happening—something centuries in the making.

Timing now was everything.

And though he still had control—barely—it was slipping. Events were in motion. The ancient game was being played once more, and the stakes were higher than ever.

If anything faltered now—any piece out of place—it could all come crashing down.

André inhaled deeply, then exhaled, sharp and slow.

They would need more than luck.

They would need precision.

And a bit of old-fashioned French audacity.

Almost as soon as Director André Molineux ended the call with Ambassador Moreau, his cellphone rang again.

The screen flashed RAYLAN STRETTON.

The American Ambassador to Egypt.

André raised the phone to his ear without hesitation.

"Ambassador," he said, mustering a calm he didn't feel. "An unexpected surprise."

"Director," came Stretton's warm, Southern-tinged voice. "Good afternoon to you in Paris. I hope I'm not intruding."

"Not at all. I assume you're not calling just to exchange pleasantries."

"No, sir," Stretton replied, his tone sharpening. "We've got some intel you'll want to hear. We've been monitoring chatter—intercepts from our listening stations in the eastern Sahara. Communications traffic between General Hassan Nasser and your friend Dr. Samy Khoury has spiked."

André straightened in his chair. "Spiked?"

"Increased by a factor of four. Several calls a day—short, urgent, highly encrypted. Something is happening. And Nasser..." Stretton paused. "That sociopathic bastard... we've triangulated him."

André already knew what he was about to hear.

"He's in Siwa."

André's eyes narrowed. "Siwa?" His voice dropped, barely above a whisper. "That's where the team is. But how did you—?"

"NSA's monitoring the cellular footprint," said Stretton matter-of-factly. "Samira, Claire, Louis, and Alex—all four are pinging from the oasis. Don't worry, we're not eavesdropping. This is passive. Location only. Just in case we need to 'act judiciously,' as it were."

André nodded slowly. "Judiciously. Of course."

"Please don't take this as snooping, André," the Ambassador continued. "We believe something significant is unfolding. A convergence. You're not the only ones watching this unfold."

André turned slowly to the window, staring out over the rooftops of Paris. "I thought Nasser was still in Cairo. Last I heard, Khoury had him tied down."

"He was," said Stretton. "Until yesterday. Khoury called him in directly—requested immediate redeployment to the western provinces. It seems they're both hunting a certain Captain Hafez Abdel-Rahman. Ring any bells?"

Molineux let out a faint breath. "Abdel-Rahman was stationed in Bawiti. We believe he attempted to intercept our team during their excavation at Bahariya. But..." he hesitated, "...it seems he ran afoul of the locals."

"The local militia?" Stretton prompted.

"No," said André. "Not militia. The Bedouin."

Stretton gave a low whistle. "That's worse."

"Indeed," André continued. "The captain had a reputation. Antiquities trafficking. Artifacts stolen from western sites and sold on the black market. He made enemies, Ambassador—powerful, tribal ones. We think they turned on him."

"So he's dead?" asked Stretton.

"No confirmation," André said, "but... let's say once you've angered the Bedouin, your survival chances drop to almost zero. They do not forgive. And they do not forget."

"Well," said Stretton slowly, "it seems no one's told Khoury or Nasser. They're still searching. Hard."

André went still. "That means they're desperate. And desperation is dangerous."

"Agreed," Stretton said. "Especially with Nasser. We both know what he's capable of."

The line went quiet for a moment. Then the American continued, voice lower.

"Listen, André. I need to be clear. The United States can't intervene. Not directly. We can provide intelligence—whatever you need—but we can't put boots on the ground. Not in Egypt. Not for this."

"I understand, Raylan," said André. "And I appreciate what you've already done."

"But you need to know," the Ambassador added, "we're watching very closely. And if things go south—really south—you call me. You'll have support. Quietly. Off-book."

André nodded slowly, even though the Ambassador couldn't see it.

"The team's walking into a trap," he said softly. "And there's nothing I can do to stop the jaws from closing."

"They're smart," said Raylan. "You've got Louis with them. He's sharp. He'll see it coming."

"Let's hope so," André replied, though his voice betrayed little confidence.

There was a pause, then a final exchange.

"We'll speak again soon," said Stretton.

"Thank you, Ambassador," said Molineux. "For everything."

The line clicked dead.

But the silence that followed was heavy—no longer filled with just unease, but dread.

Nasser was in Siwa.

The team was in Siwa.

It was only a matter of time before their paths crossed.

And when they did—it would not be peaceful.

Alex, Claire, Samira, and Louis had climbed to the first summit of Gabal Dakrur. Though the elevation was modest—perhaps thirty or forty metres—it stood proud above the surrounding plains like a citadel. From here, the vast Siwan landscape unfurled in all directions. Beneath a pale sun and a curtain of dry haze, the ruins of the Temple of Amun shimmered in the near distance, just under two kilometres away.

Claire squinted toward the southeast and gestured with her hand. "The Temple of Amun… the Temple of Umm Abayd… and Cleopatra's Spring," she said, her tone sharpening with curiosity. "They're almost in perfect alignment."

"Almost?" Alex asked, turning to her.

"Well," Claire said, "if we were standing just a little south of this spot—maybe two-hundred metres—it would form a straight line."

"That can't be by chance," said Samira, her voice hushed with awe.

"Nothing that's led us here, to this exact point, mes amis, has been by chance," added Louis.

Alex turned to Claire. "Can you bring up that image again? The one of the outline on the temple floor."

Claire nodded and knelt down, unzipping her backpack. Within a minute, her MacBook was up and glowing. She navigated to the file and tapped it open: the same geometric outline etched into the temple's stone floor—stylised, abstract, and yet oddly organic.

"If that image," Alex said, pointing to the screen, "is meant to represent this hill range, then we need to understand what these mountains looked like thirteen hundred years ago. When Malik was here."

"Most likely conjoined," said Claire.

Samira leaned in. "How so?"

Claire tapped the keyboard and zoomed in on a 3D terrain render of the area.

"Well," she explained, "look at the erosion patterns here, especially along the northern faces. The prevailing wind direction is from the northeast—"

"Is that accurate?" Alex interrupted.

Claire nodded. "Yes, I checked meteorological data last night. The northeast wind has dominated this region for thousands of years. That means the windward side—the north—would be worn down far more over time than the southern face."

She used her fingers to trace the terrain.

"See this saddle? It's narrow now, but back then, it might have been shallower, less eroded—making the hills appear more joined. And that bluff here"—she zoomed in again—"would have been more prominent. It fits the stylised 'nose' Malik marked."

She paused, then looked up.

"If we follow the geometry of that outline, and take erosion into account, then I'd say the tomb Malik indicated lies to the south of this summit, at the base of the northern hill—on the southern slope, just inside the valley."

They all stared at her in astonishment. The logic was seamless, her explanation so effortlessly blended geology, geography, and archaeology that none of them had anything to add.

Alex blinked. "I have no argument."

"Me neither," said Samira, clearly impressed.

"Sounds logical," Louis added. "Let's put up the drone."

"Agreed," said Claire, already unpacking it. "We'll cover ten times more ground by air. And it's already past one o'clock—light's perfect. Once I map the coordinates, we can check the likely sites on foot."

"Also logical," said Alex.

"Totally," Samira nodded.

"Reconnaître depuis le ciel… bon, bon, ma chérie Claire!" Louis added with a grin.

Claire smiled faintly as she laid the drone case flat and opened it. She extended its arms, powered it on, linked it to her controller, then ran a video link test. Everything was green.

Louis picked up the drone and held it above his head. Claire adjusted the gimbal, checked wind speed, then hit the thrust control.

The drone launched skyward with a soft mechanical whine and shot off to the south. Claire guided it in a sweeping arc—south first, then curling west, and finally a sharp turn east. She focused most of her attention on the southern-facing slope of the northern hill.

Just as she'd predicted, it was steeper and smoother, with fewer signs of wind-scouring or landslip. The bluff just south of the saddle rose nearly vertical, carved from hardened sandstone. Intact. Ancient. Stark.

The northern side of the saddle, by contrast, had softened over centuries—a more gradual incline, weathered and wind-blown.

Her final pass was around the southern hill. Its shape was more irregular. Gentler slopes, but two smaller hillocks sat nestled on its northwestern edge—like sentries. Between them was a narrow vertical face, half in shadow, half sunlit.

"There," said Alex suddenly. "That face. Which way is it oriented?"

Claire glanced at the controller's readout. "Drone's facing 155 degrees. So that cliff is facing… 335."

She paused. Then her eyes widened.

"Directly toward the Temple of Amun."

There was a silence. The desert wind whispered across the summit.

"Recall the drone," Alex said quietly. "I think we may have found our spot."

Claire hit the 'home' command and the drone arced swiftly back across the sky, returning to their coordinates in under two minutes. It hovered, slowed, and landed softly. She packed it away quickly and slid the memory card into her laptop.

Alex was already leaning over her shoulder. "Claire, when you said the temples and the spring were almost aligned, what if we drew a line through them all? Where does it hit Gabal Dakrur?"

Claire opened Google Earth. She plotted the points carefully: the Temple of Amun… through Umm Abayd… Cleopatra's Spring… and extended the line straight to the sandstone ridges of Gabal Dakrur.

The red path on the screen sliced cleanly through the landscape—and directly into the narrow face between the twin hillocks.

She stared. "It aligns perfectly. Not almost. Perfectly."

"That must be the nose," Alex said. "The spot the lion faces."

"Oui," said Louis softly. "Malik did not work with guesswork. Everything he's shown us has been exact. Pinpoint. Mathematically precise."

"I agree," said Samira. "It makes sense contextually, symbolically—even spiritually. The lion watches the tomb. The tomb lies in the lion's sightline. Just as Malik described."

There was no need for further discussion.

Alex slung his pack over his shoulder.

"Let's go," he said.

Without another word, they set off down the southern slope, the sun dipping westward behind them, casting long shadows over the desert.

They were close now.

So close they could almost feel the dust of the past stirring at their feet.

Chapter 11

Alex led the team southwest, down the slope of the first hill and into the narrow basin between the two sandstone peaks. The descent was steady, the ground sloping in gentle, crumbling waves beneath their boots. Around them, the desert air shimmered with the early afternoon heat, and the rocks burned warm to the touch. They circled the base of the second hill cautiously, keeping to the natural shadows. As they approached the northernmost hillock from the northeast, Claire, who had been mostly quiet, stopped and turned her gaze upward.

"You know," she said, almost to herself, "thirteen hundred years ago… these might have looked like grand pillars. Not carved like the stylised ones in temples, but natural obelisks—shaped by time, not hands."

The others paused and followed her gaze. From this angle, the twin hillocks did seem almost symmetrical, like ancient guardians marking a sacred threshold.

"I can see why Alexander would have approved of being buried here," she added softly. "This place is naturally magnificent. Humbling, even."

They walked on in silence, letting her words settle.

As they rounded the northern hillock, the gap between the two outcrops revealed itself—a narrowing funnel of rock and shadow that faced directly toward the Temple of Amun. It was a dramatic sight. The façade of the hill sloped gently backward, its sandstone face pocked with centuries of erosion. Near the top, where the

incline steepened sharply, was a narrow ledge etched halfway up—
about twenty metres off the ground.

Alex stopped and shaded his eyes. "That ledge," he said. "About
halfway up the slope. It looks… unnatural. Like it's been shaped."

Claire squinted at it. "It does. You think that's the nose, Professor?
Could we really be looking at the entrance to the tomb of
Alexander the Great?"

There was awe in her voice—real reverence.

"There's only one way to find out," Alex replied, already
tightening the straps on his pack. "But it's going to be a slippery
climb."

The scree slope ahead of them was steep—nearly forty-five
degrees—and treacherously unstable. Centuries of erosion had
deposited a loose mixture of sand, gravel, and dust that slid like
dry snow underfoot. They had no choice but to go on all fours,
clawing their way upward like mountaineers without gear.

Each metre gained was earned with gritted teeth and stinging
palms. More than once, Alex lost his footing and skidded
backwards, crashing into Samira, who yelped and tumbled into
Claire and Louis. Each time, they gathered themselves in a dusty
tangle of limbs and laughter laced with frustration, then tried again,
slower and more methodically.

They found no footholds, only persistence.

Eventually—sweating, panting, and coated in a fine layer of dust
and grime—they reached the ledge.

One by one, they scrambled onto the narrow stone platform,
pausing as they caught their breath. The ledge was just over a
metre wide, stable, and surprisingly smooth beneath their boots.
Above them, the sandstone face rose another fifteen metres into the
blue. Behind them, the view was breathtaking.

To the east-northeast, the desert unfurled like a golden sea, waves
of sand rolling towards a narrow cluster of mudbrick houses half a
kilometre away. Beyond that, stretching toward the horizon, was
the emerald canopy of Siwa's date palms—dense and swaying,

vibrant against the arid surroundings. In the middle of this living sea stood the Temple of Amun, rising above the palms like a fortress, stubborn and eternal.

Alex exhaled slowly. "It's like time hasn't touched it."

The ledge extended along the hillside for about fifty metres to their right. From where they sat, it was clear to the trained eye that this was no natural shelf. The chisel marks were subtle, nearly lost in the weathered stone, but they were there—repeating grooves, shallow indents, faint pockmarks from a mason's hammer.

To the untrained eye, it might have looked like nothing more than a weathered perch—a place to rest or carve graffiti into the rock face. Thankfully, no one had yet marred it.

"This was hewn deliberately," Claire murmured. "Malik's geometry led us here for a reason."

Alex nodded but didn't speak. He was staring ahead, letting the reality of the place settle over him. The ledge had an eerie calm to it. Cut into the living rock, its craftsmanship lost to the centuries, it was both primitive and profound.

For now, they were content to rest. The northern breeze was blocked by the twin hillocks, and the heat clung to their skin like wet cloth. But they didn't complain. Water bottles were passed around. Sips were taken in silence.

The sun had begun its slow descent to the west, lowering the temperature slightly but lengthening the shadows.

"We're close," Samira said quietly.

Alex nodded again, eyes fixed on the stone ahead.

"Yes," he said. "Closer than anyone's been in two thousand years."

Hassan was still at his desk, poring over a tangle of operational maps and field reports, when the door burst open and a young corporal skidded to a halt in front of him. Dust clung to his boots, and a sheen of sweat glistened on his forehead. He came to an abrupt, awkward salute—arm stiff, eyes wide, lips trembling with urgency.

Before Hassan could bark an order, the corporal blurted out, "We've found them, General—the two Hilux's from Bawiti. They've been spotted near Gabal Dakrur, just off the southern approach."

For a fraction of a second, Hassan's eyes narrowed as he processed the report. Then he stood, fast and smooth, his chair scraping backward with a harsh screech.

"Quickly, Corporal—recall the men. We're going to throw a net so tight around that mountain that not even a rat will crawl out unnoticed."

"The men, General?" the corporal asked, hesitating.

"Yes, the men! Now!"

The corporal swallowed hard. "Sir… most of the men are two or three hours away. They're manning the checkpoints and roadblocks between here and Bawiti, and on the Marsa Matrouh–Siwa road."

Hassan's jaw tightened. He took a slow breath through his nose. "How many do we have at the station now?"

The corporal fidgeted. "Four of us, General. One on the radios, one manning the phones. I'm on the front desk, and then… yourself, sir. That's all."

Hassan looked past the corporal toward the arid desert light filtering in through the station's barred window. Gabal Dakrur rose in the distance like a crouched beast—silent, waiting.

"Roundup everyone," he said flatly. "Even the radio man. Shut down the phones. Lock the station. Full kit. We roll out in five minutes."

The corporal gave a sharp nod and dashed away, shouting orders as he ran, his voice echoing down the stone corridor.

Hassan remained still for a moment, staring down at the maps on his desk as his mind raced. How the hell had Hafez gotten into Siwa? He had ordered checkpoints on every road, trail, and goat path within a 50-kilometre radius. And still the bastard had slipped through. He'd underestimated him—again. That mistake would not be repeated.

He clenched his jaw.

Hafez was here. But was he alone? Or did he bring others with him? How many? Armed? And what was he after?

At the moment, Hassan had just three men and a limited supply of weapons. It was barely enough to secure a warehouse, let alone surround a rugged hill and confront a rogue officer. But what he lacked in numbers, he would compensate for with guile—and superior firepower. More troops were inbound. If he could box Hafez in long enough, they would finish this.

His thoughts were interrupted by the corporal's return, voice sharp and crisp this time. "General, we're loaded up and ready. Gear is in the trucks, weapons distributed. The men are standing by."

Hassan nodded once, curt and resolved. "Good. Inform all other units—rendezvous at Gabal Dakrur. Tell them to move at speed, maximum urgency. I want that place surrounded."

The corporal saluted again, this time without hesitation. "Yes, General."

"Then let's move," Hassan said, striding toward the door.

As he stepped out into the late afternoon heat, the desert wind hit his face like a furnace blast. Dust swirled around the station yard, and the engines of two blacked-out jeeps were already rumbling, their silhouettes blurred by heat shimmer. Hassan climbed into the lead vehicle and slammed the door behind him.

Gabal Dakrur loomed on the horizon.

And Hassan, his teeth clenched with purpose, was coming.

Sightseeing time was over.

Alex stood, brushing the dust from his trousers, and glanced along the rock face. The others followed his lead, stretching limbs and adjusting their gear. The sun was beginning its slow descent, casting long shadows across the ledge, and time was ticking.

"We have to be methodical," Alex said, voice calm but purposeful. "This has stayed hidden for thirteen centuries. It won't announce itself. And frankly, I don't even know exactly what we're looking for—just something... off. Unnatural. We'll start at the southern end and work our way north. Agreed?"

There were nods all around.

They spread out, moving cautiously along the narrow ledge, pressed flat against the rock wall like a line of mime artists mimicking invisible barriers. Each of them scrutinised the stone face with studious intent, fingertips brushing lightly across its weathered surface, eyes searching for the smallest anomaly. Every crack, every groove, every discolouration was a potential clue.

It wasn't until they reached the central portion of the ledge that Samira stopped and raised a hand.

"Here," she said, tapping the wall lightly. "This section feels smoother than the rest... almost polished. Like it's been manufactured."

Alex and Claire moved in quickly. Claire knelt beside Samira and ran her fingers along the surface. "She's right. It's like render or plaster—made to imitate natural rock. But look here—too uniform. Too clean."

She stepped back to the edge of the ledge, squinting from a few feet away.

"You wouldn't notice it unless you were right on top of it. It's a damn good facsimile."

"Do you have a pick handy?" Alex asked, eyes narrowing.

Claire rummaged in her pack and produced a compact archaeologist's pick—triangular blade on one end, flat pick on the other. "Here."

Alex took the tool, glanced quickly up and down the valley. Still clear. No one around. Then, with a sharp breath, he raised the pick and drove the point into the wall.

The impact rang out—a dull, crisp thonk—and a chunk of the wall fell away with ease.

"You were right," he said, grinning at Samira and Claire. "This isn't natural at all."

He struck again, more of the false surface falling in dusty fragments. On the third swing, the pick struck something harder—denser. It wasn't sandstone. It gave a clunk—a solid, satisfying thud that vibrated up his arm.

Alex leaned in. "We've got something behind it."

Louis stepped in. "Let me take over." He and Alex worked in tandem, chipping away at opposite edges while Claire and Samira brushed loose debris clear.

After a few more minutes of careful work, the shape behind the plaster began to reveal itself: a massive plug—circular, recessed, and about six feet high. As the plaster fell away, it became clear they were looking at red granite. Not just any granite—the same type used in the altar of the Temple of Amun.

They stepped back in reverence. The plug was perfectly formed, with intricate relief carved into its face. At the centre of the carving was a lion—its body stretched out, head raised above crossed paws. Its expression was regal and alert, eyes wide and forward-facing, with such precision that the gaze seemed to follow them.

Claire caught her breath. "It's magnificent. That detail—look at the mane. The paws. It's like it's alive."

Samira moved closer. "The resting lion! This was carved by a master. Those eyes—there's depth in them. They're almost... watchful."

"Mon Dieu," murmured Louis. "C'est... magnifique. The symmetry, the line work... this is a work of art. Truly."

Alex stepped forward, wiping sweat from beneath his fedora. "But how do we move it? That plug must weigh nearly a hundred kilos."

"It's circular," said Louis thoughtfully. "Can we not roll it to the side?"

"Worth a try."

They braced themselves, pushing together—but it didn't budge. Stuck fast.

"Claire, do we have anything long and thin? Something we could work behind it?" Alex asked, already scanning the ground for leverage tools.

"How long? How thin?" Claire replied, distracted, digging through her bag.

"Would this work, Professor?" Louis held up a steel ruler—about 450mm long, flexible, and springy, from his map kit-.

"Perfect." Alex took it, inserted it into the crevice beside the granite plug, and began working it side-to-side, sawing slowly. He reached the top, then worked down the other side before handing it off to Louis to do the same from his end.

"Claire, Samira, are we documenting all of this?" he asked without looking up.

Claire raised her iPhone, still recording. "Haven't stopped since we hit the ledge. 4K, wide lens."

"I'm taking stills every step," Samira confirmed. "Lighting's good. Contrast is perfect."

Louis finished with the ruler, the last of the base section nearly free. Alex wedged the flat blade of the pick behind the plug and gently levered. It shifted—barely.

"Again," said Alex.

Louis did the same from the other side. The plug gave a reluctant creak and moved a fraction more.

Together, with slow, careful movements, they worked the plug loose. Inch by inch, the ancient seal gave way. Then—

"I think it may roll now, Professor," said Louis, sweat glistening on his brow.

"Let's do it," Alex said.

With combined strength, they heaved the granite disc to the right. At first it resisted—then, with a final, grinding groan, it rolled aside.

Behind it, a circular black opening yawned wide, flanked by perfectly hewn sandstone blocks with the recess for the granite plug carefully inset. A narrow corridor, cloaked in shadow, stretched inward—silent, dark, and deep.

Alex stepped forward, staring into the void.

They had found something. And the tomb—if that's what it was—was no longer sealed.

"Okay," said Alex, his voice steady but hushed, "I'll go in first—just to see what's inside. I'm not expecting any surprises, nothing dangerous anyway. It's more about the fragility of the space, if this really is what we think it is."

He paused, as if trying to let the gravity of the moment settle over them all.

From his satchel, Alex pulled out his Olight Seeker 4 Pro, the torch he trusted more than any other. He thumbed the power button—click—and a blistering beam of white light cut through the gloom, punching a hole into the darkness beyond the plug.

"Blinding," he murmured with satisfaction.

He adjusted the strap of his satchel across his shoulder, took a calming breath, and ducked into the narrow passageway. The cool air inside was thick and still, unmoved for centuries. With each step, his torch revealed more of what had been hidden from human eyes for over a thousand years.

Dust danced like motes of gold in the beam as he moved forward, revealing chisel marks in the stone walls, perhaps made by hands long dead. Symbols—faint, but unmistakable—lined the edges of the corridor: Kufic Alex thought, worn but not erased by time.

Behind him, the others leaned in, breath caught, watching as Alex stepped from the modern world into a hidden chapter of history.

He was inside.

And what the light touched next, no one could have predicted.

Minutes ticked by. Then more.

The three outside had taken to resting on the ledge, backs pressed against the stone wall, legs stretched out and twitching with anticipation. They passed the time speculating restlessly about what could lie within, casting anxious glances at the dark void beyond the granite plug.

Suddenly, Alex's head emerged from the entrance. His grin was a mile wide.

Claire almost stumbled in her haste to stand. She didn't dare speak, bouncing on the balls of her feet, eyes pleading for confirmation. Samira stood frozen, her hands clenched, heart hammering. This could be the greatest archaeological discovery of the century—and she was here to witness it.

"I hope you all brought torches?" Alex asked, his voice dancing with restrained excitement. "It's huge in here."

"Of course!"

"Yes!"

"Bien sûr!" Louis added, eyes gleaming.

Alex's expression shifted subtly. "Just so you're forewarned: there are bodies inside. Mummified. It's not gruesome, just… unexpected. Let's go."

They stepped inside.

The corridor opened into a vaulted chamber, perhaps twelve feet high, the walls and ceiling roughly hewn but structurally sound. Three of the walls were adorned with detailed reliefs and faint frescoes depicting the life of Alexander—from his youth in Macedon, to his campaigns across Persia and Egypt, and finally to his final journey into the desert. The narrative was sequential and deliberate: battle scenes, royal processions, sacred rituals. Louis was instantly captivated.

But it was the fourth wall that drew Samira.

It had been expertly smoothed and plastered, painted bone-white, and covered in ancient Kufic script from floor to ceiling. Her eyes scanned it hungrily. "It's telling the story of how he came to be here," she said, awe lacing her voice. "And look—down here, it's signed. Malik ibn Harun al-Sahiri — Year 24 AH. That's 643 CE. It matches."

Claire stepped forward, but her breath caught in her throat. She had seen it.

Toward the rear of the chamber, resting on a carved stone plinth about two feet high, lay the funerary casket of Alexander the Great—Dhu al-Qarnayn. The bronze had oxidized over the centuries, leaving a patina of rich green hues across its surface. It was once burnished and bright, but now it sat dull and ancient, its weight and silence pressing down on the room.

The casket itself was a masterpiece of craftsmanship. Along its sides, a relief unfolded the legend of Alexander: his taming of Bucephalus, his campaigns in the East, and the anointing of him as Pharaoh of Egypt. At the head of the lid, a sculpted likeness of the Macedonian king stared upwards, serene in death. His face was regal and youthful, framed by the stylized curls of his hair and the suggestion of a laurel crown.

Claire couldn't speak. Louis was dumbstruck. Samira had tears running down her cheeks. Alex removed his hat and stood in silent reverence. Over two thousand three hundred years had passed since the death of Alexander in 323 BCE, and now—finally—his tomb had been found.

And not in Alexandria. Not in Babylon.

Here. In Siwa. Exactly where he had wanted to be.

Beside the casket lay two mummified bodies, long dessicated and drawn into themselves, skin shriveled tightly over bone. They were more like husks than corpses, their robes the only indicator of their status: finely woven linen, edged in gold and dyed in once-vibrant blues and reds. In each of their hands rested a clay oil lamp, blackened from ancient use.

Samira returned to the Kufic inscription.

"These two," she said, eyes scanning rapidly, "were Brother Kallistos and Brother Mareon. They chose to be entombed with the Great King-God to ensure the seal was closed both from within and without."

She turned to the others, tears still brimming. "They sacrificed themselves to ensure the secret remained hidden."
Claire gasped. "Oh my God. That's… that's awful."
"Or noble," Alex countered, his voice quiet. "Such devotion to a king who had been dead for a thousand years by then."
Louis stepped away from the scene, blinking into the shadows at the rear of the chamber.
"Monsieur Professor," he said slowly, "this tunnel... it continues. What lies beyond?"
Alex turned. "Another passage. I haven't gone down yet. Let's take a look."
The team regrouped and moved steadily toward the back wall. A narrow passage revealed itself, no more than six feet high and three feet wide, sloping upwards into the stone. Claire paused and shone her torch back toward the entrance. It was barely visible now, a distant sliver of light.
"Wow," she whispered. "It must have taken them months, maybe years, to carve all this."
"Luckily this sandstone is soft," Alex said, running a hand along the wall, "but even so, an enormous feat."
The incline continued for roughly fifteen metres before ending abruptly at a set of steps—carved from the living rock—rising up to a low ceiling. At the top, a wooden trapdoor was nestled against the stone above.
Alex raised his torch and examined the hatch. "Sealed tight. Probably hasn't moved in centuries."
"Allow me, Professor," said Louis, stepping past. He climbed the steps until crouched beneath the door, then sat, pressing his feet against the hatch and bracing his back against the stairs.
He pushed.
The old wood creaked, flexed, but held.
"Le règle, professeur!" Louis said, grinning. "The ruler!"

Claire darted back down the passage and returned moments later, breathless, clutching the thin stainless-steel ruler they'd used before. She passed it to Alex.

He wedged it into the seam between the hatch and the stone, sawing gently. Like the granite plug before it, this door had been sealed with plaster or render to keep it airtight and invisible.

At last, he nodded to Louis.

Louis braced himself again and shoved upward. This time, the hatch cracked, then burst open with a sharp thunk. A shaft of sunlight pierced the darkness like a blade, spilling golden brilliance into the stairwell and illuminating the swirling dust.

Daylight.

The past had finally met the present.

Louis was the first to climb through the opening. The narrow stone passage had curved subtly back to the south-southeast, on the same 155-degree bearing they'd followed earlier. As he emerged from the cool interior of the tomb into the brilliance of the early afternoon sun, he found himself on the gentle saddle between the twin peaks of the southern hill. The air was drier here, and warmer—thin wisps of wind rolled lazily over the ridge.

He turned, crouched, and extended a hand. Claire emerged next, brushing dust from her knees and blinking in the sharp sunlight. Samira followed, then Alex, who paused at the top of the steps, glancing back into the gloom for just a moment—almost reverently—before adjusting his Fedora and stepping out into the afternoon sun.

They stood together in silence. Around them the land opened in grand, sweeping arcs. To the east the endless sea of the date palms, green and dark against the golden sands. To the south, the desert rolled on endlessly, golden and sun-scoured. To the west, more dark green date palms shimmered through the heat haze. Behind them, the northern hill loomed—slightly taller, and steeper, and now oddly familiar. They had been on its summit just an hour earlier, gazing around in hope. Now, they were a whole world away.

The realization washed over them like a wave. They had just made history.

No fanfare. No trumpets. Just the wind, the sun, the silence—and four dusty, wide-eyed explorers on a forgotten saddle between two hills in Siwa.

"We did it," said Claire softly, as though afraid to disturb the moment.

Samira wiped her brow with a scarf, her voice thick with emotion. "I can't believe we've actually found it. After all these years. All the myths, the maps, the theories…"

Alex turned slowly in place, drinking it all in. "Alexander wanted this place. This exact place. And now we know why."

Louis gave a low whistle and planted his hands on his hips, his eyes scanning the dunes. "Magnifique," he whispered. "Completely and utterly magnifique."

The breeze picked up, stirring the fabric of their shirts and tousling their hair. Below them, unseen and undisturbed for nearly two and a half millennia, lay the tomb of Alexander the Great—Dhu'l-Qarnayn—the Horned King, conqueror of the known world. And they were the first to see it in over 2,300 years.

"Come on," Alex said finally, his voice calm but resolute. "We still have work to do. And the world… the world needs to know."

They turned together, backlit by the sun, four shadows cast long against the sand.

US Ambassador for Egypt Raylan Stretton had marked the meeting as 'High Importance,' and when the clock struck 1:00 p.m. sharp, the encrypted conference platform blinked to life on André Molineux's laptop. The French Director of the INHA sat back in his Paris office, the daylight filtering softly through the tall Haussmann windows behind him. On his screen, the familiar faces of Raylan Stretton in Cairo, and French Ambassador Étienne Moreau also in Cairo appeared simultaneously.

"Gentlemen," Stretton began without preamble, "thank you for making yourselves available on such short notice. I'll get straight to it—we don't have time for diplomacy."

André leaned forward.

"We're picking up increased comms traffic out of Siwa," Stretton continued, his voice clipped and urgent. "Both radio and cellular signals are spiking. Nothing is encrypted, but the volume alone is significant. We've confirmed that Major General Karim Hassan is now in the oasis itself, and his focus appears to be on locating one Captain Hafez."

Etienne's brows rose.

"And?"

"And," said Stretton, "we've just learned that Hassan has ordered an immediate recall of all personnel from roadblocks and security posts to the east, south, and north. They're converging. Something's happening now—not tomorrow, not tonight—now."

André frowned. "But it can't be Hafez," he said. "He's dead. We know that."

"Yes," Stretton said quietly, "we do. Which leaves only one possible target."

"Samira and the team," André said, his voice dropping into a grave tone.

Stretton nodded. "I'm afraid so."

Etienne Moreau, seated in a high-backed chair in his office at the French Embassy in Garden City, leaned forward. "You want me to activate the unit?"

"How soon can they be operational, Etienne?" Andre asked.

"They've been on standby for the past eight hours, just as we discussed," the Ambassador replied. "They're stationed at a forward staging ground near the Libyan border—close enough to move quickly but far enough to avoid suspicion. They could be inside Egyptian territory in minutes."

Enemy territory, thought André grimly. Let's hope it doesn't come to that.

"Do it," said Stretton firmly. "I don't want to sit on our hands while Hassan goes rogue. We can't risk another international incident."

Moreau nodded. "Understood. The order will be sent immediately."

"And Etienne," Stretton added, "if this turns out to be nothing—if it's a false alarm—then we blame it on a GPS error. Solar interference. Technical glitch. The usual excuses."

Moreau gave a tight smile. "The Americans always have the best stories."

"And make sure they're prepared for trouble," Andre Molineux continued, his tone harder now. "We don't know Hassan's state of mind. If he feels his authority is being challenged, especially by foreigners... things could turn violent very quickly."

"I'll relay the message myself," Moreau said, his face grave. "No risks, no visibility, and no hesitation if things turn south."

"Good. We'll be monitoring from here," Stretton said. "Let's keep this clean."

Moreau gave a single, solemn nod and terminated the call.

André sat back, staring at the blank screen for a long moment. Siwa. Of all places.

He reached for his cell phone to call Samira, maybe give some advanced warning. Anything, was better than nothing, but he knew how quickly things spiral out of control, especially if they were three thousand kilometres away!

Major General Karim Hassan stood amidst the swirling dust, hands on his hips, frustration mounting with each passing second. They had found the two Toyota Hilux's parked beneath the sparse shade of a palm cluster at the base of Gabal Dakrur—but there was no sign of Hafez, nor of any of his usual entourage. The so-called 'Mountain Camp Ali-Khaled' had been shuttered for days now, locked and lifeless. The only other structure of any interest for miles was Marina Siwa House, some distance to the south. No, if Hafez was still in the area, then he was hiding here—and hiding well.

Hassan's jaw tightened. He needed answers.

"Break into the vehicles," he barked to the corporal.

Without hesitation, the young soldier smashed the side windows of both Hilux's, sending shards of glass scattering across the sand. They unlocked the doors and began rummaging through the contents—bags, books, clothes, notepads, water bottles, and printed maps. The General rifled through one of the glove compartments himself.

It didn't take long to realize something was off.

The documents were all in English. The books were marked with foreign university logos. The clothing tags were American and French. There were no signs of the usual DSD gear, no prayer beads, no sand-worn keffiyehs, no tobacco tins. Whoever these vehicles belonged to, they weren't Egyptians—and they certainly weren't Hafez.

Hassan checked the license plates again, just to be sure. Yes, these were the patrol vehicles assigned to Bawiti! So how in God's name had they ended up here? And who the hell were these foreigners? His mind whirled. Had Hafez been working with them all along? Was this the crew Khoury had warned about—'the Greek,' that fat bastard, and his so-called agents? If so, Hafez had made a fatal mistake. The black market in antiquities was already cutthroat, but trying to outmaneuver Khoury and the Egyptian state by colluding with outsiders? That was treasonous. Khoury had been right all along. Hafez was carving his own empire, and these foreigners— posing as officials perhaps —were helping him do it.

A movement caught Hassan's eye.

He turned toward the southern summit of Gabal Dakrur—and froze. A group of people had just emerged from the earth. Literally popped out of the ground, like spectres. No more than three hundred and fifty metres away, silhouetted against the bright sandstone saddle between the peaks, four figures stood blinking in the sun.

"Corporal," Hassan growled, "your binoculars."

The soldier sprinted to the open jeep and returned swiftly, placing the binoculars in Hassan's waiting hand.

He raised the lenses to his eyes, the polished steel of the Steiner Military-Marine 10x50 binoculars gleaming in the sun. He adjusted the focus with a twist of the diopter, bringing the distant figures into sharp clarity.

His stomach turned.

There, unmistakably, was the French woman—the one he'd interrogated in Tora Prison—and beside her, the same American man with the attitude and the arrogance. Two others stood with them. One appeared to be a heavyset male—maybe the muscle in this group. The fourth looked like a young woman—the one Khoury had said was a linguist or scribe, perhaps the translator.

Four of them. A cabal. A team.

They weren't archaeologists. No way. Not anymore.

They were looters. Graverobbers. Black market agents.

And worse—they had found something. He could see it in their posture, the way they paused and looked back toward the ground beneath them, before disappearing back into the ground.

Vanishing. Gone as if swallowed by the hill itself.

"Corporal," Hassan said through gritted teeth, lowering the binoculars. "Get the gear. We proceed on foot from here."

The corporal saluted. "Yes, sir!"

Hassan took one last look toward the saddle. He clenched his jaw, fire in his gut. The job he had started in Tora Prison would be finished here—without interference. No meddling embassy officials. No human rights lawyers. No international journalists. Just him, the sand, and the final reckoning.

And this time, there would be no escape.

Chapter 12

The team had descended once more through the hatch, closing it carefully behind them. Alex ensured the timber sealed tightly against the rock. For now, the last thing they needed was the unwelcome complication of a wandering tourist—or worse, a local shepherd—stumbling upon the hidden entrance to what could be the most valuable archaeological discovery of the century. One careless footprint could contaminate a priceless history, or worse, expose it to looters and opportunists.

Back in the tomb, the air was dry and still, carrying with it the faint metallic tang of age-old stone, bronze, and dust. The torch beams danced across the chamber as they moved into place.

Alex took charge quietly, handing out assignments with the calm clarity of a man who had done this a hundred times before.

"Samira, I want you on the Kufic wall," he said, gesturing toward the pristine plastered surface where the ancient script marched like sacred calligraphy across the whitewash. "Translate, annotate, document everything. We need to understand how Alexander came to rest here."

Samira nodded, already unrolling her leather toolkit of brushes, pencils, and high-resolution scanning equipment. She whispered softly to herself in Arabic, tracing her fingers just shy of the inked lines before reciting: "Dhu al-Qarnayn… Malik ibn Harun al-Sahiri…" She smiled faintly—names were anchors.

"Claire, you're on the frescoed walls," Alex continued, motioning to the three sides of the chamber adorned in vibrant motifs, faded but still awe-inspiring. "Start left and go clockwise. Document every panel, every brushstroke. Sequence them historically if you can—his youth, his campaigns, the march through Egypt. We'll need that context."

Claire was already unzipping her camera case. "On it," she said, clipping a light diffuser onto her lens. Her voice carried a low hum as she began work—an old habit from hours in the Louvre's archives—nothing melodic, just the rhythm of concentration.

"Louis," said Alex, turning to the burly Frenchman now unrolling a heavy grid notebook, "measure everything. Heights, widths, distances. Where the casket is located in relation to the walls, the elevation of the floor, the width of the rear passage. Diagram it all in planform. We'll need scale drawings when we present this."

Louis gave a crisp nod, retrieving his now heavily scuffed and barely readable steel ruler. "Understood. I'll start with the casket platform and work outward."

Alex turned back toward the centerpiece of the chamber—the green-patinated bronze casket resting atop its stone plinth. The face of Alexander, rendered in low-relief on the lid, stared eternally upward, serene and imperial. Around the casket's sides, intricate friezes depicted his victories at Issus and Gaugamela, his meeting with Darius, his crossing of the Hindu Kush, and finally, an unfamiliar scene—perhaps his procession toward the Oracle of Amun at Siwa.

Alex took a slow breath. His job would be to document the funerary chamber in all its sacred detail. The casket. The carvings. The position of the two mummified priests still clutching their extinguished oil lamps. Each detail might rewrite everything the world thought it knew about Alexander's death—and his legacy.

They set to work, each falling into a rhythm of their own. The only sounds were the occasional snap of a shutter, the scratch of a graphite pencil, Claire's humming, and the soft murmur of Samira translating Kufic to English in a voice barely above a whisper. The silence of the tomb—broken only by the past—wrapped around them like a protective shroud.

They were alone with history.

Major General Karim Nasser stood atop the second rise of Gabal
Dakrur, scanning the rocky terrain with military precision. The sun
beat down from almost directly overhead, casting stark shadows
across the hilltop and baking the ground beneath their boots. He'd
been certain—he was certain—he had seen them emerge from this
very summit not twenty minutes prior, four of them, rising from
the rock itself like ghosts. He just needed proof now.
He turned sharply to his left. "Corporal Fathi, take a wide sweep
around the western flank. If there's another exit, I don't want them
slipping out behind us. Cut them off and keep your radio on silent
unless it's urgent. Go."
The corporal saluted crisply and disappeared over the slope, rifle
slung across his back, boots crunching with purpose as he made his
way down the incline and around the base.
With that done, Nasser addressed the remaining two. "It should be
around here somewhere," he muttered, scanning the rocky surface.
"They didn't vanish into thin air. Look carefully—this entrance
will be hidden, disguised. We're not leaving until we find it."
The three men began combing the summit, eyes sharp and feet
testing every crack and crevice in the rock. Minutes passed. A soft
wind blew over the hilltop, rustling their uniforms. Then—
"Here, General! Over here!" one of the corporals called out.
Nasser strode over briskly, and there it was—just as he had
expected. At the corporal's feet was a subtle, square outline,
perhaps two feet by two, almost invisible unless you knew what
you were looking for. Dust had been swept away recently, and the
edges were too perfect to be natural.
Nasser crouched beside it. "Yes. This is it."
He extended his hand. "Your bayonet."
The corporal handed it over, and the General went to work. He
jabbed the blade into the thin seam and began to pry, grinding at
the edges with practiced determination. After several tense

moments of sawing and levering, the hatch began to shift. It groaned softly as it gave way, then lifted a few centimetres.

"Get your fingers under—now. Lift with me," Nasser ordered.

The three men hauled the hatch open just wide enough to reveal a dark shaft beneath. Stale air rose from the opening—cool and still, untouched by time. A narrow staircase descended into the gloom, carved directly into the bedrock. The darkness inside was absolute. Nasser peered down. "No torches, radio's off. We go in silent. They're somewhere inside, and I want them caught by surprise." The General drew hi Beretta sidearm, and swung one leg down into the shaft, boots testing the stairs. Behind him, the two corporals followed, weapons drawn, nerves taut. They left the hatch open just in case a fast egress was needed. Down they went, single file, hands brushing the rough walls for balance, footsteps muffled against the ancient stone. The further they descended, the more distant the outside world became, swallowed by the thick silence of the underground.

Somewhere below, those foreign interlopers—the ones he had seen at Tora Prison, the woman and the man—were trespassing in Egypt's secrets, no doubt working with Hafez's and his allies. Nasser's jaw tightened at the thought. And now, finally, they would be cornered.

He motioned for silence again as the tunnel began to level out, their boots landing on flat stone. The chamber had to be close now. It was time to finish what he had started.

The soldiers crept silently along the narrow passageway, swallowed by the pitch-black confines of the rock. With no lights and barely enough space to walk upright, they moved by touch, brushing their fingertips along the rough stone walls for orientation. The floor sloped gently downward, just enough to pull them forward, deeper into the unknown.

Fortunately for them, the passage was uniform and straight, a rare mercy in what was clearly an ancient and treacherous place.

After perhaps twenty metres, a faint glow began to bloom ahead—
soft, golden, flickering.

General Karim Nasser slowed his pace, raising a closed fist to halt
the corporals behind him. The glow intensified as they neared the
mouth of the corridor, revealing the outline of a large chamber
beyond. Even before they entered, he could sense the presence of
activity. A gentle hum—movement, scraping, maybe murmuring—
but no loud voices, and certainly no Arabic.

They were in there. Working. Oblivious.

He pressed himself to the wall and surveyed the scene: a vast
subterranean cavern, its walls awash with the harsh lighting of
LED torches. The flickering lights revealed ancient frescoes, tools
neatly laid out, and the unmistakable dust of careful excavation.
Four figures moved about—focused, diligent, unaware of the
intruders watching from the shadows.

Nasser's eyes narrowed. No uniforms. No weapons. And, most
crucially, no sign of Captain Hafez.

He studied them intently. One of the men—tall, lean,
bespectacled—was brushing dust away from a funerary casket with
a fine brush. Another woman was photographing a mural, her
mouth moving silently as she interpreted the ancient text. A third—
a younger woman—was photographing the many frescoes on the
walls, moving diligently, annotating every frame in her notebook.
The fourth man stood at the far end, scribbling into a leather-bound
ledger with military precision.

The General raised two fingers and motioned for the corporals to
fan left and right, taking flanking positions around the entrance. He
waited for just the right moment, then stepped out of the shadows,
his sidearm raised.

"Stop what you are doing and put your hands up!" he barked.

The command rang out like a gunshot, bouncing off the stone walls
in echoing thunder.

All four jumped. The bespectacled man dropped his brush with a
clatter. One of the women—Claire—screamed in fright. Samira

froze mid-sentence, her lips still parted. Only Louis Delon, the man with the military bearing, kept his composure, eyes instantly locking on Nasser with the calm wariness of a trained operative.

"Back up," Nasser snapped. "Against the wall. Now!"

Slowly, the team complied, laying down their tools with deliberate care and retreating until their backs touched the cool stone of the entrance wall. Hands went up. No sudden moves.

"Yes, I see what this is," Nasser sneered as he stalked toward them. "Looting. Black-marketeering. So this is who you are. Where is that dog Hafez?"

"Who?" Louis said flatly, stepping slightly forward, his accent calm but challenging and Hassan picked up on the French lilt.

"Don't be stupid with me, Frenchman. That dog—Captain Hafez— from Bawiti. Where is he?"

Louis raised an eyebrow. "If you mean the DSD officer who tried to execute us in the desert with his pack of murderous thugs, then I'd say he's dead by now."

Nasser paused, lips parting slightly. "Dead?"

Louis nodded once.

"Was it you?" he barked suddenly, stepping closer to Louis. "Did you kill him?"

"I didn't," Louis said, his voice steady, "but I'd have done it gladly if given the chance. I think he had a disagreement with the local bédouine."

The General stared at him but saw no trace of bluff. Louis' eyes were hard, unwavering. No fear.

Behind him, Nasser caught movement—Alex and Samira. Recognition flared.

"You two," he spat. "I know you. The false UN inspectors with their forged permits. I am looking forward to seeing you again… under more favourable circumstances." His lip curled in contempt.

Alex said nothing, meeting his glare with silent defiance. Samira, however, shivered. She remembered Tora Prison too well. So did Nasser.

It was then that Louis heard it.

Just at the edge of perception—whump… whump… whump…

His head tilted slightly. Years in the military had honed his ear to the subtleties of rotor acoustics. He knew that sound. It wasn't an Egyptian Gazelle or MiL 8. It was modern, heavier, cleaner.

It was a very familiar, very French rotor beat.

A second later, Claire heard it too. Then Samira. Then even Nasser turned, eyes narrowing, head cocked toward the ceiling.

A shadow of satisfaction crossed Louis' face.

"My reinforcements," Nasser said with smug certainty. "They've arrived just in time."

Louis smiled.

It was the wrong reaction—and Nasser caught it immediately.

"You find this amusing?" he asked coldly. "You're all trapped. It's back to Tora for the lot of you. With… enhanced interrogation."

His gaze landed on Samira as he said it.

Louis straightened. "You don't know your helicopters too well, General."

Nasser scowled. "What?"

"That's no Egyptian aircraft. That's an NH90 TTH. European build. More specifically—French."

Nasser blinked.

Louis' grin widened. "Which means Special Forces. Or more likely, the Legion. And if it's the Legion, they're operating out of Libya. Which means they're not here for you, General. They're here because of you. And they know exactly where we are."

Nasser glanced toward the passage entrance. For the first time, doubt flickered in his eyes.

Louis leaned forward slightly.

"I suggest you put that gun down, General. You've just gone from captor… to complication."

The sound of the rotors grew louder now—closer, heavier, unmistakable. The whump-whump-whump beat reverberated through the stone, a dull vibration that rolled down the tunnel and echoed softly within the chamber. They were directly overhead.

From her position near the wall, Samira looked up instinctively. Of course they had seen the trapdoor from the sky—black and geometric, a perfect square incongruously etched into the natural stone, standing out like an ink stain on a canvas of sand. They'd be landing any moment now.

Rescued again, she thought, half in disbelief.

Then she saw it—just a flicker in Hassan's posture. A twitch. A brief, involuntary glance back toward the passage. It was all the confirmation she needed. He knew it too. He was stalling. Buying time. Or looking for a way out.

Samira acted.

In rapid-fire Arabic, her voice sharp and cutting she addressed the two corporals:

إنها الفِرْقة الأَجْنَبِيَّة الفَرَنْسِيَّة. لقد جاءوا من أجله!

"It's the French Foreign Legion. They're here for the General!"

The two corporals flanking the chamber froze. They looked at each other—then back at their commander. For a moment, everything held in stasis.

The Legion.

Their reputation needed no translation. No embellishment.

Ruthless. Unrelenting. Born from outcasts and hardened in exile.

They gave no quarter and asked for none. No diplomacy, no trials.

Only war.

A crack of fear spread through the two men like lightning. Then, without a word between them, they bolted—shoving past each other in blind panic as they scrambled into the tunnel. Boots slipped on stone, elbows cracked against walls, breath came in ragged gasps as they stumbled upward into the darkness, leaving their general behind.

"Looks like you're out of friends, General," Louis said quietly, stepping forward. "I suggest you surrender."

Hassan stood alone now, the shadows crowding in around him, the noise of the approaching chopper growing louder with every second. He didn't respond. His eyes flicked back and forth—calculating, searching, cornered.

Then he saw her.

Claire. Standing half behind Louis, visibly shaken, her eyes wide with fear.

She was the smallest. The lightest. The least likely to resist.

His voice came low and venomous. "Give me the girl."

Louis shifted slightly, positioning himself directly in front of her. "You can't have her, General. Give yourself up."

"I said—give me the girl!" Hassan hissed, his voice rising in desperation.

"No, not now, not ever sac à merde!"

Hassan's gun hand jerked, now swinging toward Samira.

"Give me the girl… or she dies."

It happened fast.

Louis saw his opening—a moment of reckless threat, not tactical precision—and he took it.

With a roar that echoed like a battle cry, he surged forward. "Nooooo!"

He slammed into the General with the full force of a charging bull, both hands clamping onto Hassan's jacket lapels. Hassan's eyes went wide, but it was too late. Louis lifted him from the ground, boots scrabbling for traction, and hurled him backward across the chamber.

They hit the far wall with bone-cracking force. The sound of flesh and stone colliding was lost beneath the detonation that followed.

BANG.

A pistol shot cracked through the chamber like thunder in a cathedral, amplified by the cavern's vaulted ceiling. The sound rang in their ears, deafening and final.

Claire let out a gasp. Samira pressed her back to the wall, hand to her chest. Alex stood still as stone.

Then—silence.

Everyone froze.

The French Legionnaires poured into the narrow passage like a tide of silent, methodical vengeance, their boots thudding against the packed earth with precision and purpose. At the entrance above, the two Egyptian corporals had surrendered without resistance, overwhelmed by the sheer professionalism of their adversaries. They now knelt on the sand, wrists cuffed behind their backs, silent and ashamed, under the stern gaze of the entry team's rear guard.

Down below, the lead fireteam advanced into the cavern at a run, weapons sweeping, torch beams flickering along the frescoed walls and the shadows that danced across ancient stone. The moment the sergeant entered the chamber, he paused—eyes narrowing—taking in the scene with a soldier's instinct for battlefield geometry.

Louis Delon was sprawled over the prone form of an older man— Major General Karim Nasser—who was clawing weakly at Louis' prone form, trying to roll him off. The General's face was streaked with blood and dust, but still conscious. Louis, on the other hand, was motionless.

The sergeant stepped forward and swung his barrel-mounted torch down, illuminating Louis' side. The growing red stain left no doubt.

"Médecin!" he barked, voice sharp.

"Medic!"

A young corporal with the red cross stencilled on his Kevlar helmet rushed past, dropping to his knees beside Louis. He moved quickly and calmly, checking vitals, rolling the injured Frenchman gently onto his back, already applying pressure to the wound with one gloved hand.

Meanwhile, the sergeant grabbed Nasser by the collar and yanked him upright. The Egyptian officer gave a weak grunt but didn't resist, his expression dull, almost dazed. With practiced ease, the sergeant wrenched the pistol from Hassan's hand, tossed it aside, then spun him around and drove a brutal knee into the back of his legs.

Nasser crumpled to his knees with a stifled cry.

The sergeant stepped forward, leaned down, and pressed the cold muzzle of his Beretta into the soft flesh at the base of Nasser's neck—a final punctuation mark. No words were needed. The message was clear.

"Vérifiez les autres."

 "Check the others."

Another Legionnaire peeled off from the formation and approached Alex, Samira, and Claire. Their faces were drawn and wide-eyed, caught in the strobe-like flashes of torchlight, uncertain whether they were witnessing a rescue or another armed takeover.

The soldier barked a single word into his comms. "Clair."

 "Clear."

Alex took a step forward, craning to see past the commotion toward Louis.

"Non, laissez-les faire leur travail."

 "No—let them work," said the Legionnaire, gently but firmly, spreading his arms and blocking the way. His eyes were not unkind, but they were firm—this was no place for civilians right now.

The sergeant kept his pistol steady behind Nasser's neck as he turned back toward the medic. Hassan remained kneeling, limp and broken, eyes glassy. The weight of failure—and perhaps mortality—seemed to hang over him like the heavy air of the tomb itself.

The medic remained crouched beside Louis, still applying pressure, checking for breath, a pulse, any sign of response. His hands moved with mechanical precision, but his face slowly tightened with grim finality.

After a long few seconds, he sat back on his heels and looked up at the sergeant. He said nothing.

He didn't have to.

He simply gave a small, almost imperceptible shake of the head. The sergeant exhaled slowly through his nose and his jaw tightened. A moment passed. Then another.
Behind him, Samira gasped and covered her mouth with both hands. Claire began to weep softly, the reality sinking in. Alex closed his eyes and bowed his head.
Louis Delon—soldier, protector, comrade—had died in silence, a hero's end in the shadows of ancient stone.
The sergeant holstered his sidearm, stepped back from Hassan, and gave a quiet order into his radio.
"Un KIA confirmé. Préparez l'évacuation."
"One confirmed KIA. Prepare extraction."
The rotors above were circling closer now. The rescue was still underway.
But for Louis, the mission had already ended.

Chapter 13

The funeral of Louis Delon was held on a Wednesday.

The sky was grey and low, swollen with unspent rain—a ceiling of sorrow drawn taut above the hills of northern France. The air was crisp and damp, as though the very earth had paused in reverence. At the Cimetière de Notre-Dame de Lorette, the largest French military cemetery in the world, rows upon rows of white crosses stood in silent formation, eternal sentinels over the land. Today, they would receive a brother into their midst.

It was a full military affair.

The French Foreign Legion had spared nothing. The hearse—a black ceremonial vehicle draped in the French tricolour—moved slowly along the gravel path, escorted on foot by Legionnaires in their full tenue de cérémonie. White kepis gleamed beneath the gloom, boots were polished to mirror shine, bayonets fixed to vintage FAMAS rifles held at the slope. The Legion band played the sombre notes of "Le Boudin", its martial rhythm slowed to a funeral march, echoing through the cemetery like a final heartbeat.

Alex, Samira, and Claire had never seen a turnout like this. The choreography, the formality, the profound silence broken only by precision commands—this was not pageantry. It was respect, distilled into ceremony. The kind earned in battle, in brotherhood, and ultimately, in sacrifice.

The service was attended by dignitaries and soldiers alike. Rayland Stretton, the U.S. Ambassador to France, stood stiffly beside Etienne Moreau, who had flown in directly from Egypt. The full complement of Sentinel Security was in attendance, standing in a tight block off to one side—stoic, respectful, visibly shaken. Behind them, more than fifty members of Louis' old COS unit and fellow Legionnaires filled out the ranks. Each man wore the Class A dress uniform with medal ribbons displayed; some wore their sashes, others bore scars that needed no adornment.

Front and centre, seated with quiet dignity, were Louis' estranged widow Maryanne and his teenage daughter, Phoebe. Few even knew he had a daughter—Louis had always guarded his private life with a fortress-like resolve. But there she was, straight-backed, jaw clenched, dressed in black. The pain behind her eyes was deep and unadorned.

To her left sat André Molinieux, his usual reserve softened by genuine grief. His hands folded neatly in his lap, his gaze fixed ahead, unblinking.

Alex, Samira, and Claire sat just behind them.

The hearse came to a slow, dignified halt beside the open grave, its black chassis gleaming under the grey sky like wet onyx. Six Legionnaires in pristine dress uniform moved forward in perfect synchrony, their white gloves stark against the deep varnish of the casket. Not a word was spoken—only the soft thud of boots on gravel, the quiet scrape of the hearse door opening.

The casket, draped in the French tricolour, was borne out with solemn precision. The pallbearers moved in flawless cadence, each step measured, each breath held. The silence was reverent, oppressive—thick with meaning.

At the graveside, the cavalletto—a mechanised bier with polished chrome arms—waited over the mouth of the earth. The pallbearers halted beside it, and on command, gently lowered the casket onto the waiting cradle. The tricolour, now smoothed flat by unseen hands, shimmered faintly in the breeze.

A senior officer stepped forward. With ritualised care, he reached down, lifted the flag from the coffin and folded the flag with the help of two junior officers—first in half, then again, then into a perfect triangle. There was no saluting, no flourish. Just quiet, practiced grace. When finished, he turned, walked to Maryanne, and—bowing slightly—placed the folded flag into her waiting hands. She nodded once, tightly, lips pressed into a line. Phoebe clutched her mother's free hand, eyes wide and glassy.

And all stood still.

When the casket was slowly lowered into the ground, all of them rose. Some of them snapped to attention and saluted.

Alex stood in composed silence, eyes locked on the lonely black coffin as it descended. Grief came to him in logical increments—processed, assessed, understood, and then stored away, labelled and sealed like a file in an archive.

For Samira, it was different. Her tears were quiet but constant, like a faucet barely turned off. She would dry out eventually, she knew, but she would never forget the man who had shielded them in the dark, who had died so that they might live. His courage had been silent, his loyalty unshakable.

Claire said nothing. She showed nothing. Her face was a mask—calm, clinical, untouched. But Samira had said to Alex the night before, "She hasn't processed it yet. But she will. One day soon. It always comes."

As they filed past the grave, each of them took a handful of earth from the small basket near the edge and scattered it gently into the void. The sound of soil on the coffin's lid was jarring, final. A strange, surreal moment where the symbolic and the literal collided. Louis Delon was no longer a soldier, no longer a protector. He was part of the ground now.

A three-volley salute followed. The seven Legionnaires raised their rifles in unison and fired into the sky—three sharp reports that cracked across the cemetery like the snapping of celestial chains. A bugler stepped forward and played 'La Sonnerie aux Morts', France's own haunting equivalent of Taps. No one moved. Not even the wind.

The coffin was sealed. The grave was covered.

The ceremonial part was over.

As the crowd dispersed, small groups formed like islands in a sea of remembrance. The military men found each other and spoke in clipped, low tones – some had been here before. The diplomats conversed quietly near the gravel path. The security contractors gathered in the shade of a yew tree, smoking in silence.

Alex, glancing around, noticed Claire and André standing off to the side, engaged in quiet, intense discussion. They spoke for a few minutes. Then, André placed a hand on her shoulder—fatherly, warm, comforting. Claire extended her hand. They shook—an oddly formal gesture, given the day.

André then turned and, seeing Alex watching, gave a small wave and sauntered over, Claire falling into step behind him. They were soon joined by Ambassador Stretton and Attache Moreau.

"So," said Alex, more out of habit than impulse, "what now?"

"Well, some good news at least," began Stretton, adjusting his scarf against the wind. "We handed Hassan over to the Egyptian authorities. He's been indicted on several counts—antiquities fraud, black marketeering, money laundering… and, of course, murder. He is the scapegoat of course!"

"Where are they holding him?" asked Samira.

"Tora Prison," said Etienne Moreau grimly.

"But will he be found guilty?" she followed.

Stretton gave a sly smile, eyes narrowed. "Let's just say… Hassan put a lot of people in Tora. I doubt he'll last two weeks."

They all nodded, understanding without words.

"And Khoury? And this Greek shipping magnate, Soterakis?" asked Alex.

"Khoury's turned informant, just as we expected," said Stretton. "In exchange for giving us a full map of the smuggling routes and some very juicy names for Interpol, he keeps his job… and his wealth. For now."

"Another marked man," muttered Etienne.

"Indeed," said Stretton. "Once his former associates figure out who talked, well… live by the sword and all that."

"And Soterakis?"

"Ah, now there's the interesting part," the Ambassador said. "We intercepted several of his vessels—thanks to Khoury. We found precisely what we were looking for. The U.S. has frozen his assets, the EU has blacklisted his company, and all his ships have been impounded. He's under house arrest on his little island fortress in the Aegean. Apparently, when the Greeks raided it, they found some things that... well, should not have been there."

Samira exhaled. "Phew, that ties everything up." she added with a glance toward the grave, "Well, almost everything."

André cleared his throat.

"There's one final matter," he said gently. "The Egyptian government has officially invited the INHA to collaborate on the full documentation of the tomb. The first exhibition of the funerary casket of Alexander the Great will be unveiled next month at the Louvre. That was part of our little side deal around Khoury."

He looked to the three of them.

"Alex. Samira. Claire. The INHA would be honoured if you would oversee the work. Until the exhibition. If... you're ready to resume."

Alex nodded without hesitation. "Of course."

"Yes. Definitely," said Samira, with a steadier voice.

Claire gave a gentle nod.

"Excellent. The Dassault departs tomorrow morning for Cairo. The site is locked down at the moment—even the Egyptian Antiquities Department is barred entry. But the sooner we begin, the better."

"We'll be there," said Samira.

The wind picked up then, as if to carry the final words of the day away into the heavens. The ceremony had ended, but remembrance had just begun.

Limousines waited on the gravel drive for the ambassadors, ready to return them to their diplomacy. André's sleek black BMW 8-Series stood a few metres away, a driver at attention. It would take him—and them—back to the French military base at Camp de

Saint-Cyr Coëtquidan, the staging post for the COS. There, the glasses would be raised, the stories would be shared, and the weight of loss would be momentarily lightened by camaraderie. But for now, the sky remained low. The wind remained cold. The universe was still in mourning.

Epilogue

It had taken weeks, but the display was finally finished—ready for its grand unveiling tomorrow. The Long Range Desert Group and Special Air Service exhibition at the Imperial War Museum in Duxford had just received its finest addition yet: a fully intact, meticulously cleaned but totally unrestored Chevrolet CW30. Courtesy of the Institut National d'Histoire de l'Art, it was not only a tribute to the ingenuity and bravery of the desert raiders of World War II—but also a deeply personal memorial.

This was the very vehicle Claire and Louis Delon had discovered, half-buried beneath a dune during their desperate flight across the Western Desert from Bahariya to Siwa. Battered, sun-scarred, and partially buried, the truck had once been a ghost of the past. Now it stood resurrected, proud and defiant in the centre of the museum's most revered gallery.

The Imperial War Museum had been elated. Any addition to the collection was welcomed, but this? This was exceptional. This was a crown jewel. It was history with a soul.

Claire had overseen every detail—every part of the Chevrolet was as they found it that day – the fuel cans, the ammunition boxes, the Spam tins – everything! She had taken leave from the excavation of Alexander's tomb, personally pausing her academic passion for something more visceral. It had mattered to her—so deeply that nothing else could come first.

Tomorrow would be for the public, for historians and veterans, for school children and curious tourists. But tonight… tonight was for Louis.

She had asked Alex Carey, Samira Rahmani, and Andre Molineux to meet her here—just one last time, the night before the unveiling. She wanted them to see it with her, to bear witness to the tribute. And of course, they came. They wouldn't have been anywhere else.

The museum was silent, its great halls emptied of staff, the click of their footsteps swallowed by the cavernous stillness. Only the soft lights from above the exhibit remained, casting a reverent glow upon the desert truck.

Claire approached slowly, her fingers brushing the dented fender of the CW30, worn and sand-scoured, its old scars now made sacred. Mounted behind it was an enormous photograph taken by Claire—Louis Delon, tall and suntanned, standing beside the truck the moment they found it. He was smiling in that easy, rakish way of his—equal parts soldier and adventurer, the kind of smile that suggested he'd always find a way.

It hit her then.

A shudder, imperceptible at first, curled her lower lip. Then came the breath—a sharp, stolen thing. She took a step back, one hand gripping the fender as though it were an anchor. A tremor in her shoulders. Then a gasp.

Then the tidal wave broke.

It wasn't weeping. It was collapse!

A sound tore from her that shouldn't come from a living soul—it belonged in ancient catacombs, in echoing tombs, in the aching heart of loss. She fell to her knees, sobbing, hand still clutching the metal like it could bring him back, like it was him.

Her whole body trembled under the weight of it—the guilt, the sorrow, the disbelief that he was truly gone. She wailed, not with words, but with pain—raw and unhindered, something primal and sacred. The grief that had lain dormant, kept tidy and clinical, exploded into the air like shrapnel.

Alex stepped forward instinctively, heart pounding, thinking she might be hurt. But Samira caught his arm gently.

"No," she whispered. "Let her cry. She's held it in for too long. If she doesn't let it out now… she never will."

So they watched. Helpless, hearts breaking.

Claire sobbed until her voice gave out, until her strength was spent. Her head hung, chest heaving, the tears soaking the knees of her jeans. She looked small, fragile. But she never let go of the truck. Her hand remained curled on that fender, white-knuckled and trembling—like a child holding onto the edge of a dream before it vanished.

When the grief had finally ebbed, when the wailing quieted into shallow breaths and aching silence, the others moved as one. No words. No hesitation. Samira knelt beside her, gently taking her other hand. Alex crouched on her opposite side, and Andre, dignified and solemn, bent down and placed a steady hand on her back.

Together they lifted her—not away from the truck, but into their arms. A silent circle formed around her, each holding the others, each giving what strength they could spare. Claire, tucked gently in the centre, eyes shut tight, finally allowed herself to lean into their embrace.

This wasn't closure. Not yet.

But it was the beginning.

The pain would linger—months, maybe years. But so would the memory. And thanks to her, and to Louis, that old Chevrolet would now whisper stories of courage, friendship, and sacrifice to generations who had never met him… but would never forget him. And in that moment, beneath the soft museum lights, the universe—if only for a heartbeat—seemed to hold its breath.

The Alexander the Great exhibition had been delayed by weeks. Wrangling between the Egyptian Supreme Council of Antiquities and a coalition of international museums had dragged on—politics, prestige, and ownership all colliding in a diplomatic waltz. Who would get to display the funerary casket of Alexander the Great first? How long would each host country be granted? Which flag would be nearest the display? Which museum would claim pride of place on the official UNESCO posters?

But in the end, they agreed.

A three-year world tour would take the casket through the greatest museums on earth—The Louvre in Paris, The Smithsonian in Washington, The British Museum in London—before it would travel to the newly opened Grand Egyptian Museum for a two-year national showcase. Its final resting place would be the National Archaeological Museum in Athens. That announcement alone had sent a shockwave through the Hellenic world, and Athens had immediately begun a €70 million renovation to house their most extraordinary treasure yet.

But tonight was the beginning.

The Louvre.

Opening night.

It was a spectacle worthy of legend.

Searchlights lit the Parisian sky as black sedans rolled through the glass pyramid's inner courtyard. The air was crisp, the plaza glowing in the warm hues of floodlights and flashbulbs. Inside, the Louvre had been transformed—red carpet lined the marble floors, velvet ropes cordoned off the exhibit space, and champagne flowed freely in crystal flutes borne on silver trays by white-gloved staff.

It was strictly black-tie.

Even the security personnel wore tuxedos.

The great and the powerful had gathered: ambassadors, presidents, prime ministers, cultural attachés, curators, collectors, scholars, socialites, and stars. UNESCO had sent a full delegation. So had the UN. The archaeological elite mingled with the political aristocracy beneath the towering works of da Vinci, Vermeer, and Gericault.

Alex Carey tugged uncomfortably at his bow tie.

He felt like a fraud in this penguin suit—a scruffy academic trapped in a magician's costume. It pinched at the neck and clung to his shoulders like wet parchment. But beside him stood Samira Rahmani, and she was radiant.

She wore a floor-length emerald gown, sleeveless and sinuous, with a high neckline and a sheer panel down her back that shimmered as she moved. Her dark hair had been swept up into a sleek bun, a cascade of gold earrings adding movement and sparkle. She glowed with poise and strength, the desert diplomat in gala regalia.

"You look fantastic," Alex muttered, still adjusting his collar.

"You look like you're being slowly strangled," she replied sweetly.

Claire had flown home in the interim—to Flagstaff, Arizona. She needed time. Time with her family. Time to speak of Louis, of Siwa, of what they'd found and what they'd lost. Time to begin healing.

Alex had caught himself more than once, staring into the middle distance during those quiet weeks—thinking of Louis. Of the man who had saved them, not once, not twice, but three times. A soldier. A friend. A brother-in-arms. He was gone. But never far.

And then, in a moment of serendipity, they spotted her.

Claire.

But it was not the same Claire who had left Egypt.

Gone were the sun-bleached jeans, the oversized sweaters, the battered boots and horn-rimmed glasses. Gone was the shy, academic intern in the shadow of professors and diplomats.

She descended the gallery stairs like a woman born to royalty.

She wore a red satin gown, off-the-shoulder, with a plunging neckline and a thigh-high slit that revealed long, sculpted legs made taller by crimson stilettos. Her hair—longer than Alex remembered—curled in polished ringlets that framed her striking face. Her makeup was subtle but surgical, drawing out the sharpness of her cheekbones, the depth of her dark eyes, and the shape of her full lips.

She turned every head. Men, women, everyone.

"Holy cow," Alex murmured, eyes wide. "Is that you, Claire?"

"In the flesh," she replied with a smile, easing out one leg to reveal her heels and the flash of thigh beneath the slit. "What, you thought I'd be in cargo pants and a clipboard?"

"I just… wow. I mean, wow," he said again, stunned.

"Fucking-A it's me," she grinned.

"Ah, there you are," said Samira dryly, joining them with a raised brow. The three of them laughed, a pressure valve releasing after months of tension.

The speeches began soon after.

The Chairman of the Louvre thanked the French government, the Egyptian Ministry of Antiquities, UNESCO, and the Institut National d'Histoire de l'Art. The INHA had, after all, funded the lion's share of the expedition, and much of the display.

Then came Andre.

He took the stage with the composure of a statesman and the sincerity of a friend. His speech was passionate, sincere. He spoke of the team, their devotion, their sacrifice. He named Louis. When he called him "more a brother than a friend," a hush fell over the hall, and several eyes misted over.

He thanked Harvard. The UN. But saved his final praise for last. He raised his glass toward the audience.

"To the three who walked the path no one else could. Who followed the Path of the Four Lions. Who cracked a mystery two-thousand, three hundred years buried. Alex Carey. Samira Rahmani. Claire Marlowe."

Applause thundered across the atrium as the trio joined him onstage. Cameras flashed. Glasses clinked.

Alex, blushing, spoke for them all.

He thanked the INHA for their belief. He praised Andre for his leadership and for never losing sight of what mattered. He turned to Samira and said, "You are the best liaison I've ever worked with. I only wish I spoke Arabic like you."
The audience laughed, warmly.
He turned to Claire last.
"She was the best intern a professor could ever ask for. Diligent. Methodical. Relentless. And of course, totally brilliant. And today, she stands as my equal in every way that matters."
Then, quieter, with gravity:
"To Louis Delon, our friend, our companion and our protector. Who sacrificed everything as only a soldier can. Je te salue, tu ne seras jamais oublié. " Glasses were raised and champagne sipped in his honor around the exhibition. Even those who never knew the whole story understood the reverence of this moment. Alex continued.
"And I want to honor one more name. Someone not in this room, but whose fingerprints are on everything we achieved. Malik ibn Harun al-Sahiri. A man of vision who, over a millennium ago, left a trail for us to follow. The mastermind of this grand puzzle. Without him, none of this would have been possible."
The applause was softer, more reflective. The moment hung, golden and heavy in the air.

Later, after the handshakes and congratulations, the group found themselves gathered before the funerary casket of Alexander the Great. It stood in a hermetically sealed glass chamber, spotlit in silent reverence.
"So," Samira whispered, exhaling. "What do we do now?"
It wasn't a question of schedules. It was a question of what happens after the mountaintop.
Claire nodded. "We need another adventure."
Alex was smiling.
They both noticed it.

"What?" Claire asked, eyes narrowing. "Out with it, Professor."
"Can you both keep a secret?"
Samira raised a brow. "You know we can."
Alex lowered his voice. "When I went into the tomb that first time, alone… I found something."
"What kind of something?" asked Samira.
"A codex," he said.
Claire blinked. "From where?"
"One of the priests. He was holding it. Clutched in his hand, wrapped in cloth. I… I took it. Slipped it into my satchel. Nobody asked, nobody searched. I've still got it."
"Holy shit, Alex," Samira gasped. "Have you examined it?"
"Not yet. But something tells me… it's important."
Claire leaned in. "Do you think it's our next one?"
"I know it is."
Samira grinned, raised her glass. "I'll drink to that."
"Fucking A" said Claire with finality.
The three of them stood before the great casket of Alexander the Great, the past behind them, the world at their feet—and another adventure waiting just beyond the horizon.
They clinked glasses.
And smiled.

---END---